The guilt of innocents

Candace Robb studied ... Saxon Literature and h... medieval history and ... Archer series grew out ... York and the tumultu... series, *The Apothecary Rose*, was published in 1994, at which point she began to write full time. *The Guilt of Innocents* is the ninth in the series. Published worldwide, she is also available in the UK on audiobook and in large print. In addition to the Owen Archer novels, she is the author of three Margaret Kerr Mysteries, set in Scotland at the time of Robert the Bruce.

To find out more about Candace Robb's novels, read the Candace Robb Newsletter. For your free copy, email enquiries@randomhouse.co.uk with 'Candace Robb Newsletter' as the subject.

ACCLAIM FOR CANDACE ROBB

'It's . . . the Machiavellian intrigue that makes this such an enjoyable read. When the iron curtain came down people said the spy-thriller genre was dead. They were wrong. This is as full of intrigue as a Deighton or a Le Carré'   *Guardian*

'A vivid portrait of fourteenth-century England which gives us a hero who is cunning and capable, whether navigating the Court or the open moors'   *Time Out*

'A superb medieval mystery, thoroughly grounded in historical fact'   *Booklist*

'Enthralling and evocative . . . Candace Robb recreates medieval York with ease'   *Yorkshire Evening Press*

Also by Candace Robb

THE GUILT OF INNOCENTS

CANDACE ROBB

arrow books

Published by Arrow Books 2008

10 9

Copyright © Candace Robb 2007

Candace Robb has asserted her right under the Copyright, Designs and
Patents Act 1988 to be identified as the author of this work

First published in Great Britain in 2007 by
William Heinemann
Random House, 20 Vauxhall Bridge Road
London SW1V 2SA

www.randomhouse.co.uk

Addresses for companies within The Random House Group Limited can be
found at: www.randomhouse.co.uk/offices.htm

The Random House Group Limited Reg. No. 954009

A CIP catalogue record for this book
is available from the British Library

ISBN 9780099497899

Typeset in Sabon by Palimpsest Book Production Limited,
Grangemouth, Stirlingshire

The Random House Group Limited supports The Forest Stewardship
Council® (FSC®), the leading international forest-certification organisation.
Our books carrying the FSC label are printed on FSC®-certified paper.
FSC is the only forest-certification scheme supported by the leading
environmental organisations, including Greenpeace. Our
paper procurement policy can be found at
www.randomhouse.co.uk/environment

MIX
Paper from
responsible sources
FSC® C016897

Printed and bound in Great Britain by Clays Ltd, St Ives plc

TABLE OF CONTENTS

DEDICATION

As I was completing this book, I learned of the sudden death of a dear friend's grandson, from diabetic ketoacidosis, and I knew that I wanted to dedicate this book to his memory.

Andrew Kyle Henderson,
15 April 1985–9 December 2005

'Full of zest and the joy of life, he laughed often and had a wonderful sense of humour. From his earliest years he quickly caught on to jokes and enjoyed making them. He was loving, and had the gift of attracting very good friends. Young men are so much more vulnerable than they know – or would be willing to admit.'

acknowledgements

I want to thank historians RaGena D'Aragon, Jo
Ann Hoeppner Moran Cruz, and Compton Reeves
for their generous help, and the wonderful gang
on Chaucernet for all sorts of incidental information and inspiration; Joyce Gibb for a careful first
reading of the manuscript; the members of
Medfem for feedback on birthing crosses; Kate
Elton and Georgina Hawtrey-Woore for asking
all the right questions, and all the talented people
at Heinemann and Arrow who work behind the
scenes.

Special thanks to Charlie for the 24/7 support
and tlc he provides. I'm a lucky woman.

LIST OF CHARACTERS

Owen Archer (Captain Archer)	captain of guard and spy for Archbishop of York; steward of Bishopthorpe
Lucie Wilton	master apothecary; Owen's spouse
Nicholas Wilton	deceased, Lucie's first husband, master apothecary
Hugh and Gwenllian	Owen and Lucie's natural children
Jasper de Melton	Owen and Lucie's adopted son and Lucie's apprentice in the apothecary
Dame Phillippa	Lucie's aged aunt
Alisoun Ffulford	nursemaid to Owen and Lucie's children
Kate	Lucie's housemaid
Bess and Tom Merchet	owners of the York Tavern
Edric	apprentice in the apothecary

Sir Baldwin Gamyll	Aubrey de Weston's lord; father of Osmund, husband of Janet
Abbot Campian	abbot of St Mary's Abbey
Alfred	member of arch-bishop's guard, Owen's second
Rafe, Gilbert	members of arch-bishop's guard
*Dean John	dean of York Minster
*Chancellor Thomas Farnilaw	chancellor of York Minster; in charge of the schools
*Canon William Ferriby	member of minster chapter, brother of Nicholas and Peter; actual name John (see Author's Note)
Nigel	journeyman goldsmith
Edward Munkton	goldsmith, Nigel's master
Alice Tanner	tanner's wife
Dame Lotta	Nigel's landlady
Robert Dale	goldsmith

*real historical figure

GLOSSARY

churching	a woman's first appearance in church to give thanks after childbirth
mazer	a large wooden cup or bowl, often highly decorated
mystery	craft, or trade, particularly used in connection with craft guilds
pandemain	the finest quality white bread, made from flour sifted two or three times
scrip	a small bag or wallet
staithe	a landing-stage or wharf
toswollen	pregnant

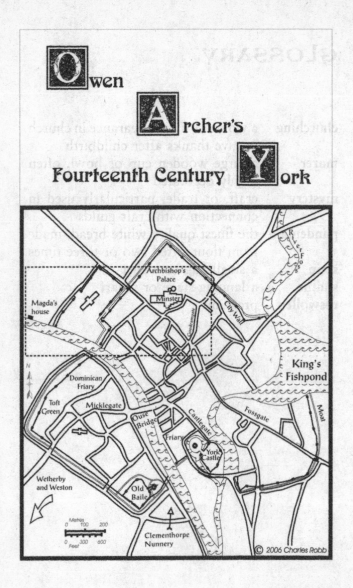

Owen **A**rcher's

Fourteenth Century **Y**ork

River Fiss

Archbishop's
Palace

Minster

Magda's
house

City Wall

Petergate

King's
Fishpond

N

Dominican
Friary

Toft
Green

Micklegate

Ouse
Bridge

Castlegate

Fossgate

Moat

Friary

York
Castle

Wetherby
and Weston

Old
Baile

Metres
0   100   200

Feet
0   300   600

Clementhorpe
Nunnery

© 2006 Charles Robb

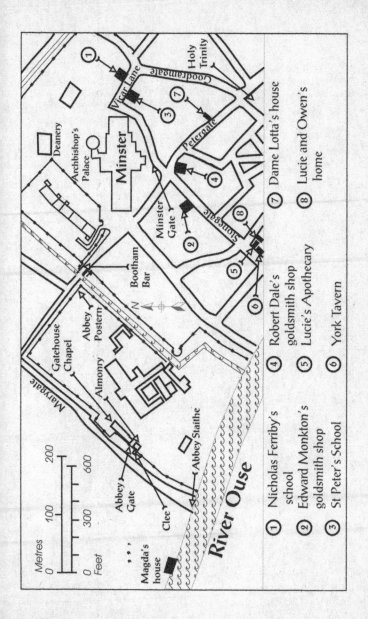

Metres
0   100   200
Feet
0   300   600

River Ouse

Magda's house

Marygate

Gatehouse Chapel
Almonry
Abbey Postern
Abbey Gate
Clee
Abbey Staithe

Deanery
Archbishop's Palace

Minster

Bootham Bar

Minster Gate

N

Vicar Lane
Goodramgate
Holy Trinity

Petergate

Stonegate

① Nicholas Ferriby's school
② Edward Monkton's goldsmith shop
③ St Peter's School

④ Robert Dale's goldsmith shop
⑤ Lucie's Apothecary
⑥ York Tavern

⑦ Dame Lotta's house
⑧ Lucie and Owen's home

PROLOGUE

York, late November 1372

The tavern noises swirled above Drogo's bent head, but he found them easier to ignore than the constant chatter of his daughters and wife in his tiny home. He loved them more than his life, but when he was home they could not let him rest. After a week piloting ships on the Ouse he was weary to the bone but they thought he was home to make repairs and listen to their tales of woe. So he'd come to the tavern intending to drink himself into a comfortable stupor and then stumble home to pass out, blissfully oblivious to all.

He had just begun his first ale when the man he least wished to see appeared at his table.

'Behind the tavern,' was all the man said before turning sharp and walking back out into the chilly afternoon.

Fearing him too much to ignore him, Drogo gulped down what remained in his tankard and pushed himself from the table, clumsily spilling the drink of the well-dressed man across from him.

'Watch what you're doing,' the man muttered.

Drogo apologised aloud, but beneath his breath he cursed as he walked away. 'Mewling merchant. Thinks he's the centre of God's kingdom on earth. He can afford to spill ale.'

Outside the wind encouraged Drogo to duck quickly into the narrow alley. The overhanging roofs blocked what little light remained in the sky, and Drogo had not yet adjusted to the dark when he felt a sharp blade slice across his cheek. 'For pity's sake!' He flung up his hands to shield himself but too late to prevent another cut, this one on his neck.

'I warned you what would happen if you crossed me,' his attacker growled. 'Thieving and telling tales.'

Another flick of the blade sliced Drogo's hands.

'Keep your cursed money!' Drogo shouted. 'I wash my hands of you.'

He turned and bolted down Petergate and through Bootham Bar, the streets blessedly empty, not looking back until he stumbled just without the city walls. The bastard was not following. Drogo slowed his pace and hurried on towards the Abbey Staithe and the safety of his fellow bargemen.

'Dear Lord, I swear I'll stick to my proper work from now on, I'm a pilot and a bargeman, not a trafficker. I swear.'

One

BEST INTENTIONS

The Benedictine Abbey of St Mary dominated the northern bank of the River Ouse just upriver from the city of York, and it also owned extensive lands throughout Yorkshire and elsewhere in the realm whose rents and crops supported the community of monks. Its staithe, or dock, at the foot of Marygate served as the hub for moving the abbey's products, supplies, and personnel, as well as the frequent visitors both clerical and noble. A group of liveried bargemen operated the staithe, chosen for their strength and knowledge of the river and its moods, not for their education or piety.

At St Peter's School, the song and grammar school of York Minster, Master John de York presided over twelve endowed choristers and at least sixty paying young scholars, many of whom lived in the Clee, a house owned by the minster although attached to the Almonry of St Mary's Abbey in Marygate, not far from the Abbey

1

Staithe. The high-spirited boys often tangled with the bargemen. The bargemen taunted the scholars for their privileged lifestyle and useless learning, and the boys retaliated by clambering about the landing place and sometimes onto the barges wreaking innocent havoc. Occasionally, the uneasy relationship erupted into violence . . .

As was his custom, Jasper de Melton had lingered in the classroom after the lessons ended for the day to copy an additional reading into his precious notebook of old parchment scraps that Captain Archer had bound for him. Master John hummed as he tidied the room, occasionally stealing a peek at Jasper's work. The grammar master's interest annoyed Jasper a little because he did not want to feel rushed. He'd make a mistake for sure, tired as he was by this time of day, and he hated scraping and recopying. That would be one less layer for a future reading. He sighed with relief when he came to the end of the brief passage. Even without the master he would have felt the urge to hurry this afternoon, for he wanted to accompany his fellow scholars to the Abbey Staithe.

Frosty air shocked him out of his late afternoon drowsiness as he pushed wide the door of St Peter's School, and it momentarily killed his enthusiasm for the coming drama, an attempt by his fellows to recover a schoolmate's scrip, or purse, from a less-than-honest abbey bargeman named Drogo who had just been seen back at the

2

staithe. Jasper must head to the staithe now if he meant to participate, and then board the barges anchored there. The mere thought made him shrug up his shoulders to protect his neck and ears in anticipation of the cold – it was a week past Martinmas and winter had taken hold. He'd forgotten his cap this morning, and his hands, which stuck out of his sleeves, were already stinging from the icy air. He'd suddenly grown quite a bit. His foster mother Dame Lucie said that it was his recent burst of growth that caused his legs to ache at night, waking him, not unusual at the age of fourteen. A restless night was certainly the cause of his oversleeping this morning and then, in his hurry to be on time, forgetting his cap and gloves.

Jasper was glad to be back at the minster school among his friends – he enjoyed being caught up in the energy that bubbled up to the surface now and then, as it had today when the more senior boys heard that Drogo had been seen at the staithe. Timing was critical because Drogo frequently travelled up and down the Ouse piloting ships between York and the sea, so he might not stay long in the city. The older boys had quickly devised a plan to confront the man about Hubert's scrip: the main body of scholars were to rush the bargemen and distract them while the older scholars dealt with Drogo.

Jasper wasn't convinced that Hubert's absence from school the past week had to do with the loss of his scrip. That had happened more than a fortnight earlier, and Hubert had attended class for a week afterwards. He knew that the lad had more on his mind than his lost scrip. In the autumn Jasper had come upon him behind the school, all curled into himself and weeping. Jasper had heard that the lad's father was feared dead. Having lost his own father when younger than Hubert, Jasper understood the fear in the boy's eyes when he loosened up and began to talk of his mother's troubles with the farm, how suddenly they were poor. In Jasper's opinion such a loss and the subsequent fear about the future were more likely to keep Hubert away from the classroom than would the loss of a scrip. Although if it had held money its recovery might comfort the lad a little.

Perhaps that was sufficient reason to help recover it, even though Jasper had promised the captain that he would not get involved in the skirmishes between the scholars and the bargemen. He was still debating whether to follow his fellows or to head straight home to the apothecary. He doubted he would contribute much as he was unfamiliar with the barges, but he knew he'd feel left out when the others talked about it afterwards. He was sympathetic to Hubert's situation as well.

It was plain that he must quickly choose, for those leading the band of scholars were already out of sight. In fact, the light had faded enough that Jasper could see only the last few stragglers.

Surely he might be late to the apothecary this one afternoon. He'd been a diligent apprentice the past year, having withdrawn from school the previous autumn when Dame Lucie was injured in a fall and could not spare him from the apothecary – she was his master as well as his adoptive mother. Dame Lucie had regretted cutting short his education, so she'd worked to convince the guild to provide her a second apprentice in order that Jasper might complete his studies. A few months ago Edric had joined the household, an experienced apprentice a few years Jasper's senior whose master had recently died. Edric could mind the shop.

By now his fellows were out of sight and it was a long way to the staithe – through the minster grounds to Petergate, out Bootham Bar and into the grounds of St Mary's Abbey by the postern gate, and then out into Marygate and down to the landing. He shut the door behind him and took off into the fading light. Slipping occasionally on frozen mud, Jasper was breathing hard by the time he caught up with the last of the group at Bootham Bar, and his hands and ears were numb. He ignored his physical discomfort as he hurried with them across the abbey grounds, but that was just part of his discomfort now, as he noticed they were being joined by curious onlookers, adults, strangers, not their fellows. He was growing increasingly uneasy about what else might be happening, about what he might be heading into.

As shouts echoed from the staithe, he and the stragglers ran the last few yards, then slowed upon reaching the barrels and covered flats that had been offloaded from the barges. The long, flat-bottomed vessels were bobbing on the water with the movements of several dozen people darting about, shouting, waving arms. The fading light made it difficult to tell bargemen from the older boys at first, and Jasper thought he'd made a mistake in coming. Glancing around at the gathering crowd he saw fists clenched and heard tension in the voices muttering about privileged scholars and hard-working bargemen, poor lads defending their own and bullying staithe workers. This was growing into something much larger than merely recovering a friend's purse.

'How will we know if we come upon the bargeman who took Hubert's scrip?' asked one of Jasper's companions.

He hesitated to respond, considering whether it would not be wise to make a run for home, but he resolved to stay – he was already here, and his reasons for wanting to help Hubert had not changed. 'Ned said Drogo wears a green cap, has a much broken nose, and a tooth missing up front,' Jasper said. Ned was one of the raid leaders.

'Come on, then,' cried one of the others, grabbing Jasper's frozen hand.

They'd just stepped onto the nearest barge when

someone crashed into Jasper, and the two went sprawling on the slippery wooden deck.

The human missile groaned as he sat up, rubbing his head. 'I almost had him!' It was Ned.

Jasper stood and brushed himself off. 'Now what?'

Ned had pulled himself up and leaned out over the water to peer at the neighbouring barge. 'I can't see him now. I hope one of the others grabbed him. But I tell you, one look in that man's face and I knew there'd be nothing left of value in that scrip. He has the eyes of a thief, mark me.'

'The eyes of a sick man – that's what I saw,' said another lad. 'He was pale as wax and stumbling like he was unwell or drunk.'

Jasper moved away from the argument that commenced, and in towards the action, remaining wary of sudden movements. He found several lads looking towards the next barge, which was wildly rocking.

'I have it!' someone cried from there. Voices rose in a victory shout. A splash inspired more shouting that gradually softened to anxious queries and responses.

'Can you see him?' a man shouted.

'He's gone under,' cried another.

'There he is, towards the stern,' one of the boys called out.

'I've lost him.' The speaker's voice cracked with defeat.

* * *

7

An icy blanket enveloped him, slaking the fire in his cheek, his neck, his arm. *God be praised*, Drogo thought, almost whimpering but knowing somehow even as confused as he was that he must not inhale. It did not matter that the current tumbled him for the water eased him, it smoothed away the pain, the guilt, the anger. *Forgive me, O Lord*, he prayed, *and let me return to my Cissy and my daughters, more precious to me than gold or silver*.

Jasper grabbed the elbow of his nearest fellow. 'Who's in the water?'

'Drogo, the one who took Hubert's scrip.'

'Was he pushed?' Jasper whispered. He could not imagine any of the older scholars taking such a risk.

'I don't know.'

God help him, Jasper prayed. Drogo had stolen a scrip, which to the thinking of his foster father, Captain Archer, was hardly a crime deserving death. The captain said a thief should be executed only if he'd also taken a life. Jasper didn't understand how this evening's worthy goal could have led to this horror.

After another splash, there was a hush, except for a whispered, 'A swimmer's gone in to help him.'

'Someone fetch Brother Henry from the abbey,' a man cried. Henry was the abbey infirmarian.

Before Jasper could think to go, he saw that

two other students were already running from the staithe down Marygate. Jasper prayed for both the good Samaritan and Drogo as he followed the bargemen and scholars returning to the riverbank, all pushing, shoving, cursing as if frightened – as if as frightened as Jasper now was. The wind had picked up, adding the danger of fire to his worries. He watched a man cup his hand dangerously close to a burning taper as he lit a lantern held by his mate, cursing as the flame licked his hand. Several lanterns already illuminated the worried faces of the townsfolk, boys and bargemen who now gathered about the two men holding a rope attached to the rescuer, ready to assist him in fighting the current to the shore. Another stood close with a long pole.

'Why don't all bargemen learn to swim?' one of Jasper's companions asked.

'Do you know how to swim?' asked Jasper.

'No, but the ferrywoman near our farm does. She says only a fool works on the Ouse without the knowledge.' The boy was quiet a moment. 'Can the Riverwoman swim?'

Jasper had never wondered that, but he could not imagine the midwife and healer Magda Digby giving in to the rushing water. The elderly woman was too wise to live on the river as she did if she feared it. 'I've no doubt she can do anything she decides to do. Hush now. They're bringing him out.'

As the swimmer climbed up the bank, the two

on the rope dropped it to relieve him of his human burden.

'Is he dead?' folk asked as Drogo's limbs gently swayed with the men's gait.

They laid him face down, and the one who'd held the pole knelt beside him and went to work pressing the Ouse from Drogo's lungs. When he coughed weakly the growing crowd cheered, but grew quiet as Brother Henry, the abbey infirmarian, pushed through to the prostrate form. After listening with bent head to the comments of the man working on Drogo, the monk turned to the crowd and asked them to pray for the man's soul. Jasper knew Brother Henry, and he read resignation in his expression.

'He is very weak,' said Brother Henry.

'We'll carry him to the statue of the Virgin,' said one of the abbey bargemen.

'The Virgin! Yes, she saved my Tom,' a woman cried.

It was custom to bring the victims of river accidents to the life-sized statue of the Blessed Mother that graced the main gate of St Mary's, for she had worked many miracles. Jasper was glad someone had thought of that.

With Brother Henry solemnly leading the way, Jasper and his fellows, the bargemen, and the townsfolk all walked the short distance to the abbey gate. Drogo was laid before the Virgin on a pallet that had been brought out by abbey servants. Jasper found himself standing beside

10

Master Nicholas Ferriby, the Vicar of Weston and Master of a small grammar school in the minster liberty. He'd offended the dean and chancellor of York Minster by locating it so close to their grammar school, the one Jasper attended. It did not seem to help that Master Nicholas was brother to one of their fellows, the keeper of the minster fabric. Jasper knew the Ferriby family because another brother, a merchant, was married to one of Dame Lucie's closest friends.

Shaking his head, Master Nicholas said, 'It is a sad afternoon's business, young Jasper. I understand the pilot is dying.'

Jasper crossed himself. 'He was not long in the water, but it's so cold.' He shivered at the thought of it.

A well-dressed young man joined them, though in truth he joined Master Nicholas for he did not seem to notice Jasper at all.

'This will go ill with the dean and chancellor, Father Nicholas,' said the newcomer in what seemed to Jasper a goading tone. 'I pray none of your scholars were involved.'

'They were not,' Nicholas said with undisguised irritation. 'What brings you to York, Master Osmund? I should think you'd be in Weston celebrating your father's safe return.'

'I've already toasted Sir Baldwin,' said Osmund. 'Why aren't you tending your flock in Weston?'

Jasper recalled that Hubert's father was fighting for a Sir Baldwin of Weston. 'Did Hubert de

Weston's father return as well?' he asked Nicholas.

The priest nodded and said quietly, 'I pray that's where the lad's gone, to see his father.'

'We should dine together while I'm in the city,' said Osmund, ignoring Jasper.

Noticing that Brother Henry was alone despite the crowd of people clogging Marygate, Jasper pushed his way towards him in the hope of finding out more about Drogo's condition. Brother Henry's predecessor as infirmarian of St Mary's, Brother Wulfstan, had been Jasper's good friend, and through him he'd known Brother Henry since the monk's novice days. It took him a little while to work through the gossiping, excited people.

Henry met Jasper's greeting with a distracted, worried expression.

'This is a terrible evening, terrible,' he said. 'I was just thinking of Captain Archer when you hailed me.'

Jasper glanced round. 'The captain? I didn't see him.' What he did see was a man lying on the pallet, blankets and hides now wrapped about him like heavy winding sheets, his face the only part of him visible.

'The captain's not here,' said Brother Henry. 'I was considering whether to ask my lord abbot's permission to seek the captain's advice. I fear that what happened to this man was no accident.'

Owen Archer was captain of the archbishop's guard and noted in the city for solving crimes for the archbishop.

'Is Drogo still alive?' Jasper asked, still staring at the body placed before the Blessed Mother as if an offering.

'He is, God be praised, but I doubt he will be for long unless we move him in to the infirmary so that I might care for him.' The servants who had brought out the pallet for Drogo waited nearby with poles ready to turn the pallet into a litter.

'*Benedicite*, Jasper, Brother Henry.'

Abbot Campian's arrival stirred them both to straighten up as if they'd been discovered at some mischief.

'If the poor man dies I shall insist that the scholars of St Peter's pay for his funeral mass and burial,' said the abbot. 'Perhaps that will put an end to their warfare.' Campian believed order to be man's greatest virtue, and so deplored the feud between the students and the bargemen.

Jasper felt his face grow hot under the abbot's stern gaze. 'We meant only to help one of our fellows.' He felt unjustly accused.

'I have heard the story,' said the abbot. 'Had you informed your schoolmaster of the boy's loss he would have seen to it.'

Of course he would have. Jasper bowed his head, feeling more than a little foolish despite not having been involved in the planning. It hadn't even occurred to him that Master John might intercede for them, and obviously it had not occurred to the older boys.

'My Lord Abbot, if I might call your attention to the dying man.' Henry drew the abbot towards Drogo. 'Certain marks on his left cheek, near the ear, and his neck and hands suggest that he'd been engaged in a struggle before he fell into the water.'

'I'd not heard of this,' said Campian.

'The wounds had been cleansed by the cold waters,' said Henry.

'Then this earlier struggle might be why he fell in?' The abbot nodded to himself.

'Perhaps,' said Henry.

Jasper stepped closer to Drogo in the abbot's shadow. Slashes, they looked like, made by a very sharp blade. 'Perhaps this did not happen on the barge, my Lord Abbot,' Jasper said, keeping his voice low. 'One of my fellows said he'd looked ill when he arrived at the barges.'

'Did you see him arrive?' asked Campian.

Jasper shook his head.

Abbot Campian thanked Jasper, then took Brother Henry aside.

'What are you suggesting?' the abbot asked the infirmarian.

'Perhaps this man had a falling out with someone else besides Hubert de Weston's friends,' said Henry loud enough that Jasper could hear him, 'someone armed and far more aggressive than the boys.'

Campian frowned down at the ground. 'Why then did he go to the barges, I wonder?'

'He felt safe amongst his friends?' Henry

shrugged. 'He might not have realised how badly injured he was, how weak.'

'I'd thought it an unfortunate accident, but it certainly looks otherwise,' said Campian. 'Still, the lads should be taught a lesson.'

Sensing a disturbance behind him, Jasper glanced back. Master Nicholas Ferriby was making his way through the crowd towards Drogo. He bent close to the drowned man, whispering a prayer.

It was not Master Nicholas but a man close behind him and a little to one side who gasped and then cried out, 'He bleeds!'

To Jasper's astonishment he saw blood oozing from the wounds on the man's face and neck. He glanced back up to see the schoolmaster's reaction.

Master Nicholas looked towards the crowd with a puzzled frown and then down at Drogo. He staggered backwards with a cry. 'Sweet Mary and all the saints!' He crossed himself.

'Holy Mother of God,' a boy cried. 'Master Nicholas drew blood from the corpse.'

His exclamation was repeated throughout the crowd accompanied by gasps and cries of dismay.

Nicholas turned to the young speaker, his eyes flashing in the lantern light. 'I did nothing but pray for his soul.'

'Drogo is not dead,' Brother Henry loudly reminded them.

Abbot Campian stepped forward, and taking

15

Nicholas by the elbow he guided him aside. 'The crowd's mood grows dangerous. I advise you to withdraw into the abbey close as soon as you can do so without notice,' he said softly, though Jasper heard it, and apparently so did some of the monks who had drawn near, for they silently shifted just enough to give Master Nicholas cover in which to withdraw.

'Am I to be a scapegoat for Master John's scholars?' Nicholas protested.

'Accept my offer or be damned,' hissed the abbot.

'Forgive me, my Lord Abbot,' Nicholas murmured, and with head lowered slipped away.

Abbot Campian turned to address the crowd. 'This is no corpse,' he said in an arrestingly authoritative voice. 'This man yet lives.'

'But he was not bleeding before Master Nicholas approached him,' cried a woman.

'His wounds were so chilled by the waters of the Ouse that the blood clotted,' said Brother Henry. 'We have managed to warm him enough so that it flows again.'

But the murmuring in the crowd was not friendly.

'A corpse bleeds when the murderer is near,' a man far back in the crowd shouted.

'A corpse, perhaps,' said Henry. 'Not a living man.'

Abbot Campian put a hand on Henry's arm. 'I've sent for the bailiffs. I don't like the temper

16

of the crowd. Such confusion is a sign of trouble.'

'God help us that the scholars' charitable intention should turn so foul,' said Henry.

'Where is Master Nicholas, my Lord Abbot?' a man asked much more loudly than necessary. Others echoed the question. There was much jostling, and angry words flew as people's tempers rose.

Jasper recognised the speaker – he was frequently escorted from the York Tavern for drunkenness.

A bargeman spoke out. 'The schoolmaster was not on the river when Drogo fell. Brother Henry is right, he was too cold at first for his wounds to bleed.'

Brother Henry knelt and gently cleaned Drogo's face, then rose and quietly said, 'My Lord Abbot, I would take him to the infirmary where he will be warmer, and send for Captain Archer to come look at his wounds.'

'Why is that?'

'The colour of the skin is not as it should be. I believe he was cut with a poisoned blade.'

The abbot paused for a heartbeat, then turned to Jasper. 'Can you find the captain for us?'

With a nod, Jasper set out in the direction of the abbey gates, shivering now not only with the cold, but also about the miserable result of his fellows' actions and the jagged tempers of the people.

* * *

17

Now Drogo whimpered in pain and cursed his mate for plucking him from the kind waters of the Ouse. He cursed him for bringing back the pain, the threads of fire that radiated ever farther out from his wounds, torturing him for the sins for which he'd already been shriven by God and the river. *My girls – God protect my daughters and my wife.*

Owen Archer had spent the afternoon in the barracks of Archbishop Thoresby's guards with Alfred, his second in command. For almost eight years they had worked together protecting the archbishop and keeping the peace in the minster liberty, the north-western section of the city surrounding the archbishop's palace, York Minster, and the school and residences connected to both. Owen's duties had often been extended to include protecting other dignitaries who had asked for the archbishop's protection – as the second most powerful representative of the Church in England and former Lord Chancellor of the realm, John Thoresby was a man of influence.

But even the powerful slow with age, and as Thoresby had been ailing for the past year he no longer travelled to Westminster or King Edward's court, but rather spent his time now in Yorkshire. Today Owen and Alfred had been discussing the logistics of Thoresby's imminent move to his palace of Bishopthorpe for Advent. In addition to his other duties, Owen was steward of Bishopthorpe;

18

he had just returned from his monthly visit to the estate and was informing Alfred, who was to lead the half-dozen guards who would attend the archbishop, of changes, projects in progress, and new considerations for guarding the archbishop in his failing health.

Alfred, who had been frowning down at his hands and occasionally nodding, suddenly interrupted Owen's monologue. 'I don't understand why His Grace wishes to bide at Bishopthorpe in this season. There's such a wheezing in his chest, and that palace sits right on the Ouse, it's damp and chill.' Alfred shivered. 'There will be flood waters soon, mark me. It's no place for His Grace.' He took off his cap, his pate shiny where it had once held a shock of straw-coloured hair, and scratched his scalp, leaving trails of reddened skin.

Owen agreed with Alfred; a mere fortnight past Thoresby had returned to the city saying he wished to escape the late autumn rains on the river; but he later confided that he could not bear the isolation of Bishopthorpe for long. 'His Grace means by returning to Bishopthorpe to appease Dean John. They complain he's spent too much time in the city of late.'

Although Thoresby was Archbishop of York, the dean and the chapter of canons were the administrators of the great cathedral and its properties, and his chancellor was in charge of the schools. They had become accustomed to little supervision by their archbishops and felt threatened by Thoresby's frequent and extended residence in the city.

'But His Grace has spent the better part of the year at Bishopthorpe,' said Alfred.

'Aye. It's his frequent returns to the city they don't like, no matter how brief. They claim folk are gossiping about how he distrusts them, though I've heard no such talk.'

'Can't they see he's ill!'

'Of course they see. Perhaps it's just as well. In truth, he's glad to escape the controversy over Master Nicholas Ferriby's grammar school. Chancellor Thomas has threatened Nicholas with excommunication, Dean John supports the threat, and Nicholas's brother Canon William has voiced his support – now they cannot understand why His Grace will not.' Owen was glad of Thoresby's stance, for his children's nurse, Alisoun, was thriving in Ferriby's school.

'And no wonder His Grace won't support their complaint,' said Alfred, 'excommunication for competing with the minster school? It's daft. His brother William has no backbone.'

'William's reacting to the early rumours that he was protecting Nicholas,' said Owen. 'Their enemies said the Ferriby brothers were building power, that they meant to have Peter mayor and William dean.' Owen and Lucie were close friends of Peter and Emma Ferriby, so they had heard much of the rumours when they were first spread about. Both Peter and William had tried to distance themselves from their brother Nicholas once it was clear he intended to stay in the liberty. The dean and chapter felt that over the years the chapter's influence in the city had been chipped away by the mayor, council, and bailiffs, and the existence of competing schools in the city threatened the income from students' fees that covered the upkeep of St Peter's School and the master's expenses. Although neither Peter nor William had high ambitions in the city they did not want to risk losing what comfortable success they enjoyed – Peter was a successful and prominent member of the Mercers Guild and William, as keeper of the minster fabric, held great responsibility for the upkeep of the magnificent cathedral and claustral buildings.

As for the archbishop's support, Owen understood why the dean and chancellor might have assumed Thoresby's cooperation. Five years earlier he had censored the opening of song schools in the city, but their purpose was ecclesiastical, not practical like a grammar school, and Thoresby now insisted the difference was everything. To Dean John and Chancellor Thomas it was another sign of the rising power of the York laity.

'In the long run it would be far more comfortable for everyone, particularly Master Nicholas, if he moved his school out of the minster liberty,' Owen said. 'Surely –'

A banging on the door interrupted him. He opened it with such a jerk that Jasper almost fell into the room.

'What is it, lad?' Owen asked as his foster son slumped down onto a bench and fought to catch his breath. 'Alfred, is there anything to drink?'

Alfred picked up a jug on a windowsill and shook it. 'Aye, though it's only well water,' he said as he poured a cup.

Jasper took it with thanks and drank it down.

'A bargeman fell into the river and almost drowned.' Jasper paused to burp. 'They took him to the Virgin at the abbey gate. As Master Nicholas approached him he began to bleed, and people are saying he's a murderer, though Drogo – the bargeman – isn't dead. Brother Henry would have you look at the wounds because he thinks they are poisoned.'

'Whose wounds?' Owen asked.

'Drogo's,' said Jasper.

'Who went in the water?' Alfred asked as he refilled Jasper's cup.

'Drogo, the pilot, the one we were looking for.' Jasper drank down the second cup.

'Are his wounds mortal?' Owen asked.

Jasper shook his head. 'Slits on his face, neck and hands. They didn't look deep. But if the blade was poisoned . . .' he raised his eyebrows.

That would make all the difference. Owen nodded, and was about to remind Jasper that he'd promised not to participate in the battles between the scholars and the bargemen – the latter being a rough lot – but he decided to hold his tongue until he heard more. 'Why were you looking for him?' he asked.

Jasper pressed his hands to his eyes and shook his head slowly, as if wondering that himself. 'We wanted to recover a scrip that Hubert de Weston lost a fortnight ago. This Drogo had grabbed it and then refused to return it.'

A bargeman teaching a boy a lesson. It seemed innocent enough. 'That's all?'

'Aye. But none of us would attack him with a poisoned blade.'

No, Owen did not think that likely. 'How was Master Nicholas involved?' he asked.

Jasper shook his head. 'He wasn't. Drogo was warm at last and the bleeding started again. But the people wanted to blame him. Is it such a terrible thing he did, to open a school in the minster liberty?'

'No it is not,' said Owen, 'and I can't think why most folk would care one whit about Nicholas Ferriby. Unless there's a rumour I've not heard. I don't know that I'd risk my soul's salvation for the prestige of teaching in the liberty. If they say he's up to something more than education . . .'

'Has someone gone for the bailiffs?' Alfred asked.

Jasper nodded. 'And Abbot Campian told

Master Nicholas to go into the abbey grounds to escape the crowd. They've taken Drogo to the abbey infirmary.'

Owen nodded. 'The abbot is a sensible man. You look half-frozen yourself, Jasper. Go straight home. Tell your mistress what has happened and where I am.' He shook his head as he saw the argument form in Jasper's eyes. 'You'll hear all that I learn. Now go. I am off to Brother Henry.'

Shrugging his disappointment, Jasper slumped out of the barracks.

Lucie and Owen's house sat on the corner of St Helen's Square and Davygate, next to Wilton's Apothecary, the shop Lucie carried on from her first husband, Nicholas. When he was alive and then when she and Owen were first wed the building that housed the shop had also been her home. Her father, whose manor of Freythorpe Hadden was in the countryside south of York, had purchased the large house across the garden so that he might spend more time in the city with his grandchildren, and on his death he'd left the town house as well as the manor to Lucie. It was a beautiful home in which to raise her children and provide a comfortable home for her aged aunt, Phillippa, who'd been crippled in body and mind by a palsy. Joining the gardens had allowed Lucie to grow a greater variety of *materia medica* for the apothecary. All in all she felt very blessed in her marriage, her children, her career, her life – and especially this healthy pregnancy.

The afternoon light faded quickly at this time of year in the North, and though the hall boasted casement windows looking out onto the extensive garden Lucie was glad of the light from the hall fire and several wall sconces. Phillippa napped by the fire near the table at which Lucie was working on the shop accounts. Alisoun Ffulford, the children's nursemaid, had just risen from her seat across the way and lit an oil lamp, placing it beside Lucie – unasked for.

'Bless you, Alisoun,' said Lucie, trying to keep the surprise out of her voice, for she knew the young woman would take it as a subtle criticism.

It had taken some time, but Lucie had ceased fretting over the volatility of Alisoun's moods, having witnessed how the young woman struggled to smooth them out. Certainly Jasper seemed immune to Alisoun's moods except when she snapped at him – for he greatly admired her. Lucie suspected that Alisoun felt likewise about Jasper. She was consistent with the children, firm but kind and always ready to sing or read to them. It was in the idle moments, especially after Gwenllian and Hugh were abed, that Alisoun fought her devils, her resentment of the kin who were her guardians and her frustration with Magda Digby's elusiveness. She'd wished to apprentice to Magda, but so far she'd had little opportunity to work beside the midwife and healer.

Lucie had never expected Alisoun to be so long

a part of her household – she'd been Gwenllian and Hugh's nurse for more than a year. Her understanding had been that the girl was temporarily assisting her after she'd fallen and miscarried and suddenly needed more help in the house. Indeed, at the moment Lucie shared some of Alisoun's impatience with Magda. When Lucie had realised she was again with child she'd told Magda that it was time to replace Alisoun with a wet nurse. Magda had assured her she had already begun to look for one, and more recently that she had someone in mind. Yet not a word of Alisoun's replacement had come in many a week. Lucie was quite satisfied with Alisoun most of the time, but she agreed with Owen that even if a wet nurse was not required, Alisoun was still too inexperienced to take on the care of a newborn in addition to Hugh and Gwenllian. Now, with only a month until she delivered, Lucie was growing anxious about the arrangements.

But it was not her wont to complain these days, so happy was she that she'd conceived again. The loss of the baby she'd carried the previous year had sent her into such a sinful despair that she had feared her penance would be to bear no more children. Then just as she'd set her mind to being content with Gwenllian and Hugh, her courses had stopped. Still she had feared saying anything to Owen or to Magda. It was Owen who had coaxed her to talk of it, noticing with delight her swelling breasts.

'I fear to speak such hope,' she'd whispered in the darkness of the night.

'Hope, my love?' Owen had said. 'You are much farther along than hope might bring you. Would you not like to make a special offering in the minster for your safe delivery?'

Owen had known just what to say. Lucie did not think any woman could have a better husband.

This evening Alisoun's woes concerned her grammar master. She was sitting at the hall table practising her letters on a slate while Lucie worked on the shop accounts. Kate, the cook and housemaid, had Gwenllian and Hugh in the kitchen feeding them an early supper.

'If it were only Master Nicholas's school being in the minster liberty I would not worry so,' Alisoun said, sitting stiffly straight as was her habit of late, 'but I'm certain that some of the students will gossip about the beliefs he holds that border on heresy.'

'Heresy? Master Nicholas?' This was the first Lucie had heard of heretical teachings. Word of this could get him stripped of his parish of Weston as well as his little school here in York.

It had been Owen's inspiration to send Alisoun to Master Nicholas's school. He'd noticed how closely she watched Lucie writing up the shop accounts and how eagerly she asked Jasper about his lessons. Owen's guilt over his insistence that she leave her post when the baby was born was assuaged by her obvious appreciation of the gift.

27

She was careful to fit her school work in around her duties in the household. She would be horribly disappointed if her grammar master brought ruin upon himself by insisting on keeping his school where it was – or, even worse, teaching heresy to his students. York had few good schools that accepted girls. How awful if Alisoun lost both her job and her school at the same time.

What a wealth of worry because of the girl's chatter, Lucie thought, and in her condition she was a consummate worrier. She wished Alisoun would quietly work at her letters or at least take up a happier topic. Or that Aunt Phillippa would wake from her doze by the fire and join them. Lucie looked forward to the end of the children's meal when Kate handed them over to Alisoun and she would be busy once more.

Relief came from an unexpected quarter. Lucie's good friend Bess Merchet, mistress of the York Tavern just beyond the apothecary, knocked on the street door and then opened it to announce herself. She entered the hall before Lucie was on her feet. Her ample curves and the pale red hair that escaped her cap belied her age. She breathed life into a room merely by entering it.

'Sit, my friend,' Bess said as she hugged Lucie, always the hostess even in another's house. The ribbons on her cap quivered as she glanced around the room. 'Where are your men?'

'Owen and Jasper are not yet home,' said Lucie. 'Edric is in the shop.'

'Pity.' Bess eased herself down across from Alisoun. To Lucie, at the head of the table, she said, 'Your new apprentice is a comely lad.'

Lucie laughed. 'Trust you to notice, Bess.'

'Edric is no lad,' Alisoun blurted. 'He's eighteen.'

Her outburst and its accompanying deep blush surprised Lucie. Edric had not seemed to her a young man who would catch a young woman's interest. But considering him now, she realised he was comely in a delicate way, though part of that impression might be his shy demeanour. Still, she'd thought Alisoun preferred Jasper.

Bess leaned forward on her strong forearms to peer at what Alisoun was doing. 'I see you are practising your letters. What a fortunate day it was for you when you joined this household, eh? *And* when Nicholas Ferriby opened his school. Let us pray that the dean and chancellor hear nothing of your grammar master's peculiar ideas about the bible being translated into the common language or, even worse, how unacceptably wealthy the canons of York Minster are.'

So these were his heretical ideas. He sounded like a follower of John Wycliff, an English priest both famous and infamous. Lucie's stomach burned, and she took a slow, deep breath for the baby. With the dean and chapter already feeling threatened by the laity they would certainly pounce on the heretical idea of lay people

29

bypassing their priests by reading and interpreting the bible for themselves.

'Master Nicholas's ideas are tavern talk?' Alisoun asked in amazement.

'On dull evenings,' Bess said with a wink. 'But tonight people have something of more substance on their minds – or less, depending on your taste. Have you heard that Drogo the steersman almost drowned today?'

'Who is he?' Lucie asked.

'He's a pilot on the Ouse?' Alisoun asked. 'I should think they were often nearly drowned.'

'That is so.' Bess crossed her arms, relaxing. 'But not from the barges anchored at the Abbey Staithe, and not because one of the scholars of St Peter's School pushed him overboard.' She grinned at the surprise in both her listeners' eyes. 'Let us pray that he lives, or Captain Archer will be sent out to find the lad who pushed him in.'

'I pray Jasper was not among them,' Lucie said, worried because he was not yet home, though she could not imagine him doing such a thing. But neither could she imagine his fellows pushing a man overboard, and said so.

'Ay, but this steersman had kept a scrip one of the scholars lost in their last skirmish onboard the barges,' said Bess.

'Jasper told me about that,' said Alisoun. 'Hubert de Weston. He's a charity student at St Peter's this year. His father was in a siege in France – all of our countrymen died there. The

Spanish devils got them. Master Nicholas told us about it.'

'La Rochelle?' Bess asked.

Alisoun nodded. 'Jasper said that Hubert was very upset when he lost the scrip.'

Lucie vaguely remembered hearing something about the incident from Jasper. 'It sounds as if the lad can ill afford a loss like that. But why didn't the boys send Master John to speak to the man?'

'Why would they think he'd still have the scrip?' Bess asked. 'Sounds to me as if they just wanted to punish him, and it went much further than they'd intended.'

'You keep saying "they",' said Lucie. 'So it was not Hubert who pushed the man into the river?'

Bess hesitated, frowning as she considered all she had heard. 'Everyone speaks as if the lad wasn't there.'

'What will they do to the boys?' Alisoun asked.

'I don't know,' said Lucie, distracted by her concern. 'Owen might know what –' She paused, hearing the street door.

Jasper stepped into the hall, red-faced from the cold outdoors. He took in the occupants of the room and then took a step backwards as if wanting to retreat. Lucie could imagine his discomfort with all their eager eyes fastened on him, and him most likely tired and hungry.

'You're just the man we need,' Bess said. 'Come,

sit beside me.' She patted the bench on which she sat.

Jasper shuffled towards the table with a glance towards Lucie that appealed for help.

'Are you hungry?' she asked. 'Kate is feeding the little ones and I'm sure she'll give you something. You've only to go ask her.'

But Bess was not to be cheated of hearing an account of the excitement from a potential witness. 'Alisoun, why don't you see to some food for Jasper while he rests his growing bones beside me?'

Alisoun grudgingly pushed herself away from the table and rose.

At that moment, Edric stepped into the hall through the garden door. Throwing a smile his way, Alisoun stepped quite cheerfully towards the doorway in which he stood, brushing against him as she slipped out to the kitchen.

Edric, for his part, did not turn to watch Alisoun depart, but was already bobbing his head in greeting to Lucie, Bess, and Jasper.

'There's much talk of someone almost drowning,' he said with excited delight as he took the seat Alisoun had vacated. 'Do you think Captain Archer will be the one to catch the guilty one?'

'I pray that he isn't,' said Lucie. She wanted the baby to be welcomed by both its parents. 'Was the shop busy this afternoon?'

'Yes,' said Edric. 'The weather has folk sniffing and coughing, and their bones aching from the damp cold. I shut the shop to come eat something, but I promised several folk they might return later for their physicks. Why don't you want Captain Archer to search for the one who pushed the pilot, Mistress?'

'Because it's dangerous work and keeps him away from home,' Jasper snapped.

Edric blushed. 'Oh. Of course.'

Bess glanced towards Lucie, lifting her eyebrows in curiosity. Lucie noticed, but did not meet her friend's eyes, not wanting to irk either of her apprentices. Jasper had appeared so glad of Edric's presence at first, but gradually he'd begun to behave as if he resented him, and that resentment seemed to have grown stronger and stronger, for no cause apparent to Lucie. Edric worked hard and deferred to Jasper's long experience in the shop while also sharing the things he had learned from his former master. Now she wondered whether Alisoun was the thorn. That would be a great pity, for there was no remedying that sort of rivalry.

Still eyeing Edric, Jasper said, 'You would not be smiling had you seen the man pulled from the water.'

'Were you there?' Edric's eyes were alight.

Lucie suspected that he had no idea how Jasper felt about him.

'Yes.' Jasper turned to Lucie. 'The captain has gone to the abbey infirmary to see the man's wounds.'

Lucie inwardly groaned – Owen was involved.

'Wounds?' Bess murmured. 'I hadn't heard of wounds.'

'Do tell us what you saw, Jasper,' said Edric.

Jasper loudly sighed as he raked his straight, flaxen hair from his forehead. 'There was a crowd, and I saw little. I only heard that Drogo had gone into the river. I did not see him until he was pulled out.'

Lucie wondered whether had Jasper not been there Owen might have avoided becoming involved. She wished the lad had kept his promise to stay out of the skirmishes between the scholars and bargemen.

Alisoun had returned with a tray of food, and cups for both young men.

'So what of these wounds?' Bess asked.

'Someone had cut him on the face and neck, but most people did not see the cuts until they began to bleed.' Jasper glanced at Alisoun and sat up straighter when he found her eyes on him. 'Unfortunately Master Nicholas had just approached Drogo when his wounds began to bleed. The crowd began murmuring that he was a murderer.'

'Heaven help us,' whispered Lucie. 'Why him?'

'Because he was there when they saw the blood,' said Jasper. 'By then everyone was cold and tired and ripe for trouble. They'd been pushed around and their feet had been stepped on and their stomachs were growling. Rumours spread that didn't need to make any sense once the people were ready to explode. So when they saw the blood I wasn't surprised they cried out that Master Nicholas was a murderer even though Drogo's still alive.'

'My grammar master would never hurt anyone!' Alisoun cried.

'They've already hanged him in their hearts,' said Bess, 'especially Drogo's fellow bargemen. They protect their own and they're not gentle about it.'

All at the table crossed themselves, and grew quiet.

'I did hear some good news,' said Jasper, smiling at Lucie. 'Hubert's father and his lord are safely home in Weston.'

'God be praised,' said Lucie.

Later, after Edric and Jasper had returned to the shop and Alisoun had retired with the children, Bess said to Lucie, 'I thought Jasper was for the monastery. Did his calling die with Brother Wulfstan?'

'He still speaks of it, but now it is usually as a threat when he feels unappreciated.' Lucie smiled, remembering how she'd mourned that such a handsome young man would close himself off from the world. 'I have some doubt that he has a true vocation.'

'Not with the way he looks at Alisoun,' said Bess.

Indeed. 'This evening it appeared as if her heart

lies elsewhere,' said Lucie. 'I am both relieved and sorry for that. Poor Jasper.'

'Aye, but she would be a difficult partner, wilful and moody.'

'He sees none of that. But what do you think of Edric's behaviour? I didn't notice his eyes lingering on her.'

Bess shook her head. 'No, they linger on his mistress. And don't pretend to me that you've not seen that.'

Of course Lucie had noticed, and God help her but in her clumsy stage of pregnancy she enjoyed the flattery, though she took care to discourage it and keep Edric focused on his work. 'He is under my roof, in my protection. I do not allow myself to fret about it, and Owen is blind to it – at least he seems to be. Faith, he sees little of Edric, which is for the best.' In fact it felt to Lucie that Owen saw little of *her*, which was *not* for the best. She did wish he were not away so often, that Thoresby did not rely on him so much. When Lucie had been pregnant with Gwenllian, their firstborn, Owen had taken pains to tell her how beautiful she looked, how she still stirred his desire, how excited he was about the life they had begun. Now he seemed merely worried about her health and relieved when she reassured him that she felt well.

Smiling, Bess patted Lucie's hand. 'Owen would understand, I think. Edric is comely, but to his elders he's coltish, young and awkward.' She tidied her cap. 'Speaking of your handsome husband, I dare not linger until he returns. I've already stayed away from the tavern longer than is wise.'

'God go with you, my friend. I pray the tavern is quiet.'

Bess chuckled. 'If I thought it would be quiet I'd feel free to bide with you a while longer. The customers will be eager to recount what they saw and heard at the staithe and the abbey gate over and over, and it will take several tankards for most of them.'

Lucie walked Bess to the door and watched her turn towards St Helen's Square. She felt restless now, not at all in the proper temper to work on the accounts. In the kitchen, she found Kate drowsing beside the hearth. She thought of her apprentices working into the evening. Jasper's day had been long already, and Edric had been alone in the shop for long stretches. They might welcome her help for a little while.

She slipped past Kate and, taking an old cloak from a hook by the door, went out into the garden. Breathing in deeply, she felt the crisp air begin to revive her spirits. No wonder Magda advised her to walk outside as much as she found comfortable. She took the path through the garden to the apothecary. She found Edric in the workshop, hands on hips, considering an assortment of jars, a scale, and a mortar and pestle.

'Dame Lucie, what a blessing that you've come.' He drew up a stool for her at the work table.

'Are you in need of my advice?' she asked as she took a seat.

'I am. I'm mixing a headache powder for the Master of St Leonard's, but I've just noticed that there are three different mixtures for him.'

Sir Richard de Ravenser, the archbishop's nephew, suffered from a variety of head complaints, varying in intensity. 'How did his servant describe his condition?'

Edric made a face. 'It was not his servant.'

'His clerk Douglas?'

Edric nodded. 'He's threatened to return before I close up.'

Lucie thought it was the first sarcasm she'd heard from her new apprentice.

'Douglas is an unpleasant man in the best of times,' she said, 'but when Sir Richard is ailing he's desperate and so even worse than usual. How did he describe his master's condition?'

'Sir Richard is blinking against the light and wants nothing to eat,' said Edric.

Lucie nodded. 'Poor Sir Richard, that is his worst. Make him the third one, with the sleeping draught. I'd forgotten he's been away, to court. I'm not surprised he used all he had and needs more. Double the recipe.'

She reached for a jar of sufficient size and felt Edric step close, his hands ready to catch her by her swollen waist if she stumbled. She was flustered by the scent of him, the warmth of his breath on her cheek. Perhaps he was merely concerned for a mother-to-be, not wooing her; in fact, that is surely what it must be. He had no doubt heard that she'd lost her last child in a fall. Turning round and handing him the jar, she said, 'You are kind, Edric, but you must not fuss over me. After all, I am your master.' She said it with a smile.

He blushed and moved aside. 'I meant no disrespect, Mistress.'

'I doubt you did, Edric.' Perhaps she needn't have said anything, but if it had flustered her what might he have felt. He must learn propriety. 'Do not make Douglas wait,' she reminded him, then moved on into the shop to assist Jasper.

She was glad to find him intent on listening to a customer's lamentations regarding his bowels. Not that the subject was pleasant, but Jasper seemed himself, as if he'd already shrugged off the event on the river.

Later, back by the fire in the hall, Lucie remembered her apprentice's gesture and wondered whether he understood the difference between feeling protective of a woman and feeling attracted to her. He was so young, so earnest – so charming. She knew that it was just such a complication that worried some of the guild members about her being a master apothecary, with male apprentices. Most likely because Jasper was her adopted son, he'd never seemed confused about his relationship with her. But Edric – she was unsure how to know whether she was reading too much into his behaviour or not enough. After all, Bess had noted it.

That worried Lucie. But she need not fear that Owen would notice. She wished he were less protective of her and more flirtatious and affectionate. She felt huge and unlovely. A passionate kiss would go a long way towards brightening her spirit.

Two

PUZZLING CONNECTIONS

The near drowning and a priest and school-master suspected by the gossips of attempted murder brought many to the York Tavern that evening. Bess's husband Tom growled about her long absence when she returned from Lucie's house.

'You'd be more than a little angry if I'd disappeared just as half the city arrived thirsty and cranky with frostbitten fingers and toes,' he grumbled.

She hugged him, and as she stepped back noted his bemused expression. A hug was the last thing he'd expected from her. She was suddenly poignantly aware of his sagging jowls and swollen eyelids and thanked God he came from a long-lived family.

'The fire's smoking,' she said. 'See to that while I fill tankards.'

He nodded and pushed a pitcher towards her. 'It's plain I'll be brewing again this week.'

Bess noticed a pair she knew to be abbey bargemen in the corner and made her way towards them in the hope they might be in a mood to talk. Heads bowed, they seemed like two monks in church this evening, quiet and solemn-faced.

'Have you news of the pilot?' she asked as she stood over them unnoticed, another clue to their mood.

Bart shook his shaggy head, and as he raised his tankard for a refill he surprised Bess with such a grief-stricken look that she almost spilled some of Tom's best ale.

'You are good friends with the man who almost drowned?'

'My wife and I are godparents of his lasses,' he said. 'I was the one to tell his good wife of the accident. I had to repeat it because she just couldn't believe what I was saying, and then she screamed and frightened the little ones. I pray he recovers. I've got a knot in my belly that all the ale in York won't loosen.' He took a long drink.

It wouldn't be for lack of trying, Bess thought as she made sympathetic noises.

'Had he been but a little later returning today it wouldn't have happened,' said the other.

'Aye.' Bart nodded. 'Hal's right. He came just before those cursed scholars. Pampered pets.'

Hal winced at his friend's words. 'I don't think

42

we can really blame them,' he said. 'Drogo didn't look right when he walked up to me. He was rubbing his eyes like he couldn't see clear. I think there was blood on his hands. He asked me for some water. By the time I fetched it, he was in the river.' He crossed himself.

'Blood on his hands?' Bess thought that significant. 'But you aren't certain?'

Hal held up his own hands. 'We can never get off all the pitch or the river filth.'

It looked as if all the creases on his hands were picked out in black, as well as the greater part of the joints. 'I see,' said Bess.

'Those scholars are still the ones pushed him in,' Bart growled.

'We don't know that,' Hal maintained. 'If Drogo was sickening, a nudge might have sent him in, the barges were rocking so with all the folk moving about. I'm not easy blaming the lads.'

Bart grunted.

'What if someone in the city is after bargemen, and not just Drogo?' Hal added, frowning down at his tankard, then up at Bart.

'Why would that be?' Bess asked.

Hal shrugged. 'Why Drogo?'

Bart snorted. 'That's what makes it plain the *scholars* did it. They're angry about his keeping the scrip. He was a fool to do that. Why would he think the lad carried anything of worth in it?'

'Because he carried it with him that day?' The words were out before Bess knew it. But if she did say so herself, it was unusual for a lad to go about wearing a scrip.

Hal held her gaze. 'I'd not thought of that. But now you mention it, it is odd.'

'If I have any more thoughts, I'll let you know,' said Bess. She leaned down to Hal and added in a low voice, 'Watch your friend. I want no rowdiness tonight. Folk need to feel safe here.'

'I'll clear him out soon,' Hal promised. 'He'll not wake happy as it is.'

As Bess moved on she tucked away the fact that Drogo had been thirsty and perhaps bleeding already when he'd arrived at the staithe, and the question of what Hubert de Weston had carried in his scrip. She could not follow the idea now for she needed full use of her wits to keep tab of how much of what folk were eating and drinking. Tragedy was good for business, as ever.

A man moved out from the shadows, blocking Owen's access to the abbey infirmary. Owen cursed silently; when he'd entered the abbey grounds through the postern gate he'd thought he was alone. Drawing out his dagger – for it might be the would-be murderer intent on finishing his work, Owen called out, 'Who goes there?'

The man moved closer so that Owen could see his hawk-nosed face. 'It's George Hempe.'

Relieved, Owen said, 'I'm glad you're here.' Hempe was a city bailiff, and the very one Owen would have sent for. He'd disliked Hempe until they had been thrown together in an investigation the previous year and he'd learned that the man's intentions were good despite his stubborn and brusque manner, that he earnestly wished to bring criminals to justice. Bailiffs usually saw their duties as keeping the immediate peace, not preventing future trouble. Hempe was not so short-sighted.

'Have you seen the pilot?' Owen asked.

'I had a glimpse of him as they carried him into the abbey grounds. But that is all. I'm not as welcome in here as you are. I can tell you he looked near death.'

'How could you not be welcome? Were you not sent for?'

Hempe laughed. 'I was, yes, but as soon as he saw me Abbot Campian made certain I understood that the man had fallen from the *abbey* staithe, not the *city* staithe, though it was *possible* he'd been attacked in the city. I'd been called upon to keep the peace among the city folk, not to interfere in abbey concerns. He sent for you as well?'

'Yes. I might have avoided it, but my son Jasper was in the crowd of scholars at the staithe.'

'Has Jasper an explanation of what happened?'

Owen was shaking his head as they came upon the outcast of the evening, Nicholas Ferriby.

'Captain Archer, Master Bailiff, I must speak

with you.' The schoolmaster's deep voice trembled. 'I am condemned of a crime that did not happen.'

'Calm yourself,' said Owen. 'From what I've heard you did nothing wrong tonight.'

'But the crowd out on Marygate,' Nicholas gestured towards the abbey gate, 'they accused me. Their voices were so angry. I wasn't at the barges, Captain. I don't know why they would even connect me with that man.' He paused to catch his breath.

'You are safe here in the abbey grounds,' said Hempe.

Owen was impatient to move on, but he could imagine how unsettled the man must feel. 'Some quiet prayer in the abbey church will calm you, Master Nicholas. Now I fear I must leave you. I've been summoned to the infirmary.'

'Why?' Nicholas asked.

'To see Drogo's wounds.'

'The wounds – they complicate the story,' said Hempe, considering Master Nicholas. 'You swear you had not been seen with Drogo earlier in the afternoon?'

'I swear!' Nicholas cried, then groaned. 'Even you?'

'You are not in danger here,' said Owen, shaking his head at Hempe to quiet him. He had no time to calm the schoolmaster. 'Abide in the hospitium tonight, Master Nicholas.'

'By morning the crowd will have forgotten you,' said Hempe.

'I pray you are right,' said Nicholas. 'But what if the man dies?'

'Then we have much work to do,' said Owen. 'I must pass now.'

The schoolmaster stepped aside. 'I shall go pray for his recovery.'

'And I'll see that the crowd has dispersed,' said Hempe.

Inside the warmly lit infirmary, Owen found Brother Henry bent over an ailing monk, and he left him in peace for a moment. Scanning the room for Drogo, he was startled by memories. The hanging herbs, tidy rows of pallets, indeed the smell of the room reminded him of many visits with Brother Wulfstan. Owen had seldom come here since his friend's death three years earlier. Brother Henry was capable, but not gifted like his predecessor; neither Lucie nor Owen came to him for advice.

'Drogo lies over near the brazier,' Henry softly called out.

Owen pulled himself back into the present and noticed the man now, or the shape of him beneath the blanket. Henry joined him.

'He is dead?' Owen asked.

Henry nodded and then crossed himself. 'He died just a little while ago. I waited to move him to a more public place until you'd seen him.'

'Did he ever wake?'

'No. He made mewling sounds towards the end, as if in pain but too weak to cry out.'

'That doesn't sound like drowning,' Owen said. 'But a poisoned blade – that is no sudden quarrel but deliberate murder.'

Henry bowed his head and crossed himself. 'The devil is loose in the city.'

'The method is only too human,' said Owen. 'Let me see him.'

Henry uncovered Drogo's head, then drew back the blanket to expose his right hand. The skin on his face already looked waxy and slightly grey, though around the cuts it was much darker and there was a trace of crust that did not look like a scab. It was too small a sample for either Owen or Lucie to detect the presence of poison, too little to smell or taste.

'He tried to protect his face,' Owen noted.

Henry nodded. 'That is what I thought. The slits must have stung, but I wouldn't think they were terribly painful. I suppose that's why he went to the barges and not home to clean the wounds. What do you think?'

'I think his attacker was confident of the poison. Depending on what it was, Drogo might have sought relief in the river as the pain worsened.'

'May God grant him peace,' said Henry.

Owen released Drogo's hand. He crossed himself and said a prayer for the pilot's soul. 'Did you know him?'

Henry muted a sneeze with his hand. 'A little. I'd spoken to him at the staithe now and then. He seemed a quiet man, though I heard murmurs tonight that he was too ready with his fists when drunk.'

'That is not an unusual trait in our fellow men.' Owen noticed lines of weariness encircling the infirmarian's eyes and mouth despite his youth. 'You found no other marks on his body?'

'This bruise.' Henry touched a faint discolouration high on the man's left arm. 'I thought it might be where his rescuer clutched him.'

It was the size of a man's hand. 'You may be right. Anything else?'

Henry shook his head as he tried to cover a yawn, but his exhaustion won.

Owen empathised. 'You are already weary, and I expect you have a long evening ahead of you. I'll not keep you long. Have you had much illness here?'

Henry shook his head as he tucked his hands in the opposite sleeves and moved away from Drogo. 'I made a nettle draught for myself yesterday that was far too strong, and then I could not sleep.'

'Ah, the healer has no time to be ill.' Lucie often pushed herself far past signs of exhaustion.

'I don't think of it as illness,' said Henry. 'My sneezing upset my patients. I am accustomed to fits of sneezing after mixing some powders. The nettle quiets it. But I was distracted while measuring the draught. Brother Paolo was . . .' His voice trailed off and he frowned down at his sandals. 'He's grown wicked in his illness.' Glancing up at Owen, Henry blushed.

49

Owen tried to erase his grin. 'Pleasuring himself?'

'How did you guess?' asked Henry as he averted his eyes.

Owen found it difficult not to laugh outright, imagining the monk distracted by a vigorously fluttering blanket, or startled by the old monk crying out in pleasure. 'I've seen it in the camps, men comforting themselves, taking heart from a healthy response.' Owen shrugged. 'Of course it is more appropriate for soldiers than for monks.'

'It is a sin regardless,' Henry said sternly, his face very red.

Owen had forgotten Henry's primness. 'I pray you forgive me, Brother Henry. I should not have spoken so boldly.' He searched for another topic, having no cause to offend the monk. 'Warn those keeping vigil with the body that Drogo's murderer is abroad. I am most concerned about his family, if he had one.'

Henry quickly regained his composure. 'He had a wife and two daughters, I believe. They are waiting in the chapel with several of our brothers. I must get word to them of his death.' He crossed himself. 'I shall warn the others of the danger. Did you hear about Master Nicholas Ferriby being accused of the murder even before Drogo died?'

Owen nodded. 'Jasper told me. Indeed, Master Nicholas accosted me outside your door. He fears for his life. The man's death will be a blow to him.'

'It was his misfortune to approach Drogo when he did, and someone saw a chance to stir them to violence. They will forget him tomorrow.'

'You will offer him a bed for the night?'

'I would have thought he'd bide with his brother William, but I suppose they are at odds. Abbot Campian suggested that he take refuge here, so I've no doubt he is arranging a bed for him. I would guess he'll be off to Weston as soon as he's able.'

'That depends on whether he's willing to repay the parents of his scholars. They have already paid a year's fee.' Owen had for Alisoun.

'I'd not considered that,' said Henry.

'Before I go home to my dinner I must talk to the lads biding in the Clee.'

'May God watch over you, Captain,' he said. 'I would not wish to meet the person who so subtly murdered the steersman.'

'Keep me in your prayers, Brother Henry.'

Hempe waited without. 'How is he?'

Owen shook his head, then crossed himself. 'Dead of poison on the blade that cut him.'

Hempe cursed. 'I spoke to one man who'd seen Drogo running from a tavern in Petergate late this afternoon. I'll see what I can learn there. Let us meet in the York Tavern.'

Owen agreed, then headed out the abbey gate towards the Clee, where he was quite sure Master John, the schoolmaster of St Peters, would be with his scholars.

Light shone from the chinks in every shutter of the Clee, and spilled out as Dame Agnes opened the door to Owen's knock, her snowy white cap glowing in the brightness. Young voices also spilled out into the night, as well as thuds and a dog barking. Dame Agnes, a pretty woman with a pious devotion to her charges, beamed at Owen.

'Captain Archer, praise God that you are here. Several of my boys are eager to tell someone all they noticed at the barges today. I am so grateful it is you who is come to talk to them. You understand boys.'

She was also talkative. But he was heartened by her greeting.

'Is there someplace I might talk to them one at a time, beginning with the older scholars?' he asked. 'After I've spoken to Master John and you.'

She smiled. 'And how did you guess that Master John would be here?'

'He would not leave the lads until he was certain they were all calmed,' said Owen.

'You know him well. These boys are blessed in their schoolmaster.'

'And their matron,' he added, falling into her rhythm.

As they spoke he'd noticed the youngest scholars joining her, crowding around her. Now she glanced around (for they were not much shorter than she was) and exclaimed, 'Oh my boys, Captain Archer is going to help us discover the truth of what happened to the pilot this

52

afternoon.' Her expression, when she raised her eyes to Owen's once more, was dramatically changed. 'We must learn the truth.' There was fear in her eyes, fear for her lads. She understood this was no mere schoolboys' tussle.

Owen was never confident that he would learn the truth. He knew full well that the truth was not always in the best interests of the powerful, and they could, and often did, control the outcome of his investigation. But looking at the trusting faces lifted to his he prayed that he was able to resolve this in a manner that would restore a sense of safe order to the lads.

Dame Agnes asked the boys to fetch one of the servants and ask Master John to attend her.

The schoolmaster was the first to appear, dividing the pulsing crowd of boys as Moses had the waters of the Red Sea. 'Archer!' he boomed. With his deep, strong baritone and his animated yet kindly face he seemed born to his calling. 'So His Grace the Archbishop has taken an interest in our tragedy?'

'I am not here at his request,' said Owen. 'But I've no doubt he will wish to have this resolved.'

'He's taken precious little interest in Chancellor Thomas's concern about Nicholas Ferriby's school,' said Dame Agnes with a sniff.

'Because it is a needless concern,' said John in the tone of one tired of repeating himself, 'and absurd to threaten him with excommunication. I agree with His Grace on that. Ferriby's scholars have no hope of entering St Peter's.' His smile was affectionate.

Dame Agnes hesitated with a little frown, but then bobbed her head at a servant who had just joined them. He was out of breath and smelled of onions. 'Watch the lads while we retire to my chamber, Stephen.'

The servant grinned and thanked her. Owen guessed he was relieved to have a reprieve from chopping onions.

Agnes's chamber was a screened-off corner of the hall, large enough for a small bed, a table, a few stools, and a large trunk. She settled on the bed and gestured to them to take the stools.

'I hoped you might tell me what the lads have said about their part in Drogo's death,' said Owen.

'Death?' Agnes whispered, looking over at Master John.

'God grant him peace,' said the schoolmaster, his face grave. 'This is terrible news, Captain, and all the worse for my scholars' part in the bumping and jostling that might have caused his fall. But how did he die? I understood his fellows quickly pulled him from the water.'

'The blood, Master John,' Dame Agnes murmured.

John lifted his eyes to Owen. 'I'd almost forgotten about that. What really did happen today?' .

'That is what I seek to discover,' said Owen. 'Why do you suppose your lads did not seek your help in retrieving young Hubert's scrip?'

A fond smile broke through the concern. 'Their sense of adventure, Captain. The older ones love to lead.'

'They should know better than to engage the bargemen. What is innocent fun to the lads is threatening to the bargemen's livelihood. I've explained that to Jasper many times, but he was there this evening despite my warnings, and despite promising he'd not go to the staithe.'

'He was not there long, I assure you. He'd stayed behind to copy a passage.'

'But he did go.'

'And this time it was not a game with the lads. They did find the scrip, but it was empty.'

'They *did* retrieve it?' Owen had not heard this. 'How?'

'When Geoffrey, one of the older scholars, demanded it, Drogo tossed the little purse to him, just like that, and then moved deeper into the crowd.'

'I would talk to Geoffrey,' said Owen, glancing at Dame Agnes.

She was quick to understand. 'I'll fetch him at once.' She slipped away.

'But it was empty, you said.' Owen thought about how the lad might have responded to that. 'Did he charge after Drogo when he found it empty?'

'I don't think he realised at once that there was nothing in it,' said Master John.

'Where is the scrip now?'

The grammar master produced it. It was the

size of Owen's hand, clearly a woman's scrip, and the pouch was indeed empty. 'Keep it safe,' he warned. 'We may need it.'

The grammar master nodded uneasily.

'What else have you heard from the lads?' Owen asked.

'I heard about the poor man's bleeding face, and about Nicholas Ferriby fleeing into the abbey grounds in fear of his life.' Master John shook his head. 'Foolish man. He is such a foolish man.'

'The crowd was angry, or so I am told,' Owen reminded him.

'Yes, yes, they do say so.' Master John nodded as he lowered his gaze to the unremarkable floor. 'Yes.'

'Abbot Campian advised him to retreat into the abbey.' Owen wondered whether John's earlier claim of indifference about Nicholas Ferriby's school might have been an attempt to deflect questions about the conflict. 'It is natural that you would resent Nicholas for threatening your income.'

John gave an elaborate shrug. 'The status and funding of St Peter's School are Chancellor Thomas Farnilaw's responsibilities. I am merely the schoolmaster. I've no cause to resent Master Nicholas. I am glad that Abbot Campian is giving him sanctuary.'

Owen believed John did resent Nicholas, but that his feelings embarrassed him, being of a mercenary nature.

Dame Agnes had returned with a tall, well-built

older scholar with a man's stubble on his chin and a sullen set to his mouth. 'This is Geoffrey Townley, Captain,' she said. 'Geoffrey, this is Captain Archer, who wishes to ask you about what happened on the barges.'

'I did not push him into the river,' said Geoffrey in a wounded tone.

'That is a good start,' said Owen. 'I understand you saw Drogo. Can you tell me all that happened? All that you noticed about him?'

The young man still looked uncertain. 'You're not accusing me?'

'No. I'm asking for your help.'

Geoffrey seemed to think about that for a moment, then nodded. 'I am sorry I spoke to you so, Captain.' By his blush Owen understood that he'd been frightened, which was hardly surprising. The young man repeated what Master John had already told Owen about Drogo tossing the scrip to him, but with an additional piece of information. 'He smelled of ale, Captain, and I thought he was drunk, the way he moved, like he had to think about lifting his hand and turning his head. But when he bled in front of the Virgin I understood that he'd been injured.'

Ale. He hoped Hempe learned something at the tavern. 'Did you see him go into the water?' Owen asked.

Geoffrey shook his head. 'The crowd was thick round him. I feared the barges would start taking on water.'

'When did you realise the scrip was empty?'

'The lads crowded round me while we waited for Drogo to be pulled from the river. They asked me to look inside.' Geoffrey paused, shifting a little, shrugging. 'I wasn't going to look, thinking it wasn't right without Hubert there. But I thought I might feel around, see what I could learn from it, and I felt just the leather. Then I looked, and my fingers had been right. I was holding just the scrip, nothing in it.'

'How did that make you feel?'

'Tricked. Cheated. So were we all. But I don't understand. Why return it if it was empty?' Geoffrey nodded as Owen was about to speak. 'I know, he satisfied me and was able to get away, but he did growl something about returning it to Hubert.'

So he'd mentioned the boy by name. Owen wondered whether Drogo had known him or had learned the lad's name after he'd taken the scrip. 'Even if you'd looked right away, it sounds as if he quickly disappeared.'

Geoffrey sighed. 'He did. He was very fast.' The sullen expression had softened into disappointment. 'When I realised he'd tricked me I was glad he'd fallen into the river.'

'Geoffrey!' Dame Agnes need say no more, all the shock and disapproval clear in her tone.

The young man crossed himself. 'I didn't feel that for long. I was just angry.'

'I would have been angry to find I was holding

an empty scrip,' said Owen. 'Did anyone else catch your eye? Odd behaviour? Someone out of place?'

Geoffrey shook his head.

'Do you know who Master Nicholas is?'

'Who? Oh, yes. He was blamed for Drogo's wounds.'

'Did you see him on the barges? Take a moment to think back. They sound as if they were crowded.'

The young man lifted his gaze to the ceiling, frowning as he thought, and finally shaking his head as he lowered his gaze to Owen once more. 'No. Do you think it was Master Nicholas who was drinking with Drogo?'

'I doubt it, though I can't say why. If you hear anything or remember anything else that you think might be of use, I need to know.' Owen was about to give him leave to go, but thought of one more question. 'Were you at the abbey gate when Drogo bled?'

'I was, Captain.'

'Did you see Master Nicholas approach him?'

'I did.' Geoffrey frowned. 'Why?'

'Did he carry a weapon?'

'Not that I could see.'

'Did he try to sneak up to Drogo?'

Geoffrey shook his head.

'Did he seem worried? Frightened?'

'No, Captain.'

'I am grateful, Geoffrey. And – you might tell

59

the other lads what I've asked. I would like to hear from anyone with anything to add.'

Geoffrey nodded and hastened out.

Hempe awaited Owen at the York Tavern, thoughtfully staring at the ceiling beam, a tankard of ale firmly in hand. As Owen greeted him he seemed to remember that he was cross, and pulled his brows together.

'He'd been in the tavern, a cloaked man entered, said something and left, and then Drogo left.' Hempe shrugged his powerful shoulders. 'Precious little in that.'

'No one recognised the man?'

'Cloaked and hooded.' Hempe snorted and shook his head. 'It could not be much more useless, could it?'

'So it might have been a priest?'

'I suppose it might have been a woman for all they could tell.' Hempe cursed under his breath.

'You are so caught up in this?' Owen asked, curious about this man who was becoming a friend.

'I don't like the smell of it,' said Hempe. 'What did you learn?'

Owen filled him in, by which time Hempe thought he ought to head home.

'Being raised to a bailiff of the city has been a mixed blessing for my trade.' Hempe was a mercer. 'I have more business, but I'm far less efficient.'

'You're likely to hold public office for the rest

of your life,' said Owen. 'You're a worthy man, and it's noticed.'

Hempe grumbled something as he departed, but it was plain he appreciated the compliment.

He was no sooner out the door than Bess Merchet joined Owen. She did not like to be seen socialising with the city officers – it made some customers uncomfortable. Over an ale she recounted for Owen her conversation with the two bargemen.

'Already bleeding when he arrived,' Owen said, realising Brother Henry might have been right about the attack happening elsewhere. 'What else?'

Bess told him how, to her thinking, Hubert's carrying the scrip about with him was unusual.

'I'd not considered that,' Owen admitted, as much to himself as to her. He would ask Jasper what he thought of that. 'Did the one who suggested someone having cause to be after the bargemen say why he thought that might be?'

'That was Hal who suggested it,' said Bess, glancing towards the corner of the room. 'I did not ask, Bart was so certain it was about the lad's scrip.'

Owen followed her gaze, but saw only a pair of travellers and a young man in a goldsmith's livery in the corner. 'Are they still here?'

She shook her head. 'No. Hal honoured my request to take Bart away before he grew restless. I could find out where they bide.'

'Would you, my friend?' Owen pressed her hand. 'I may need them before I'm finished.'

'Lucie looks herself again,' said Bess, 'you've naught to fret about there, though she'll be less pleased than I am that His Grace has already set you to the task of finding Drogo's murderer.'

'He hasn't,' said Owen, leaning back to drain his tankard. Wiping his mouth, he rose. 'But he will. Abbot Campian sent for me, and in the next day or so he'll begin to worry about the safety of the abbey bargemen – after all, we have no idea why someone attacked Drogo, and he'll ask His Grace for my assistance. His Grace will be only too happy to agree in order to bring peace to St Peter's School. So I have begun to ask questions while folk still remember what they thought they witnessed. Though some are already confused.'

'Not everyone has spoken sense?' Bess leaned over to wipe the table top with one efficient flourish. She was eager for gossip.

'No. A lad had told Dame Agnes at the Clee that he'd been standing beside the older scholar who pushed Drogo into the Ouse, but what he saw was the student help the man who dived in to save Drogo. He'd freed the man's sleeve from a nail that had snagged it. Others had witnessed it and laughed at the lad's mistake.'

Bess laughed. 'Poor chick! He'll regret ever having said a peep.'

'It's a difficult lesson he's learned, that he should

not jump to conclusions,' Owen agreed. 'Keep your ears pricked, my friend.'

He headed home, looking forward to discussing the evening's events with Lucie, his most trusted advisor. He was still smiling about the lad's mistake when he entered the hall. Lucie and Jasper were sitting at the table quietly talking. Dame Phillippa nodded by the fire – she seemed to sleep all the day of late. Alisoun's voice curled down from the solar – she was softly singing to the children. He said a prayer of thanksgiving for the peace in his household. Lucie lifted her head, then rose to greet him, but he told her to sit and rest herself and went over to kiss her. The child in her womb slowed her steps and swelled her ankles. He admired Lucie's courage in carrying this baby and tried not to think how with each pregnancy – this was her fourth in the eight years they'd been wed – she aged a little more. He thought God cruel in making them choose between children of their flesh and each other. He caught himself, wondering why his thoughts had gone from cheer to gloom so quickly. He turned to Jasper.

'Are you rested? Might we talk of Hubert and what you saw today?'

'I didn't have a chance to tell you before – the best news is that Hubert's da and Sir Baldwin are alive. Master Nicholas told me.'

'God spared them? I am glad of that,' said Owen. Nicholas had said nothing of this to him, but then he'd been worried about his own survival.

Lucie rose again. 'I'll tell Kate to serve us.'

'Let Jasper ask her. Then we'll talk,' said Owen, having known full well that he would be rewarded with the frown that she now gave him. 'You are my beauty and my love, wife, and I'll cherish you as I may.'

Lucie blushed and could not hold the frown. She kissed Owen's cheek.

Jasper grinned as he rose. 'The captain and his Welsh charm win the match!'

Owen noticed Alisoun's wax tablet beside where Jasper had been sitting. 'Her schoolmaster is not easy in his mind this night.'

Lucie studied Owen's face for a moment. 'You are involved even before His Grace has commanded you.'

'And how do you know whether or not I've spoken to Thoresby?'

Her eyes twinkled. 'You were smiling when you returned. He always leaves you in a temper.'

Jasper rejoined them, sliding back onto the bench across the table. 'Have you learned much else?' he asked Owen, reminding him that he'd promised to let him know what he heard.

'A little.' Owen summed up his evening's gleanings while Kate set trenchers of stewed fish and root vegetables before them. 'Drogo was bleeding when he arrived at the staithe,' he concluded. 'And Bess reminded me that lads don't often walk about with scrips. What say you?'

Jasper rolled his eyes as he chewed a mouthful.

'She is right,' said Lucie.

'He's worn it every day since he returned to school,' said Jasper. 'Some teased him about it, those who bide in the Clee. They said he convinced the matron to let him sleep with it beneath his pillow.'

'I should think many of the lads hid something dear to them such as that,' said Lucie. 'I did at St Clement's.' Lucie had lived at St Clement's Nunnery after her mother died. Her father's gift of the house had been in part an attempt to make amends for having sent her away.

'Dame Agnes has some amusing rules,' said Jasper. 'Pillows must be flat on the pallet or the lads will grow crooked. She reminds them to lie on their backs in bed. Though no one checks them during the night.' He chuckled.

'She is a dear, God-fearing woman,' said Lucie, 'but I'm grateful she wasn't my matron.' She and Jasper laughed.

Though he was enjoying the lightness of the conversation, Owen was very tired and wanted to hear what else Jasper knew so that he might head for bed. So once more he turned to his son. 'Tell me about Hubert's disappearance.'

Jasper shrugged. 'There is little to tell. Several days back Master John missed him in class. The lads said he'd awakened that day at the Clee. One was sent to ask Dame Agnes if he was ill. She'd thought he was in class. Then Master John sent word to his ma in Weston, hoping that's where he's gone, but he's still waiting for a reply. They've had the crier and the parish priests in the city ask for news of him. None of the gatekeepers had noticed him passing through, but I know they don't see all who pass. I was able to hide from them when I needed to.' Jasper had witnessed a murder and had been on the run when Owen and Lucie took him in. 'Some close to Hubert said he was that upset about losing the scrip it sickened him.'

'Weston? That's a long way for a lad to travel,' said Owen. 'And dangerous.'

'And with his scrip stolen, he's no way to pay the ferryman,' said Lucie, pressing Jasper's hand. 'It takes me back to when you were on the streets.'

Owen did not like the sound of this. He did not want Lucie sinking into fear for her children as she had the previous autumn. 'Tell me about Hubert,' he said. 'He must be well liked for you lads to go to such trouble to help him.'

'He's one of the younger scholars, so I don't know him well. As I said, he's a charity student this term. His da was away fighting for the king in La Rochelle, but, as I said, he and his lord survived. But we didn't know that earlier today. I wonder whether he knows?'

'So you thought to help the family,' said Lucie.

'Yes. But I think we've made it all worse.'

'What more do you know of the lad?' Owen asked.

'He lost a brother and sister to the pestilence,

so his ma's alone now – was alone. He thought his place was at his mother's side, not at school.'

'Sounds like a serious young man.'

Jasper nodded. 'He's quiet, but he's not strangely quiet. Everyone likes him.'

'He sounds like a model student,' said Lucie.

'Master John does not favour him in any way. *Too* quiet, I think – the master likes the spirited ones.'

'Where would you guess he is?' Owen asked.

'Trying to find his way home, if not there already,' said Jasper. 'It's all about his ma, I think, and feeling like he's all she has left.'

'I would say you should go to Weston, my love,' said Lucie, beginning to rise. 'Young Hubert is the person you must talk to.'

Owen bowed his head. Only last night he'd returned from a few days at Bishopthorpe and he was not keen to set off again.

Lucie and Owen lay in bed the following morning bundled up so that they would not freeze with the shutters open, watching the first snow of the season in the soft early light. It was a sweet moment for Lucie, with her joy in being in the arms of her love and feeling their child move in her womb. Yet even so, there was a shadow on her heart; it had been on the day of the first snow nine years earlier that her late husband Nicholas had fallen ill and what she thought she knew of those she loved had been turned on its head.

'I hate to speak and shatter the grace of this moment,' said Owen, reaching for her hand and holding it in both of his, 'but I am worried that you will spend the morning kneeling in the garden.'

It was Lucie's custom to honour this anniversary with a vigil at Nicholas's grave. Archbishop Thoresby had consecrated a grave for Nicholas in the back of the garden, for the apothecary garden had been his master work. Lucie was not surprised that Owen worried about her. She knew he'd never been comfortable about the ritual because of the customary weather.

'Not today, my love,' she assured him, kissing one of his battle-scarred hands. 'I would not risk the health of our child.'

She drew his hand to her stomach and watched his expression as their child kicked him roundly. Owen's eye opened wide in wonder, and his face crinkled into the most beautiful smile in God's kingdom.

'Now that's a sturdy kick,' he said in a voice tight with emotion.

'Or a punch,' said Lucie, enjoying the moment and wishing it could be prolonged.

A knock on the street door down below distracted both parents, but not the baby, who flailed away.

'Quiet,' Lucie whispered, rubbing her great stomach.

Someone clattered up the stairs.

'Hugh,' said Owen with a laugh. 'Do you think he'll ever walk a straight line?'

The boy proceeded to pound on their door. When Alisoun called him away, he stomped in protest.

'We're awake,' Owen called out. 'Save the door and let Hugh in.'

Lucie laughed with him, hiding her disappointment in Owen's allowing the interruption.

The door eased open and Hugh peered around it, his fiery red hair unmistakable for anyone else's. Seeing Owen and Lucie watching for him, he squealed and raced into the room.

From the hallway, out of view, Alisoun said, 'I am sorry about Hugh. I was too slow to catch him. A messenger is here from His Grace the Archbishop. He said he is to bring Captain Archer to the palace at once.'

Lucie and Owen exchanged looks of regret over the moving head of their son.

'I told you he'd send for me.'

'You've not broken your fast,' Lucie said, wanting him healthy.

'He'll feed me,' said Owen. 'But I can't go at once. I want to say good morning to Gwenllian.' He was already up and dressing. 'I'll tell him I'll come to the palace bye and bye.'

The snow had stopped before Owen stepped out into Davygate, and already what had fallen was turning to a slippery slush underfoot, the sort of surface he'd hated since losing half his sight. Long ago, while in the service of the Duke of Lancaster, he'd been blinded by the *leman* of a prisoner of war, a debility that had ended his career as captain of archers. Neither the duke's physician nor Magda Digby had been able to save Owen's sight. It was then that he'd learned to read and write in order to be the duke's ears in the court circles, and it was these abilities as well as his fighting skills that had interested Archbishop Thoresby when the old duke died – for as Lord Chancellor of England the archbishop also had need of a spy. Owen had loved and honoured the old duke, Henry of Grosmont, a fine commander and a deeply pious man. Owen had not trusted the new duke, the husband of Henry's daughter Blanche and a younger son of the king, and had therefore agreed to enter Thoresby's service, naïvely believing that an archbishop would be as moral as the old duke. He'd quickly learned to his regret that although Thoresby was a man of God, he was also an ambitious man, a man who believed that it was often best to look the other way in order to protect strategic alliances. Falling in love with Lucie Wilton had tied Owen to the archbishop's service. It was not only that in deference to his lord the guild had allowed Lucie to continue in her late husband's apothecary upon marrying Owen, but even more importantly the circumstances of her husband's death might have remained a blot on Lucie's name but for Thoresby's influence. For that, Owen owed him his allegiance.

With his faulty depth-perception challenging him in the half-light of the snowy November streets, Owen picked his way past York Minster and into the grounds of the archbishop's palace with a caution that frustrated him – he was aching to stretch and move. When he found that the stone steps leading up to the palace doors had already been swept of snow, he took them two at a time. He found Brother Michaelo, secretary to the archbishop, awaiting him in the doorway to Thoresby's private hall in his characteristically spotless Benedictine habit, an amused expression on his aristocratically bony face.

'You are restless in the city, Captain?' he asked in his Norman accent. 'Or were you impatient to reach the top?'

'Both,' Owen said, catching his breath. For that to have winded him meant he needed far more activity than he had managed of late.

Michaelo responded with an elegant shrug. 'His Grace awaits you in his parlour.'

'This is about the drowning?'

Michaelo lowered his head slightly, his manner of nodding. 'I warn you, His Grace rose quite early and is not in good temper.'

'Thank you for the warning.'

Owen found Thoresby sitting by a brazier in his parlour, his hands steepled before him, staring out the glazed window opposite that opened onto the winter garden. He slowly turned to acknowledge Owen.

'You came in your own good time, Archer.' His sunken eyes were difficult to read, but the irritation in his deep voice was quite clear.

'I was filthy, Your Grace, and I did not wish to insult you with my state, so I washed.' It was a safe lie, for Thoresby had an unusual fondness for bathing. Owen bowed to him and then took his seat beside a small table set with bread, cheese, and ale. 'Your Grace is kind to think of me.'

To Owen's surprise, Thoresby broke out in deep-bellied laughter.

'Kind? I did not think I would live to see the day when you called me kind.'

'You are in a better humour than I expected.' Owen wondered why Brother Michaelo had misled him. But it was a passing thought as he reached for the food; it was always a boon to be offered the hospitality of Maeve's kitchen. He broke off a piece of the crumbly cheese and popped it into his mouth, followed by Maeve's unparalleled pandemain, the softest, whitest bread under heaven.

'Do you know about yesterday's tragedy on the Abbey Staithe, Archer?' Thoresby asked, serious once more. He poured water and wine from delicate flagons of Italian glass into a matching goblet, then sat back in his throne-like chair to sip it.

Owen had not seen the flagon and goblet set before. As he washed down with the strong ale what he'd managed to eat so far he wondered whether the mayor was still trying to win Thoresby's trust with valuable gifts.

'The abbey infirmarian sent for me,' said Owen. 'And Jasper had been on the staithe when Drogo went into the Ouse. I've not yet spoken to the bargemen.' He went down the list of what he knew so far.

Thoresby interrupted only when Owen came to Nicholas Ferriby's unfortunate timing.

'Do you believe it was pure chance?'

'More than likely, Your Grace. Why would a guilty man risk stepping close to the man? But the fact is, Drogo was not yet dead at that point. It was hardly a miracle that his wounds bled. It is the way of crowds, forgetting their wits in their excitement.'

'I don't want the outcry about that incident to become part of the conflict between Ferriby and St Peter's School,' Thoresby said.

'How would it?'

Thoresby held his goblet with both hands and swirled the contents as he gazed down at it. 'Such a crime would seal Nicholas Ferriby's damnation – a scandal for both the clerical Ferribys. William would also suffer.' He glanced up at Owen. 'You think I'm losing my wits.' He sighed. 'I'm slower, more tired, but my wits are in order, Archer.' He rose with a grunt and crossed over to the window, his simple clerical robes hanging loosely on his tall, increasingly gaunt frame. 'They cannot understand why I count Ferriby's school as nothing more than an annoying flea in the minster liberty, perhaps not even so much. They should have made certain of my support before threatening him with excommunication. It carries no weight without my support, and now they are angry with me.'

'They might recall your censoring the opening of a song school in the city, Your Grace.'

'You know that was different, Archer. The song school is a Church affair. A grammar school is useful to all who would enter a trade, learning reasoning, reading, a little writing.'

Owen did see the difference. 'I am surprised that the dean supports the chancellor's excessive anger.' As it was the chancellor's role in the liberty to oversee the grammar and song schools, it was understandable that a rival school might anger him. But Owen would have thought the dean would have a cooler head. 'Would the Pope agree with this even if you were to support them? Is holding a rival grammar school such a terrible sin against the Church?'

Thoresby turned from the window, smiling. 'Of course not. But they'll use the incident with Drogo against Ferriby. They'll find a way, mark me, Archer.'

Owen thought it best not to mention the grammar master's Wycliffite opinions. Thoresby would only resent his giving him a reason to question his support of Nicholas. 'That someone mortally wounded Drogo is of more concern to the folk of this city,' said Owen. 'The lad whose scrip is at the centre of all this must be found.'

'Indeed,' said the archbishop, thoughtfully nodding. 'I am aware that the lad might be in danger.'

Owen had been ready to argue that point, as was his custom with Thoresby. Sometimes he wondered whether Thoresby's contrariness had always been a game meant to irk him.

Returning to his chair, the archbishop took up his cup, sipped, and then asked, 'What is your plan?'

He decided to be glad of the archbishop's improved attitude. 'The lad's almost certainly not in the city, and from what Jasper tells me it's quite likely he's tried to return home. He might have learned that his father survived La Rochelle and has gone home. Master John of St Peter's has received no reply to the message he sent to the lad's mother, but then Master Nicholas, her parish priest, is not there to read it to her. I propose to head to Weston in the hope that the lad is at home, or if he is not to search the countryside between here and Weston.'

'And if you find no trace of him?'

'Perhaps his parents might suggest another likely place. But if not . . .' Owen shrugged, not at present having a further plan. 'At least we'll have tried all we could think to do.'

'Yes.' Thoresby shifted a little. 'What might the lad have carried? Have you any idea?' He sought Owen's good eye and held his gaze.

'None,' Owen admitted. 'Anything that would fit in a lad's scrip and is of value to someone. That is little to go on.'

'A fool's errand, going to Weston?'

'Perhaps.'

'Take horses from my stables,' said Thoresby, 'and what men you see fit to accompany you. I would offer my barge, but I think the River Wharfe has too many rapids for it.'

Owen had hardly expected such a generous offer as the barge. He was a little sorry that it wasn't appropriate for the journey. 'Aye. It is not so navigable as the Ouse. Who will you be taking with you to Bishopthorpe?'

'You need not concern yourself with that in choosing men. I intend to remain in York until this matter is settled. I don't like the idea of Ferriby being made a scapegoat for the minster's financial problems. If they need more money for the upkeep of the school they should raise fees or accept more students, not threaten a good man with excommunication.'

'Is that at the bottom of your support? Not the lad's fate?'

'Both their fates are at present intertwined, Archer. Now who will accompany you?'

'Not Alfred. He's of more use to me here, in charge. I'll take Rafe and Gilbert.'

Thoresby nodded. 'Do you know young Hubert de Weston by sight?'

'I'd thought of that. No, I don't, but Jasper

76

knows him, and his presence would be reassuring to the lad.'

'You might take Nicholas Ferriby,' Thoresby suggested. 'There is no need to involve more in your household.'

'Jasper already feels a part of all this, Your Grace. He's fond of Hubert, and remembers how he felt when his father died.'

'You don't trust Ferriby,' said Thoresby.

'If that were true I would not have sent Alisoun to his school. Even so, whether or not I trust him is beside the point, Your Grace.'

'Do you think Drogo's bleeding was a sign of Ferriby's guilt?' A hint of a smile played on the archbishop's thin lips.

'No. But his imprudent decision about the grammar school –' Thoresby had touched on something Owen had been trying to ignore – 'I do question his motives now.' *And I worry about what he's teaching.* 'But there was no bleeding corpse, Your Grace. Drogo was alive.'

'So be it,' Thoresby said. 'I am counting on you to save my friend Emma Ferriby from more grief.'

So that was his interest in this. Lucie's good friend was the daughter of an old, very dear friend of the archbishop's. His death the previous year had aged Thoresby even more than had the death of Queen Phillippa, whom he'd worshipped. Owen and Lucie had both become involved in the aftermath of Sir Ranulf's death, and he understood why Thoresby wished to spare the family.

'Emma considers her brother-in-law a fool for placing his school in the liberty,' said Owen.

'He is still her husband's brother,' said Thoresby. 'I want this settled as quietly and as quickly as possible.' The fire was visible in his eyes now.

Owen emptied his cup of ale.

Thoresby rose. 'I'll tell Michaelo that you will be choosing some horses from the stables, and he'll prepare a letter of introduction for you. It might be helpful to talk to the family's landlord, Baldwin Gamyll.'

Owen bowed. 'Your Grace.'

'Do not disappoint me, Archer.'

'That is not my intention I assure you, Your Grace. I shall do my best; the rest is in God's hands.'

Thoresby grunted and waved him out the door.

The archbishop rarely took Owen's faith as sincere. It was one of many aspects of their relationship that puzzled Owen, that Thoresby trusted him, counted on him, but considered him a man of little faith.

As he stepped out into what had become a sunny but chilly day, Owen decided not to leave the minster liberty at once, but to stop at the lodgings of Nicholas Ferriby. He assumed the man was not still hiding in the abbey.

Unfortunately, Nicholas already had a guest, his brother Canon William.

Nicholas gestured to Owen to take a seat by

the brazier. His brother had taken the one seat with a back, which Owen guessed to be the school-master's chair during the school day. The room was tidy except for a cupboard from which books, papers, rolls poked out every which way, giving the impression that the knowledge was reaching out into the room to grab the nearest mind.

Nicholas settled down near him. The sweat on his brow and upper lip belied his assurance that he and William had been idly chatting and welcomed another participant. Something uncomfortable had transpired between them, Owen thought.

'This is a pleasant room,' said Owen. 'My children's nurse, Alisoun Ffulford, is one of your scholars and speaks highly of your skill in teaching.'

The schoolmaster forced a smile. 'Alisoun. Yes. She has a quick mind, Captain. I am gratified to hear she speaks well of my little school. I am delighted to have several young women attending.'

After a pause, in which Owen tried but failed to come up with a comment that could not be construed as referring to his troubles with the dean and chancellor, Nicholas filled in the silence.

'Did Archbishop Thoresby assign you to guard me, Captain?' he asked. 'The crowd was vicious last night. Vicious.' He pressed his hands together and shook his shoulders as if shivering. It was an incongruously comical gesture as it was plain in his eyes and voice that he was upset.

'I heard, yes, but they were clearly wrongheaded – the man was still alive. Did you know Drogo?'

The schoolmaster shook his head, wide-eyed and quick to add, 'Why would I?'

'I thought perhaps you might have the occasion to travel by boat between Weston and York and might have had occasion to hire him as pilot.' Owen did not actually believe this, but he thought he might see something in the man's response.

'A costly means of travel,' William noted, 'and slow, considering the weirs and rapids on the River Wharfe. It would waste time.' Weston sat on the Wharfe's north bank west of Leeds.

Owen was disappointed to learn nothing from Nicholas's reaction. 'So you'd never met Drogo, but you stepped up to say prayers over him last night?' Owen allowed his tone and frown to add that he found that puzzling.

'I am a priest, Captain.' Nicholas's voice cracked slightly, and he blushed and glanced away. 'I would do so for any poor soul.'

'For that I can vouch,' said William. The canon was a quiet, expressionless man, quite a contrast to his brother.

Owen pretended to be satisfied. 'My business is with Hubert de Weston, whose lost scrip seemed to be at the core of this trouble. The lad's been missing a week. As you are pastor of Weston I wondered whether you might have had news of him.'

80

Nicholas shrank back a little, and had begun to shake his head when William spoke up.

'My brother saw his father at Mass on Sunday, didn't you, Nicholas?'

A pale nod met this betrayal. Owen wondered why Nicholas had not wished him to know the father was safely at home. 'I did see Aubrey de Weston, yes. But not young Hubert.' He avoided looking at William.

Owen wondered whether Nicholas hadn't wanted to reveal that he'd been in Weston the previous Sunday, or whether he was merely picking up echoes of the brothers' conflict.

'It would have been a kindness to tell Master John of St Peter's that Hubert's father was safe at home.'

'Tell Master John?' Nicholas sputtered. 'I am hardly one to say anything to Master John at present, though he is not as vicious as the dean and chancellor.' He glared at his brother, who dropped his blank gaze to the floor.

A mere courtesy might go a long way to soothing tempers, thought Owen, but he went straight to his purpose. 'I've come to ask the way to the lad's home.'

'You're off to Weston?' asked William.

'I am.'

'But why, Captain?' Nicholas asked.

'In the hope of finding the lad and talking to him about Drogo,' said Owen. 'So. Can you tell me how to find him? And the Gamyll manor?'

'Why the Gamylls?' Nicholas asked.

'As a courtesy. I'll be on their land.'

'But of course,' said Nicholas, and pulling a wax tablet from a stack nearby he drew a map.

As Owen left the minster liberty he found himself anxious to arrive in Weston before something more happened. He was quite certain that Nicholas had not wished to be completely open with him, but why he felt that he was not sure. He would have Alfred keep an eye on him.

Three

JOURNEYS

Several days earlier, Hubert de Weston had approached his home with caution. Despite being hungry, thirsty and sore of foot, he'd hesitated to make himself known to his mother, for the closer he'd come, the more he'd doubted she'd be glad to see him. She had insisted that he return to school, believing that with an education he would be ensured a good life. So she would not be happy that he'd run away. But he would be so relieved to see her – that was his goal, and to make sure that she was all right. Then he could return to school with a clear conscience, though he dreaded the journey back. He'd also dreaded discovering that his mother was not well, or – he'd feared even imagining 'the something worse' because if evil thoughts were sins then thoughts had power, just as charms did. He'd crossed himself and prayed that his mother was well, that the cross he'd lost did not have the power of a charm.

On his approach a rhythmic sound had caught his attention – it was like something sliding and thumping, sliding and thumping, and he'd recognised it as the sound of chain mail being rocked, spun in the rocker barrel with wood chips and oil. But Aubrey had taken all his chain mail with him. Hubert had had a sinking feeling in his belly as he'd considered the possibility that his father was alive and here. This was not the something worse that he'd feared, but it was bad enough.

He'd pressed his palms against the house and prayed that he would find his mother rocking something other than chain mail, that her cheeks would be rosy with the cold air and her eyes bright, and that she would turn towards him and light up with joy at his coming. Then he'd peered around the corner and seen Aubrey about ten paces from the house, his face screwed up in anger, his lips moving in a silent rant as he'd turned the rocking barrel on its stand. Hubert had imagined he was cursing about doing his own work; he was never satisfied with his family, never.

'Aubrey?' His mother's voice had come from the house – she must be at the door.

Hubert not only had not stepped forward to see around the corner, he'd retreated a little, unsure he wanted either of his parents to see him yet.

'Husband,' she'd called out in a stronger voice tinged with irritation.

Aubrey had not stopped turning the handle at

once, but he'd slowed and looked up at Ysenda, who had now stepped out far enough into the yard that Hubert could see her. She wore a coil of rope dangling on one arm, like a huge, clumsy bracelet.

'May I go to collect firewood?' She'd been trying to keep her tone humble, but Hubert could hear the angry edge.

'No, damn you, woman. I'll fetch it.' Aubrey had stopped turning and kicked the rocker. 'You can finish cleaning the mail. And do it right. It might lie in the chest for years now, till Hubert is summoned by Osmund Gamyll to fight by his side, as I was by Sir Baldwin.' They were Sir Baldwin's tenants, and owed him service when the king summoned him.

Hubert had almost laughed out loud, trying to imagine Sir Baldwin's son going to battle. In truth he feared and despised Osmund Gamyll and dreaded a time the man would be his lord.

'I know where the storms have torn at the trees, Aubrey,' said Ysenda. 'There is no need for you to quit your work when I can find the wood faster than you could.'

'I said I'll gather the wood.' Aubrey had snatched at the rope.

Ysenda had hurriedly slipped it off her arm before he tugged too hard and had handed it to him.

Hubert hated how his father treated his mother like a prisoner. She had a temper, especially when

85

she'd been drinking, but she was the mistress of the house and needed to go about her duties. Aubrey did not like her going to Sir Baldwin's wood for fuel, he did not like her going to market, he did not even like her to go to Mass without him. So she sneaked out more often than not, which was the cause of most of their arguments, though Hubert was certain that had she not gone out they would have argued about there being no food, no drink, no fuel for the fire. Aubrey was a fool to fuss about her going to the wood after he'd been away so long. He must realise she'd been fetching for herself all that time, at least when Hubert was in school.

But at least he would be gone for a time and Hubert could be alone with his mother. Unfortunately, since it was only hours till the early dusk of November he must spend the night there, with his parents. He'd sunk down with his back to the wall to await Aubrey's departure.

Despite the cold, he must have fallen asleep for a while, for the sun had deserted him and when he'd looked out he'd seen his mother removing the chain mail from the rocker. He must have been very tired to have slept through that noise.

Taking a deep breath, he'd stepped out from the side of the house. 'Ma!'

Ysenda had turned to him and pressed the chain mail to her breast. 'What are you doing here, Hubert?' Her words had been oddly pronounced, and as Hubert reached her he'd seen the cause –

her left cheek was bruised and swollen, obliter-
ating the pretty dimple.

He'd hugged her, then stretched up to gently
kiss her injured cheek. 'I wanted to see you.'

'He's home,' she'd said.

'I know. How long has he been here?'

She'd blown a strand of hair from her eyes,
still clutching the chain mail. 'Perhaps a week.'

'And he's already beaten you.' Hubert had
touched his mother's cheek again, wondering how
anyone could want to hurt her.

She'd taken a step backwards, frowning
crookedly. 'Did Master John send you home? Did
someone accompany you? Is this what was in the
letter? I'd no one to read it to me.'

Her questions and her faraway eyes confused
him. 'You're not glad to see me?' he asked.

She must have remembered the mail she had
clutched to her, for now she shook it out. 'Does
this look clean to you?'

He dutifully ran a hand down it, trying to
discern any flaws in it. The rings felt intact, but
that did not mean they were free of dirt and rust.
'The light's faded too much to see,' he said.

She cursed under her breath and tossed the mail
back into the rocker. 'I pray you, work on it a
while longer, there's a good lad.' She bent to peck
him on the cheek, a hand at the small of her back.
'I *am* glad to see you, son. But I'm worried, as
well, with your da being here. And you haven't
answered me. Did Master John discharge you?'

What did you do to displease him? I pray it isn't anything your da won't like. Did someone escort you?'

'I came alone, and Master John doesn't know I'm here. I was worried about you, all alone, with winter coming on.' He'd hoped she would not ask for details of his journey. He did not wish to worry her.

'Oh Hubert, as you see I'm not alone. And you were to learn and make something of yourself, not fret about me. What will Master John say?' She'd pressed a hand to her swollen cheek. 'I'm a grown woman. It's not your place to worry about your mother.' She'd massaged her temples and closed her eyes. 'I'll lie down for a little while.'

Hubert had watched her until she disappeared inside, hoping that she'd turn around and say she was glad to see him. But she had not turned, not to say that or to ask how he'd made his way alone from York, or comment on how thin and dirty he was. He had not wanted her to ask about his journey, but it hurt that she had not. He never should have gone away. He had not wanted to. He remembered how angry he'd been when she'd insisted he return to school. He'd gone mad, lashing out at a goose in his anger.

It had been a hot summer afternoon. The geese, ever-vigilant, had watched as Hubert crossed the yard, apparently sensing his mood. They were ready to attack if he showed any interest in moving towards them. He'd ignored them until he'd moved far enough in the opposite direction for them to lose interest; then he'd turned and, raising his arms above his head as he bellowed at the top of his lungs, he'd charged them, startling all into flight but one stubborn male.

He'd lunged towards the defender, who'd flapped his wings and shot his beak towards Hubert's leg, almost managing a nip. But Hubert's energy had been equal to the gander's and he'd spun away in time. What happened next was what haunted Hubert – again he'd lunged for the gander with a temper so vicious he'd stopped himself just short of wringing the fowl's neck – he knew he'd intended to do so – and he'd earned a painful bite on the wrist.

Holding his bleeding arm, Hubert had fled to the empty stable and crumpled down onto the hard ground long swept clean of hay, breathing so hard he'd thought he might burst; but in time he'd caught his breath and sat back to suck on his wound until the bleeding slowed. Out in the yard the goose had noisily dared him to try again. Through the chinks in the rotting wall Hubert could see it kicking up dust as it paced and fluttered its wings. He'd been grateful that his mother had gone to Sir Baldwin's woods to collect firewood and had not witnessed his behaviour.

My Lord, forgive me. Hubert hadn't understood this anger. He'd seen his father wring the necks of animals out of anger, but in Hubert's eleven years of life he'd never been driven to such an act. He'd prayed he would not grow up to resemble his father; Aubrey de Weston's temper darkened the family's life. Even the plague deaths of two of his children, Hubert's siblings, had driven him to outbursts of anger rather than grateful affection for his wife and surviving son, leaving Hubert to comfort his mother.

But Hubert was home now. He pushed the memory aside and settled down to rock the chain mail until his arm tired, his mood careening from embarrassment to anger to disappointment to relief to fear, and then they all jumbled together. Nothing had changed at home, and nothing ever would. For the first time he understood that he was quiet at school because it felt good to be quiet, to enjoy the stillness that he felt, the peace – until he'd begun to worry about his mother. He supposed she might be right in saying that he need not worry about her.

Later, when Aubrey had returned, Hubert had made an effort to greet him with a smile and a show of joy that he'd survived.

Aubrey had made an approving sound. 'Well, they've taught you something this time.' He'd patted Hubert on the shoulder.

Encouraged by the reception, Hubert had asked, 'Would you tell me about France? And the channel crossing?'

Aubrey had settled back with a cup of watered wine and began to speak in a low voice that Hubert seldom heard. He talked about the work they'd had calming the horses on the crossing, how many men were sickened by what were in truth merely moderate waves, how mild the weather felt as they travelled south.

Hubert had so enjoyed his father's tales. It had been an evening filled with delights, unlike any other that he could remember at home, and he'd dared to hope that he had indeed learned something from his time at school, a way to cope with his father. Perhaps his maturing would ease the strife in the household.

But no sooner had Hubert gone to bed than his parents had resumed their arguments. He'd wriggled down under the covers as far as he could and still breathe, and wondered how soon he might return to school.

And now, a few days later, they were at it again, arguing about the amount of cider she had in the outbuilding. Hubert hated to hear his mother weep.

He liked to daydream that he was brother to one of his fellow students who lived in a house in the city or on a prosperous farm, but even more importantly he chose the ones who spoke of their fathers with affection and admiration. Then he'd have his imagined mother die in childbirth or something and his imagined dad would meet and fall in love with Hubert's real mother, for he had no desire for any other mother. Her new husband would come home from travels with exquisite cloth and jewels to adorn her, and her eyes would shine with love as she looked on her happy family. God was omnipotent, so surely He'd created families like that. Hubert could not understand why God would create such a beautiful woman like his mother and then give her such a mean husband, as well as allowing two of her children to succumb to the plague.

His mother deserved happiness, not the misery Hubert was trying not to witness right now. He sat on the bench outside the kitchen, hands cupping his ears against his parents' voices – his angry, hers tearful. Aubrey de Weston was a heartless man, a man who trusted his lord, but not his family, particularly not his wife. Hubert avoided calling him 'Da'; it felt better to him to think of his father by name rather than by relationship. Fortunately, Aubrey didn't seem to notice. Hubert knew it was sinful to wish Aubrey had died at La Rochelle as Father Nicholas had reported, but he could not keep his thoughts from going there. If Hubert were older, stronger, he would have defended his mother's honour with his fists whenever Aubrey accused her of lying so she wouldn't be pushed to defend herself. Surely it was the humiliation she felt that resulted in the foul language she sometimes spewed, frightening Hubert.

He hadn't even been able to keep her pretty cross pendant safe. Its loss was unforgivable. He'd come home to see with his own eyes whether his carelessness had made his mother vanish as well.

The fear had gnawed at him for almost a week before he'd worked up the courage to run away from school. He'd not confided in either Master John or Dame Agnes because he thought they would tell him that the loss of a trinket could not make his mother disappear, and would therefore refuse to give him leave to journey to Weston, and most assuredly not alone. But he could not sleep, could not eat, could not study, could not think of anything else until he saw with his own eyes that his mother was unharmed. He'd stolen the cross to have something of her near him, by which action he'd made it a charm. He knew of charms, and knew that they had power beyond the ordinary. It had been his responsibility to protect it, to keep it safe, and he'd failed. He hadn't expected to see that man on the barges, and his questions about the scrip had frightened Hubert. That's why he'd run, seeing the man his mother had always tried to keep away from Hubert.

The snowfall on the morning after Drogo's drowning caused Edric and Jasper to be late in coming into Owen and Lucie's hall for their morning bread, cheese and ale, for they'd first swept the snow from the threshold of the shop and the paving stones between the shop and the hall. Lucie was glad that the activity had warmed their relationship. Some mornings they arrived from their shared quarters above the shop in chilly silence, but this morning they were trading complaints about Sir

Richard de Ravenser's clerk Douglas and seemed quite companionable.

Alisoun had already brought Gwenllian and Hugh in from catching snowflakes on their tongues to warm up by the fire.

Seeing all the youthful faces bright with the crisp air made Lucie momentarily impatient with her awkward body, feeling confined and idle, but she caught herself and assured God that she loved and cherished the child who moved within her. She could not bear to lose another child, no matter her present discomfort. She'd fallen into such a terrifying despair when she'd miscarried the previous year, fearful that she was now too old to carry a child full term, fearful that Gwenllian and Hugh might be taken from her by illness or accident. Her mind had been so heavy and dark with fear – she thanked God every day for lifting her despair and blessing her with another child.

When Edric and Jasper were sated and warm, they came over to her as usual to join them in returning to the shop.

'Not this morning,' she said. 'I'll wait for the stepping stones to dry.'

'We'll escort you, Mistress,' said Edric with an enthusiasm that almost coaxed Lucie to reconsider.

But Alisoun prevented any such change of heart. 'Dame Lucie dare not risk a fall, Edric.'

Jasper leaned down and quietly asked Lucie if she would like him to escort her to the back of the garden later.

She shook her head. 'This year I'll keep the day in my heart. But bless you for remembering the anniversary. I am grateful.'

He kissed her cheek and pressed her shoulder. 'I'll come for you if we meet with a challenge that cannot wait.'

She nodded, too overcome with emotion to trust her voice. More than the clumsiness, she disliked her changeable, exaggerated moods when with child – and for a while afterwards. She dreaded most the darkness that had overwhelmed her when she'd lost the child the previous autumn, and prayed throughout the day and night that God would deliver her from such horror this time. She sensed that she'd almost lost Owen's comfortable affection last time, that she'd almost driven his heart from her, though she knew he would never physically desert his family. His love and friendship were precious to her and she could not bear to lose either.

She took out her spinning and had regained her sense of well-being when a visitor arrived. It was her friend Emma Ferriby. Kate took Emma's cloak and announced her, a funny behaviour the maid had taken up of late, amusing because voices carried quite clearly from the hall door to the interior, there being only a small screen blocking the draught, and no screen passage that might have muted the sound. Emma hugged Lucie with affection. She smelled of snowy air and lavender, and her silk gown richly rustled. Kate and Emma's maid slipped away to the kitchen.

'You look very well,' said Emma, having stepped back to observe Lucie. 'And I envy you. I should so love to have a chance at bearing a daughter to dress in Peter's beautiful cloth.' Her husband was a merchant and traded some of the loveliest cloth in York in his shop. Emma held out a package. 'But since I'm not so blessed, I thought we might pass some time this chilly morning choosing some cloth for the two of us. No doubt you'll want a new gown for churching.'

'You are a dear, dear friend to think of that,' said Lucie, her spirits definitely improving. It would feel wonderful to slip into a new gown once she was able to go abroad. 'Come, let's sit at the little table by the window so we can see the colours in daylight.'

'Such as it is today,' said Emma, following Lucie across the room. 'I have never cared for snow. I never feel steady on my feet.'

'But it has stopped snowing for now,' said Lucie, 'has it not?'

'Yes it has, but the wind is rushing down the streets and keeping the shadowed pavements and frozen mud quite slippery. I was glad of my maid's arm in several places.'

Before he continued his investigation Owen thought it best to tell Lucie and Jasper about the trip to Weston on the morrow. He found Jasper and Edric in the shop, both busy with customers. At the house he was unhappy to find Emma

Ferriby. He was fond of her, but he imagined she was there to find out whether her brother-in-law was in trouble, and Owen could not honestly reassure her that all was well, having come away from Nicholas's house with a gnawing feeling that the man had lied to him about knowing Drogo.

She and Lucie were bent over swatches of cloth. After the customary greetings Owen decided to do what he'd come home to do and hope that Emma kept her peace.

'His Grace has offered me horses and men so that I might ride to Weston on the morrow, Lucie. I would take Jasper if you can spare him in the shop. He knows Hubert de Weston, he'll recognise him if we encounter him. He might also be a comfort to the lad – someone familiar.'

Lucie had nodded her agreement halfway through his determined speech, and now asked only, 'Do you know that the boy is in Weston?'

'No, but Emma's brother-in-law saw his father there on Sunday. Perhaps the boy learned of that and headed home.' Owen glanced at Emma, expecting her questions to begin now.

But she said, 'Thank God his father is safe. So Nicholas has been helpful?' Emma was now sitting back and giving him her full attention. She was a plain, small woman who practised the art of making the best of her features with beautiful clothes well cut.

Owen valued her intelligence and absolute support of Lucie, and so although Nicholas had been helpful only because his brother William had betrayed him, Owen said merely, 'He has.'

'You don't think –' Emma glanced over at Lucie. 'We've been talking about my husband's brother, how Peter worries about Nicholas's strange choice in situating his school, his childish enthusiasms.' She shook her head as she would over the unfortunate antics of her sons. 'But I do not think him capable of attacking that river pilot.'

'Any man might attack another with cause,' said Owen. 'I cannot protect him, Emma.'

She looked hurt. 'I hope you don't think that is why I am here, Owen, to ask you to watch over Nicholas.' She glanced at Lucie, who smiled and pressed her friend's hand. 'For your thoughts about his situation, yes, but my first purpose was to while away a gloomy day with Lucie.'

Her honesty beguiled him. 'I do not know what to think of your Nicholas,' Owen said. If he was innocent, why was he not straightforward? 'Do you know of any connection he might have with the pilot?'

Emma shook her head.

'That may be a good sign. Do you by any chance know Sir Baldwin Gamyll?'

'Yes, though not as well as my mother does,' said Emma. Less interested in the new topic, she went back to fussing with the cloth samples.

'Do you know the son?'

She shook her head. 'I've not seen him for a

dozen years or more – not since my wedding, I think. He was little more than a boy then.'

There was a guardedness in her response that Owen wondered about. 'But you've heard of him since then?'

Emma glanced up. 'My mother has spoken of him, and of course she would not mention him were his character above reproach. He is of interest for being sharp-tongued and wanton.'

'Wanton?' Owen was curious.

'According to Ma he is ill-mannered and un-governed. He does not favour one sinful pastime over another.' Her sudden grin was impish as she spoke the last words in her mother's imperial tones.

Lucie laughed and clapped her hands. 'And we know how you agree with Lady Pagnell.'

Emma's father had been a knight. Marrying down – it was one of the things she and Lucie had in common, Emma marrying a merchant, Lucie the captain of the archbishop's guard, and before that an apothecary.

'So he is likely a bad sort, but no worse than many other idle young men awaiting their inher-itances?' Owen asked.

'I recall hearing his name mentioned regarding some unpleasant matter,' said Lucie. 'I remember only because I thought what a contrast he must be to his father.'

Emma was nodding. 'I pray the Gamylls are not taking Chancellor Thomas's side against Nicholas's school?'

'I've no idea. I am merely curious. His Grace is preparing a letter introducing me to Sir Baldwin.'

'Oh. That should be helpful.' Emma looked relieved. 'As I recall Sir Baldwin's new wife was not moving to the manor until he returned. She must be a happy woman.'

Owen was glad to leave Lucie and Emma to their cloth samples, having many people to talk to before he returned to prepare for the journey. But at the door he turned, remembering that he'd not wished to disturb Jasper in the shop.

'I've not told Jasper about Weston. The shop was busy.'

'He will be told,' said Lucie. 'I shall enjoy giving him such news – he'll be delighted. Though I can feel my own worries rising.'

'I'll bring him safely home, my love.'

Lucie blew him a kiss.

A biting wind caught Owen's breath at the street corners, but the snow had not resumed. He thought it wise to pray for a few days of still, mild weather, though November in the North was seldom favoured with such days. At the statue of the Virgin by St Mary's gates he paused, bowing his head to pray for Drogo's soul. He noticed that the man beside him wore the abbey livery.

'Did you know Drogo?' Owen asked.

'Aye, and you?'

'No. Abbot Campian has asked that I try to discover what really happened last night.'

'Good. That is good. I'm Hal. You're Captain Archer, aren't you?'

'I am. Did you know him well?'

'As well as any of us on the barges did. He wasn't much of a talker until he was drinking, and when he was drinking I wanted no part of his company.'

'Drogo was an angry man in his cups?'

The man nodded. 'Violent sometimes, which you've no doubt already heard.'

Nodding, Owen said, 'I would like to talk to your fellows on the barges. Would you accompany me?'

'With pleasure, Captain.'

They were watched with curiosity by the men on the staithe, almost all of whom wore the abbey livery. Hal introduced Owen, and once they understood what he wanted they seemed eager to answer Owen's questions. Unfortunately they were able to provide little new information. No one recalled seeing Drogo and Master Nicholas together.

'But he was secretive about many of the trips that took him away down the river,' said the man who did most of the talking for the group.

Several nodded.

'Drogo was often away?' Owen asked, happy to sense in the group an eagerness to talk.

'Oh, aye,' said the spokesman. 'We sometimes wondered why he wore the abbey livery. There are other pilots in the city, but none work as much as he did.'

'Pilots are paid well, you see, and abbey bargemen live tolerably well,' said an older man who had been whittling while listening to the others.

Another man said, 'Yet his wife and daughters wear rags and eat no meat.'

'Aye, he's right about that,' said Hal.

'He drank his earnings,' said the spokesman.

The whittler vigorously shook his head. 'He'd never make it out of bed if he drank so much as that. And the wife and girls are not ragged.'

'What do you suppose he did with the money?' Owen let his eye rest on each man in turn, but he saw no sparks of insight. The spokesman merely shrugged. Owen tried another approach. 'You said he was secretive about many of the trips. Why was that, do you suppose?'

'He'd talk in riddles,' said the spokesman.

'Aye. I stopped asking him,' said another man. 'He made no sense.'

'Smuggling,' said another, 'that is what I thought he was about.'

'Then why not spend the coin?' asked the spokesman of the others.

'Mayhap he had another family downriver,' the whittler suggested with a wicked gleam in his eyes.

'Not him, Sly Pete,' said the man sitting next to him. 'He was the ugliest among us!'

That raised some hearty laughs, though the spokesman remained grim-faced.

'We have no proof of another family,' he said.

Owen left them with a plea to come to him or to leave word in the shop about anything they might recall about Drogo, assuring them that anything might be useful.

He could still hear them arguing as he entered the abbey gate. It was quiet once inside, and he was soon in the abbot's house, comfortably seated in the abbot's parlour.

After he recounted to Abbot Campian his conversation with the bargemen Owen asked, 'Why did you maintain him in the livery if he was so often gone? Did you not know about his absences?'

The abbot had listened without apparent interest. Now he frowned a little. 'I knew. But the others did not complain, and more importantly he was an excellent pilot so he'd been of use to me. When we ship our wool we want it safe.'

It seemed to Owen the abbey was wasting riches better used elsewhere if it retained a pilot/bargeman who was seldom at his station, but he kept that thought to himself. He was about to take his leave when George Hempe was announced.

Campian glanced at Owen. 'Would you care to stay?'

'I would,' said Owen, curious whether Hempe had learned anything new. He resumed his seat.

Hempe removed his hat as he entered the room, exposing his bald head, which, with his hawk-like nose and dark, beady eyes made him look like a bird of prey. 'My lord abbot,' Hempe said in a deep, inflectionless voice as he bowed. Catching sight of Owen as he rose, he said, 'Archer.'

Owen nodded to him.

'I am curious what business a city bailiff has with me,' said the abbot, motioning Hempe to take a seat.

'The dead man's wife claims that her home was searched while she and her daughters were at the abbey last night, my lord. I'd hoped you might know whether that was a likely claim.'

Abbot Campian turned to Owen. 'What say you, Captain?'

Owen was, of course, very interested in this bit of news. 'How does she know it was searched?'

Hempe almost smiled. 'So you think it is likely to be true.' He nodded to himself. 'Things were moved about, more than a stray animal wandering in might do. A jar was knocked off a high shelf. And the clothes in a chest were in disarray. There was also lamp oil on the floor where there'd been none.'

'I would guess someone is looking for the contents of young Hubert de Weston's scrip,' said Owen.

'I thought the same.' Hempe looked down at his feet, then up at the abbot. 'My lord, was Nicholas Ferriby in the abbey grounds all evening?'

'Master Nicholas?' Owen said before the abbot could respond. 'Drogo's mates don't believe he knew the schoolmaster.'

'He was here all evening,' said the abbot. 'He slept here because of the mood of the crowd when he kindly stopped to pray over a dying man.' The usually impeccably composed Campian flushed a little. 'Do you suspect a grammar master of ransacking the dead man's home? What foolishness is this?' Campian stared at Hempe until the bailiff looked away.

The abbot's emotion surprised Owen. George Hempe had a rough way about him, but he was respected in the city. Campian must be quite upset about Drogo's death.

Hempe rose. 'Forgive me, my lord abbot, I meant no discourtesy. I will call upon Captain Archer with any further questions.'

Campian also rose, slowly shaking his head. 'It is I who must apologise. I was not aware how disturbed I was by the witless crowd last night. You have had only rumours with which to work. Now the captain can supply you with more accurate details.' He bowed to both of them. 'I pray you, go about your good work and return peace to this abbey.'

Owen followed Hempe out of the abbot's parlour. 'I've never seen the abbot in such a temper,' said Owen as they walked out into the cold afternoon.

'No matter.' Hempe paused and waited until Owen looked at him. 'What was in the lad's scrip, Owen?'

'I still don't know. But if God wills it, I'll know soon.' He told him his plan.

Hempe rubbed his head and then covered it with his felt hat. 'I don't like the smell of this, I'll tell you that. And I'll tell you something else – I didn't ask you about Ferriby only because of some gossip trying to excite people. As I left Drogo's house a lad told me he'd seen the man at Master Nicholas's school.' He waited for Owen's reaction.

Owen cursed. 'Who was the lad?'

'Jenkin, Will Carter's son. To hear Will talk, his son is a wizard and it's the dean and chancellor's loss that they did not accept him into the minster grammar school, and Nicholas Ferriby's good fortune. The lad did seem quick.'

'Not quick enough to realise he was harming his master by speaking up,' said Owen. 'But we must be grateful for his unwitting help. I will want to talk to the lad when I return.'

'I thought you would.'

Thoresby would not be pleased with this possible connection. Nor was Owen. Nicholas had denied knowing Drogo.

By now they were out on the street just without Bootham Bar. A couple with a cartload of goods and a pair of wealthy merchants on fine horses were waiting to pass through the gate. Owen and Hempe joined the line.

'I'm relieved that this is in your hands,' Hempe said.

'I pray that feeling is justified,' said Owen, not at all sure himself. He'd spent the better part of a day talking to people but had learned precious little.

He parted with Hempe once through the gate. It was about the time at which Drogo had gone into the river the previous day. How quickly the lives of the pilot's family had changed. How suddenly life had lost its certainty for them.

In the early hours, with a dusting of snow falling on frozen ground already thinly covered, Jasper shivered and stomped as he waited for Kate to fetch the food she had packed for them.

'Perhaps you need more clothing,' Owen said.

Jasper grunted and shook his head. 'I'm like this in the morning. I cannot get warm, and then when I truly wake I'm comfortable. I've always been this way.'

Owen did not recall that about Jasper, but by questioning him he might undo all the good he was accomplishing by taking him along to Weston. They'd had too many arguments of late, the lad being far more sensitive to any perceived slight than he'd been in the past. Owen did not feel safe suggesting anything or asking for assistance in any task – Jasper would take it as a complaint, or criticism. Lucie said he was suffering growing pains, but Owen wondered whether the trouble-some Alisoun had something to do with it. He was hoping that this journey might rekindle the old camaraderie he sorely missed with Jasper. In the past they'd enjoyed archery and gardening together, both skills that Owen had taught him – he'd been an enthusiastic student. He missed their comfortable conversations, the delight of being sought out for advice.

They headed for the palace stables, where Rafe and Gilbert were to meet them. Once in the stables Jasper did appear comfortable, though that might have more to do with the warmth from the horses than his clothing. Owen had taught Jasper to ride when they travelled between York and Lucie's manor of Freythorpe Hadden, and he'd taken to it quite well. But this was a longer ride, and the weather increasingly unpleasant. Owen wondered whether he'd been premature in bringing Jasper. He laughed at himself and resolved to stop fussing about Jasper's comfort. It appeared that the lad considered himself in good company. He and Rafe, one of Owen's youngest men and sometimes a bit too gregarious, were discussing the merits of various saddles, and Gilbert had already managed to compliment Jasper, inspiring a proud smile. Owen relaxed. Jasper had been through more in his fourteen years than Owen had been through when he became an archer for the Duke of Lancaster.

Two grooms had been instructed to escort them, leading the horses from the stables and through the city, across the Ouse Bridge and out Micklegate.

Owen walked beside Jasper, who gazed around as if seeing the city for the first time. The bridge particularly seemed to delight him.

'You've crossed the Ouse many times,' said Owen.

'I cannot believe I'm here with you, Captain,' Jasper said, his smile radiant for a moment, after which he self-consciously straightened his mouth and affected a bored expression.

Seven years? Eight? He still called Owen 'Captain', never 'Da'. But neither did he call Lucie 'Ma'. Perhaps that was asking too much of him, for the lad had deeply loved both his parents, and still mourned them.

'Sometimes I cannot believe how you've grown,' said Owen. 'I must remember to take advantage of you while you're still in the household.'

Out in the countryside the snow brightened the ground, providing contrast with shapely limbs and dark junipers, stone walls and houses. But it also dampened the riders and Owen's companions all expressed relief when he decided they would stay in Wetherby for the night so that they might reach Hubert's home in daylight.

While Gilbert and Rafe flirted with the inn-keeper's pretty daughter, Owen and Jasper sat in a corner near a crackling fire and discussed the changes that might occur with the new baby, and whether it made a difference whether it was a boy or girl. Having exhausted that subject, Owen took the opportunity to review with Jasper what he knew about Hubert, Drogo, and Nicholas so far.

'You think Master Nicholas is lying, don't you?'

Jasper commented when Owen paused. 'Do you think it has to do with his school?'

'You're a scholar at St Peter's. Have you any guess what might have been in Hubert's scrip?'

Jasper, sitting forward with forearms on his thighs, trying to be subtle about stretching his sore muscles, shook his head. 'Coins, perhaps? I don't know. What could he have to do with Master Nicholas's school?'

'The grammar master is Hubert's parish priest,' Owen noted.

Jasper looked up at him. 'Do you think it was something belonging to Master Nicholas? Something that the dean and chancellor might find helpful, something that would help them close his grammar school?'

This conversation was proving more useful than Owen had anticipated. 'That might explain why the lad kept it so close to him,' he said, 'but what about Drogo? Why would he want it?'

Frowning down at the rushes, Jasper was quiet for a while. Owen went over to his men to remind them that they had a long ride on the morrow, and they might wish to stop drinking now. Gilbert nodded and pushed aside his tankard, but Rafe stared down into his and sighed.

When Owen returned to the snug corner, Jasper was shaking his head.

'We've nothing to suggest what it might have been, do we?' he asked. 'Nor why Drogo wanted it.'

Owen agreed. 'I think it might be best if we forget what we think we know and listen well to whatever Hubert and his mother might have to say. What sounds at first unimportant might be the very detail that will lead us to the truth.'

'I'll watch their faces, too,' said Jasper.

Owen was proud of him. 'Speaking of faces, it seems to me your face has been saying you're not fond of Edric. Is he dull witted?'

Jasper ducked his head and mumbled, 'He'll do.'

'I am not chiding you. Just talking. He has said little to me, so I don't know him well at all.'

'He works hard and means well,' said Jasper, 'but –' He sighed.

Owen poked his head close to Jasper's. 'Tell me.'

'We laugh at different things. Have fun different ways. I wouldn't choose him for a friend.' He shrugged, and made a face as if certain what he'd said made little sense.

'I see. He's not making you unhappy, he's just not much fun.'

Jasper screwed up his face. 'I think the worst part is that he tries to be fun.'

Owen laughed. 'For me, the one who annoys me is Alisoun. She is such a brown, brittle young woman.'

Jasper had straightened and now looked into the fire as he spoke. 'Hugh and Gwenllian love her.' His voice was a little tight.

So this was where his trouble lay. Owen and Lucie had wondered whether it might be so. 'I think you like her as well.'

Jasper shrugged. 'She can't be bothered with me since Edric came. We've not gone together to St George's Field to practise at the butts since then, have you noticed?'

Alisoun was a skilled archer, as was Jasper. It was their shared interest that had made possible their friendship. At another time Owen might be relieved to hear that the friendship had soured, both of them needing more maturity, but he heard in Jasper's voice and saw on his face the distress that he felt. Owen did not wish that on Jasper.

'Alisoun will soon return to Magda Digby's service. Edric will have no cause to go there, but you might.' Owen grinned.

Jasper said nothing. Owen decided he'd pried deep enough and said all that needed to be said.

Four

FLOATER

For Lucie it was always so. No matter how often Owen left the city, on his first day away she felt a vague unease and tried to devise work that would so occupy her that by the time she was finished a few days would have passed. But that did not help the nights, unless the work was both physical and mental and she could fall into bed exhausted. In summer a garden project might suffice. The apothecary garden planted by her first husband was extensive, supplied much of what she sold in the shop, and she enjoyed working in it. But in November, in late pregnancy, gardening was out of the question. She was mentally and physically uncomfortable at night. She often treated the children to a night in her bed, but in her stage of pregnancy it was infeasible, for she would keep them awake with her fidgeting about in bed, her pacing, and her occasional tears.

So she was out of sorts after Owen and Jasper's

departure, until she remembered that Edric would need her in the shop most of the day. Once Alisoun departed for her classes and Aunt Phillippa seemed settled with the children, Lucie asked Kate to walk through the garden to the apothecary shop with her. As they passed through the workshop she pointed out a high stool for Kate to carry into the shop.

Edric seemed flustered by the news that Lucie would work beside him all day.

'But should you stand so long, Dame Lucie?' He blushed a little.

'No, and that is why I have this high stool.'

He rushed to take it from Kate and carry it to the counter area. 'Where shall I place it?'

She indicated a spot. 'You'll do the reaching, lifting, rushing about and I'll sit here and talk to the customers,' she said, easing herself onto the stool and smoothing out her skirt.

'I'd best hurry back now,' said Kate. 'In case Dame Phillippa becomes confused.

Edric hovered above Lucie in his most irritating way.

She smiled and patted him on the forearm. 'I will enjoy it. Do not worry about me.'

He fussed over her for a while longer, but eventually, after they'd seen to a few customers, he fell into a rhythm, understanding how their partnering would work.

Nicholas Ferriby broke the quiet of the morning, rushing into the shop and then trying to minimise himself while Lucie and Edric dealt with a customer, Dame Barbara. But being a man expansive in his movements, Nicholas could not help but be a presence in the shop, and his slightly asthmatic wheeze was just loud enough for Dame Barbara to turn to him and offer to return later if he had need of something at once.

'Oh no, I pray you, forget that I am here,' he said, holding up his hands palms out as if pressing her back.

Dame Barbara turned back to Lucie with an amused glint in her eye, and when the grammar master swept gracefully into a bow as she departed, she choked back a laugh. What rendered Master Nicholas amusing was that he spoke dully but gestured dramatically, as if his arms betrayed his attempt at a dignified demeanour.

He quickly strode to the counter as if he was in danger of being beaten to it.

'Master Nicholas,' said Lucie, 'I do not expect to see you mid-morning on a school day. I hope you have not come about Alisoun.'

His hands rose up in exclamation. 'My assistant is with my young scholars for a little while. I'd hoped to see Captain Archer, but an elderly woman at the house informed me that he is away?'

Lucie did not blame him for being uncertain whether to credit her aunt's information, for Phillippa sounded vague these days. But she had been accurate, which cheered Lucie.

'Yes, he is, for several days. Might I be of help?'

Nicholas shook his head. 'I am grateful to you for asking, but no. I must speak to the captain.' He pressed his temples and his eyes flitted side to side as if he were listening in distress to warring factions in his head.

Lucie rose. 'We might withdraw into the workshop. No one will interrupt us or hear us there.'

'Thank you, no, Dame Lucie. I apologise for disturbing you. I should not have done so.' He pressed his hands together in prayer. 'Sometimes I think too much and create problems where none existed. I have been foolish. Please remind Alisoun to inform me when the captain has returned.' He bowed out of the shop, opening the door so wide that he jammed it into a snow drift.

Edric assisted him in freeing it.

Lucie did not know whether to laugh or worry.

Hubert's home sat to one side of a broad clearing that sloped away from where Owen had paused at the edge of the wood. It was a long, low house surrounded by several small outbuildings. A pig was the only creature in sight, eyeing what Owen guessed was the kitchen garden. It was so quiet he could hear its snuffling across the clearing. Smoke trickled out from a central hole in the house's thatched roof. There was more snow on the ground here than there had been in Wetherby, though not so thick as to cover the underbrush, so it was more like lace than a blanket of snow.

'What a lonely place,' said Jasper, keeping his voice low.

'It is not so far from the town,' said Owen.

'It is a humble home for one at St Peter's School,' said Gilbert.

Owen realised that he did not know Aubrey de Weston's status, whether he was merely a tenant farmer or Sir Baldwin's retainer. It seemed a humble home indeed for a retainer. He considered how best to approach.

'We'll ride to that first building, where Jasper and I will dismount and go to the house,' Owen decided. 'Gilbert, Rafe, find somewhere to tether the animals where they'll be protected from the wind, if you can, and then join us.'

A track from the building to the house indicated that someone had been here about an hour ago, judging from the fresh snow on the bare patches. Paired with the smoke Owen judged it a sign that someone was at home. That was soon confirmed as he noticed a boy standing in the doorway holding a bow. Fortunately he held it so inexpertly that Owen had no fear of his hitting them.

'That is Hubert,' said Jasper.

'We are friends, not thieves,' Owen called, holding up his hands to show that he held no weapon. 'Tell him who you are, Jasper.'

'It's Jasper de Melton, from St Peter's. This is my Da, Captain Archer.'

Owen patted Jasper on the shoulder, more for

the two-letter word than for his execution of the order.

Hubert did not lower the bow. 'Jasper. Why are *you* here?' The boy's voice was reedy and frightened, his face tight with fear. He took a step backwards.

Owen and Jasper stopped a few feet from Hubert. He looked but a child, with tousled red hair, freckles, chapped lips from licking them in the cold wind. He seemed short for a boy of eleven, as if his limbs were not growing at the right pace.

'Invite them in, son.' It was a woman's voice, gentle and friendly.

Hubert turned to look behind him. 'Ma, are you certain?'

The woman laughed. 'Quite certain.'

The boy dropped his gaze and let the bow and arrow hang as he stepped aside to allow Owen and Jasper through the door.

'I am Ysenda de Weston, Hubert's mother,' said a pretty woman standing by the fire circle in the middle of the hall, centred in the light from a hanging lantern. It was a dramatic effect in the dimly lit room. She was a small woman with dark eyes and a smile that welcomed attention. From beneath her white cap dark curls strayed – by design, Owen guessed – and her gown was cut to accentuate her curves despite being made from humble cloth. She was a woman who knew how to catch a man's eye and hold it. What a desolate place for such a woman. 'I did not hear your names clearly enough.'

Owen introduced himself and Jasper.

'You are welcome, but I would know what is the matter of your visit?'

'There has been a death in York that seemed to have some connection with your son's losing his scrip,' said Owen, watching Ysenda uneasily glance towards her son. 'Archbishop Thoresby and Abbot Campian of St Mary's have asked for my assistance in discovering how the man died.' He found himself hesitant to say it concerned a murder – her prettiness, no doubt. 'I hoped that by finding out what Hubert carried in the scrip we might learn something that would help me.'

As he spoke he'd watched Hubert's reaction, and he was glad of it, for the lad moved into the shadow and stole glances at his mother to see her reaction. Owen guessed that he had not told his mother of the loss.

'Your scrip, Hubert?' she looked puzzled. 'Did I send you with one?' She lightly laughed, but it rang false. 'I must have.' She stepped out of the light and gestured to the benches near the fire circle. 'Do sit, Captain, Jasper. I'll fetch cider to quench your thirst.'

She withdrew, grabbing a wrap from the wall by a door opposite the one through which they'd entered.

'As we've arrived without notice, and there are

two others with us, I assure you we do not expect hospitality,' said Owen.

'Two others?'

'I left them to tether the horses out of the wind.'

Ysenda glanced towards the door with a worried look and for a moment Owen thought her face was swollen and bruised on one side. 'We've enough cider to last a good long while,' she said. 'I keep it cold behind the house. Hubert, fetch the bowls.' She slipped out the door.

The boy set his weapon aside and did as he was told, pulling four bowls from a cabinet against the far wall and setting them down on a stool near the fire. His hands shook.

Ysenda returned, carrying a large jug. Glancing at the bowls, she said, 'Four? The captain's men are here. Open the door for them and then bring two more bowls.'

Gilbert and Rafe entered and quietly moved a bench away from the others towards the door and settled there.

Hubert chose a seat in the shadows, but Owen moved one of the hanging lanterns so that the four by the fire could see one another. In this wider light he saw that one side of Ysenda's fair face was indeed swollen and bruised. She had been careful to keep that side away from them until now. Ysenda de Weston intrigued him.

Noticing his gaze, she lifted a hand to cover her cheek. A strip of cloth on her sleeve hung down, revealing a tear. She did not seem a woman who would delay mending her carefully tailored gown.

'I shall not ask about your eye if you'll not ask about my cheek, Captain.' She spoke in a teasing voice as she bent over to pour the cider.

Though Owen was sick to death of explaining how he'd lost the sight in his left eye, he did not wish to agree to her deal; but she had made it so that he would appear rude if he did not. She was clever. He wondered why she needed to be so clever.

'Agreed,' he said with a little bow. 'Before we begin, I wondered whether you would prefer to have your husband present.'

Ysenda looked startled. Hubert almost spilled the bowls he was carrying to Gilbert and Rafe.

'Perhaps I'm mistaken. I'd heard your husband survived La Rochelle.'

She bowed her head, hand to heart. 'It is true that Aubrey was no longer there when the Spanish attacked. He is alive. He's come home.' She lifted her head, tears in her eyes. 'And gone again.'

Hubert put an arm around her. 'He doesn't deserve your tears, Ma,' the boy said.

Owen wondered whether that was part of the story behind her injury and the torn sleeve.

'I beg your pardon for intruding on you like this, without warning,' he said. 'We will not stay long. Jasper, tell them of the event that brought us here.' Coming from a friend of Hubert's it might

121

seem less threatening, Owen thought. Mother and son seemed on their guard and he did not think they would say much unless he was able to ease their fears.

Jasper cleared his throat and, with an expression of dismay, asked, 'You mean at the staithe?'

'Aye, just that, and you might include Master Nicholas's unfortunate charity.'

'Father Nicholas our vicar?' Ysenda asked.

Owen nodded. 'Jasper?'

With admirable clarity Jasper thoroughly described the events of two nights past. As his son spoke, Owen observed Ysenda fidgeting, and seeming at one point to have difficulty catching her breath. When Jasper had finished his account, Hubert and his mother exchanged looks, hers agitated and his sullen.

'What could you have carried that a pilot might desire?' asked Ysenda, reaching for Hubert's hand. 'I sent you with nothing of that nature.'

Hubert dropped his head, chin to chest. 'I wanted something of yours with me at school,' he said, his voice muffled by his posture.

'I have nothing of value,' she said, but her tone subtly changed on the last two words. 'What did you take, Hubert?' Her voice was suddenly sharper. 'Have you brought the scrip, Captain?'

'No. It is safe in the city,' said Owen.

The boy looked up at Jasper and Owen. 'I don't know why a pilot would want it,' he said in a child's whine. 'It must have slipped out and he didn't even know he handed back the scrip without it.'

'Perhaps,' said Owen, 'but we still need you to tell us what *it* was. I'm sure you can see the importance in our knowing.'

Hubert took a deep breath, and still not facing his mother he said, 'It was a little gold cross.'

Ysenda's intake of breath at last drew her son's eyes.

'I swear by all the saints you'll have another, Ma.'

'Oh Hubert, you have no wealth, nothing.' She dropped his hand and turned away from him with a muttered curse.

He looked shattered.

'What did you mean to do with it?' she asked, tight-lipped, forgetting to be charming for her guests.

'It was like a charm, to give me good fortune, to have something of yours with me.' The boy had resumed talking to his lap, and did not notice his mother's hand rise once more. But he felt the slap. Holding his cheek and staring at her with wide eyes, he whimpered, 'I was so afraid for you when I lost it, that's why I came home. I was afraid losing it meant you were hurt, or – dead.'

She stared at him as if he'd grown horns. 'You foolish boy,' she breathed. 'Why am I so punished?' she asked the fire.

'Was it valuable, Dame Ysenda?' Owen asked.

She raised her eyes to his, but did not seem to focus on him. 'Gold is,' she snapped, then moaned, 'God help us.' She brought a hand to her mouth and shook her head, as if arguing with herself, then sighed loudly. 'What went through his head?' she whispered as if Hubert were not there. Her features had somehow hardened.

'Had you ever taken the cross out when you were outside the Clee, Hubert?' Owen asked.

The boy shook his head, still with hand to cheek, although Owen did not think the slap had been delivered with enough strength to truly injure him, merely his pride and his faith in his mother's love for him.

'Did any of the other students know what you kept in the scrip?' Owen asked.

'None of them, but Dame Agnes knew. I couldn't keep it from her.'

'Did she talk to you about it?' Owen asked, although he could not imagine a more unlikely culprit.

'It was a small thing,' Ysenda interposed, indicating something in length less than two joints of her smallest finger and one joint wide. 'My husband gave it to me when he knew he was leaving. I do not know where he bought something so fine, or with what. But I did not dare ask.'

'Had you worn it?' Owen asked.

She shook her head, and to Hubert she said, 'You are a sly one,' in a cold voice.

'I didn't want to leave you,' Hubert cried. 'I

told you I didn't want to. I worried about you all alone.'

'And I told you that it wasn't your place to worry about me.' Ysenda looked away from her son, making an impatient, angry sound in her throat.

'Do you think your husband will return soon?' Owen asked.

Ysenda turned her pretty face – once more seeming gentle – towards him, tilting the injured side towards the light. 'I doubt that even Aubrey can predict that, Captain.' She rose. 'I am sorry that I cannot offer you beds for the night – in case he should return and accuse me . . .' Her voice trembled and she looked away.

Perhaps it was this that made mother and son uneasy, that they both feared the father's return.

'Was he drunk?'

It was Hubert who answered. 'It wouldn't have mattered if he'd been sober, Captain. He's a beast to Ma.'

'It wouldn't be the cross he was angry about?'

Hubert shook his head. 'Ma didn't know it was gone till you came. He doesn't need a reason.'

'Enough, son,' said Ysenda in a sweet voice. She moved behind him and put her hands on Hubert's shoulders. 'If my husband finds out about the cross I don't know what he'll do. I'll never tell him that Hubert lost it.' She bent to kiss the top of his head.

Hubert wiped away tears with his sleeve.

'Will Hubert be returning to St Peter's?' Owen asked.

The boy twisted round to see his mother's face, shaking his head.

'But he must,' she said, ignoring Hubert. 'St Mary's Abbey has been so generous to sponsor him.' She took a deep breath, patted her son's shoulders. 'That is where he belongs now, where he will learn about the world.'

'Ma,' Hubert began to rise.

But she held him down as she shook her head at his imploring expression. 'It has always been my dream for you, as soon as I saw how quickly you learned.'

'He is well thought of at school,' said Jasper, 'and well liked by all of us.'

Ysenda smiled at Jasper. 'You are a kind boy. God bless you. There, Hubert, you've made me proud. You are doing well in school.'

Hubert had given up trying to implore her and sat with his chin on his chest. By his uneven breath Owen knew the boy was trying hard not to embarrass himself by crying in front of them. Poor lad.

'Why did you boys go to the staithe?' Ysenda asked Jasper, her tone sharp, disapproving. 'What lured you?'

Jasper took a moment to respond. 'I can tell you why *I* did. I don't like to feel left behind, to listen to the others talking about some fun I didn't share with them. I would never go there otherwise, except if something special were being unloaded. Or the king's barge were expected.'

Hubert had lifted his head as Jasper spoke. He tried to smile. 'He's right,' Hubert said. He turned to his mother. 'I never thought I would lose it. Never.'

'He kept the scrip with him all the time,' said Jasper.

Ysenda forced a smile for Jasper, but her eyes were dark with what Owen could only guess was fear. 'I can see my son has a true friend in you. I am more determined than ever that he should return to school.' She turned to Owen. 'I would ask a favour, that you take him with you?' It was a soft, breathless query, as if she feared refusal.

'I would, gladly.'

'No!' cried Hubert. 'You've – what if Father comes back? Who will protect you, Ma?'

It might mean nothing, but the boy hesitated before saying 'father', and it seemed odd that he used the informal 'ma' but the more formal 'father'. Perhaps Owen was merely sensitive to that at the moment. Jasper had called him 'da'. He smiled to himself.

'The days are so short now, you cannot ride far before nightfall, Captain,' said Ysenda. 'Is it possible – I would not ask such a favour but that you are here – if you are biding in Weston tonight, would you return for Hubert in the morning? As you can see, I must convince him that this is best for both of us.'

Rafe was shaking his head, but Owen did not intend to miss the opportunity to have the lad close at hand. 'We will come for him in the morning,' he said.

As they walked towards the horses, Jasper asked, 'Did you think they were hiding something?'

'Half truths and poor play-acting,' said Owen. 'You have a good nose for this, son.'

Jasper looked pleased. 'What will we do now?'

'I would like to talk to someone at the Gamyll manor. We might even find Aubrey de Weston there.'

'Hubert hates him.'

'I noticed.'

Rafe and Gilbert were discussing Ysenda's charms when Owen and Jasper joined them by the horses.

'It's a sin for a man to hit such a beautiful face,' Rafe said.

'But not a plain one?' Owen asked, releasing the reins of his horse. 'Come, men. We've more to do before sundown.' His men often irritated him with their empty chatter, but he disliked it even more when Jasper was there to hear it.

As he sat on his horse waiting for Rafe to get his bearings, Owen glanced back at the house. Someone stood at the door, peering out. He thought about Ysenda's obvious fear and prayed he was not a fool to leave them alone for the night.

* * *

The great stone walls encircling York stopped on either side of the Ouse, a tidal river that ebbed and flowed, and flooded whenever the myriad streams in the moors and dales ran fast with melting snow or heavy rains. All vessels on the part of the river bisecting the city rode the changes, high in the water when the tide was in, trapped in the mudflats at very low tides. To live on such a watercourse or along its banks was to internalise the one certainty in life – that nothing was permanent.

Magda Digby, midwife, healer, a gifted woman of youthful old age, lived in a house capped with an upside-down Viking vessel as if ever ready to carry her away on a flood. New acquaintances inevitably suggested that, but Magda only smiled, never explaining her choice of roof. Her home sat on a rock near the north shore just outside the city walls and beyond the Abbey Staithe, upriver from the city, downriver from the Forest of Galtres. At high tide the rock became an island, and in floods the dried reeds she'd spread on the floor inside were often swept away. Yet the structure stood, as if it were hovering over the rock, or was an insubstantial mirage. The dragon on the prow, glaring upside down towards land, added to the mystery of the house.

Her ever-shifting 'yard' suited Magda. It was as changeable as the folk she tended. In flood time she hoisted her few pieces of furniture up to the rafters and went journeying, gifting the housebound and the lonely with her presence. She saw no reason to cling to her rock and worry. If her home were swept away, then she would seek another that suited her. It was not perfect. She knew full well there was no such thing as perfection.

Out on her rock she felt free to go about her life according to her own moral code. She was not a Christian; she followed her own spiritual path. A few considered her dangerous, imagining that she cast spells. Only a few. Those timid about seeking healers within the city or their towns or villages knew where to find her, and trusted that their secrets were safe with Magda. She turned no one away if they appeared to be in need – she did not rely on their requesting aid, but watched their eyes and the flow of their movements, listened closely to their breath as they spoke. She often understood what people needed long before they did.

November was often a travelling time for Magda, but the stormy season had been quieter than usual, so she was still in residence. By late afternoon the dusk seemed but a continuation of the sunless day. It was that hour when, weary and oddly disoriented, the carpenter hammered his own finger, the tawyer spilled the alum, the cordwainer pricked himself, the apothecary mismeasured, the confessor momentarily nodded off and missed the sinner's most anxious confession. Magda Digby stepped out of her dim, smoky house to rest her eyes and enjoy the braw wind she'd noted gusting occasionally through the chinks in the wattle and daub and down the smoke hole. The snow of the previous day had warmed and soaked into the earth, but it felt as if more might fall. Once she'd studied the sky and reckoned the time, she moved her gaze to the river, noticing that the water was being forced upriver against the current – the tide was coming in.

It was carrying something that she did not like to see. Upon the roiling waters a body bobbed towards her, pushed towards shore on the incoming tide. The water moved the limbs gracefully, if unnaturally.

An uninvited visitor, and the beginning of much trouble, Magda thought. She fetched her shepherd's crook and placed herself where she might attempt a capture. She could see now that the body was that of a man. It gave her pause, for she was short, and though strong enough for a woman of her size, she might be overwhelmed by the man's greater weight. But a few moments more or less meant the difference between life and death in the cold currents. Taking a deep breath she braced herself, stretched out the crook, and managed to hook him by an armpit. She used the cooperative motion of the water to her advantage, slowly guiding him towards her, and then patiently waited until another strong surge lifted him enough that she was able to manoeuvre the body onto her rock.

Sitting back to rest a moment, she checked the water for signs of other bodies, or debris from a capsized boat. But she saw nothing else amiss.

Crouching down to him, she noted he wore well-made clothes, nothing fancy. She did not recognise him. More important at present was his condition. His eyes were closed. She put one hand to his neck, feeling for a pulse, while gently opening one of his eyes with the other. She felt a faint heartbeat, which tempted her to hurry. But before turning him over to push the water from his lungs, she took a good look at him so that she did not unwittingly ignore anything that needed her attention. His left sleeve was slashed on the forearm and stained with blood. Leaning closer, she saw that it was a clean, fresh cut. Now she turned him over and found the smaller, but far more sinister slash in the upper back of his tunic, between the shoulder blades. Blood stains radiated outward like the rays of the sun, but this was a dark, dark thing. She massaged the water out of his lungs, unable to prevent the blood from oozing. She did not like his losing more blood, but it was more important that she help him breathe deeply and cleanly than stanch his blood. She searched her memory for a match to his face, gradually realising that she'd known him as a lad, which was why his face was both familiar and unfamiliar. Nigel.

As water dribbled from his mouth Magda felt a shiver travel through him, but it was weak, and she reckoned such a feeble spark would not carry him through the night. The temptation to hurry faded in her. There was nothing for her to do but make his last hours as comfortable as she might.

His eyelids fluttered. 'I am thirsty,' he said, weakly lifting his arm as if to catch her attention. 'So thirsty.'

Such a weak voice, Magda thought. 'Thou has been in the Ouse,' she said, speaking to hold him present. 'Thou hast had thy fill of water. But Magda will bring thee something good to sip.'

With visible effort, his jaw clenching, he opened his eyes a little, but fell back at once, and seemed to sink deeper within.

Sitting back on her heels, Magda considered his condition. Such a wound would have bled greatly, even more so if the heart was pierced. No wonder there was so little life left in him. The river had washed away much of his blood. There would always be some of this unfortunate man in the Ouse.

He was the bailiffs' business now. She spied two boys on the north bank watching her.

'Is it a floater?' one boy cried.

'Aye. Fetch Magda a bailiff, lads. And a priest.'

Nudging one another with excitement, the pair nodded and ran off, apparently comfortable that the victim was none of their kin.

Innocence gave them a pragmatism they'd lose all too soon. Magda sighed and wondered whether she should find another to send for Owen Archer.

But she need not. He would know soon enough. She sensed that Nigel's injuries were connected to the death of the pilot Drogo. She felt it in her bones.

She crouched beside the man and lifted his head, dripping some wine into his mouth. He took little, and she saw that he was too near death to benefit from more prodding and discomfort. Gently rolling him in some warm hides, getting him close to the house and beneath the eaves, she went back inside to her work.

In Weston they had learned the way to Sir Baldwin's manor, and now, in the waning light, Owen and his party rode there. The snow had stopped, but the wind was the sort that rattles the bare tree limbs and carries a memory of wolf calls. Owen prayed that they were welcomed at the manor for the night, even an outbuilding would do. If they must make camp outside the fire would take much tending on a night such as this.

Dogs sounded their approach, rushing out from the stables. A leather-clad man with the straight, strong bearing of a fighting man followed the dogs out into the yard. He calmly watched the four come to a halt.

'What trouble brings armed men into my yard?' he asked with authority but no malice.

Owen dismounted, assisted by a groom who had hurried out from the stables.

'I am Owen Archer, captain of Archbishop

Thoresby's guard, and this is my son Jasper, and my men Gilbert and Rafe.' From beneath his travelling cloak Owen drew the letter of introduction that Michaelo had provided. 'Am I speaking to Sir Baldwin Gamyll?' One of the dogs circled tightly around him, sniffing out his character.

'I am Sir Baldwin.' The man's hat covered most of his hair, but his stylishly forked beard was mostly grey, and he bore the usual wrinkles of a grey-haired man as well as a still red scar that puckered the flesh between his right eye and ear.

Owen handed him the letter.

Jasper, upon dismounting, was surrounded by the circling dogs. He squatted down, holding out his hand. They came closer, curious, and soon allowed him to rub their ears.

'God be thanked for your safe return, Sir Baldwin,' said Owen. 'Many with such a wound would not have returned home.'

Baldwin met Owen's eye. 'Or I might have lost the eye, as you did. Come, there is a good fire in my hall and we can talk in comfort. The archbishop does not send his captain so far on a mere whim. I am honoured to serve you.'

Jasper rose with an air of regret about leaving his new friends.

It was a sturdy house and large, with a stone undercroft and a substantial storey of wattle and daub above. A covered stair led to the hall door. The dogs ran ahead of them up the steps to a woman who crouched to greet each dog, then stood and invited the party into the hall. Owen guessed her to be much younger than Sir Baldwin, but not his daughter, not with the looks they gave one another.

'Lady Gamyll,' Owen said with a bow of his head as he passed her, and she smiled as she nodded back.

Sir Baldwin introduced them.

Within the hall, wall sconces and a blazing fire gave off a welcoming glow. Owen and his companions would be blessed indeed if Sir Baldwin and his lady permitted them to spend the night in a corner of this hall.

Lady Gamyll called for wine and some food, and instructed a servant to help the guests remove their boots. Sir Baldwin had moved over to the fire, where he stood reading the letter. When Owen joined him, Baldwin handed back the letter and gestured to Owen to have a seat.

'Have you gone to the lad's home?' he asked, settling down across from Owen.

'We have come from there.'

Baldwin gave a little laugh. 'You won't have received a welcome from Aubrey.' He lifted his arms as a large, dark cat leaped up onto his lap. 'Agrippa has missed me,' he said, fondly petting him. 'But back to Aubrey, he hates any man to come within yards of Ysenda.'

'He was not there,' said Owen.

'Not there,' Baldwin said, and sighed. The cat turned round three times and then settled. Baldwin stroked him again then scratched him beneath the chin. 'I wonder what he's about on a day like this?'

'Dame Ysenda has a bruised and swollen face and seems uncertain whether or not Aubrey will return. But I think she fears his return more than his desertion.'

Baldwin cursed. 'For months he talks of nothing but his love for his wife, and when he returns he beats her. The man is a wastrel – he is wasting the time he has with her, such a beautiful woman, so –' He stopped himself, seeming to realise he'd said more than was called for, but then added, 'That too-fortunate wastrel,' as if he could not help himself.

His outburst intrigued Owen, and noticing the pale red that lingered beneath the predominant grey hair he wondered about Baldwin's relationship with Ysenda de Weston.

Lady Gamyll had withdrawn to the kitchen, Owen presumed. He was glad she'd been spared her husband's awkward moment.

Baldwin rubbed the cat's ears. 'The pity of it is, Aubrey is a good man, loyal, a skilled woodsman, and a man of faith.' His voice was now merely conversational. 'But the moment he is within sight of her, he is changed. I believe he both loves and despises her and it has eaten at his heart. They are poison to each other.'

'Poor Hubert,' said Jasper, joining them.

Baldwin smiled at Jasper. 'Do not hurry into

manhood. Enjoy this time of innocence. You are still free of love's confusion. Be at peace.'

Owen wondered whether Baldwin had ever so fallen under a woman's spell. He suspected so.

Five

the charm

With the tide in, the Riverwoman's rock was an island, and George Hempe wondered whether they'd need a coracle to cross to it. He was never comfortable going there, which he'd admitted to himself by bringing Owen's man Alfred with him. Magda Digby was the Riverwoman to Hempe, not a mortal with an ordinary name. He did not think she was entirely of this world, but had one foot in another place that fey folk inhabited. He was grateful when he found her standing on the north bank of the river with Father Goban from St Mary's Abbey and the coroner. Beyond them, two servants held lanterns over two others at the water's edge who were lifting a limp body out of a coracle. The man was wrapped in hides; he made no sound as they lowered him onto a pallet at the feet of the three standing there. Even in the darkening evening the Riverwoman's multi-coloured clothing confused the eye, creating an impression that her garments floated around her as she stood still. Hempe joined the group as she was explaining to the coroner why she had sent for him when the man was still alive.

'Magda did not expect him to linger so long,' she said. 'He was already so cold from the river and had lost much blood.' They all gazed down at him.

'Nigel,' Hempe said. 'He's an apprentice to Edward Munkton, the goldsmith.'

'We've already established that,' said the coroner. He and Hempe had recently fallen out over a judgment in the bailiffs' court that the coroner considered excessively harsh. 'He's been stabbed in the back, near the heart.'

'Or in,' said the Riverwoman.

One of the servants brought a lantern near so that Hempe now clearly saw how Nigel lay with eyes closed, breathing shallowly.

The Riverwoman met Hempe's eyes. 'He loses strength with every breath.'

Father Goban of St Mary's Abbey quietly greeted Hempe and Alfred. 'I'm to take him to the statue of the Virgin where we will offer prayers for him. Then I'll take him to the infirmary, while my brothers keep vigil for him in the chapel, praying for his recovery, or for his soul's swift journey to heaven.'

'I doubt a swift journey,' said the coroner. 'There is nothing saintly about Nigel.'

'So you know him?' Hempe said. 'Does he have family in the city?'

The coroner shook his head. 'I don't believe so. I worked with him on a pin for my wife last year. He spoke as if he were quite alone here.'

Father Goban called to the servants to proceed with Nigel to the abbey. 'God go with you, Dame Magda,' he said, following the men into the darkness.

'Wilt thou attend the priest?' Magda asked Hempe. 'Violence begets violence, and he walks through the darkness with a man someone meant to kill.'

'I'll attend Father Goban,' said the coroner.

'Before you depart,' said Hempe, 'you said the man is no saint – what are his sins?'

'His master once asked the guild to allow him to let the young man go, saying he suspected him of hoarding gold filings,' said the coroner. 'But they were never able to find evidence, so he remains an apprentice, though he boards outside Munkton's house. He's generally distrusted. I counted myself fortunate to have experienced no trouble when I worked with him.' With a courteous bow to the Riverwoman, the coroner departed.

Hempe was disturbed to have not known about Nigel's problems.

'Can the poor man survive the journey?' Alfred asked the Riverwoman.

'The priest said any man would pray to die in a chapel's grace. Magda thinks few men care a whit where they die, only that they do.'

'I'm sure many believe they'll reach heaven more quickly by dying in a sacred place,' said Alfred.

'Aye, and others believe that death in battle is a good, honourable death,' said the Riverwoman, 'but that does not mean all do. Where is thy captain?'

'He and Jasper are in the country,' said Alfred. 'They're searching for the murderer of the last man pulled from the Ouse.'

'Ah.' The Riverwoman nodded. Just that.

Hempe decided he was not a man if he could not talk to the Riverwoman. 'Did he speak at all?'

'He did. He asked for prayers. He'll have them now.'

'He said nothing else?'

The Riverwoman shook her head. 'He had ale on his breath.'

'So he might have been at a tavern this afternoon.' Hempe nodded. 'That is helpful. I am grateful.' He was beginning to feel more comfortable. 'Did you know Nigel?'

'Magda never had cause to talk to him, though after some thought she put a name to him.'

'Well then at least he wasn't bedding with young women who needed your assistance to rid themselves of bastards,' said Hempe.

'Folk come to me for other reasons,' the Riverwoman said, clearly angry.

'Forgive me,' Hempe quickly said, not wishing

to antagonise her. 'I am certain they come to you for healing far more often –'

'Magda is weary.' She stretched her arms to the sides, her clothing shimmering in the darkness. 'Magda bids thee good evening, now. She has much work to do on the morrow.'

Hempe gave her a little bow and wished her peaceful sleep, but that thought led him to thoughts of her lonely house. To Alfred he said, 'The murderer might try to silence the River-woman, believing that Nigel betrayed him to her.'

Alfred cursed under his breath. 'You want me to watch over her tonight, am I right, Hempe?' He made it sound as if Hempe were sending him to his doom.

'I'll send someone to take the later guard,' said Hempe.

'Why not you?'

'I do not know her. I sense that you do, at least a little.'

'She'll not be pleased,' Alfred grumbled. He looked over at where she was preparing her coracle for the crossing. 'But she's a good woman and a friend to the captain and his lady. Perhaps I'll earn grace for watching over her. God knows that many folk need her.'

Alfred turned and went to join her.

As Hempe was weighing whether to begin talking to taverners or Master Edward, the goldsmith, he heard a strange barking sound. Glancing over his shoulder he guessed it was the River-woman laughing. He shivered and crossed himself.

A full belly and the warmth of the hall made Jasper drowsy, but the captain was counting on him to listen and remember, so he fought sleep, wanting to hear all that Sir Baldwin said. There was so much to remember – that was his challenge today. Yesterday's challenge had been the ride; Jasper had not ridden far in a while, so his thighs had been burning by mid-morning. When he'd dismounted at midday his legs had wobbled for the first few steps and he'd been grateful that no one was looking his way. Today's ride had not been easy either, but it had not been as bad as he'd feared this morning when he'd awakened so stiff he'd worried he'd be unable to stand. But he'd managed to stand, and walk, and mount, and after awhile he'd gone numb, for which he'd thanked God.

He had also been trusted to tell Hubert and his mother about Drogo's murder. For a moment he'd been irritated that the captain had not warned him, but in the end he was proud to have done it. He would tell Alisoun how the captain had trusted him, indeed counted on him for a first-hand account. He wondered what she thought of his going off with the captain and his men. Edric could not boast of anything similar. He did not like to think of Alisoun and Edric together back in York, but he hoped that she was irritating him by imagining aloud what Jasper was doing. He often wondered whether she knew she was voicing things people would prefer not to hear, or whether she had missed being taught that before her parents died. Sometimes she seemed surprised by people's reactions to what she said, but sometimes she seemed to be expecting a reaction. Jasper's mother had always shaken her head and put a finger to her lips when he was blurting out what he should have kept to himself, and it had become part of how he thought. He *sensed* now when she would be shaking her head, and he'd stop.

Alisoun. Jasper sighed through the knot in his shoulders. She was so smart, so pretty, and she had the singing voice of an angel. Strange how different it was from her speaking voice. But she wasn't delicate like so many girls. She was strong, and that's how she could be as skilled with the longbow as she was. She would have been fine on this journey.

When he'd heard he would be accompanying the captain Jasper had been excited, but he had not given much thought to the long ride, the wind, the snow, the mud, and then the strangers' houses they would be entering, interrupting their lives, asking questions that could be embarrassing. He had in the past imagined the captain chasing down murderers and sitting in faraway taverns telling strangers about his days as captain of archers for the Duke of Lancaster, maybe singing one of his sad Welsh songs while accompanying himself on a borrowed lute. But what Jasper had seen so far was nothing like what he'd imagined. He saw how much the captain disliked intruding on people to ask questions that made them uncomfortable. He could tell when the captain was reviewing the interrogations – there was a tension in his shoulders and his jaw, and his mouth twisted into a little snarl. Jasper found his father's work decidedly unpleasant. He had felt unwelcome at Hubert's home, despite Dame Ysenda's courtesy, or maybe because of it. When she'd forgotten herself and spoken coldly to Hubert, who was very upset, Jasper had seen through her guise. She had been very careful about what she said and she'd seemed too pleasant in the circumstances, having been beaten by her husband and then deserted. Jasper was certain that both mother and son were hiding something.

Being in their house had brought back strong memories of his life with his mother after his father died. He had wanted to protect her. He'd loved her doubly for being his only parent. He had disliked her being out of his sight. He would have done anything for her, given his life for her. He could see that Hubert felt that way about his mother. But Ysenda was nothing like Jasper's mother, who had been soft-spoken, gentle, always loving, and had a beauty that was less striking but more compelling, he thought. Hubert's mother had a prettiness that made him uneasy somehow. As if she would be trouble. Alisoun would be trouble, but in different ways – she chafed at the restrictions of being a girl, not at being loyal or honest. Sometimes she was a bit too honest. Maybe it wasn't Ysenda's prettiness, but something else.

Sir Baldwin seemed an honourable man with a heart. Jasper liked him. Right now he sat by the fire, the scarred knight who'd fought bravely for his king, with a beautiful, large black cat curled up on his lap, gently stroking it as he talked to his guests.

'Did you learn what the lad had lost?' he had just asked. 'What this pilot had taken?'

When the captain described it, Sir Baldwin's demeanour changed. 'Where might Dame Ysenda –' He gave the cat a pat on the bottom. Once the cat was down, Sir Baldwin headed towards the screened end of the hall, saying he wanted to check something, that they should all be at ease. Jasper leaned over to entice the cat his way, but straightened as Lady Gamyll joined them.

'Where is my husband?' she asked, looking round.

Her face was not pretty, but she moved and spoke with such grace that she seemed beautiful. Jasper would rather a woman like Lady Gamyll any day to one like Ysenda de Weston. He was glad that Sir Baldwin had such a wife.

After the captain explained Sir Baldwin's absence, he said, 'This is a beautiful hall. You must be proud of it.'

147

'I shall be,' she said with a shy smile. 'I've only lived here for a few days, so it is still a little strange to me. I'll feel more at home when my tapestries have been hung.'

'You are newly wed?' asked the captain.

Jasper thought that a bold question, but Lady Gamyll did not seem to mind.

'We've been wed for almost a year, but my husband thought it was best I remained with my family until he completed his mission for the king.' She kept her eyes lowered as she spoke. 'I am blessed that God granted his safe return.'

As she spoke the last few words Sir Baldwin strode out from behind screens at the far end of the hall looking even more agitated than when he'd left.

'The birthing cross is gone,' he said to no one in particular. 'I must ask Father Nicholas who last had it.'

'Is there a problem, husband?' asked Lady Gamyll. 'Did you mention the birthing cross?'

He looked at her and his expression changed, lightened. He must love her, Jasper thought, pleased with that. The captain looked at Dame Lucie like that, as if being with her made everything all right, worth every struggle, every effort. Just as with Sir Baldwin's scarred face, the captain's would soften and the scars would fade a little.

'Yes, my love – have you heard of it? I'm sure I've not thought to mention it – yet.'

Lady Gamyll blushed. 'The servants mentioned it. They told me that when Father Nicholas sought it for a woman's lying in they could not find it. I would have mentioned it, but I did not think you needed that worry just yet.'

Jasper guessed the cross was a charm against trouble in childbirth.

Sir Baldwin bowed to his wife. 'That is most helpful. And now, my love, this is unpleasant business. I do not want you troubled with this.'

Lady Gamyll needed no more signal, but rose and excused herself, withdrawing in the direction in which Sir Baldwin had just come. Jasper was sorry for that, but excited that there was something troubling their host that he would speak of.

'The cross the boy lost – I think it almost certain it was the one that belonged to my first wife.' Sir Baldwin remained standing. 'I cannot imagine where Ysenda might get something so like it. They have little wealth. Aubrey has no true skill for farming. He's a fighting man, not good for much else.'

'You called it a birthing cross,' said the captain. 'What is that?'

Sir Baldwin closed his eyes and pressed the bridge of his nose as if it might help him think. 'It was passed among the women of this parish as a charm for an easy childbirth. It was my first wife's belief that it had helped her through difficult deliveries of our son and daughter, and she'd loaned it to our tenants' wives, and then the villagers, until it became custom.' He dropped his hand and for a moment the soldierly posture sagged. 'She felt so sure of its grace. Few believe with such ferocity as she did.'

Jasper could almost see the memories passing before the faraway eyes.

Sir Baldwin straightened. 'Perhaps Ysenda was with child when we left, and lost the child while we were away? But she should have returned the cross then, or passed it on. You say the boy found it among her things?'

The captain nodded. 'This complicates matters, that it is your property that Hubert lost.'

'*Probably* mine. Most likely. How did Ysenda react to his confession?'

Sir Baldwin grunted at the captain's description of how she was first confused, then angry with her son.

'She claimed Aubrey had given it to her before your departure,' said the captain.

'Unlikely.' Baldwin took a few steps, as if he needed motion. 'Were it anyone else –' He curled his hands into fists and then, seeming to remember he wasn't alone, he relaxed them. 'This is most puzzling. I find myself annoyed, though I can imagine how it might happen, the lad sees a trinket, the purpose of which his mother would not have explained to him. The women of this parish will be unhappy about her carelessness, and they've no love for her as it is.'

'Why is that?' asked the captain.

150

Jasper was surprised by Rafe's chuckling comment, 'You've only to look at her, Captain. Pretty and willing. Teasing. Flirting with any man who comes along.' He shook his head. It was the longest speech Jasper had ever heard him make. He was a quiet man, strong, not as quick as Gilbert. He usually let Gilbert do the talking.

The captain grinned. 'Oh aye, I saw that. But why would the women dislike her?'

Everyone laughed at that, but it was short-lived laughter. Jasper thought that he'd been right to be uneasy in Ysenda's presence.

The captain was already back to thinking through what had happened. 'I would like to know how Dame Ysenda obtained the cross,' he said, 'and whether another woman had requested it and was told Ysenda had it. Well, it seems not since the priest had come for it. How long before the birth do they usually ask for the cross? The lad took it at harvest time, and you and Aubrey left when? In spring? Did Aubrey mention her being with child?'

'We departed in late winter. No, he said nothing of a babe, and he would have.'

'Seven, eight months,' said the captain. 'I suppose she might not have told him yet.'

Jasper was confused for a moment, then realised the captain was counting forward.

'Your wife was not here while you were gone, but what of your son Osmund?'

Sir Baldwin's expression became unreadable to

Jasper. 'Yes, Osmund was here – in the sense that he's ever here. But Father Nicholas would have come to the house for the cross. The women do not come on their own behalf. Modesty.'

'I cannot think how the dead man would have heard of the cross, or known that young Hubert had it.' The captain sat with his forearms on his knees, a faraway look in his eyes.

Sir Baldwin shook his head. 'You said he was a bargeman and pilot. I never engage barges. For my wool shipments I have my steward use merchants in York. They know about those things.'

Jasper was still wondering what their host meant about Osmund. 'Does your son conduct business?' he wondered, then realised by the faces turned towards him that he'd said it aloud. 'Forgive me.'

'No need,' said the captain. 'That is a good question.'

'He doesn't,' said Sir Baldwin. 'He pretends to be dull-witted about running the estate so that nothing is expected of him, though he's a clever young man – too clever, perhaps. My steward saw to everything while I was away. No, I can think of no way the theft of the cross might involve anyone in my household.'

'I would still like to talk to your son about estate matters while you were away,' said the captain.

'He's not here. In York, I believe. As is Father

Nicholas. He's seldom here. More than a little negligent of the souls in his care.'

'Has Osmund business in York?'

Baldwin shrugged. 'You'll think this strange, but I let my son go about his life as he will. I suspect he's up to something reckless, but I would not venture to guess what it might be.'

Jasper could see that the captain was disappointed, but he quickly moved beyond that topic. 'Is it possible that Aubrey de Weston is somewhere on your land, Sir Baldwin? Does he perhaps come here when he's fought with his wife?'

'There are a few men he drinks with,' Sir Baldwin said. 'It is possible.' He did not sound very hopeful.

'Could you have someone escort my men around, just to make sure he isn't right under our noses?'

Sir Baldwin rose. 'I will. And you must stay the night, all of you. There is room in this hall for you, and you are most welcome.'

Jasper silently said a prayer of thanks.

Though it was the end of twilight, Hempe walked along the waterfront towards the castle on the chance that he might cross paths with someone who had seen Nigel that afternoon. He stumbled when he picked up speed, and the waterfront was so far mostly deserted, so he spent the time arguing with himself about why he was bothering. In the daylight he would find many people gossiping here. To walk here in the morning was much more likely to be useful than this stroll in the freezing dark.

The river sucked at the mud and the wind sighed around him. He noticed those sounds more than the steady rush of the river; they were more human, more intimate sounds. He could not recall the last time he'd been so alone, surrounded by a veil of darkness, with little to hear over the river and the wind. The Riverwoman chose to live in such isolation. He wondered how long it would take to become accustomed to such a silence; it turned him in on himself. It felt like the time to pray. He prayed for the souls of Drogo and Nigel, and for Drogo's family.

As he walked along the friary wall his prayers changed, focusing on himself and Owen Archer. He had learned a great deal from Archer. He found it comfortable working with him again. It gave him a confidence that made no sense, but felt good. He was glad there were men like Archer in the kingdom, who put the skills they'd honed in war to a peaceful purpose that benefited the people, not the nobles. Too few cared about the people.

He smiled at himself – a philosopher of a sudden – and decided to give up for the night. Turning upriver once more, he almost tripped over something that by its squawk he discovered was a lad. He caught hold of cloth as the boy tried to flee.

'Who are you?' Hempe demanded.

'No one, sir. No one to you.' The boy tried to make his voice reedy and frightened, but it rang falsely.

'What is a lad doing on the staithe in the dark?'

'Just walking, sir.'

Hempe wished his eyes would adjust to the dark so that he could make something of the lad he held. Why had he not noticed him before? Had he been that lost in his thoughts, or had the lad been stealthy?

'Were you set to follow me?'

A weak laughter. 'In the dark?' the lad asked, elongating the last word. He kicked at Hempe and broke his hold. Hempe reached with both hands, but the lad was gone. He could hear him splashing in the tidal mud, but he could not catch him.

'A curse on you!' he shouted, for no reason but that it spilled from his open mouth.

Cursing himself he headed for the nearest tavern.

The balding guard seemed disturbed by the whisper of the river that filled in the silences between the fire's pops or the occasional conversation.

'I should go without,' he said, beginning to untangle his legs.

Magda and Alfred were sitting close to her fire circle on low stools, sharing a fish stew.

'Thou needst not. Magda will notice sounds out of place.' But she nodded as Alfred mumbled an excuse, understanding that he was not in the habit of trusting the ears of the elderly. She had been surprised by the hawk-like bailiff's concern for her safety. It did not matter that it was unnecessary. But something was nagging at the back of her mind, a worry that she hoped would come forward.

When Alfred returned to his stool, apparently having found nothing amiss outside, he asked, 'Do you never feel too alone here, when the river rises round you?'

'Nay, then the Ouse is Magda's protector,' she said, 'and her ears can rest easy.'

'Why do you live here?'

'It is home,' she said. 'Magda can no more explain that than thou couldst explain why thou art so loyal to Captain Archer.' Ah. That is what bothered her, Owen's household was unprotected with him away.

'He's an honourable man, and he has taught me to be a better soldier,' said Alfred.

She was not interested in what he thought were his reasons. 'Magda is worried about Dame Lucie and her household tonight.'

'Why?'

'Captain Archer and young Jasper are gone. Dame Lucie is alone with only women, children, and gentle Edric.'

'But the captain is often away. The Merchets look out for Dame Lucie and the children. And Alisoun Ffulford is skilled with a bow. You would know that.'

She knew all of that, but she was still uneasy, and she'd learned long ago to heed such a gut-deep feeling. 'Magda thinks they might be in danger. If it was the same man who injured the goldsmith's apprentice and poisoned Drogo, he might wish to end the captain's questions about the pilot, and he might hie to the captain's house not knowing that he is away. Dost thou see?'

'Why do you connect the two?'

'A fair question, but Magda cannot satisfy thee with facts. She fears this. Strongly fears this.'

Alfred was on his feet. 'That is good enough for me. I should warn them. But I told Hempe I'd stay with you.' He cursed beneath his breath and looked not a little angry.

He would be like that all night. Magda had no appetite for such company. She considered the situation, and found an appealing solution.

'Fret not. Magda will come with thee to Dame Lucie's home.'

'You will?'

Magda laughed at his relief. 'Thou'rt such a boy. Come. Help Magda gather her things.'

As they passed Marygate, Magda slowed, noticing the crowd near the statue of the Virgin Mary. Hypocrites, most of them. She doubted many of them had known Nigel, and few of those who did would have welcomed him at their fires, yet they all congregated to pray over him. It was their fear of death that they prayed about, not the goldsmith's apprentice.

'Did you wish to join them, Dame Magda?' asked Alfred.

'Thou couldst leave these things with Magda and see whether the man yet lives,' she suggested.

He did so without further ado. Alfred had surprised her with his considerate manner, which she had not expected from him – this was a reminder to her not to judge hastily. A few folk clustered round him, proudly sharing what they knew. His head was slightly bowed, his walk slower as he returned, and she knew that her catch had died. Patting Alfred on the shoulder, Magda thanked him. He did not seem to notice that they'd not exchanged a word.

She was sorry the man had died without the chance to name his murderer. There was boldness in this murderer, and she feared that he would be smart enough to keep track of Owen Archer's movements. She'd told Alfred that she feared for Lucie because the killer might be after Owen, but what if he'd chosen to strike when Owen was away? He might decide to take a hostage from his household, distracting him once he'd returned.

Bootham Bar was busy with folk coming and going. It took time to get through, and Magda was almost trotting by the time they reached Stonegate, the street of the goldsmiths. A few folk stood in front of the goldsmith Edward Munkton's house and shop, their heads together, gossiping about his apprentice's death, Magda had no doubt. Folk enjoyed nothing so much as someone else's trouble except perhaps talking of things they knew nothing about. Magda was relieved to see Lucie's home at the corner of St Helen's Square. She was anxious to be proved wrong in her worry.

The maid Kate opened the door just a crack to ask their names. When they identified themselves she flung it open while announcing them at the top of her voice, which was considerable.

'Do not rise, Lucie,' Magda said as she entered. 'Magda can find thee.'

She remembered shifting herself at Lucie's stage of pregnancy.

'I am glad to see you,' Lucie said as Magda settled beside her near the fire.

Magda was pleased to see the healthy glow in Lucie's skin and no darkness around her eyes.

Lucie leaned close to ask quietly, 'Have you brought news of a wet nurse?'

'That is not why Magda has come.' She spoke as softly, not wishing to provoke Alisoun. 'But she does have one for thee. She will come a fortnight hence.'

'Will that be soon enough?' Lucie asked.

'Aye.'

'You sound quite certain.'

'Magda is.'

Lucie glanced over to where Alisoun sat with the children. 'She will soon take them to bed and we can talk more freely.'

Magda nodded. 'Hast thou heard of Magda's catch today?'

159

'How could I help but hear about it in the shop?' At Magda's frown Lucie added, 'I sat on a stool and let Edric fetch and carry for me.'

She silently chided herself for worrying that Lucie might take risks, knowing as she did how desperately she wanted this child.

'Is that why Alfred is here with you?' Lucie asked. 'Because of the injured man? I don't quite see –'

'Hempe the hawk told him to watch over Magda tonight, in case the murderer thought the poor man had told her aught.'

'Oh, then he is dead?' asked Phillippa.

Magda nodded. She had thought Lucie's elderly aunt was asleep.

'Thou art sharp this evening, my friend.' She had known Phillippa a long while and was glad when the veil of her illness lifted.

'Will you stay the night?' Lucie asked.

'Aye, that is what Magda hopes.'

Phillippa rose. 'I must prepare a bed for you.'

Lucie touched her aunt's arm. 'There is no need. Magda can share my bed. Do you mind?'

'That will be most agreeable,' said Magda. 'Now. Let Magda repay thee for thy hospitality by telling thee the tale.'

Alisoun rather loudly commanded Gwenllian and Hugh to play quietly so that she might listen to their guest.

Magda noticed that Lucie seemed annoyed by her outburst, though she said nothing. Perhaps

Alisoun had already outstayed her welcome in this household. She was a wilful orphan who had wearied all her kin in their attempts to help her. She'd come to Magda with the intention of becoming her apprentice. Magda had neither accepted nor desired an apprentice in all her years, which were considerable, but she was curious whether the girl's dogged determination might surprise her. Alisoun had expected to follow her in her daily rounds. But Magda had wished to see how the girl behaved in service, so she had offered her as nurse to the Archer children after Lucie's accident. Although Magda had reassured her that she might continue her studies and that a new position would be found for her, the girl was doubtless worried. Magda must talk with her again.

Ah well, to the matter at hand. She recounted all that had happened, speaking loudly enough so that Alisoun, Dame Phillippa, and Kate could hear her. All the women bowed their heads and prayed for Nigel's soul when she had finished her account. Magda bowed her head as well, though her thoughts did not tend towards asking a god to welcome the young man into heaven. She hoped that he'd had no fear in the end, and that no one's life would be cast into shadow by his passing.

It was much later, when Magda and Lucie were up in the solar preparing for bed and could not be overheard, that Lucie told her of Nicholas

Ferriby's discomfort in the shop that day. Magda found it troubling, and she saw that Lucie did as well.

'I would ask George Hempe to talk to the grammar master, but I fear he might make the man even less inclined to talk,' said Lucie.

'The vicar of Weston is a soft man, my friend, easily frightened, easily swayed. Magda hopes that his tale is not the only way to the truth, for he may not find the courage again to tell thy husband.'

Owen lay in Sir Baldwin's hall, the front of him that faced the fire wonderfully warm, his back cold and stiffening. He prayed that his host was right, that Ysenda would not punish her son for having taken and lost the cross. Her request that they return for Hubert in the morning had bothered him more and more as the afternoon turned to evening. He imagined her taking a whip to the boy's back, though he had no reason to think she might behave so. Still, as she could not hope to ever be able to replace the piece, she might be frightened that they'd be turned out, and such fears often drove otherwise gentle parents to violence. But Sir Baldwin could not imagine her behaving in such wise, and Owen doubted the man would abandon Ysenda – or Aubrey for that matter, for he'd spoken well of him for the most part. Owen decided that Ysenda would not have asked him to return if she'd meant harm to the boy.

Aubrey was another matter. Rafe and Gilbert had found no sign of him; none of his friends had seen him in days. Baldwin did not think Ysenda would tell Aubrey about the cross. Owen was not so certain – a slip was always possible. But it had already been too dark to go walking about the countryside spying on Hubert's family.

Owen slept fitfully, dreaming of his flame-haired son Hugh running from Ysenda who chased him with a multi-thong whip. Alisoun also figured in the dream, aiming arrows too close to Hugh for Owen's comfort. He woke in a sweat and drowsed lightly for the rest of the night, having no desire to re-enter his dreams.

Jasper snored beside him, enjoying a sleep that Owen envied. He was proud of the boy, and impressed by his endurance and perspicacity. He intended to ask Jasper to keep an eye on Hubert when they were back in York. He would be far less conspicuous than Owen or one of his men.

As a greyness showed through the chinks in the shutters, Gilbert rose to relieve himself, waking Jasper.

'You can't sleep, Da?' the boy asked, his eyes only half-opened.

If there ever was a reason to be grateful for having been awake at this moment, it was to hear Jasper call him 'da' for the second time.

'No. I dreamt that your little brother was being chased by Ysenda and barely missed by Alisoun's arrows. I did not wish to return to that!'

Jasper grinned. 'Praise God she was missing him.' He scratched himself and rubbed his eyes. 'Is it time to rise?'

'No, it's too early. Go back to sleep.'

Jasper needed no more urging. He burrowed beneath the blankets and in a short time his breathing grew slow and even.

Owen had risen shortly, and he'd been sipping mulled wine by the fire as he exchanged pleasantries with his host and hostess for a little while when Jasper finally woke. Gilbert escorted him out into the frosty morning while Lady Gamyll called to a servant to bring ale for Jasper.

'We are grateful for your generosity,' said Owen.

Lady Gamyll smiled. 'You are my first guests. It has been my pleasure to see to your comfort.'

In a short while they were mounting their horses, waving their farewells. Owen had hoped Sir Baldwin would finally say whatever it was that Owen sensed he was holding back regarding Osmund, but he had not, and so he rode away disappointed, while the others were in good humour.

It was not a long ride to Ysenda's house – they might have simply walked over to fetch Hubert, but then they would have wasted time, and Owen hoped to arrive in York in good time the following day. He wanted to discuss all he'd learned with Lucie, hear a wise woman's view of it.

Jasper rode up beside him. 'I've noticed that you don't like Alisoun. Why not?'

'What? Is she still on your mind?' He chuckled at the boy's earnest expression. 'I find her sullen and unpleasant to be around.' Owen thought it best to leave it there.

But obviously Jasper was not satisfied. 'She's been a good nursemaid.'

'Yes. She has, son.' Owen was glad to see Ysenda's lonely house just ahead. 'I think we'll let Hubert ride with Rafe.'

They dismounted close to the house this time.

'Rafe, Gilbert, wait out here. Watch the house. I would not like to be surprised by Aubrey's return.'

'And what if he's in there?' asked Gilbert.

'Then I'll have Jasper call you in.'

Both men nodded and moved to opposite sides of the door.

Jasper knocked and took a step back as Ysenda opened it. Owen stood right behind him and noticed Hubert hovering in the dimness just behind her. Ysenda's smile seemed forced.

'You came back,' she said. 'I half thought you might not.'

'I'm a man of my word,' said Owen. 'May we come in?' He reached over Jasper and put his hand on the door.

Ysenda did not miss the gesture. 'Do come in.' She stepped away from the door, her movement hesitant.

Inside the cottage the first thing Owen noticed was that Hubert was not dressed for travel. He was sullen in his greeting, as he'd been the previous day.

'I have spoken with Sir Baldwin,' Owen began, taking a seat by the fire.

'Oh?' Ysenda moved to stand behind Hubert, her hands on his shoulders. 'I have changed my mind, Captain. Hubert does not wish to return to York just yet, and I won't force him. In truth, I will be grateful to have him here for a while.'

'Has your husband returned?'

She shook her head. 'Hubert can help me.'

The boy seemed to relax a little, looking less sullen, and Owen was in part happy for him. But he wondered how the lad would feel about some of the matters he intended to discuss.

'We must talk about something, Dame Ysenda. Something that might not be entirely comfortable for Hubert. Is there somewhere he might go?'

'I want to hear whatever you have to say,' said Hubert, puffing out his chest in a boyish way that reminded Owen of his own unwavering confidence in himself as an archer long, long ago.

Ysenda patted her son's shoulders. 'Then you shall, my young man.'

'Will you sit?' Owen invited them.

'I'm comfortable as I am,' said Ysenda. 'I'm sorry I've no more cider to offer you.'

Either she'd consumed a great deal since they'd been there the previous day or she resented their presence of a sudden. 'We are not thirsty.' Owen dropped his head for a moment, weighing various approaches. Ysenda was either expecting a fight, but he did not know what about, or she was simply eager to see them on their way. In either instance, he decided that an abrupt approach was necessary in order to have any chance at all of discussing the origin of the cross with her.

'While we dined with Sir Baldwin and his lady the subject of your son's loss came up, and naturally our host was curious as to what had been so precious to Hubert that he wore his scrip at all times.' He was irritated when Ysenda dropped her head so that he could not see her expression. 'When I described the cross Sir Baldwin excused himself, and when he returned said that his late wife's cross, which he would describe precisely as you did, was missing. He wondered if you'd perhaps been with child when he took Aubrey to France.'

'Ma?' Hubert turned around to look at Ysenda, who wore an indecipherable expression that Owen thought might be the result of warring impulses. 'That wasn't Lady Gamyll's cross, was it?' the boy asked, his voice slightly cracking with discomfort. 'I didn't lose hers?'

Ysenda tilted her head, and shook it once. 'Why Sir Baldwin would think to find it at home is a sign of how little he's cared about the manor in recent years. The cross is passed around the tenants and villagers for an easy birth. It is seldom in his care.' She did not speak in anger, but as if gently correcting her lord's error.

'I am relieved to hear that the cross Hubert lost was not Lady Gamyll's. I'll inform Sir Baldwin that he has only to check in the village and among his tenants for the one called the birthing cross.'

'You will find that difficult,' Ysenda said. 'With Father Nicholas so often away there is no one –' She abruptly broke off and slipped down onto a bench, covering her face with her hands.

'Ma?' Hubert knelt on one knee trying to see her face. 'Why are you crying?'

She pulled him to her and kissed the top of his head. 'I am tired, so tired. I should have let you leave with them last night. Then you need never have known the value of what you lost.' She lifted her face to the ceiling. 'God in heaven, was it so wrong of me to want more time with my only son?' She dissolved again in tears, holding onto the boy so hard that her knuckles paled.

Her inconsistencies were beginning to annoy Owen.

Hubert squirmed out of her clutch. 'Ma, are you saying that the cross didn't belong to you?'

She shook her head, still crumpled in on herself. 'No,' she whimpered. 'I forgot to return it when I lost the baby.'

And had concocted a story for Owen about Aubrey having given it to her.

The boy sat down a little away from his mother. 'I didn't know.'

'I did not think you would have had any idea

what it was, Hubert,' said Owen. 'It's not the sort of thing a mother tells a son about.'

'I didn't even know about the baby,' Hubert whispered, hugging himself.

'Your ma wanted to spare you the worry, I'd guess,' said Jasper, yet again making Owen proud of him. 'Mothers don't always know how much we guess, or how strong we are. Sometimes they just make it all harder for us, don't you think?'

Hubert nodded without looking up.

'Aubrey's been hopeful that his fighting skill had improved his standing with Sir Baldwin, that he might be honoured with more land, some of the richer land by the beck. That will never happen now. We can never hope to replace the cross even if we starved from now till the Last Judgement.' Ysenda had given her moan to the fire, but suddenly glanced up at Owen. 'What did the dead man do with the cross? Surely he wasn't wearing it when he died? There is still hope. Have you gone to his house?'

This brightened Hubert. 'I had not thought of it being found. What do you think, Captain?'

Owen thought that it was now time to leave them, now that they were buoyed with hope. He rose. 'We will do all we can to find it and return it to Sir Baldwin,' he said. 'If Hubert came to York with us, he might be one of the first to know if it is found.' He looked at the boy.

Hubert shook his head. 'I'll not come yet, Captain. I will stand by Ma if our lord makes much of this.' He was not so confident as before, but Owen admired the boy's spirit. He would grow up to be a fine lad, like Jasper.

Ysenda rose. 'Have you asked the man's family? Was there anyone else he might have given it to?'

'That is what I must discover back in York,' said Owen, 'now that I know what was lost, what I'm looking for.'

They took their leave quickly, and were mounted and into the town of Weston before anyone might ride after them. Owen needed distance and time in which to ponder all he'd learned.

'Did she mean to lie about the cross?' Jasper asked when they stopped to warm themselves by a fire while enjoying the food and wine Lady Gamyll had ordered prepared for their journey.

'Does your asking that question mean that you think she did?' Owen asked.

'That's Dame Magda's trick, answering a question with a question,' Jasper said. He looked healthy and content, thought Owen. Lucie should be proud of the life she'd given the lad, an apprenticeship that had given him a sense of his own place until he'd felt part of the family.

'I expected Dame Ysenda to lie, or to avoid directly answering us. Something warned her that she would regret that and she took back the lie. Or traded it for another.'

'She's canny,' said Rafe. 'I could see that yesterday.'

'I feel sorry for her husband,' said Gilbert. 'I

do not think she would be an easy woman to live with.'

'Certainly not an easy woman to leave!' said Rafe, slapping Gilbert on the thigh.

Perhaps that was what bothered Owen about Aubrey's absence. 'You heard what Sir Baldwin said, the man talked of his lovely wife all the while he was away from her. He is a most contradictory man to abandon her once he's returned to her, don't you think?'

All three of his companions nodded. Owen wondered what Aubrey was up to.

Six

A RIDDLE OF A MAN

Hubert observed his mother humming as she swept up the snow and mud that the captain and Jasper had tracked in; her happy mood disturbed him. He'd thought she would be humbled and worried about the loss of Sir Baldwin's cross, and worried about Aubrey's disappearance as well, even though at the same time glad he was not there. But she appeared to be light of heart. That bothered Hubert.

He was sick at heart for having taken something that had not even belonged to his mother. His relief about the possibility that the cross might yet be found and returned to Sir Baldwin was quickly fading. His having lost what not only belonged to their lord but was also of value to the entire parish felt like an unbearably heavy guilt. He'd already feared he'd never make amends for having worn the scrip, tempting the pilot and unwittingly leading him to the action that caused his death. He wondered whether Drogo had shown the cross to someone, and they'd decided they wanted it for themselves and killed him for it. Perhaps Drogo had meant to return the cross in the scrip, but by then the other man had taken it and cut Drogo with the poisoned blade. Hubert felt like he'd awakened in a nightmare and could not find his way out, but it was even worse, for it wasn't just a horrible dream, it was real.

Worst of all was his confusion about his mother's state of grace. Jasper had been right when he'd said that parents did not credit their children with half the knowledge they possessed – his mother didn't. He was as certain as he could be that his mother had not lost a child of late. She had not been large with child before he departed for York – he knew that because he'd hugged her often, and tightly, and he'd also caught sight of her bathing in the beck on Sir Baldwin's manor grounds. He would have seen or felt if she'd been with child, and he'd felt nothing out of the ordinary. It followed that he could not account for her having the birthing cross hidden among her things. She should not have had it. And he would be willing to make a bold wager that women had needed the cross in that time, and yet no one had come to her seeking it, so that meant to him that no one had known of her supposed pregnancy. Hubert did not like what he was thinking, that his mother was up to something sinful, even if it was only wanting a pretty thing that wasn't hers.

To his shame he found himself regretting that he had not departed with the captain and Jasper.

He picked up the buckets to take to the well, but his mother asked him to stay a moment. Setting aside the broom she came to sit near where he stood and patted a stool nearby.

'Just a moment, Hubert. Someone the three of you talked about, the bargeman who stole the scrip. What was his name?'

She had to look up at him because he had not sat down. He itched to escape into the fresh air.

'His name was Drogo,' he said. 'Why?' He could not make out her expression as she craned her neck, but he did not wish to sit. 'Do you know a Drogo?' He did not really want to hear more, but he must know.

She shrugged, trying to seem indifferent, but she'd reacted almost as if it hurt to hear the name. 'I was merely curious. Now off with you. I can see that you are eager to be without, to stretch your growing bones.'

Hubert hitched up the buckets and continued out, but once he'd passed the outbuildings, he set down his load and breathed great lungs full of the brisk air, trying to ease his trembling and nausea. He prayed that he was wrong about his mother, that she hadn't stolen the cross.

In the morning Kate had called Alfred inside to break his fast with the family, and then Magda had ordered him off to the barracks to sleep.

'Thou needst not watch Magda and the captain's family during the day,' she'd assured him. 'Nosy neighbours will keep the household safe.'

Shortly afterwards, when Lucie and Edric had gone to the shop and Alisoun off to school, Magda settled down with her old friend Phillippa, who was still quite clear in her head this morning. She chose a spot not too far from the children, who were quietly playing with Kate, though far enough that she and Phillippa could quietly discuss Alisoun. By merely observing Alisoun for the past few hours Magda could see that the children loved her and responded to her with an ease that bespoke a firm but loving hand on her part, so as a children's nurse she was satisfactory. But that came as no surprise as Alisoun had held that post in the households of several of her kin before she'd insisted that she wanted only to apprentice to Magda.

Why she wished to be a midwife and healer was a puzzle to Magda, for Alisoun seemed judgemental and impatient with the fully grown. She had followed Magda's orders in nursing Lucie back to health, but she had not managed it without complaints from her patient and others in the household. When Magda instructed her in preparing healing potions and powders she would often argue, skip steps, or pay no heed to the order in which she added ingredients. But what most disturbed Magda was her apparent lack of any compulsion to be of help to people. She must be told that someone needed help, she did not see that and act of her own will. And yet Magda's usually reliable feelings were that there was a healer somewhere within Alisoun.

Phillippa told Magda how Alisoun had shifted her affections from Jasper to Edric, and how plainly jealous she was of Edric's admiration for Lucie.

'She is causing much unease in this house morning and evening,' said Phillippa.

'She knows that a wet nurse is soon to supplant her,' said Magda. Once again she resolved to talk to the girl.

'I do hope that the wet nurse can also take care of Gwenllian and Hugh,' said Phillippa. 'God has made it so that I cannot be counted on to help with them, though I love them with all my being.'

Magda patted her friend's bony hand. 'Thou wast a mother to Lucie most loving and skilled in healing. Thou hast done thy part. Magda has also done her part. She has arranged for Kate's cousin Maud, who was recently widowed and has an infant to raise, to be nurse for all three children, and wet nurse if Lucie's milk ceases. Kate has promised to keep it a secret until Magda feels the time is right to tell thy niece.' The wet nurse requirement had been an excuse to let Alisoun go. Lucie had always nursed her own children, which she had the freedom to do having not wed a knight like her father. 'Maud is eager to meet the children and join the household in which her cousin serves.'

'Kate's sister was a great help to me at Freythorpe. God be praised, they seem a hard-working family,' said Phillippa. 'I know you're going to say God had nothing to do with it, but I believe otherwise.'

Magda sniffed. It was exactly what she'd been about to say. She must be growing old if she repeated herself so often that Phillippa knew what she would say. Maybe she did need an apprentice. But was Alisoun the one? She'd waited for more than a year for the girl to prove herself compassionate and perceptive, but she'd seen no sign in all that time. Yet she must now discuss Alisoun's future with her.

A knock at the street door sent Gwenllian and Hugh racing to answer it, but Kate had reached the door first and shooed the two in Magda and Phillippa's direction.

From the doorway Magda heard Kate say, 'No, the captain is away.'

Sensing a tension, Magda hurried to the door. Kate began to explain, but Magda recognised the woman on the doorstep.

'Dame Alice. What a pity thou hast crossed the river to see Captain Archer and he is not here. Might Magda help thee? Or Dame Lucie?' She wondered what the tanner's wife wanted with Owen.

Alice was a timid woman, but she knew Magda, having needed her as midwife many times, though most of her many children had not lived past their first years, being a sickly family. She stood apologetically hunched into herself, her eyes wide with the anticipation of trouble, though she tweaked her mouth into a brief smile on seeing Magda.

'I heard about the apprentice who died last even, pulled from the river,' she took a deep breath, 'and that Captain Archer might be looking for the murderer.'

Well aware that Owen could have no knowledge of the most recent murder, Magda said, 'Thou hast guessed rightly. If thou hast something to tell him, thou canst trust it to Magda.'

'God bless you, Dame Magda, for it was all I could do to find a friend to watch the children once.'

Magda invited her to step into the hall, and sat down on a bench near the door.

Alice shuffled in, and only then did Magda realise she was with child again, poor woman. It might be time to teach her how to avoid quickening. Her boots were worn to nothing – and she a tanner's wife. She shook out her skirts as she sat down, shedding mud and what looked like dried vomit onto Kate's clean floor.

Phillippa limped over to ask whether Alice would like something warm to drink, and receiving a shy nod she went to fetch it.

'Now, Dame Alice, what dost thou know about the dead man?'

'I don't know that it's of use, but it seems to me it was likely him I saw yesterday afternoon. Two men were down on the bank near the Old Baile just as the tide was boiling up the river – a storm surge it looked like. I thought to warn them.' Alice paused to take the bowl of mulled cider Phillippa brought her. 'Bless you, Goodwife,' she said, tears forming in her frightened, tired eyes.

Phillippa smiled, bobbed her head, and limped away. Magda sensed that her old friend was about to slip into confusion again.

But it was Alice she must attend. 'Who was on the riverbank, Dame Alice?'

'Two men. Arguing. One was finely dressed, a youngish man, and the other I guessed to be his servant, perhaps the same age, perhaps a wee bit younger, dressed plainly. They were flailing their arms as they argued and I thought it best not to call out. But I was curious and looked again, and now I did not see the plainly dressed one, just the fine young man climbing up from the mud and brushing off his gloved hands.' She stopped abruptly to sip the cider, wiggling her toes which must have begun to thaw.

'How many weeks toswollen art thou?'

Alice pressed her lower back with her free hand. 'This one will come in mid-spring, I think.'

Too late to stop it safely for such a worn

woman. 'Magda will bring thee a rub for thy back, to ease it as thou swells.'

'God bless you, Dame Magda.' Alice took another sip.

'Thou dost not know either man?'

Alice shook her head. 'No.' After weak laughter she said, 'I heard the one who died was a goldsmith's apprentice. Why would I ever meet such a one? But I reckon he was the one I thought a servant. The other –' She shook her head again. 'Such a man did not notice me even when I was my prettiest, many bairns ago.'

'Canst thou describe the finer one?'

'He was straight-backed and quick on his feet, and it might be that he is fair-haired, but it might have been part of his hat that looked so. It was trimmed in fur and feathers.'

She might be describing any one of a number of men in York. 'Why hast thou come to tell the captain this? Thou didst not know either man, nor wast anyone to know of thy witnessing the argument.'

With a little shrug, Alice said, 'I hoped Dame Lucie would give me a draught for my night cough. It wakes me all the night. My husband says I have no need to spend what little we have on that.'

Magda silently cursed the man who valued his cock over all else. 'That will be thy digestion, not unusual in thy condition. Tell Dame Lucie what thou hast done and she will not charge thee.'

'You are kind, Dame Magda.'

'Thou hast done a good deed that should be repaid,' said Magda.

They talked a while longer, Alice describing how that part of the riverbank was seldom busy with people because the mud was particularly deep there, and then Magda saw her out with a promise to tell Owen all Alice had said. She would, too, for it was possible that poor Alice had been the last to see Nigel the apprentice alive. She wondered who the gloved man with the fancy hat might be. For if the other had been Nigel, this one might be the murderer. She wondered how many men with feathered and furred hats had been seen in the city recently.

'Amélie is late. Why does she linger so long in the garden? What can she be thinking, letting Lucie run wild?' Phillippa had risen to pace the hall, wringing her hands and worrying about something that had happened in the past. Amélie was Lucie's mother, who'd died long ago.

'Who is Amélie?' Gwenllian asked Magda. 'Why is Aunt Pippa so angry?'

'Thy aunt is confused,' said Magda. 'Shall we sing to soothe her?'

Gwenllian shook her head so hard her dark curls wildly danced about her head, and her dark eyes were frightened. Magda knew that the child's curiosity would only confuse Phillippa more, so she drew her friend out to the kitchen, asking Gwenllian to mind her little brother.

'Magda would like thy company whilst she talks to cook, old friend,' she said to Phillippa.

'I should never have let her marry,' said Phillippa as they crossed the walkway to the kitchen, still within the hearing of those in the hall.

Magda chuckled. Gwenllian would drive Kate mad with questions when next she fed her.

'Who is this girl?' Phillippa demanded when she spied Kate rolling out dough. 'Are you the new kitchen maid?'

Kate was accustomed to the elderly woman's confused states. 'I'm a hard worker, Dame Phillippa, and not so above myself that I complain about scrubbing and fussing with the straw.'

Phillippa sniffed. 'I'll be watching you, and I'll be the judge of your value.'

With a smile and a little curtsey, Kate acknowledged her comment and returned to her dough. Magda approved of her and was glad that the young widow Maud, soon to join the household as the children's nurse, was her kin. Kate's sister Tildy had worked in the house before her. They were a poor family, all entering into service as soon as they were old enough. Tildy was now living at Freythorpe Hadden, Lucie's inheritance, the manor young Hugh would claim when he was of age. Tildy had married the steward and in a short while had borne several healthy children. It was a pity that Phillippa could not manage that household, as she had for her brother, Lucie's father, for many years. Magda knew that with this elderly confusion it was best if the person could remain in their most familiar surroundings. But Phillippa needed closer watching than Tildy could manage, and Lucie was very good with her.

A sack of roots and dried herbs that Magda had brought as trade for Lucie's hospitality soon absorbed Phillippa with the very familiar routine of tying the herbs to the rafters and brushing the roots clean, then storing them.

They'd not been there too long when through the open doors Magda heard George Hempe's deep voice. She patted Kate on the arm and went out to meet the man, shutting the hall door so that Phillippa would not get curious and wander in.

The hawk was almost humorously angry, standing with legs wide, hands on hips, as though he ruled there. He'd apparently been civil to Gwenllian and Hugh, who seemed proud to have greeted him at the door.

Magda asked Gwenllian to entertain Hugh at the far end of the hall for just a little longer. The girl's dimpled smile was reassuring. She was enjoying the responsibility.

'You should have sent word that you'd come here last night, Dame Magda,' Hempe said once Gwenllian had led Hugh away.

'Was it not a wise decision, Bailiff?'

'The matter is not whether it was wise, but that I've wasted the morning searching for you.'

'Thou wilt be repaid with helpful news. Sit down and listen to Magda.' She told him about Nicholas Ferriby's odd visit to Lucie and Alice Tanner's tale of the men on the riverbank. 'The one might well be the murderer.'

His face relaxed as he listened. 'A hat like that has surely been noticed by someone. I am most grateful to you, Dame Magda.' He rose. 'Will you stay here for a few more nights?'

'Until the captain returns. Alfred has vowed to set night watches on this house until such time.'

'Owen's return will not make your solitary home safe,' said the hawk. 'I suggest you stay here until we have Nigel's murderer.'

Magda wagged her head. 'Thy advice will be considered.'

'You will slow me down if I am worried about you.'

He was getting angry again, which amused Magda.

'A bailiff of York worried about Magda, who does not live in his city.' She shook her head and tsked, then let out a barking laugh. 'Thou art so like a hawk when thou'rt angry! Thou mightst sprout wings. Magda takes orders from neither bird nor man, Bailiff. But thou seemst to Magda a good, honourable fellow, so she will consider thy advice, as she said she would.'

'You are a contrary woman.' Hempe seemed about to explode, but bowed to her and thanked her for her help.

Grateful that he was not staying to argue, Magda saw him off and then returned to the kitchen, where Phillippa was quietly and efficiently completing her sorting and cleaning.

Kate smiled. 'You bring calm with you, Dame Magda. It is a gift.' Of course she was relieved that Phillippa was absorbed and not fussing.

'It is a skill,' said Magda, 'learned by observing, listening, trying and discarding. Thou couldst do the same.' She was relieved to have passed on Alice Tanner's information. 'Magda will attend the children.'

Hempe had done his best to leave with his dignity intact, despite the crone's grinning ear to ear. He wondered at Owen's willingness to count her as a friend. She behaved as if she held the secret to life and everyone else was welcome to flail about in the darkness.

He took a deep breath and admitted to himself that it was his anger chattering in his head, and that he was aware of all the good she did. Besides, he might now have a description, however incomplete, of Nigel's murderer.

The shadows of Stonegate reminded him that he'd yet to talk to the goldsmith Edward Munkton about his late apprentice. Recalling that the man had tried to break his contract with Nigel over suspicions of theft, Hempe hoped he would not have any pangs of disloyalty about telling all he knew of the dead man, good or bad, including whether he had a friend who wore showy hats.

In fact, Munkton seemed reticent to speak to Hempe, but he led him through the busy, oven-heated workshop to his screened corner and offered him a cup of watered wine. Though Hempe preferred his undiluted, he accepted with grace, consciously on his best behaviour.

'Nigel.' Munkton shook his head. 'I had such hopes for him. He was a skilled craftsman – a journeyman he was, past apprenticeship. He was clever, a quick learner, but alas, he grew secretive and untrustworthy.'

The crooked jaw that twisted the goldsmith's face produced a speech so slurred that Hempe's response was delayed as he reckoned what he'd heard.

'I'm not gossiping,' Munkton added, apparently worried about Hempe's silence.

'No, you are assisting me,' said Hempe. 'Secretive and untrustworthy, you say? I should think such flaws made him ill-suited to be a jour-neyman in a goldsmith's shop, working amidst such wealth.'

'That was my very argument to the guild,' said Munkton. 'But they wanted proof, and Nigel had been far too clever to leave any trace of his theft.'

The goldsmith lifted a beringed hand to his mouth, stifling a cough, but he could not mask the rheumy rumble in his chest. Hempe felt a tickle in the back of his own throat, and sensed a fine dust in the air. Something floated delicately atop his watered wine and the lamplight caught sparkling motes on Munkton's fine clothing. He wondered whether it was gold dust.

'At least they permitted me to board Nigel elsewhere. I felt better without him biding under my roof,' Munkton continued. 'I'd planned to bring another complaint about him at the next guild meeting.' He tapped his fingers on the table, apparently considering what he'd just said for he added, 'But I didn't murder him.'

'I had not even considered accusing you, Master Edward.'

Munkton bobbed his head in approval. 'Some might be simple enough to think I'd risk all to commit such a crime.'

'What was the matter of your latest complaint regarding Nigel?'

Munkton covered another gurgling cough.

'Unexplained absences,' he wheezed, then cleared his throat. 'He was away three full workdays not long ago.'

'He had no excuse?'

The goldsmith sniffed. 'Illness. He always claimed illness. But his landlady is no one's fool and she knew he was away. I confronted him with that and he said he'd gone to a friend's house but could not on his honour betray her. Honour. Humph. He was just bedding some wife whenever her husband was away, that is what I think, and that is not proper behaviour for a guildsman. He was but nineteen years and already so dissolute.'

'So young.' Hempe shook his head, doing his best to gain the goldsmith's trust. 'The guild would surely have supported your complaint this time. Do you have any idea who the woman was?'

'No. Neither did his landlady.' Munkton coughed again. 'I pray you, if we are to be a while longer, I would step away for a moment to dispatch a servant to the apothecary. This cough is worsening. I feel a churning in my chest.' He patted his well-clothed chest with both beringed hands.

'Of course. I'll wait quietly.'

When his host was gone, Hempe helped himself to a cup of unwatered wine. It was much more satisfying. The screens that separated Munkton's little space from the workshop were painted with scenes from the bible, Moses with the tablets of stone floating in the air before him, Christ at the wedding feast changing the water to wine. Law and miracles. It seemed a peculiar pairing. He guessed the screens were cast-offs from the hall above.

'There. Now what was I about to tell you?' Munkton settled down once more, taking a sip of his sickly watered wine. 'Oh yes, the complaints I had from customers and neighbours. He was a surly fellow, and too attentive to the daughters of Stonegate. Robert Dale, whose shop is at the corner, complained that his daughters would not walk out if they saw him in the street, and his wife had called him lewd and dangerous.'

Robert Dale's wife was one of the most beautiful women in York, and also perhaps the most sumptuously dressed and bejewelled. 'Perhaps his murder should be no surprise, eh?' Hempe suggested.

'I pray he had done no one such harm as to provoke such an attack.' Munkton looked sincere as he crossed himself.

'But someone did murder him,' said Hempe. 'You have heard of the murder of the pilot Drogo, also fished out of the Ouse?'

Munkton nodded. 'Do you think their deaths are connected?'

'That is the question, to be sure. I believe they might have been. Have you ever used Drogo as a pilot?'

'No, I go through other merchants to ship for me. But I thought he was an abbey bargeman.'

'That was his official post. Do you use the Abbey Staithe?'

Munkton shook his head. 'But another of my apprentices saw Nigel with a man in the abbey livery. He wore a green hat as I've heard this Drogo wore. It was perhaps a fortnight ago, maybe not so long as that, and shortly afterwards was when Nigel disappeared for several days. Might that be important?'

Why didn't you come to me with this information earlier, damn you? Hempe silently cursed

189

as he worked to keep his voice and visage calm. 'Indeed it might be important.' He sipped his wine. 'I am grateful for your openness with me.'

'We will all sleep more soundly when we know the murderer is rendered impotent, Master Bailiff.'

'Speaking of hats, did you ever see Nigel with a blond man who wore a feathered and furred hat?'

Munkton frowned as he thought. 'No. But my wife's sister's husband wore such a thing. Ugly, it was. And didn't one of the mayor's men own such a hat?' The goldsmith was apparently beginning to enjoy this.

'I'd hoped it was a more unusual combination.'

'I wouldn't call it common, God be thanked.'

'Have you any notion what Nigel's business might have been with Drogo?'

'Perhaps this Drogo was buying the shavings Nigel stole from me,' Munkton said, then shook his head. 'Shall I fetch young Rob, whose witness I'm repeating, to talk to you?'

Hempe asked him to do so.

The lad resisted all Hempe's efforts to put him at ease, and he added little to his master's report, except that the exchange seemed friendly, and the man in the abbey livery seemed grateful to Nigel.

'Did you hear anything that they said?' Hempe prompted.

The lad shook his head.

Hempe left Munkton with a promise to inform

him of any significant news, though he had no intention of keeping the promise. He was discouraged. Irritated. He considered the pleasure of having another cup of wine, perhaps at the York Tavern, but he remembered the Riverwoman's account of Nicholas Ferriby's behaviour in the apothecary the previous day and decided to continue on into the minster liberty. Then he would be even more deserving of a cup of wine.

Once again Owen and Jasper stayed in a quiet corner of the tavern where they were warming themselves. Rafe and Gilbert were enjoying themselves flirting with both the taverner's wife and daughter. Owen had asked Jasper to recount to him what he'd heard and observed at both Hubert's and Sir Baldwin's houses. He was impressed with the boy's memory and how much he had observed. In some details they disagreed, but they were for the most part insignificant. The most significant difference was that Jasper had had a strong sense when they were leaving Hubert's home that morning that the boy regretted having chosen to stay with his mother. Owen had not noticed it, which bothered him if it were so, as much as Aubrey's disappearance was bothering him. Baldwin had described Aubrey as yearning for Ysenda all the while they'd been gone. He wished he knew what could have happened to make that same man beat the wife he'd so sorely missed, and leave again within such a short time, whether it could have anything to do with Drogo's taking Hubert's scrip.

'Jealousy?' he wondered aloud. That is what kept coming to mind.

'Who's jealous?' Jasper asked.

'Aubrey. Perhaps he found evidence that Ysenda had been with another man. She might have thought she was with child, the child of a lover, and that's why she took the cross. If it was clear that Aubrey could not be the father – but she did not seem pregnant.'

'So what would he find?'

Owen had forgotten for a moment that he was talking to Jasper, and studied his face to see whether this talk of pregnancy and lovers embarrassed him. It did not seem so. 'I wish I knew what he found. Tell me what you saw that made you believe Hubert had changed his mind about returning with us.'

'He'd stopped looking at his mother as if he was ready to protect her. There was something in his eyes when he looked at us too, as if – oh, I don't know, it's little things.' Jasper ducked his head over his tankard, fair hair falling over his face so that it almost touched the rim, then he suddenly lifted his head, raked his hair back and took a drink.

'How did he look at us, Jasper? I'm trying to understand what you saw, what I missed. I believe you. You have helped me far more than I'd known you could.'

192

Jasper's face was again hidden by his hair. He sighed and rocked the tankard on the boards. 'Do you mind when I call you "Da"?'

'Mind? God help me, it's all I can do not to hug you right there. I'm proud of you, son, I am, but, even if I weren't as proud of you as I am right now, I'd still be proud to have you call me "Da".' He shut up, hearing himself going on like a blithering fool.

Jasper nodded and sat rocking the tankard for a good long while, head bowed, face hidden.

Owen glanced over at Gilbert and Rafe and considered telling them that they'd already had enough ale, they had a long ride ahead of them, but he was loath to break into the moment. He sat back and watched the fire.

Finally Jasper straightened and raked the hair from his eyes, which looked red and a little swollen.

'He looked like he hoped we'd save him,' said Jasper in a gruff voice. 'That's how he looked. Like he wanted us to order him to come with us.'

'Dear God watch over the lad.'

'You're thinking a lot about Hubert's da as well. I think it's strange he left, but it sounds as if it's happened before.'

'Yes, it's happened before, but both Sir Baldwin and, subtly, Ysenda behaved as if this time he was gone longer than usual, and not to the usual places – where it's his custom to drink.'

Jasper suddenly slapped the table. 'The lover attacked him, and he's lying injured somewhere!'

'That would be a nasty welcome home from war, but I was thinking more in terms of why he's hiding from us.'

Jasper was shaking his head, still building his drama. 'But Hubert said nothing. A son would always choose his father over another man, wouldn't he?'

'Fathers and sons can disagree, and a father can seem cruel – or be cruel,' said Owen. 'But enough of your lover story – I just want to talk to the man, get a sense of him. We don't really know anything at all of him, but others' opinions – that he loves his wife and is a good fighter, a good drinker, a poor farmer. An honest man. Did he not beat his wife he'd seem an uncommonly good man. But he's avoiding us. Or is he?'

Owen wondered whether Thoresby would give him leave to send Rafe and Gilbert back to Sir Baldwin to ask for his help in searching for Aubrey de Weston.

A dozen or so boys and girls of varying ages were solemnly listening to Master Nicholas explaining the value of committing passages to memory. The classroom door was open to the alleyway yet those closest to the brazier in the room looked sweaty and sleepy. Hempe hesitated, loath to interrupt a lesson, but neither did he wish to return later, when he might very well find the same situation. He stepped into the doorway.

A young girl gasped to see him and tugged on

the sleeve of her neighbour. Soon all were looking his way, which at last drew the grammar master's attention.

'Master Bailiff,' he said with a nod. 'Are we disturbing the King's peace with our lesson?' He smiled and winked at the young scholars, some of whom giggled or chuckled, some of whom were not comforted by his demeanour.

Hempe forced a laugh. 'Nay, your lesson is blessed noise. I pray you, would you step out with me for a moment. I would talk to you, but I will be brief.'

The grammar master forced his smile to stay and asked his assistant to read a passage from the bible while he stepped out with Hempe.

'I trust you believe that their lessons are important?' Nicholas said when they were a house away. 'I hope that your behaviour in interrupting us does not bespeak your opinion of education.'

'It is in your power to make this very brief, indeed,' said Hempe. He sensed that Nicholas's expression of irritation was an attempt to cover fear. 'Why did you seek Captain Archer's counsel yesterday?'

Nicholas squirmed as he glanced up and down the alleyway. But he looked Hempe in the eye at last. 'I merely wished to know whether Captain Archer felt my name had been cleared, whether he'd heard any more gossip concerning the poor man who bled as I prayed over him.' He lifted his chin as he completed his little speech.

'But surely Dame Lucie might have answered that for you. Why did you not ask her whether you had won back your good name?'

'I did not consider that Dame Lucie would know of all that Captain Archer had heard. Is that all?'

Hempe shook his head. 'Nay, I doubt that is all. You sought out the captain for more than that. You seemed worried. Perhaps a little frightened.'

'You were not there. How can you know how I behaved?'

'I ask questions. I am working with Captain Archer at present, so I can tell you that the journeyman's death has quieted the rumours about you and Drogo.'

Nicholas crossed himself. 'I'd heard of another death on the river. But what has that to do with Drogo's death?'

'Perhaps people think it unlikely that you would attack two men. But I don't know that. Where were you that afternoon?'

'In the schoolroom.'

'What are you fearfully worried about?'

Nicholas shook his head, but now he did not meet Hempe's eyes. 'My good name, that is all. You must understand, as a schoolmaster and a vicar I must be above suspicion, else parents will not trust me with their children, and my flock will not trust me as confessor. Not to mention my trouble with the dean and chancellor of St

Peter's. I've no doubt you are well informed about that issue.' He paused to catch his breath.

He had resumed eye contact, and Hempe did not doubt that all he said was true. It was what he was not saying that Hempe wished to know.

'I know about that, yes, and I am aware of the import of scandal attached to the name of a priest and grammar master. But I trow you have more to tell.'

'Is it not enough that my livelihood is threatened?' Nicholas cried. 'You say you are aware of the *import*. You aren't. You've no idea.'

Hempe was glad of the emotion and thought he might push a bit more. 'You've more to tell, Master Nicholas, and I'll keep asking you until you satisfy me.'

'You may believe whatever you please, Master Bailiff, but you'll get no satisfaction from me, for there's no more to tell. I've answered your questions in all honesty and now I must return to my scholars.'

With a huff, the grammar master tugged at his gown to smooth it over his belly and marched back to his classroom. Hempe had no authority to keep him away from his scholars, and he knew to relent before he'd made an enemy. With a sigh, he headed for the nearest tavern outside the minster liberty. It was time for that cup of wine.

Brooding over a claret quite inferior to that which he'd served himself at the goldsmith's, he eventually let go of his irritation with the grammar master and considered what would be most useful. It was mid-afternoon by now. He was spending far too much time on this. Investigations were not his job, but he could not shake thoughts about it so he'd might as well do something constructive. That the murders were connected he felt in his bones. He had only to find the link, and that might lead him to the murderer. He thought about Drogo and remembered someone searching his house. He'd forgotten to ask Master Edward where Nigel had lodged. The man down the bench, deep into his cups, growled as Hempe rocked the seat in his haste to leave.

The lad who greeted him at Munkton's was glad to give him the information, and Hempe was off at a trot to Petergate and the house of Dame Lotta, a wealthy widow known for her charitable gifts to the churches of the city. Munkton had certainly settled his journeyman in respectable lodgings. Perhaps the guild had insisted.

An elderly manservant opened the door, 'Master Bailiff? How did you know my mistress –?'

'Did she send for me?' How strange.

'Aye. Just now.'

The elderly servant was eased aside by the tiny widow. 'George Hempe, I think?' Her dark eyes seemed intense in her exceedingly pale face, and a beautiful contrast to the fair hair braided beneath her veil. Hempe thought her one of the handsomest women of York. 'Come in, I pray you. I've made an unpleasant discovery and need your counsel.' She led him to a door at the end of the hall farthest from the street.

'Dame Lotta, I've come concerning your lodger, Nigel, the journeyman –'

'For Master Edward. Do you mean you know why I sent for you?'

'You sent for me?'

'What else would a bailiff of York want with me?' Her dark eyes watched him with lively curiosity.

'I wished to ask you about your tenant.' Hempe wondered how she remained unwed. Might she consider a mere bailiff? He shook his head to rid himself of the thought.

'You shake your head, Master George?'

'A crook in my neck, that is all. Pray ignore my twitches. What was your unpleasant discovery?'

Obeying a nod of her head, the manservant slipped past Hempe to the door and swung it wide.

'Behold my late lodger Nigel's room, Master George,' said Dame Lotta with a sweep of her arm.

Bedding twisted and mounded on the floor, a good mattress slit open, feathers everywhere, the contents of a chest spilling out.

'I assure you, had the young man done such damage, even once, he would have been back at Edward Munkton's.'

'When did you find this?'

'Just a while ago.' Lotta bowed her head and apologetically said, 'I did not like to go in last night, not with him just murdered. I feared his spirit might be flitting about in agony, and where would he come but his last home. Nor did I want my servants frightened.' She peered up at him with the sweetest expression of fear Hempe had ever seen. 'Perhaps it is unwise to say this of the dead, but he was not a nice man, though tidy and quiet. I'd thought about asking him to leave.'

Hempe asked permission to go into the room and look around, which Lotta readily gave. Clothes, a writing slate, a small book of notes regarding the working of gold which had been his mystery, a pair of worn boots, prayer beads – Hempe found nothing of interest. But of course whoever had searched before him would have removed anything that might point to his murderer, assuming that his murderer was the searcher. He tried the door leading to the side alley and found it locked.

The servant, standing in the doorway to the hall, said, 'I found it unlocked this morning, sir. Mistress told me to lock it.'

'Had the lock been damaged? Or the door?'

'The lock, sir. I had to put another one on it.'

Dame Lotta kept a supply of padlocks, it seemed. Returning to the hall, Hempe asked her what she meant by 'not nice'.

'I did not care for the way he looked at me,' she said. 'And of late I'd heard another man's voice a few times. His guests were to come to the street door so that I might know who was in my house.' She nodded her head as if to emphasise the correctness of the rule. 'But this one would come by way of the alley door. Nigel also seemed secretive in other ways. Not that I cared to know much of his life, but he'd grown rude in his responses to my questions.'

'And yet he looked at you with too much interest?' asked Hempe.

She raised her eyebrows. 'There was variance in his behaviour. I do not dissemble with you.'

'I never thought that you did, Dame Lotta. I beg you, forgive me if I have offended you.'

She smiled and gave him a little bow. 'Of course, Master George.'

'Did this visitor by any chance wear a fancy hat? Fur and feathers?'

'As I said, I did not see the visitor.'

'Ah. Yes, you did say.' He learned little more, and as he left her home he wondered whether she was truly God's most adorable creation, or whether he'd had too much wine too early in the day.

Jasper guided his horse close to the captain's. 'Da, I just remembered something. Osmund Gamyll was in the city the night of Drogo's death. It was when he was talking to Master Nicholas that I learned Aubrey and Sir Baldwin were alive and home.'

'Are you certain?'

'Yes.'

The captain grinned and nodded. 'You are proving to be an excellent spy, my son.'

Seven

SECRETS
OF THE HEART

While Kate instructed Gwenllian and Hugh in some kitchen chores and Phillippa napped by the fire, Magda tried to engage Alisoun, just home from school and rosy-cheeked from the cold, in a discussion about her future.

'I never wished to be a nursemaid,' said Alisoun, her pouting face above her thin neck giving her the look of an indignant bird. 'I'll be relieved to quit this house.'

Magda could tell by the girl's jagged breath that it was not so, but she did not intend to argue with her.

'Kate's cousin Maud needs the warmth and healing of this household, so Magda is glad thou hast no desire to remain here. Thou needst not worry about thy schooling – it will not be interrupted unless thou shouldst choose to journey with Magda when the floods begin.'

Alisoun sat a little straighter, subtly fluffing her feathers. 'You'd let me come with you?'

Magda nodded. 'Unless thou art needed in the city. Thou needst a lodging, so it is thy choice whether to bide with Magda or accept another post. Magda thinks thou couldst do much for an ailing young woman, the daughter of a shipman. Thou wouldst get much practice in healing by attending her.'

Conflict shone in Alisoun's eyes. 'You would teach me how to care for her?' she asked.

'Aye. Her healing requires both physicks and a supportive presence, a listening friend. Wouldst thou have the patience for that?'

'I want to be a healer, not a friend.' Alisoun almost growled the last words.

Now she reminded Magda not so much of a chick as a small, testy dog. 'Thou hast much to learn about what a healer does. When Maud is ready to come here, Magda will take thee to meet the young woman and thou canst decide for thyself.'

'And if I don't choose to take care of her?' Alisoun barked.

'The city and the countryside overflow with people in need, young Alisoun. Thou shalt not lack for work if thou art willing.'

The question remained in Magda's heart – was the girl willing? She must be patient, for only time would provide the answer to that troubling question.

* * *

Her lower back aching and her ankles swollen after a full day of sitting on the high stool in the shop, Lucie was glad to accept Edric's offer of his arm for support as they crossed the garden to the hall. Frost softened the winter twilight, and where the lamplight spilling from the hall window illuminated the wisps of air and the stark winter garden, Lucie felt as if she'd stepped into another world, one more magical, with different standards of beauty. She mentioned this to Edric and he paused to look around.

'It *is* wondrous,' he said in a reverent whisper. 'The world must be so beautiful seen from your eyes, Dame Lucie.'

Sometimes it was difficult for Lucie to remember that he was older than Jasper, he seemed so artless in his youthful infatuation.

'I was so caught up in how cold I am that I had not noticed how the fog swirls,' he said.

Lucie had noticed that he seldom seemed aware of his surroundings. 'Your apprenticeship is a time for learning how to live a good life in your mystery as well as how to mix physicks, Edric. You will be a better apothecary by knowing life.' She stopped herself. This was not the moment for such a discussion. 'And you are right, it *is* cold out here.' Lucie picked up her pace, still with her hand in the crook of Edric's arm.

As soon as they entered the hall, Lucie noticed Alisoun's eyes fastened on her hand on Edric's arm. She dropped it, irritated by how guilty the girl made her feel with that look.

Magda's multicoloured gown caught Lucie's eye as the healer approached her, and she thought how fortunate she was in her friend. She noticed Magda glancing over at Alisoun with a thoughtful expression, but then she was smiling at Lucie as she guided her to a high-backed chair by the fire.

'How dost thou?' Magda asked as Lucie settled. Lifting Lucie's hem Magda shook her head at her swollen ankles.

'I'm aware of those,' said Lucie. 'My back aches as well. I am truly toswollen. It all seemed easier when I was younger.'

'It was,' said Magda, 'but thou wilt soon feel better.' She went over to the fire and stirred something in a small pot.

Gwenllian pushed a low stool under Lucie's feet and then knelt next to her. Lucie reached down to stroke her raven curls.

'You are my angel,' she said.

Gwenllian gingerly bent over to rest an ear on Lucie's belly. 'Baby is sleeping?' she asked.

'Your brother or sister has been dancing a jig all the long day, so I think he or she is tired. I am, too!' But at this moment Lucie felt content.

Straightening, Gwenllian leaned on the arm of Lucie's chair, trying to look her in the eyes. 'Aunt Pippa was confused today. She was worried about someone named Amélie. Who was she?'

Lucie glanced over at her aunt as she smoothed her daughter's hair. 'She was my mother, your grandmother from Normandy, remember? Aunt Phillippa must have dreamt about her and woke confused.'

Gwenllian shrugged and sighed. 'I don't like that she thinks grandma is still alive. I don't like when Aunt Pippa's confused.'

'Neither does she, my love.'

Magda brought a cup of steaming liquid from the pot on the fire, and now thrust it into Lucie's hands, startling her. 'For the swelling and the backache,' she said. 'Now, drink.'

Gwenllian ran back to Hugh and Alisoun. Lucie watched as her two children began a tag game around Alisoun's chair.

'Thou art blessed with healthy bairns,' said Magda. She'd pulled a stool up to join Lucie.

Edric made a move to join them.

'The bailiff George Hempe came to Master Nicholas's school today, Edric,' said Alisoun.

He changed his direction and sat down near her, but not so near as to become part of the tag game. 'What was wrong?' he asked.

'I don't know. He asked to speak to Master Nicholas in the alleyway. After that, Master Nicholas kept forgetting what he'd been saying.'

'It's no wonder that the controversy about his school and the gossip about what happened when he prayed over Drogo has shaken him,' said Lucie.

'I did not mean to disturb your rest, Dame

Lucie, I was speaking to Edric.' Alisoun spoke in a tone far too familiar for a nursemaid.

Lucie would not tolerate such disrespect from the girl. 'Take the children to the kitchen, Alisoun, and calm them with supper. You might eat with them this evening.' She used a firm though not unfriendly tone.

'But Kate feeds them,' Alisoun said, her colour high.

Edric studied his shoes.

'Not this evening,' said Lucie. 'She will be up late in case the captain and Jasper return. You are apparently at ease, so it is no inconvenience to you to feed the children.'

Alisoun rose and snapped her skirts.

'Have a care,' said Magda. 'Thou hast fire in thy eyes, Alisoun, and it is blinding thee.'

Bobbing her head to Lucie and glaring at Magda, Alisoun rounded up her charges and led them out of the hall. Lucie let her breath out only when the door closed behind them.

Magda looked disgusted. 'Where is the healer in her soul?' she muttered as she rose to give the fire a poke.

'Did I cause trouble for Alisoun?' asked Edric.

He looked abandoned, and Lucie felt for him. It would take a sturdier man than he would ever be to carry the burden of Alisoun's affections.

'It was nothing you did, Edric,' she assured him. 'I think she is bored with her duties here. It is well that a wet nurse will soon come to take her place.'

'What will she do then?' he asked.

'We will continue to support her schooling,' said Lucie, 'and Dame Magda is arranging a post for her.'

'Magda spoke with Alisoun earlier.' She settled back down. 'Do not fret, lad, for she is surrounded by those who wish her well. Enough of that girl.' She turned to Lucie. 'Magda also talked with George Hempe, the hawk himself. He called here, and Magda told him about Master Nicholas's queer behaviour. That is why he sought out the man. And a tanner's wife came to tell the captain of a pair on the riverbank yesterday who might have been the goldsmith's lad and his murderer. But then thou knowest she was here. She did come to thee?'

Poor Alice, pregnant again. 'Yes. She has all that she needs for a while, and I was glad to give it to her. She is a sweet woman, too sweet.' Lucie knew Magda would divine her meaning.

'Aye, she should not have –' Magda glanced up at Edric's eager expression and fussed with Lucie to finish the cup of herbs. 'Magda will not be here tomorrow, but she will leave more of this beverage for thee.'

'Where will you be?' Lucie had slept so soundly the previous night and believed that Magda's mere presence had provided such a gift, a night of unbroken sleep that was such a rare blessing when pregnant. 'You are not safe at home.'

'That is thy opinion, but Magda won't be at

home. She has a thought that a baby who is due is about to proclaim her arrival.'

'Then it's true what they say,' said Edric in a hushed tone of wonder, 'you can see the future.'

Lucie knew to expect Magda's barking laughter, but Edric looked startled and confused.

'Thou hast leaped from a thought that it is time for the baby to wondrous powers of divination,' Magda said. 'Thou hast honoured Magda, but she cannot accept thy praise.'

Edric could not help but smile in response to Magda's gleeful expression, her clear blue eyes twinkling. Lucie was glad that he was able to laugh at his mistake, but she worried about how easily the young man was befooled. He would be prey to tricksters if he did not learn to discern what was probable and what was not.

After dinner, Edric went off to his chamber above the shop and Phillippa went off to her own bed, still fretting about the dead who yet lived in her confused mind. Alisoun had apparently chosen to remain in the solar after putting the children to bed for the night.

Lucie, Magda, and Kate sat in the kitchen, and Magda announced Maud's imminent arrival, which delighted Lucie. As Kate had been in the household long enough to be trusted as family, Lucie and Magda were free to continue, talking of Alice Tanner's overabundance of children, George Hempe's visit, the possible connections between Nigel and Drogo, and most of all

Alisoun's feelings about Edric and his for Lucie.

It was quite late when they heard Owen's and Jasper's voices in the hall. Kate hurried out of the kitchen to see to their comfort while Lucie and Magda followed more sedately.

Seeing the midwife with Lucie, Owen jumped to the wrong conclusion. 'What is amiss? Is the baby all right?'

'Our baby is healthy, my love, and the most active one I've carried. Magda had the trouble, not I.'

'The second murder, aye,' said Owen, rubbing the scar beneath his eye patch, which Lucie took as a sign of his concern over the 'coincidence' of two men knifed and then drowned. 'Alfred just explained why he was guarding the house. He's a good man. And this young man,' Owen put a hand on Jasper's shoulder, 'is a fine spy in training. He has been a great help to me.'

'Da's work is nothing like I've imagined it,' Jasper said. Lucie saw that the boy was exhausted but excited to tell all. 'We found Hubert, but he wouldn't return with us. I'm hungry, Kate.'

'So am I,' said Owen. 'But first things first.' He swept Lucie up in his arms. 'I am so glad to see you looking so well, my love. Now to bed with you. It's late for you to be down here. You need your rest.'

She gladly accepted the ride up the stairs. 'I missed you,' she said as he gently lowered her to the bed. 'But Magda was a peaceful bed mate,' she teased.

'You shared our bed with Magda?' Owen looked incredulous. 'Does she mutter charms in her sleep?'

They laughed together, a moment of intimacy that Lucie extended by pulling him down beside her.

'I'm filthy from travel, my love,' Owen protested.

'When did I ever mind that?' she whispered into his thick dark hair. Christ but she loved him.

They kissed long and tenderly.

'So, *does* she mutter charms in her sleep?' Owen asked when they paused to breathe, his breath tickling her face.

'You know she has no truck with charms,' Lucie said, laughing. It was so good to have him in her arms. 'Do you think Hempe was right to worry about her after she'd fished Nigel from the Ouse?' Unfortunate question, she realised at once.

Reminded of his work, Owen sat up, moving a little away from her. 'I do, and I'm glad that Magda agreed to have a care. A goldsmith's journeyman.' He shook his head. 'I wonder whether Drogo asked him the value of the cross and he coveted it. But such a small piece.' He explained what it was that Hubert had lost.

'A birthing cross,' Lucie said, feeling sorry for the women who had been deprived of a good luck piece for their lying ins. 'The poor lad. Where is the cross now?'

Seeing the frustration in the set of his jaw and

his shoulders she knew his response before he gave it. 'I wish I knew,' he said. 'I hope that George Hempe has spoken to Edward Munkton about Nigel.'

'Hempe was here today,' said Lucie. 'Magda spoke to him.' A yawn escaped her and she realised how sleepy she was. 'Now go have some food and ale, and Magda will tell you about all that has happened while you've been away. I look forward to hearing about it all in the morning.'

As Owen was about to leave Lucie said, 'Jasper looks happy.'

Owen's smile bespoke his own happiness. 'Aye. We both are. Now sleep, my love. I can see that your eyelids are ready to close.'

'God be praised for bringing you both home safely.' She loved them so fiercely at this moment.

Owen crossed himself. 'God be praised for keeping my family safe while I was away. Now rest, Lucie my love.' He closed the door behind him.

She lay in bed turning over what Owen had said about his inquiry in order to quiet her emotions. A gold cross belonging to Ysenda's lord. Drogo finding it in the scrip, perhaps going to Nigel for advice on what it was worth. She'd heard from Julia Dale that the goldsmith's journeyman was unpleasant, and suspected of theft. As Lucie drifted towards sleep, she floated between concern over Edric's gullibility and wonder about whether Drogo had been equally gullible, to have shown his spoils to Nigel, a man of such negative reputation.

When Hubert heard the horse he groaned to think Captain Archer and Jasper had returned, but he soon saw that it was worse than that.

'Ma, it's Master Osmund.'

She had been chopping roots at a table in the far corner and now paused, the knife in mid-air, glancing over her shoulder towards the door with a worried expression. Her reaction was not at all what he'd expected. 'Stay close to me, Hubert. I would not be alone with him.'

'But you always want to be alone with him.' It had been her custom to shoo him out of the house when Osmund appeared. In fact Hubert had believed his mother to be in love with their lord's son though her behaviour was usually more anxious than delighted. Osmund had spent much of the past summer in their home. Hubert suspected that Osmund had spent even more time there while he was at school. They'd been lovers – he was almost certain of that. But now the expression on his mother's beautiful face was fear. 'What has frightened you? Has he hurt you? Does it have to do with the cross?'

'No!' his mother said. 'I would not have your father walk in on us, just the two of us. You know how he makes up his own story of what is happening. He might hurt someone.'

Hubert did not respond. Aubrey's 'own story'

would be accurate. She thought Hubert didn't know. It hurt that she could think he did not have a good idea that Osmund was her lover, that she could think she had fooled him. Osmund had so far shown none of the virtues of Sir Baldwin. He hadn't even run the estate while his father was gone. Hubert did not trust him, and he'd heard enough gossip about others feeling likewise, including Aubrey, that he felt he was right not to. But his mother had not seemed to see that in him at all. Had something newly opened her eyes? He wondered whether Osmund had *given* her the birthing cross, but pushed that thought aside, not wanting to believe his mother would have accepted it knowing that the women of the village and the manor might need it.

Osmund knocked on the door.

'See him in,' said Hubert's mother, staying by the table.

Hubert opened the door and stepped back. 'Master Osmund,' he muttered with the slightest bow he could manage. He found himself wondering where Aubrey was, wishing he would appear.

'Young Hubert! I did not think to find you here. When did you return from school? Are you ill?' Osmund Gamyll surprised Hubert by sounding and looking sincerely concerned.

'He was worried about me,' said Ysenda, 'working the farm without his father. He had not heard that Aubrey has returned –' She did not move from her corner.

Osmund handed his hat, gloves and cloak to Hubert. 'Take care of these, and then find some occupation elsewhere.'

'No, son. Stay here with us. You might tell Master Osmund how you like school. What you have learned, and how comfortable it is at the Clee.'

Hubert grumbled to himself as he carefully put the gloves in the hat and hung it over the cloak.

'Will you not leave your work to welcome me home, Ysenda?' said Master Osmund.

His mother had left her corner and stood at the far end of the fire, brushing the roots off her hands and her sleeves and skirt. 'I am so untidy. I had not expected you.'

'Where *is* Aubrey?'

Hubert hoped she would tell him the truth, for Osmund probably already knew from Sir Baldwin that Aubrey had disappeared.

'I wish I knew,' said his mother.

'What happened?'

Ysenda sank down on a bench, looking weary, one hand to her forehead. 'We argued and he walked out the door. It's been several days since he left. I cannot think where he might be.' She looked truly worried, and sounded tearful. Hubert wondered whether this was a ruse to get Osmund's sympathy, or whether she had changed her mind about Aubrey.

'Have you looked for him?'

She had not, as far as Hubert knew, and neither

had he, nor had they asked the men who worked the fields. One of them should have.

'I was angry at first,' she said to Osmund. 'Now I'm worried. It's best that you go.'

Osmund took a seat instead, reaching his hands out to warm them at the fire, playing the lord. 'When does Hubert return to school?'

'Not until Aubrey is home.' She rose and went around the fire to Osmund, cocking her head and giving him an uncertain smile. 'He will go back to school. He's doing very well, aren't you, son?'

Hubert shrugged.

Osmund sat back and nodded to Hubert to sit. He reluctantly did so, but stayed close to the door, in case he needed to escape.

'I heard that you'd lost something in the city, lad, and that it caused trouble,' said Osmund. 'I'm curious about it. What was it that the bargeman kept from you?'

Hubert searched for a lie though he knew Osmund would learn the truth soon enough, if he did not already know. He could not bring himself to tell him now, in the house, with his mother already frightened. He could not look at her face, he must think. 'A badge I'd won in school. The first thing I'd ever won,' he said, hating how breathless he sounded.

'How odd that a bargeman would want such a thing.' Osmund's tone was mocking, as if he did not believe Hubert but meant to play along with him until he slipped.

'He hoped I had money, Master Osmund. He probably threw away the badge.'

'Tell him what the badge was for, Hubert,' said his mother.

They both turned to look at Hubert, and he felt himself getting warm with anger. He looked from one to the other. She wanted him to lie even more. She'd never before even wanted him in the house when Osmund came, but suddenly he was expected to be the entertainment and also her saviour. He rushed for the door and was out of the house before either of them had a chance to say a word.

After sunset, when it was too cold to remain wandering in the fields, Hubert returned home. His mother cursed him for his discourtesy to Master Osmund despite Osmund's having been clear about wanting Hubert out of the house, and then sat by the fire and proceeded to drink bowl after bowl of cider until she grew sloppily drunk and cruel. Hubert had witnessed her attacks on Aubrey before, but it was his first experience being her target, her butt. She droned on and on about how he'd embarrassed and humiliated her.

'Are you afraid of Master Osmund?' he asked.

For a moment there was a glint in her eyes, a softening in her face that made him think he'd guessed the truth, but then she changed. 'I'm afraid of what he'll think of us.'

'Why do you care, Ma? Master Osmund might

never be your lord. Sir Baldwin's new wife will keep him healthy for a long while, you said so. And if Master Osmund does become your lord someday, he'd have forgotten my running out of the house by then – though I don't believe he minded at all.' Hubert rarely made such speeches to her, but she was not making sense and he hoped to reach her. He hated to see her drunk. It made her ugly. She frightened him.

'Why do I care?' she shouted. 'Why do I care, you ask me.' She contorted her face as if she were being tortured. 'Because Osmund Gamyll sponsored you at St Peter's this year, you ungrateful wretch, and you've made him think that was a mistake.'

That washed over him like icy water. 'I thought St Mary's Abbey sponsored me.'

'No, you fool. What would they care about you?'

Hubert felt sick to his stomach. 'Did he say I couldn't go back?'

'Not yet. But he will. You stupid boy.'

There was worse to come. Once she'd begun her attack, she became infatuated with her power to inflict pain.

'Do you want to know why your da never smiles? Do you know what he's gnawing on like an old bone that he sucked dry long ago? The pestilence took his two children and not you. You were spared, the bairn that wasn't his, the one I used to trick him into wedding me.' She sat back

219

with her hands to her hips, her head cocked to one side, a sickening grin on her sweaty face. 'There. How do you like that?'

Not at all. He did not like that at all. He felt alone, unloved. He snapped with her taunting attitude and, picking up a pot, he rushed at her, lifting the pot to bash in her head and be done with her.

'How dare you threaten your mother?' she shouted, throwing up her arms to deflect the blow.

Her shout brought Hubert to his senses. He might have killed her. 'You're drunk!' he shouted as he dropped the pot, just let it drop and bounce on the earthen floor thinly covered with rushes.

He covered his ears, but she tore his hands away. Her breath smelled foul, her face was red and swollen, her eyes wild, and in that moment he hated her with all the fervour with which he'd loved her before.

'So who's bastard am I?' he shouted.

She slapped him on the cheek. 'Don't use that word in my presence.'

'You're the one who made me a bastard, aren't you?' He was crying, blubbering, and hated himself for it.

'You don't deserve to know who your father is, you with your foul mouth.'

How he could have adored the slovenly woman before him, stinking of sweat and cider, her hem filthy, her cap crumpled, spewing such hateful words, he could not now understand.

'I've learned foul words from you when you use them on Aubrey,' he said.

She slapped him again. He grabbed her wrist and squeezed, but she was strong and broke away.

'You ruined all my hopes when you stole the cross, you snivelling sneak.' She stopped for a moment, her head turned slightly away and her gaze towards the floor, as if trying to catch a faint sound. With a little cry, she took an oil lamp and knelt before the chest in which she kept her clothes and little treasures. Opening it and precariously balancing her lamp on a corner she began digging through her things. She rose to lean over farther and the lamp fell, fortunately out and onto the floor. Hubert rushed over to shove the rushes away and stamp on the ones already caught. He took the lamp back to the fire, but hurried back to lift his mother's skirts from the pooling oil.

'Look what you're doing. You might have burned down the house.' He was weeping again, frightened by this woman he'd called mother. He clawed at her, trying to pull her up. He didn't understand what he'd done for her to turn on him so. He would never have thought the cross could mean so much to her.

She pushed him away, letting the lid of the chest drop with a dull thud, and then struggled onto her feet. Her expression had changed dramatically. Now she looked as if ready to weep, suffering a terrible sorrow.

'The scrip also. The one –' Her voice caught

and she stumbled to the bench on which she'd sat. She shook the jug, checking for more cider. 'I should send you to town for more. You've done this to me. All this time, trusting you, feeding you.' She dropped her head into her hands and wept. After a short while she cursed him and then curled up on the bench. Soon she was snoring.

He let her stay there, sleeping till the wee hours when her cries woke him – he didn't know how he'd managed to fall asleep. She'd tumbled off and burned a hand on the smouldering fire. Experienced from years of tending her injuries he greased her hand with celandine and goat's grease and wrapped it for her. She crawled to bed moaning about the pain in her head, whimpering that she needed water. He broke the ice on a bucket outside and brought in a bowl for her, sitting beside her to help her sip it. He tended her without feeling, without any of the tenderness he'd always felt for her, the comfort of being needed by her.

In his mind he felt as if he'd been looking at her upside down all his life, and suddenly he'd been righted and saw that she was the very opposite of all he'd believed her to be. He tried to retrieve his old love, but her smell, her cruelty, her lies kept crowding his head.

The morning dawned with a brittle sun, and Jasper suggested that he wait until the following day to return to school. But Owen would not hear of it.

'I've kept you from your lessons long enough. I'll walk there with you to tell your Master John that you've been away with me in the service of the archbishop.' Owen could see that appealed to Jasper.

'How much will you tell him?' Jasper asked. 'I would know what I can say.'

'I don't think I'll tell him more than that we spoke to Hubert, and he intends to return after spending some time with his father. I'm considering whether to mention the cross – he might be able to help us if he knows what we seek. Do you agree?'

Jasper frowned a moment. 'I doubt he could help you with the answers you still need, so I see no gain in telling him what was in the scrip or any more about the family.'

'You've a good mind, son. I still might tell him about the cross, but we shall see.' Owen noticed Lucie watching them with quiet joy. She knew how much he'd hoped this journey would bring them closer once more.

An icy wind tore at their cloaks as they walked down Stonegate. Jasper tried to speak but the wind forced him to cover his mouth with one hand. The few people who were out in the street were bundled and bent against the wind. A woman's empty basket was suddenly lifted from her crooked arm and became airborne. Jasper leaped to catch it, handing it back with a mute nod to her thanks. Owen was glad to catch sight of St Peter's School past the scaffolding around the minster's lady chapel, and even happier once inside. The students who boarded in the Clee had not yet arrived, so Owen was able to take Master John aside to explain Jasper's absence.

The schoolmaster nodded throughout Owen's explanation. 'I heard a rumour to that effect,' he said in response. 'His absence was for a good cause. God be praised that Hubert reached home safely. He is a good lad, and I can understand that he would want to spend time with his father. After all, he'd thought him dead. His homecoming must have been cause for great joy and thanksgiving.'

It had certainly not seemed so to Owen, but he smiled. 'I do hope the abbey does not withdraw their support of the lad now that his father has returned. The farm does not appear prosperous. In fact, Sir Baldwin hinted at that.'

Master John glanced over at Jasper. 'May we speak freely, Captain?'

'Yes.'

'Abbot Campian's sponsorship is the public story. His mother did not wish Hubert to know of his benefactor, though I could not see why not, for he is their lord, after all, and Aubrey accompanied him to battle.'

This was an unexpected twist. 'Sir Baldwin sponsored Hubert here?'

'His son Osmund arranged it in his father's name, yes, as his father had requested.'

Owen wondered whether that had something

to do with his sense that Ysenda was not telling him everything. But the lad had also seemed secretive. 'You are certain Hubert doesn't know?'

'We've taken care that he should not, Captain. Tell me, did you discover what the lad had in his scrip?'

Hesitating, Owen decided that the schoolmaster might have some insight, and he knew the man to be trustworthy.

'It was a small gold cross, a pendant,' said Owen, indicating that it was but a few inches long and one wide, small enough to cup in the palm of his hand. 'Something belonging to his mother.'

'That small?' Master John shook his head. 'But you saw the size of the scrip, it must be at least six times that size. Why had he worn that to carry something so small? He might have worn the cross round his neck on a chain or leather thong.' He sighed. 'But it is like a lad to not think things through. I see it all the time. Poor lad. His mother will not be happy to lose a piece of gold.'

'No. They can ill afford to replace it.'

'I'd wager Drogo hoped for a better catch than that,' said Jasper.

Owen was glad he'd listened.

'I wonder whether he even saw it in the scrip?' Master John wondered, scratching his chin.

Master John's comments about the size of the scrip and the size of the cross gave Owen pause. There had been an elaborate buckle on it – might the boy have thought it of value? Or perhaps there was a hidden pocket. 'Where is the scrip now?' he asked.

'Why, here.' The schoolmaster lifted a leather box from a high shelf and set it down on a bench. 'I keep my scholars' forgotten items in here.' He eased off the tight-fitting lid and rummaged through a collection of scarves and gloves, then looked up, perplexed. 'It isn't here. I am certain this is where I put it.'

Owen bit back a curse. 'You live in the chamber behind this hall, do you not?' he asked.

John's face flushed as he nodded.

'Do you spend time in here in the evening?'

'God help us.' Master John removed his felt hat and mopped his head with a cloth. 'I do spend some evenings in here, when I'm preparing lessons. I know what you're thinking, I was a fool to leave it in an unguarded schoolroom. But I can't imagine when someone might have felt sure they would not be caught. God's blood, this is – I can't believe –' His face crumpled.

'Did anyone see you place it in the box?'

'William Ferriby was here. We'd been discussing his brother's stubborn insistence on keeping his school in this liberty, whether there was any way William might dissuade him. But none of the boys were here.' He moaned. 'I've been a fool. I'd brought the scrip from the Clee, thinking it would be safer here.' He looked distraught. 'This is terrible.'

'I won't deny that it worries me, Master John. Have a care when you first enter this room.' He made certain that the schoolmaster met his eye, saw his concern. The other scholars had begun to file in. 'I should leave you to your students.' Walking past Jasper Owen patted him on the shoulder. As he stepped outside he heard the scholars asking Jasper whether he'd been helping the captain. It would be a good day for the lad, but not for his grammar master.

The wind almost pushed Owen into George Hempe, who awaited him outside the school.

'I thought I'd find you here or with Archbishop Thoresby,' Hempe said, hunching his shoulders to protect his neck from the icy wind.

'I haven't seen the archbishop yet.' He weighed Thoresby's anger at a delay in reporting to him against having more news for him, and decided that he might at least speak with the goldsmith. He needed to see William and Nicholas Ferriby as well, but he first wanted to consider how to approach them. 'Before I talk to His Grace I would see Edward Munkton. Would you care to join me?'

'I don't know what use I would be to you,' said Hempe. 'I've been unable to connect the goldsmith's journeyman with the bargeman.'

'I'm surprised you've taken the time out of your responsibilities to continue to work on this.'

'I cannot seem to let it go.' Hempe gave an embarrassed laugh.

As they walked towards Petergate Hempe told Owen what he'd learned about Nigel.

'You're a good friend,' Owen said. 'I thank you.' He told Hempe about the cross. 'I believe the cross is how Nigel became involved with whatever is driving the murders.'

They were turning towards Stonegate when Hempe asked, 'Why do you think Ysenda de Weston had kept the cross?'

Owen wished he knew. 'Whatever her reason it was not so simple as a woman coveting a piece of gold jewellery, I'm certain of that. And now that the scrip the lad had carried it in is missing, I'm worried that there was more in it.'

'Or the scrip itself was worth something?'

'I wondered that, but I doubt it. As I recall it was good leather, not the best, with a brass clasp fashioned like a buckle. I cannot think that worth sneaking into St Peter's School to steal.'

'Nay.' Hempe tucked in his chin and braced against the wind whistling down Stonegate.

Edward Munkton looked dismayed by yet another visit from Hempe, but was more civil to Owen, no doubt because he'd bought a mazer, a beautiful wooden drinking cup decorated with delicate gold filigree, from the goldsmith a few months earlier. He'd wanted something special to present to Lucie when she was brought to bed with the child. The visit was well worth it, for Munkton jerked to attention as soon as Owen described the cross.

'Nigel, may he rest in peace, asked about such pendants a few days ago. He wondered about their worth and who made them. I sent him across to Robert Dale. He makes such pieces.'

That was good news to Owen, for Robert Dale was a friend.

'Have you presented your wife with the mazer yet?' Munkton asked.

'No. I've avoided temptation by hiding it.' He'd taken it to Brother Michaelo for safekeeping, knowing that he would be able to retrieve it at once – there was not a better organised man in all York, in Owen's opinion.

'Admirable constraint, Captain,' said Munkton with a conspiratorial wink as Owen and Hempe left the shop.

Across Stonegate, a servant showed them in to Robert Dale's workshop to stay warm while he fetched his master. Several of the journeymen were working on a large piece and their hammering was deafening. The goldsmith soon joined them and, making a show of covering his ears and wincing, led them outside and up to his hall.

Swearing him to secrecy, Owen told Robert about the Gamyll cross. The goldsmith sat with his head down, nodding to indicate his attention, but he perked up at the name.

'The Gamyll cross, did you say? Sir Baldwin Gamyll of Weston?'

'Yes,' said Owen, 'did you make it for him?'

Robert trained his myopic gaze on Owen as he

slowly nodded. 'I did. And you are not the only one who has asked about it of late. Disturbing.'

'Who else has mentioned it?' asked Hempe.

'Father Nicholas – the merchant Peter Ferriby's brother – was inquiring about what quality of chalice he might purchase with money left to his church in Weston and mentioned in passing a birthing cross in his parish. I was curious about it, and he said it had been a gift to the late Lady Gamyll from Sir Baldwin. Is this the same cross?'

'It is,' said Owen. 'Did he say anything else about it?'

Robert puckered up his face, thinking. 'Oh yes. He asked how many such crosses he might purchase with the money, and then laughed. But then he asked again. I told him quite a few, that a chalice requires far more gold. He did not press me further.'

'Master Edward said he'd sent his journeyman, Nigel, here when he'd asked about small gold crosses. Did he talk to you?'

'He sent him here? That horrible man? God grant him peace, but he would not have been welcome in this house.' Robert frowned. 'He might have spoken to someone in the shop. Shall I inquire for you?'

Owen and Hempe were offered watered wine by a maid while they waited for the goldsmith to return.

'Nicholas Ferriby,' Hempe said, staring into his cup. 'Now why would he have that cross on his mind?'

'Perhaps he thought it lost and wondered whether he might replace it,' said Owen. But he was bothered by Nicholas's interest as well. He'd been in York the night Drogo died. Was there something to that, he wondered, something he wasn't seeing? Then there was the missing scrip. Might Nicholas's brother have mentioned seeing it at St Peter's School?

Robert returned with an apprentice about Jasper's age in tow, who hesitated just inside the doorway.

Robert gave him a little push. 'Do not be afraid, Michael, you are not in trouble. In fact, this might earn you the day off you have asked for.'

The boy's face lit up with that, and he quickly settled down on a stool by the fire. Owen noticed gold glitter on Michael's simple hat.

'Tell them about Nigel,' Robert said.

'We were standing in St Peter's after Mass on Sunday last,' said Michael, 'and he asked me if we made gold crosses for ladies to wear as pendants round their necks. I told him we did, and some bore pretty sayings, or prayers – short ones.' He looked to his master for approval, which he received as a smile and a nod.

'Did he want to purchase one?' Owen asked.

'A journeyman?' Michael laughed. 'He asked if Sir Baldwin Gamyll had ever been in the shop, and I said yes, we had just made a delicate gold circlet for his new lady to secure her veil.'

'Anything else?' Owen coaxed.

'He wondered whether Sir Baldwin and Master Robert spoke as if friends. I said as much as a merchant and a lord might be friendly, they were. After all, Master Robert knew that the circlet was for Sir Baldwin's second wife, so he knew something of the family.' Michael winced as he glanced at his master.

Robert nodded his approval and thanked him.

That was enough for Owen. Nigel had been asking about the Gamyll cross, there was no doubt of that.

Owen and Hempe were quiet as they walked out into Stonegate.

'I'll see His Grace now,' said Owen. 'We've matters to discuss.'

'I'll be at the York Tavern if you have need of me,' said Hempe. He began to walk away, but paused and turned back to Owen. 'They might have worked together, Drogo and Nigel. Stealing and selling downriver.'

That had crossed Owen's mind. 'But who caught them then?'

Hempe shrugged and continued on his way.

Owen almost changed his mind about seeing Thoresby before the Ferriby brothers, but he'd already delayed long enough that the archbishop would be in a fine fury.

Eight

SCAPEGOAT
OR CRIMINAL?

Brother Michaelo met Owen in the archbishop's hall. 'His Grace expected to see you earlier.' His elegantly sculpted face was set in an expression of mild irritation.

Owen bowed slightly to the archbishop's secretary. They had known one another a long while, and were friends in their ways, but Michaelo's loyalty was to the archbishop, not Owen. When Thoresby was irritated with Owen, so was Michaelo. 'I've more to tell His Grace now than I had earlier. I pray he will be glad of that.'

'Will Emma Ferriby be pleased with your findings?' Michaelo asked.

'Is she here?'

'No. But you know that His Grace wishes above all to lift the pall of suspicion from her brother-in-law, Master Nicholas.'

Owen might have known more had he not

followed his conscience to call on His Grace before calling on William and Nicholas. Frustrated and irritated with himself, Owen snapped, 'I would see His Grace, Michaelo.' His words echoed in the hall, despite the tapestries and cushions on the elegant seats.

Michaelo smirked as only he could do. Bowing, he said, 'If you will follow me, I shall announce you.'

Thoresby was pacing in his parlour when Michaelo opened the door. That did not bode well for Owen, but he'd weathered worse. At least his family had nothing to do with the matter at hand, so there was nothing with which Thoresby might threaten him.

'Your Grace,' Owen said, bowing.

'You have kept me waiting half the day, Archer,' Thoresby said, still prowling about the room arrayed in his archbishop's robes. Owen wondered what official appearance had required them.

'I was working for you, Your Grace. I have much to tell you. But if you've more important matters to see to, I could return.'

'Is Nicholas Ferriby innocent?' Thoresby lifted a document from a shelf and tapped his other hand with it for a few beats, then put it back. The archbishop had a gift for thrusting to the heart of the matter.

'I cannot say for certain as yet.' Owen wished he would sit down. This prowling was so uncharacteristic of late that he did not know how to interpret it. It felt like dark, anxious energy.

Thoresby paused with his back to Owen, bowing his head for a moment, hands clasped behind his back, his archbishop's ring catching the light from the brazier. They were old hands now. The archbishop had aged greatly in the nine years that Owen had known him.

'Shall we sit, Your Grace?'

'Emma Ferriby has suffered much of late. You are aware of that, I know, her father's death, her mother's feud with the Bishop of Winchester.'

'That all happened a year ago, Your Grace. Since then life has been calm in her household, and with her mother.'

Thoresby grunted. 'I met in the chapter house today with the dean and chancellor. They now suggest that the rumours surrounding Master Nicholas are proof that he is unsuited to take charge of young scholars. Canon William was also present.' Thoresby perched on his chair, hands on knees, and shook his head at the brazier. 'You would say the same?'

Owen relaxed his self-recrimination about not going to William at once upon learning he'd witnessed the storing of the now-missing scrip, as he'd perhaps been spared having the dean, chancellor and archbishop present when he spoke to him. 'What had William to say?'

'He mentioned that a large landholder in Nicholas's parish had asked him why his brother deemed it necessary to set up his school in the minster liberty. William wondered whether the man was concerned about the character of his parish priest.'

'What was his opinion about his brother's motives and his character?'

Thoresby shook his head. 'He merely reported the visit, no more. He was otherwise present merely as a courtesy, I believe.'

'Did he name the landholder?'

Thoresby sighed, signalling impatience. 'No. I told you all he said.'

Owen bit back a frustrated curse. 'I wish you had asked. I would like to know if it was Sir Baldwin or Osmund Gamyll.'

'Are you criticising me, Archer? Have a care.' Thoresby emphasised the warning with a brief pause. Then, with a dismissive shrug, he said, 'It would be wise to talk to William Ferriby in any case.'

'I intend to.' Owen wondered about William's loyalties. 'To explain my hesitation about Nicholas Ferriby's guilt or innocence requires that I tell you all that I have learned, Your Grace.'

'Then begin, Archer, begin.'

The prospect suddenly seemed exhausting. Owen took the chair opposite the archbishop and forced himself to begin with Hubert and his mother. When he reached Nicholas's meeting with Robert Dale and his mention of gold cross pendants, Thoresby snorted.

'This is the evidence that he is a murderer?'

'Your Grace knows me better than to suggest that,' Owen said. 'If I might inquire, Your Grace, would money assist Nicholas in opposing the chancellor's intention to close his school?'

'Fetch the wine and cups from the table.' Thoresby sat back, fussing with the drape of his sleeves. He nodded his thanks to Owen before he took a sip. 'Ah. Better. I found the minster air filled with stone dust. Difficult on old lungs.'

Owen settled back with his own cup, willing to wait for Thoresby to come round to answering his question. He'd managed to communicate what he'd learned without many interruptions, so he felt he should now be patient.

'If I were not opposed to excommunicating Nicholas, he would need to raise money to put a petition before the pope,' said Thoresby. 'But I am on his side, so there is little chance they will prevail. The school is small, and his own parish church is not particularly well endowed, so he might welcome more money, but so might we all. There is precedent for the chapter's reaction to a grammar school in the liberty – or at least near it. Years ago the dean and chancellor were incensed by St Leonard's grammar school. But the school remains. I believe this tempest will pass as well, and Master Nicholas's school will survive. It is a modest institution, and girls are accepted – certainly nothing St Peter's will ever consider.'

'All Nicholas need do is wait?'

'I believe so. But whether he has the wisdom to do so, I cannot judge.' Thoresby sipped his wine. 'What will you do now?'

'I must see Master Nicholas and his brother. Nicholas came to the shop while I was away but would not talk to Lucie in my stead.'

Thoresby tilted his head as if thinking. 'Do you expect another murder?'

'Until I find the murderer that is always the danger, and the motivation for dropping all other responsibilities and searching in every way I can think of.'

'God go with you, Archer, and with your family. Dame Lucie is well?'

Owen smiled. The archbishop was godfather to both Gwenllian and Hugh, and intended to stand for the child to come. 'She is as well as a woman might be as she slows and grows anxious for the babe to arrive.'

'Cherish her, Archer. Do not stint in your attentions to her because of these crimes.'

The comment confused Owen, made him suddenly wonder whether he had neglected her, whether Thoresby had heard she'd complained. But Owen knew that to be unlikely. 'I do cherish her, Your Grace.' He resented feeling the need to defend himself. But perhaps he did need to express his affection for her more.

Thoresby rose. 'I want to hear what Nicholas and William have to say to you.'

Owen had thought that would be the case. He

bowed and took his leave. As he departed the hall he wondered why he'd taken Thoresby's admonition about Lucie to heart, a cleric never wed, though with experience of women, never having lived with one so long as Owen had with Lucie. He thought of how she'd pulled him down onto the bed when he'd returned last night – there was a time when they'd lustily taken every chance to lie together. But that was before the children, and before Lucie's aunt had moved in. Perhaps since her accident the previous year he'd been reluctant to make love to her too often.

He realised he'd been so distracted he'd missed his turning and had to double back. Enough. He did not need his mind clouded with doubt about his treatment of his beloved wife. As he headed down Vicar Lane towards Master Nicholas's school he fought a twinge of anger. Thoresby meant well. He was good to Owen's family, very good.

It was the supper hour for the scholars and Nicholas was able to withdraw into his large chamber with Owen. He did not look well, as round as ever but with a pallor that seemed excessive even for the sunless season.

'Captain, I am in your debt for coming. I am not one to scare easily, but I've –' he flung wide his arms, 'well, since the goldsmith's journeyman was murdered I've not known what to do with myself to stay calm, which of course I must do for my scholars.' He'd begun to sweat.

'You knew Nigel, the journeyman?' Owen asked.

Nicholas shook his head. 'No, no, I knew him not, but –' He took a deep breath and reached beneath his collar, pulling out a gold chain from which hung a delicate gold cross. 'This is a birthing cross belonging to Sir Baldwin Gamyll. Drogo brought it to me for safekeeping the day before he died.'

'Holy Mother of God, it's here.' Owen caught his breath.

'Have you been looking for this?'

'Looking for it? You f –' Owen caught himself and dropped the fist he'd raised. 'This was in the scrip Drogo took from Hubert.'

Nicholas had flinched at the sight of the fist. 'God help me,' he murmured.

'You not only lied to me, but you kept this a secret?' Owen struggled to keep his voice low. 'How could you not guess how important this is, eh? By the rood, you had better have a good reason for keeping this from me – and the fact that you knew Drogo.'

Nicholas threw up his hands. 'Drogo came to me once, a few months past, to inquire about the fees for the school, having heard that I accepted girls as well as boys. He has two daughters. My fees were more than he could afford, but he said his circumstances might improve over the winter and he might see his way to sending one of his daughters. He was courteous and seemed a loving father. So we were not entirely strangers, but that is the extent of it.'

Owen tried to calm himself. He needed answers. He needed to ask and listen. 'Did he say how it came to be in his possession?'

Nicholas shook his head. 'Well, yes, he made up a tale about a buyer trying to trick him. But I knew what it was, having handled it in my parish so often, I know the imperfections, the wear on it – and that it's been missing for months.'

'Why did he come to you?'

Nicholas shook his head. 'He would not tell me. I asked, believe me, for it was a great puzzlement to me and he seemed frightened. He said he did not want it found on him. How he knew it belonged in my parish I don't know, but why else would he entrust it to me?'

'He did not want it found on him? He said that?'

Nicholas nodded.

'He said nothing of Hubert's scrip when he brought the cross to you?'

Nicholas sagged against the wall, his head in his hands for a moment. 'He did not mention the scrip.'

'Are you ill, Master Nicholas?'

'No. Merely – oh, this is why I said nothing to you. After that horrible moment when Drogo began to bleed as he lay before the Virgin I knew I would be suspect if I came forth with this.' He pulled the chain over his head and held it out to Owen. 'When he died, and then a goldsmith's journeyman, I feared I was next, that someone was tracking the cross.'

'Do you know whether Drogo showed it to Nigel?'

'No – how could I? But when I heard about the man's death, the goldsmith's journeyman, well, I connected the two deaths.'

'Have you shown it to anyone?'

'No!' Nicholas's colour had returned with a vengeance. 'Oh, you see, you see, I knew I was cursed by accepting it from Drogo. God's blood, what am I to do?'

'I'm sitting down,' Owen muttered. He tucked the cross into the small pouch he wore on his belt.

Nicholas gestured towards several short benches.

Owen settled on one. 'Tell me what you know about Hubert de Weston's family.'

'What?' Nicholas blinked at the abrupt change in topic.

'Sir Baldwin told me that Aubrey de Weston yearned for his wife all the while he was away, but shortly after returning home he'd disappeared, apparently in a temper. Is that surprising?'

Nicholas shook his head. 'Ysenda seems to be poison for Aubrey, and he for her. Their fights are legendary in the parish. He is a soldier at heart, a man who is quick to anger, quick to attack. I believe they love each other in their own tortured way, and I think them both good people, though she has little faith, it seems to me. In fact I worried about her that she did not know how to ask for

Divine guidance in her grief when I told her that her husband might be dead at La Rochelle. I'd thought of asking Osmund Gamyll to restore her post as housekeeper in his family hall. She'd been sent away when Sir Baldwin remarried, despite his not bringing his young wife to the house until he should return.'

This was a new twist. 'Ysenda de Weston saw to Sir Baldwin's home?' Owen wondered why Baldwin had said nothing about this. Keeping his mistress close at hand?

'She took care of the house after his first wife died, and before he wed Lady Janet. There was gossip about Ysenda and Sir Baldwin, with Hubert having the Gamyll hair, but he was born before she worked at the house. Gossips are often slack about their facts.' Nicholas nodded at the sounds growing in the hall beyond the door. 'The afternoon begins, Captain.' He rose. 'I pray I can depend upon you to protect my good name, knowing that I have told you this in confidence.'

Owen rose with a little bow and said, 'You have been most helpful, Master Nicholas. I am going to set a guard on the school. He'll be in His Grace's livery.'

'To watch me or to protect me?' Nicholas asked in a testy voice as he saw Owen to the alley door.

'To protect you, of course,' said Owen. He made certain the door did not latch tightly, and then headed towards the deanery.

* * *

Chancellor Thomas appeared behind the servant who answered the door. Recognising Owen, the chancellor thanked the servant and sent him away.

'Why do you wish to speak with Canon William?' he asked in a wary tone, his eyes searching Owen's face.

'I am here on the business of His Grace the Archbishop,' said Owen.

The chancellor was a distinguished scholar and considered himself a figure of authority, but he was not Owen's authority. It was moments like this that made his connection with the archbishop worth all the aggravation of the old man's self-interest. God forgive him but Owen enjoyed discomfiting men like the chancellor who wished to command him but could not.

'Might I know the nature of the business?' Thomas predictably asked.

Owen pressed his shoulders up to his ears and rubbed his hands together. 'I am in danger of freezing on your doorstep.'

'Of course,' the chancellor said down his nose and stepped aside to allow Owen into the hall, then snapped at a servant that Canon William might be found in the minster choir and to fetch him here.

Relieved to hear that, Owen said, 'There is no need for Canon William to come here. I'd as lief attend him in the minster.' Owen bowed to Farnilaw and thanked him, having remembered that in another circumstance he'd admired the man, and then departed.

The choir was fragrant with beeswax and incense, though only a few candles and lamps were lit at present. Canon William's sandals whispered on the tiles as he came to greet Owen.

'How might I be of assistance, Captain Archer?' he asked with courteous puzzlement. 'I pray this does not concern my imperilled brother.'

'I've a few questions to ask you, and this might take some time,' said Owen. 'Might we sit?'

Gesturing to a gracefully curved bench towards the entrance, William gave a worried shake of his head as he settled down beside Owen. Turning so that he might see Owen's face he asked, 'Is this about my brother?'

'In part. Master John of St Peter's School told me that you were with him when he put Hubert de Weston's scrip away in the schoolroom.'

William frowned at the floor for a moment, then nodded. 'Yes, I was.'

'Have you told anyone of seeing the scrip?'

Lifting his eyes to Owen, William frowned, apparently understanding the significance of the question. 'Let me think, Captain. I'd no idea it would signify.' He joined his hands as if praying, then lifted them, pressing his fingertips to his forehead. After a few breaths he dropped his hands and nodded. 'Perhaps I did.' He grimaced with embarrassment.

Owen tried to keep the irritation out of his voice. 'Is there anyone in particular you might have mentioned it to?'

'God help me, but it would have been Dean John and Chancellor Thomas. I had a small group to dinner – it might have been that same day – and they were among my guests.'

'Do you recall why you spoke of it? Did either of them ask about it?'

William shook his head. 'No, neither asked about it. I mentioned it because they'd expressed an interest in this tragedy – they are the only ones. The indifference of my fellows has been most disturbing. They were our students who rushed the barges. It is our student who is missing. It goes hand in hand with this ridiculous idea of excommunicating my brother because of where he situated his school. They all think they are superior, more than human.' By the end of his little speech William was talking loudly, and now he pressed a hand to his mouth and crossed himself with the other.

'You will be glad to hear that I found the boy Hubert at home in Weston,' said Owen.

'Thank the Lord for that.'

'I'll return to this matter, but, before I forget, His Grace mentioned that a landholder in your brother's parish questioned Nicholas's choice of the minster liberty for his school, but you'd not identified the man.'

William smiled a little, relieved. 'Pray make my apologies to His Grace for neglecting to name him. It was Osmund Gamyll, at such time when he feared that his father was lost and he was about to take his place as lord of the manor.'

246

'How did you come to meet with him?'

'I was out walking in the city and we met on the street. He seemed vaguely familiar – I was embarrassed to have forgotten his name. He was brief, and attempted to be pleasant, though he was plainly concerned about my brother's judgement and the state of the parish.'

'Strange that he should ask you, Nicholas's brother.'

'He said he'd heard that I was trying to remain impartial. I assured him that he had no cause for concern, that Nicholas is a worthy priest most devoted to his calling, and that his enthusiasm for educating the children of York was misunderstood by the chancellor.'

'How did he receive that?'

'Indifferently. To be frank, Captain, in the end I was not impressed by his demeanour. I felt that once he'd had his say he cared not a whit for what I had to say. He's a man who should study the sumptuary laws and give some of the wealth he spends on his finery to the Church. That would go a long way towards helping his parish.' As William spoke he'd straightened and begun tapping one foot in agitation.

But his description of Osmund Gamyll suited many eldest sons eager to take their seats at the high table.

'Since that meeting have you remembered whether you and Osmund Gamyll had been previously introduced? How he knew you?'

247

William nodded. 'It had been at Nicholas's table – oh – there was another occasion in which the company discussed the sad incident at the barges. Nicholas and I were in his chamber and Osmund Gamyll came to ask whether the lad had been found. Is his interest important, Captain?'

'It might be. When I was in Weston, I learned that although the scrip was empty when Drogo handed it to Geoffrey that night on the barge, Hubert had kept it close to him because within he had a birthing cross that belonged to the Gamylls.'

William looked startled. 'Now that is a peculiar connection, isn't it?'

'What was Osmund like on this occasion?'

'Oh, still a peacock of a young squire, but he spoke well, and amused us with tales of the countryside. I quite liked him that time, though it was clear my brother was ill at ease.' William sighed. 'But to the point, I fear I might have mentioned the scrip's being safely tucked away for the lad in the schoolroom at St Peter's. Why?'

He'd been so specific. Owen almost groaned with frustration. 'It is no longer where Master John hid it.'

William blushed. 'Dear God, I've done Nicholas no good, have I? My poor brother. But I tell you I cannot believe he would take it.'

'I did not say he did. Apparently the dean, the chancellor, and Osmund Gamyll also knew where the scrip was,' said Owen, 'as well as yourself.'

William moved his mouth as if trying to speak, but nothing came out. His face flowed in and out of emotions as if he could not settle on one.

Owen rose. 'You have been most helpful. I pray you, keep this conversation between us.'

Finally catching his voice, William agreed. 'But I must ask, what did the boy want with a birthing cross?'

Owen explained Hubert's unhappiness about leaving his mother alone.

William looked sympathetic. 'They feel so much at that age.' He was beginning to move away when he turned suddenly, 'A gold cross, Captain? Might that then be connected with the death of the goldsmith's journeyman?'

Owen put a finger to his lips. 'That is what I mean to discover.' He thanked William, and then, before moving on, knelt in the choir for a moment to pray for Lucie and the child in her womb.

Hubert's hood would not stay up and he did not care. He let the wind rip through his hair as he screamed out his anger and hurt up on a hill near his home. Birds startled from the underbrush. A man stopped his cart to stare up at him for a while, eventually moving on with a shake of his head.

'I hate her,' Hubert shouted. 'I hate both of them. I hate all three of them. Damn them. Damn her. I hate her. I hate me.' The litany expanded, contracted, curved back on itself, but the emotion remained steady – Hubert hated himself, his parents and Osmund Gamyll with all his heart.

After his mother had nearly burned down the house the previous night she'd slept until late this morning, almost midday. When she woke, she asked Hubert why he was so quiet. In her eyes there was a touch of fear – or perhaps it was doubt.

'How can you ask me that after last night?' he'd asked, irritated that she could be so changeable. 'You don't love me.'

'What are you talking about, Hubert?' He could see her fear deepen.

As did his. Could she not remember? Was she possessed?

She tried to smile prettily but her face was swollen, her hair uncombed and she smelled rank with sweat. 'Be a good lad and fetch me water, then stoke the fire. I'm not well today. How silly to think I don't love you. Now smile for your mother, won't you?'

Always before he'd come around, forgiving all, certain that he could prevent future outbreaks, that with his love he could keep her from drinking. But this morning he could not smile for her. Nor could he bear her presence. Pretending he'd gone to do her bidding he'd climbed the hill, trying to flee his feelings, but of course he could not outrun them.

'Hubert!'

He had not heard Aubrey's approach.

'Where have you been?' Hubert shouted. 'Sir Baldwin's servants have searched everywhere for you.'

'You'll sicken up here in the wind and cold,' Aubrey said. He wore a close-fitting hat and a heavy cloak, and even so his face was ruddy with cold. Hubert realised that he was cold. Aubrey firmly grasped his hand and despite his protests – Hubert could not imagine what he wanted – led him down the other side of the hill, across a frozen stream, through a wood and into an outbuilding they'd used for livestock when they had enough to require grazing in the far fields. A fire circle brought welcome warmth. Hubert approached it with his hands out.

'Sir Baldwin's servants didn't find me because they never search on our land,' said Aubrey, sounding weary. 'Now what was all that about, son?'

Hubert shrugged. 'So you come here a lot?'

'Yes. I know I need not go far, neither of you will come searching for me.'

'She never told me to.'

'You might have come on your own, son.'

'Don't call me that. You know it's not true.' Hubert flung himself down on a pallet near the fire. Everything stank of damp and animals long gone. 'It's all lies.'

Aubrey squatted down beside him. 'God's blood. She told you that? Is that why you're angry?'

Hubert said nothing, uncertain how much he wished to say.

Aubrey squeezed his shoulder. 'I'm glad you're disappointed that you're not of my flesh. But you are my son. I like to think that I've made that plain.'

'Don't lie to me.'

'Where's the lie in that, I ask you?' Hubert felt him settle down beside him.

'All your foul moods, like coming out here, leaving us, they're all because Rob and Bess died and I didn't. The only one not yours lived.'

'She told you that?'

Hubert nodded.

'Satan's daughter she is, I swear I don't know what I did that God cursed me with loving her.'

'I hate her.' It came out half sob, half growl. Hubert buried his face in the hay, not wanting Aubrey to see his tears.

Aubrey gently rubbed his back. 'I thought she was good to you, wanted you innocent of her evil so you would adore her. Something must be wrong for her to turn on you like that. She liked it that you thought I was the cause of all the suffering in the house. She even told you once that I'd brought back the pestilence from the market in York. That it was my fault your brother and sister died.'

Hubert had forgotten that. He struggled to sit up on the lumpy pallet. Aubrey sat with his knees up, arms propped on them, staring at the fire. He looked worn, like he had not been sleeping or eating.

'How did you find out I wasn't yours?' Hubert asked. 'Were you angry?'

Aubrey shook his head. 'I knew from the first, I knew she was with child. Sir Baldwin had a wife, so he told me her condition, knowing how I cared for her. I was only too happy to take the chance.'

'Sir Baldwin?' Hubert touched his hair – red, like his lord's. He'd thought maybe Osmund, but not Sir Baldwin. He felt a little better – at least he wasn't Osmund's son. 'I'm Sir Baldwin's son?'

'Aye. Even if he'd not been wed he'd never have taken Ysenda to wife, a bastard herself, child of the former vicar. My parents advised me to look elsewhere, to find a woman of honest birth with a good family, a bit of land for a dowry. But her beauty blinded me. I pray you are never so foolish, so stubborn, my son.'

Hubert was only half-listening, absorbing his new identity. 'I'm Osmund Gamyll's half-brother?' He spit into the fire.

'Your father is an honourable man, Hubert. He's been good to me.' Aubrey patted Hubert's leg. 'Your half-brother will change when he is lord. They all do.'

Hubert was digesting the fact that his mother had slept with Sir Baldwin and now was bedding his son.

'I hate her,' he hissed. 'How can you love her?'

'You know how – you've loved her all your young life. My guess is that she drank too much last night and turned on you. Am I right?'

Hubert nodded.

'I pray she's in no danger,' Aubrey said, shifting a little on the pallet to look at Hubert. 'Poor lad. How often did that happen while I was away with Sir Baldwin?'

'She's never been as bad with me.'

'That worries me.'

'Most of the time when she drank she complained about you.'

'God be thanked for that. I worried about you, and her. I wish I knew what to do to make her happy.'

'Can she really not remember what she said, what she did the night before?'

Aubrey closed his eyes and dropped his head, as if ashamed. 'I can tell you from experience – yes.'

Hubert found that a little reassuring.

'Did she weep when she thought I was dead?' Aubrey asked.

'Yes, oh, yes.'

'Who brought the news?'

'Father Nicholas.'

Aubrey nodded. 'He's a good man.' He stretched his legs and resettled. 'Enough of that. Something has been troubling me, son – how did you travel from York home?'

Hubert was glad to be asked even though he

was reluctant to talk about the experience. 'I walked.'

Aubrey grunted. 'Well I know that, lad, but how did you find your way? I had to be shown the way a few times before I could ride it myself, and even then I was worried I'd stray. Tell me – did you have a guide?'

Hubert shook his head. 'I asked here and there.' He turned away from Aubrey's searching eyes.

'God in heaven, Hubert. You trusted strangers to tell you which way to go? You might have been killed or – did anyone harm you?'

'I didn't let them. I ran.'

Hubert's stomach felt funny now that he was allowing himself to look back at the journey. He did not like remembering how frightened he'd been, how he'd lay awake at night even though he was so tired and, when he accidentally fell asleep, the terror he'd feel when he woke and remembered that he shouldn't sleep. He burst into tears.

Aubrey drew him close and held him.

When he was calm again, Hubert sat up by himself and wiped his eyes.

'Never again, son. You must promise me you'll never make a journey like that alone again, not until you're able to defend yourself against the worst of them.' Aubrey's pale eyes held Hubert's gaze.

'I promise.'

'I've neglected your training in arms and hand-to-hand combat. But when you're home from school again we'll begin.'

Hubert was more than a little surprised – his father had never offered to teach him to fight. 'Promise?'

'I promise,' Aubrey said, laughing. He patted Hubert's shoulder. 'You seem calmer now. Are you ready to go home?'

The thought made Hubert want to retch. 'I don't want to ever go back.'

'It's your home, son. She's your ma. She'll want to see you before you return to school, which is where I'm thinking you should be.'

'She says I won't be going back.'

'Not going back? Why not?'

'I ran out when Osmund Gamyll was talking to me.'

'Why does that warrant?'

'It's Osmund who sponsored me at St Peter's.'

Aubrey sighed. 'For his father. Sir Baldwin has sponsored you from the first. He felt it his duty as your father. Damn her. She just wanted to hurt you. She's cruel and dishonest when she drinks.'

Yesterday Hubert would have hated Aubrey for saying that, but he didn't today. 'I don't know what to believe.' Hubert wanted to wake up and be back at school, before he'd lost the scrip. *Please, God, let me out of this bad dream.*

'Do you think she's afraid of Osmund?' Aubrey asked.

Hubert nodded. 'I think she may be.'

'God help her,' Aubrey murmured. 'Hubert, believe that I've always thought of you as my son, and that I'm proud of your learning, and of how you've always helped where you could and looked after your mother.'

Hubert wondered why Aubrey was being so nice to him. 'I'm not worthy of your kindness.'

'Not worthy? Oh, Hubert. I was there when you were born and from that moment I've loved you.' Aubrey put his arm around Hubert's shoulders and smiled at him. 'What a voice you had from the start!' He laughed.

Hubert had never thought about being born. 'I'm sorry I listened to her about you. I thought it was all you, all the fighting.'

Aubrey's smile was sad. 'She knows what to say to anger me, that's a fact. I've prayed for patience, I've tried to harden myself against her words, but I'm no saint, that is for certain. Sir Baldwin knows of what I speak. And now you. I am sorry she turned on you. Tell me – does she argue with Osmund?'

Hubert nodded.

Aubrey rose to place another thick branch on the fire, poking the coals so that it would catch, then settled back on the pallet beside Hubert, who was content to listen to the crackling and popping for a while. How strange it was to feel so comfortable with Aubrey, to know him as a person, how he felt, why he'd wed. He hoped Aubrey did not regret it later. It would be nice to have a father like him.

'What did Osmund Gamyll want with you?' Aubrey asked. 'What did he come to talk about?'

Hubert had dreaded the question. He did not want to betray his mother, despite hating her. But Aubrey had not asked what Osmund wanted with his wife.

'He's been in York and heard all about –' Hubert stumbled, not knowing how to begin. 'I lost something of Ma's that turned out to be Sir Baldwin's.'

'Is that it? Did Osmund accuse her –' Aubrey shook his head. 'Go on, son.'

'I didn't really *lose* it, it was stolen by a bargeman. With Ma's scrip – I'd put it in there. And he returned the scrip, I guess, but not the cross. And a man died. The man who stole it.'

He wasn't surprised that Aubrey looked confused.

'Why did you have something of your mother's in one of her scrips?'

'I was stupid and thought she loved me and I wanted something of hers to keep close to me.' Hubert began to cry again. He pressed his fists into his eyes to stop the embarrassing tears.

Aubrey had risen. 'Here, have a little.'

It was a jug of cider. Hubert shook his head, thinking of his mother.

'Go ahead. When you calm a little more you can explain the rest. I won't let you have so much you cannot walk and talk, I promise.'

Hubert took the jug and drank, then handed it to Aubrey.

'When you are ready, you can tell me more.' Aubrey put the jug into a sagging trunk and left the hut.

Hubert lay back on the pallet, praying for help to stop thinking for a while or to at least slow down his thoughts. He felt as if he had bees in his head, buzzing so loudly that he could not hear his own breath.

Owen and Hempe slipped through the alley door into Nicholas Ferriby's room to search it. Such a tidy room should not take long, they had reasoned, and they would be away before the school day ended. Hempe took a large semi-circular vestment press that looked full of clothing, Owen searched the shelves. Nicholas had a simple but still costly book of hours, some letters from parents and guardians, several hats. He took the hats down one at a time and at the bottom made a discovery. Tucked within one was the scrip he'd seen that night at the Clee.

'Hubert's scrip,' he said softly.

Hempe stole across to him. 'The cross, the scrip, what more do we need?'

Remembering his idea that there might be more to the scrip, Owen carefully felt every inch of it. He noticed a slight bulge beneath the clasp and slipped his fingers beneath it. He found a tiny pocket, and within – he drew out a gold ring set with a single ruby. 'Now this is a beautiful thing. I wonder to whom this belongs?'

'We'll ask him,' Hempe said.

'Not yet.' He tucked the ring back in the little pocket.

'I wonder how he'll explain this?'

Owen shook his head. Scrip in hand, he stepped out into the alley, and Hempe followed close behind him. The wind kept them silent for a moment.

Turning his back to it, Hempe asked, 'Now what?'

'We confront him after the scholars depart for the day.'

Hempe leaned close to be heard. 'Do you suppose the owner of the ring was another victim? One we have yet to discover?'

'I intend to find out.' Even with this evidence in hand, Owen did not feel satisfied. 'Can you imagine Nicholas Ferriby purchasing poison for a knife? And what of the well-dressed man who argued with Nigel on the riverbank? I found no furred and feathered cap.'

'He is not what he seems,' said Hempe. 'And we do not know that Alice Tanner saw Nigel and his murderer. She might have seen two men unrelated to Nigel's death.'

Of course that was possible. But Master John had remarked how difficult it would be for anyone to be sure they would not be caught breaking into St Peter's School – for Master John's rival to take that risk seemed so foolhardy as to suggest madness, and Nicholas did not strike Owen as a madman. It also seemed madness to murder two men for a simple gold cross. The ring was almost certainly of greater value.

And Owen very much doubted that it had been in the scrip when Drogo handed it to Geoffrey on the night of his death.

Nine

THE MILLER'S SON

A quiet afternoon in the shop allowed Lucie time to send Edric into the workshop to prepare more calendula and aloe salve for dry skin and various other cold weather balms that would go quickly now that snow had arrived. She settled on a long bench with Jasper's cat Crowder who looked as if he had been neglected of late. As she combed his ginger and white fur his purr grew louder, just the sort of cheery sound her spirit needed. Lucie had been sad when Magda departed midday, and as the afternoon wore on her gloomy mood had turned darker with fears of losing the child she carried or giving birth to a sickly, mewling baby over whom she would fuss and fret through its brief life. It was as if she feared that Magda's departure had deprived her of grace.

She was startled when Crowder suddenly nipped the hand in which she held the comb, his characteristic signal that he'd had quite enough fussing. He jumped down, shook himself, fluffed his groomed fur, then trotted off into the work-shop. Lucie was still smiling and shaking her head at the enormous dignity of cats when a woman entered the shop. Lucie guessed by the ashen colour of her complexion that the woman sought a physick for herself. She was not well-to-do, but proud – though her clothes were drab and patched, the patches were delicately sewn and her wimple was starched.

'What might I do for you this windy day?' Lucie asked.

'I need something to ease my heartache and my fear so that I might sleep. My children need me.' The woman's voice shook and she seemed near tears.

Moved by the woman's apparent suffering, Lucie put her arm around her. The woman allowed herself to be led to the long bench, tears falling.

Lucie settled beside her. 'For such things it is helpful if you tell me more about this difficulty. You said "heartache". You have no injury or illness of the body?'

'No. My Drogo was murdered. Our house was searched. I am so frightened I cannot properly mourn my husband.'

Drogo's widow. This was not some chance encounter. Lucie took the woman's cold hands and pressed them between her overheated palms. 'Now I understand your pain and fear. May God watch over you and your daughters.'

'Are you Dame Lucie Wilton?'

'Yes. I don't know your name.'

'My name is Cecilia, but Drogo called me "Cissy".' She had regained her composure. 'I know that your husband is searching for my husband's murderer, and I am grateful. I pray he finds him, and quickly.' Her eyes moved in jerks and her hands had still not warmed. 'God bless and keep you and your family, Dame Lucie.'

'And may he bless and keep you and yours, Dame Cissy.' Already considering what might be best for the woman, Lucie asked, 'Are you able to sleep at all?'

Withdrawing her hands, Cissy wiped her tear-streaked cheeks. 'Since Drogo died I cannot stay asleep for the slightest noise wakes me. Then the devil starts whispering of all the evil that might be brought down on my little family. I have no husband, we have no protector.'

'Much of your fear will pass when you know that his murderer is found,' said Lucie. 'For the nonce you can drink something before sleep that will calm you. How are your daughters?'

Cissy gave a little shrug. 'They are young and, God forgive me for saying this, but Drogo paid them little heed when he was at home and he frightened them with his temper. Already they forget that we are in mourning.'

'Perhaps that is best for them,' said Lucie.

Cissy nodded and tried to smile. 'They are good girls. I am blessed.'

She was missing a few teeth among what seemed

264

healthy ones, and there were scars on her face, around her nose and mouth, that Lucie guessed were from beatings.

'I don't know why, but the loss of his mother's ring made me cry more than his murder,' said the widow. 'Both his parents died of the plague. Some say that millers are always among the first to go, I don't know why.'

'I had not heard you'd been robbed. Does Captain Archer know this?'

Cissy shook her head. 'It seemed such a small thing beside Drogo's murder, I did not want to complain of a bauble. If they find the murderer they will find the ring.'

Lucie did not think that was necessarily so. 'Knowing to look for the ring might help them. When did this happen?'

'My daughters and I were at St Mary's for Drogo's burial service. When I walked into the house it felt strange. I knew someone had been there. Searching. They had tried to put things back, but there were things in odd places. I didn't notice at first that the ring was gone for I seldom wear it. But it must have been taken that day.'

'No wonder you have difficulty sleeping,' said Lucie. She excused herself to tell Edric what to mix for Cissy while they talked. As she returned she was mulling over what the widow had said that might be of use to Owen. She was curious about Drogo's background. Perhaps it would suggest something to Owen.

'What mill did Drogo's parents work?' she asked.

'You would not know it – the Gamyll family's mill near Weston.'

Lucie's pulse raced at the hope of answers at last. 'Weston. Are you from there?'

Wiping away tears, Cissy shook her head. 'I've always lived in the city.'

'How long ago had he lived there?'

'Years now. I've never seen it and we wed eleven years ago.' She wiped her cheeks again. 'He'd no family left, nothing from them but the ring. That is why it meant so much to him – and to me.' She bowed her head and breathed deeply as if to control her tears.

Edric brought a cup of watered wine from the workshop, mouthing to Lucie that he'd put in a pinch of valerian. Confident in his judgement of how much to add, she nodded to him to offer it to Cissy. While the woman sipped, Lucie tried to think what else to ask her. She wondered whether Drogo could have recognised the birthing cross and so kept it.

'When you realised the ring was gone, did you check to see whether anything else was missing?'

Cissy nodded. 'I looked through everything. They'd taken a few coins I'd hidden away. Pennies. Nothing else.'

'Did you find anything that you'd never seen before?'

She frowned at Lucie. 'No.' Her eyes were

steady now; the wine was taking effect. 'My Drogo was no thief, Dame Lucie. I'm sure he kept that lad's scrip so long because he was away, but he'd always meant to return it. He wanted to teach him not to bother the bargemen, that is all he meant to do.'

'I do understand that the young scholars irritate the bargemen, Dame Cissy. Did he ever show you a small gold cross, a pendant?'

She shook her head, frowning. 'Why do you ask?'

'It was a thought, just that. Would you describe the ring for me?'

'It is a gold ring with a small but pretty ruby. The gold is patterned, like lace around the ruby, and I've always worried that I'd bend it. That's why I didn't wear it much. It's not a ring for every day.'

As Cissy relaxed she spoke of Drogo's frequent travels downriver and back, jobs he seldom knew about until the day he must depart. She knew nothing about who employed him as a pilot or what the boats carried. What he told the children about was Kingston-upon-Hull and the great estuary, especially the water fowl.

'He painted such pictures with words.' Cissy looked away, dabbing her eyes. 'They will miss that, my girls. Then they'll remember him kindly.'

Glancing up from his reading Master Nicholas groaned to see Owen and George Hempe enter the schoolroom. 'More questions? For pity's sake, I swear I've told you all I know of Drogo and his story.' But he looked more frightened than frustrated, and the hand that closed the book trembled a little.

'Let us withdraw to your chamber,' said Owen. 'I would not like someone to walk in while we are talking.'

Nicholas looked from one to the other, his neck so tensed that his head shook. 'Why?'

'Look at you,' said Owen, 'you are already upset. You do not want a student to enter and see you so.' He walked over to the connecting door.

Nicholas rubbed his bald head as if it helped him decide what to do, then crossed over to open the door. He stood back to let them through. As he passed, Owen smelled the man's fear. Nicholas followed them into the room with an air of dread, his usually lively arms pressed to his sides, hands clasped. He glanced around and noticed the disturbed pile of hats.

'What is this?' He looked at Owen with growing anger, his face darkening. 'Have you been in here without my permission?'

'Yes, we searched your chamber.' Owen did not like that he'd done so. He could well imagine Nicholas's sense of betrayal.

'What right had you?' the schoolmaster hissed. 'This is outrageous.'

'I remind you that two men have been murdered,' said Hempe.

'I need no reminding,' Nicholas said to Hempe, then turning to Owen. 'I've cooperated with you, Captain, and this is how you treat me?' There was a catch in his voice.

'I am acting on behalf of Archbishop Thoresby,' Owen said.

Nicholas said nothing for a moment, apparently waiting for more of an explanation. When none came, he said, 'Then I'll speak to His Grace, not you, the captain of his guard.'

'In good time,' said Owen. 'First I would ask you for the truth of how you came to have the Gamyll cross and this.' Owen held out the scrip. 'This is the one that Drogo the bargeman tossed to a lad on the barges the night he died, young Hubert's scrip. You knew where Master John of St Peter's had hidden it.'

His eyes wide with alarm Nicholas shouted, 'Why do you persecute me? What do you want of me? I've never seen that before.'

'I do not purpose to persecute you, but it's difficult for me to believe you've never seen it, Master Nicholas, for I found it tucked inside your dark red hat. And this was in it.' Owen held out the ring.

'My hat –' Nicholas shook his head as if trying to clear it. 'I've never seen that ring, either.' He glanced over at the pile, then at Hempe, who met his gaze without blinking, then back to Owen. 'Someone must have put the scrip there. Perhaps Chancellor Thomas had someone hide it here so that I'd be blamed. Murder. Theft. Deceit. They're determined to prove that I am not fit to teach the children of York, that I'm not fit to wear the cloth. They'll have me executed for spite since the archbishop won't agree to excommunicating me.' Spitting out the words, his eyes wild, Nicholas Ferriby looked unfit indeed. He rubbed his head again, then his brow.

'They do not need to go to such lengths,' said Owen, 'you know that. Help me prove your innocence, Master Nicholas.'

'I'll help you with nothing. I will speak to His Grace,' Nicholas insisted.

'So be it,' said Owen. 'We'll escort you to his palace.'

'God be praised,' cried Nicholas. 'His Grace will hear me.'

The setting sun had already disappeared in the city streets, though now and then as they walked a beam would flicker between the roofs, and in the ray of light it seemed that Owen could yet feel the sun's warmth, but he thought it unlikely. It was a confusing time of day, the play of light and shadow, the blue sky above and the darkness below. He wondered how Nicholas must be feeling if he was truly innocent of the theft of the scrip and ring. If innocent, what overwhelmingly damning 'evidence' he must now discredit. Owen wished he knew to whom the ring belonged. He prayed that they might find out in time to prevent another murder.

* * *

Hubert must have fallen asleep, because the next thing he knew Aubrey was gently shaking him.

'The sun's going down. Your ma will be worried,' he said.

At first Hubert went rigid with unease that his father was so close, but as he rubbed his eyes he remembered their conversation. Aubrey loved him even though he was Sir Baldwin's bastard. He'd loved him from the moment he was born.

'I don't want to go back to her, Da. Can't I stay with you?'

Sitting down on the pallet beside Hubert, Aubrey shook his head. 'I'll return to her soon. She is my wife, and I love her.'

'Even when she hurts you?'

Removing the hat that covered his dark, thinning hair, Aubrey scratched his head, then replaced the cap and sighed. 'You're still so young, Hubert. I'm not sure how much of all this you understand. But the love between a husband and wife who chose one another is not necessarily a happy love. We need each other, and it might be because of that need that we hurt each other, when one of us isn't paying enough attention to the other. I don't know. God knows I've done what I believe is expected of a husband.' He bowed his head. 'What was it that you lost?' he asked, looking up again. 'You mentioned a cross? A piece of jewellery belonging to Sir Baldwin?'

Hubert nodded. 'I didn't know then. I thought it was Ma's.'

'I wonder – perhaps she's frightened that he'll accuse her of stealing it.' Aubrey spoke so softly he seemed to be talking to himself.

'He already knows *I* took it.' Hubert thought this would be a good time to tell Aubrey about Osmund's visits. He opened his mouth, but he couldn't get out the words. He didn't want to hurt his father. Instead he scrambled to his feet and crossed to the door. With his back to his father, he thanked him for the afternoon. 'I love you,' he said, and was ready to hurry out.

But Aubrey joined him at the door. 'I'll walk with you to the top of the hill.'

In the deepening gloom Hubert was glad of the escort. The wind whipped the trees about, tossing debris in his face, forcing him to keep blinking. Even when he broke out into open sky the light was fast fading. He realised he must have slept a long while. They crossed the frozen stream and approached the hill.

Aubrey paused, sniffing. 'Who would be daft enough to light a fire in the fields in such wind?'

Hubert paused to wipe his eyes, while, muttering and huffing, Aubrey began the ascent. As Hubert started after him he started coughing. The smoke was thicker now.

'Christ God Almighty!' Aubrey shouted at the top and disappeared down the hill towards home.

When Hubert reached the top of the hill he did not at once comprehend what he saw. Down below it was all smoke and flames, like a field burning. But he should be able to see his house. As he resolved the layout in his mind he did not want to believe it and tried to figure out a different explanation. He could no longer follow his father's progress for the smoke and flames were all that he could see. His house stood in that field. His home. He began to run down the hill.

'Ma!' he shrieked. 'Ma!'

As he reached the field Hubert could see his house engulfed in flames, the high wind fanning them. The roar, hiss and crackle of the fire was terrifying, and it rose so high he felt overwhelmed, too small to have any effect on such a conflagration. But the large timbers still stood. It was not destroyed. He must save her. It was his fault. He should not have left her. The smoke choked and blinded him. Taking off his hood he covered his mouth and nose and pushed on towards the house.

'Whoa, son, whoa.'

Hubert was picked up and carried away from the fire, then set down but held tightly with powerful arms.

'Ma!' he shrieked. 'What if she's in there?'

'How long has it burned?' he heard Aubrey breathlessly ask and he wanted to shake him for wasting time on such a useless question.

'I've been here a while,' said the man holding Hubert. He realised it was Sir Baldwin. 'Where were you, Aubrey? Where've you been, man? My men searched for you.'

273

'God in heaven, save that for later. Has anyone seen Ysenda?' Aubrey's voice broke.

'No,' said Baldwin. 'My servants saw the flames and raised all the others they could find quickly. By the time we arrived we could do no more than soak the outbuildings. My hall is so near – I would have thought she'd flee to us. Surely Ysenda would have run for her life.'

'I pray God that she did,' Aubrey sobbed.

Hubert remembered his mother stumbling by the fire the previous evening. He did not know whether she would have been able to run in that state, and there had been more cider, plenty more for her to drink today. 'If she was drinking she might not have felt the fire until it was too late,' he cried.

Sir Baldwin mumbled something that Hubert could not understand as his son Osmund joined them.

'I saw you and the boy running down the hill just now, Master Aubrey. God's blood you took your time.'

Hubert almost spit at him. 'Don't talk to my da that way!'

'So where were you, Hubert?' Osmund asked with a sneer.

'Go help with the buckets,' Sir Baldwin snapped.

Hubert needed no one to fuel his feelings of guilt. 'I left her. I shouldn't have left her.' He gathered all his strength to push against Sir Baldwin's arms, but made no headway. They couldn't hold him here, it wasn't right. *God give me the strength to break free*. The flames boiled and flared, lighting the twilight with their ghastly glow, masking all that might yet be in the house. He could not stay still. He had no right to stand there in safety. He leaned into Sir Baldwin's arms again, but the man only tightened his grip.

'You love her, both of you. Why aren't you helping her?'

'To enter that blaze would be certain death,' said Aubrey. 'Your mother is no fool. She will have found her way to safety.'

'If she'd been injured,' Osmund said, 'she might have been trapped.'

'Dear God, don't let her die like this,' Hubert shrieked.

'Osmund, leave us,' Sir Baldwin commanded. 'Your father's right, Hubert,' he said in a far gentler tone, 'we must have faith that Ysenda is safely sitting beside a fire nearby. There is nothing we can do about anything that was in the house.'

Hubert finally collapsed against him and wept.

Looking beyond the servant who greeted them at the palace door, Owen saw Brother Michaelo reading to Archbishop Thoresby in the glow of lamps placed around them. Despite the fire in the middle of the hall a brazier burned near them. It was a scene of comfort and camaraderie that Owen was sorry to interrupt, knowing how disappointed

275

Thoresby would be to hear of the strong evidence against Nicholas Ferriby.

'If you would, ask His Grace if we might meet with him,' Owen said to the servant. 'I am accompanied by Master Nicholas Ferriby and the bailiff George Hempe.'

The servant bowed and crossed the room. Michaelo glanced towards the doorway and said something to the archbishop. Thoresby nodded and turned as the servant began to speak.

'Nicholas Ferriby, eh?' Owen could clearly hear Thoresby's deep voice. 'Show them in, and then bring chairs and wine.'

Once they were settled, Thoresby nodded to Owen. 'What has happened?'

'Your Grace, I asked them to bring me here,' said Master Nicholas. 'They are persecuting me.'

'Let us speak calmly and in good order,' said Thoresby, his deep-set eyes coolly dismissing Master Nicholas for the moment. 'Archer?'

Reminding himself that he was not the priest's keeper, Owen informed Thoresby of his meeting with Canon William, and then with Nicholas, the receipt of the cross, and his subsequent search of the chamber where he'd found the scrip and ring.

Thoresby leaned his head back against his high, cushioned chair, his expression pained. 'Nicholas Ferriby,' he said softly, 'you are a disappointment.'

'Your Grace,' Nicholas cried, rising from his chair.

'Be silent!' Thoresby commanded. 'Hempe, how do you come to be involved?'

Owen was curious how he would explain himself.

Hempe straightened up in his chair, placed his cup of wine on a small table beside him, and then cleared his throat. With an uncharacteristic deference he said, 'Your Grace, I am well aware that I have overreached my duties in assisting the captain, but I could not help myself. This city is not safe until the murderer is found and brought to justice. Since the beginning I have been uneasy in my mind about this murderer, that he has no fear of God. He did not kill in a rage and then repent. He planned his kills. I felt compelled to help Captain Archer however I might.'

'He's been of great help to me,' Owen said.

Thoresby sat with steepled hands, studying Hempe, and Owen thought he read approval in his expression.

'They had no right to search my chamber,' said Nicholas.

'Be quiet, Master Nicholas.' Thoresby had not moved his gaze from Hempe. 'You follow your conscience, Master Bailiff, I have witnessed this before in you. I thank you for assisting Archer in this distasteful search.'

Hempe's face glowed as he bowed to the archbishop. Owen was glad for him. The schoolmaster looked petulant. Owen thought it a strange little drama in the midst of something far more sinister.

'Now, Master Nicholas.' Thoresby still sat with his hands in front of his face as if his conversation was partly with himself. 'I interest myself in this business for the sake of my dear friend Emma Ferriby, not for any virtue of yours.'

Owen did not look over at Nicholas, for being blind in his left eye he'd need to turn quite obviously to see the man who sat to his left, and he was certain the man was already humbled enough. He knew how such words from the archbishop stung.

'I suppose you would say that Chancellor Thomas is also persecuting you,' Thoresby said with a sarcastic tone.

'He wants to excommunicate me for teaching the children of York who cannot attend St Peter's. Is that just?' Nicholas's face was quite red by now with righteous indignation and wine.

'Who was this Drogo to you?' Thoresby asked.

'He was a stranger, Your Grace. I wish I knew how he came to know that the cross belonged in my parish.' Nicholas tried to discreetly blot the sweat on his high forehead.

'Have you any idea how he would have known, Archer?' Thoresby asked.

Owen shook his head. 'None yet, Your Grace.'

Thoresby nodded. 'How do you suggest the scrip and ring came to be hidden in one of your hats, Master Nicholas?'

Now Owen permitted himself to turn his good eye on the schoolmaster, wanting to see how he received that question. Nicholas looked as mystified as he'd looked earlier.

'Your Grace, I cannot say. But as Captain Archer has just told us, Chancellor Thomas knew where the scrip had been hidden. I believe it possible that he ordered it put there.'

'Indeed? An interesting place to put it, in a hat.' Thoresby smirked. 'How do you suppose the chancellor came to have it?'

'Master John might have given it to him. Why would he keep it? But he might have removed it himself, or had it removed.'

'Your Grace,' Owen broke in, becoming impatient with Thoresby's baiting, 'Master John was keeping the scrip for Hubert when he returns. I was with him when he discovered it missing, and I believed his dismay.'

'And what of the ring, Archer?' asked Thoresby. 'To whom does it belong?'

'I don't yet know.'

'We'll leave that for now.' Thoresby dropped his hands and leaned forward, looking at Nicholas. 'I must ask you why you persist in keeping your school in the minster liberty when its presence there has caused so much distress. This is a large city, Master Nicholas, why not move it? I doubt that your scholars would desert you. Why must it be there?'

'The parents of my scholars deem it an honour to send their children to the liberty, Your Grace, and they count it a safe, respectable part of the city, with your guardsmen and so many clerics there. It pleases them.'

'I propose that it also feeds your pride, Master Nicholas.'

Owen found it difficult to sit still, having been Thoresby's target too often to find this comfortable.

Nicholas bristled but dropped his gaze in a gesture of humility. 'Your Grace, I swear to you that was not my purpose. I was offered a fair lease on the property, which was well suited for a schoolroom and my private chamber.'

'That may be so,' said Thoresby. 'We'll discuss this again. For now, the school is closed until your name is cleared.' He rose. All rose.

Nicholas stood with head bowed. Owen noticed that his knuckles were white as bone.

'Michaelo, have a room prepared for Master Nicholas,' said Thoresby.

Glancing up, Nicholas said, 'For me?'

'You'll bide here until such time as I know what to do with you.'

'You are most kind,' Nicholas murmured.

Thoresby had already turned to Owen and Hempe. 'Come with me to my parlour. I would talk further.'

As Owen followed Thoresby across the hall he was thinking about Canon William's presence when Master John tucked the scrip into the box. It was difficult to imagine Chancellor Thomas being so desperate as to put the scrip in Nicholas's chamber to implicate him, but excommunication was itself a desperate step. William had mentioned the scrip's hiding place to the chancellor.

In the parlour, Thoresby asked that they review with him all they knew so far and with whom they had talked. It was a tedious meeting and Owen was glad when he finally escaped into the cold evening air. He even welcomed the snow that had begun to fall in large flakes.

Standing well away from the burning house and behind the wind that fed the flames, Hubert and Sir Baldwin, along with many neighbours, watched in grim fascination the gradual collapse of the last upright pole. Aubrey was moving among the crowd asking whether any had seen Ysenda. There was an audible sigh from the watchers when the pole settled in the embers.

Sir Baldwin put a hand on Hubert's shoulder, 'There is no more to see, lad, and we've all breathed too much smoke and ash. Come to the hall. You will stay with us until you return to school.'

'And Da?' Hubert felt strange, speaking of his adoptive father with his natural father. He wondered whether Sir Baldwin thought of him as his son at all.

'Aubrey shall come as well. He has saved my life many a time in France. I can at least shelter him and help him search for your mother in return.'

They waited until Aubrey made his way back to them. He was shaking his head. 'No one has seen her. Tomorrow, in daylight –' He pressed his hands to his face.

Hubert put a hand on his forearm. 'Come, Da, let's go to the hall. Sir Baldwin says we're to bide with him there.'

Dropping his hands, Aubrey lifted his face to the sky and howled. It was a terrible sound, filled with anguish like an animal caught in a trap. Hubert crossed himself and knelt to pray that his mother had escaped the fire.

Snow began to fall again as they quietly walked to the manor house, giving Hubert a new worry, that his mother had not had the presence of mind to take a warm cloak as she'd fled, if she'd fled.

Though Hempe had hurried on, Owen was still standing on the steps to the archbishop's palace watching the snow when Peter Ferriby, Emma's husband, took the steps two at a time and halted just below him, gasping for breath and obviously concerned.

'I heard that my brother Nicholas was escorted here by you and one of the city bailiffs, Owen.' Peter was larger and more imposing than either of his brothers, partially due to his quietly elegant attire.

'He was,' said Owen. 'We found Hubert de Weston's scrip in your brother's chamber, and a ring that he swears he's never seen before. He demanded to speak with the archbishop, so we escorted him here.'

Peter looked away with a curse, then back to Owen. 'You searched my brother's chamber? Why did you think to do that?'

Owen told him about Nicholas's inability to explain why Drogo would have given him the Gamyll cross, and William's admission that he'd told Nicholas where Master John had hidden the scrip.

'I see.' Peter dropped his gaze, slowly shaking his head. 'God help him.'

'I'm certain he would welcome your company right now,' said Owen, patting him on the shoulder. 'I'm going home.'

Wrapped in blankets and sipping spiced wine, Hubert and Aubrey listened to Sir Baldwin's account of Owen Archer's visit and the missing cross, as well as the murder of Drogo.

Hubert's father slumped lower and lower as he listened with dismay to the tale. '*That* cross,' he cried when Sir Baldwin was finished. 'Why did you take that, Hubert? What could you want with a birthing cross?'

'A very good question,' laughed Osmund as he rose from his comfortable chair by the fire. 'I regret that I cannot stay to hear your explanation. I pray you, be at ease.' Despite his lazy expression he seemed in a hurry to depart.

But Hubert was glad to see the back of him. 'I didn't know what it was, Da.' He felt himself blushing. He unhappily repeated how he'd wanted something of his mother's close to him. It seemed foolish now, and worse, it had not even been hers. He wished he could forget it.

'That such a simple, innocent act could cause a man's death. God have mercy on us,' Aubrey said, crossing himself.

Hubert had expected anger and felt a wave of relief wash over him. Aubrey seemed far more concerned about why Ysenda had taken the cross in the first place. 'She said nothing about being with child or having lost one,' he said.

'Osmund found it odd when I told him about all this earlier,' said Baldwin.

'It isn't right, talking about Ma like this when she's out there somewhere,' Hubert blurted out.

A long, uncomfortable silence descended on the room.

'Drogo,' Aubrey said, suddenly breaking the spell. 'The miller and his wife who died in the pestilence had a son called Drogo.'

'The miller's son. Sweet Jesu, you are right, Aubrey,' said Baldwin. 'I wish I'd remembered that for Captain Archer.' He glanced at his young wife, who was sitting quietly, her sewing forgotten in her lap. 'It is a common name in the parish, but uncommon elsewhere.'

She smiled at him. 'It is a large estate, my lord. How could you remember the names of all the children?'

* * *

As the snow fell without the house, Lucie, Phillippa, Alisoun and the children sat close to the hall fire, listening to Phillippa's tales of life at Freythorpe. Gwenllian loved to hear about her grandfather, Sir Robert, whom she remembered. Hugh had been too small to remember him well.

Lucie kept watching the door, anxious to tell Owen about all she'd learned from Drogo's widow. At last he appeared, rosy cheeked from the cold and well dusted with snow – and looking exhausted, the lines in his face etched more deeply than usual. She waited until he'd settled with a cup of ale and appeared to be both warm and comfortable before telling him of Cissy's visit.

When she described the ring, he sat forward and excitedly asked her to repeat what she'd said. 'The ring in the scrip,' he said when she'd done so. He seemed unaware of her for some moments. 'It does not fit with the rest. But the Gamylls' miller, yes, that could tie them together.' He suddenly focused again on Lucie. 'Tell me everything, what she looks like, what she said, anything you can recall.'

She understood his interest once he told her about finding the scrip in Nicholas's chamber, with the ring hidden inside.

'Drogo might have put it there while he had the scrip and forgotten to remove it when he returned it,' she said. 'You did not notice it at first.'

'I don't believe that,' said Owen. 'Geoffrey was quite certain that the scrip was empty, and surely

Master John handled the scrip enough to have noticed the ring if it had been in there. Someone put the two together and placed them in Nicholas's chamber, someone determined to make him look guilty of something far worse than opening a school in the minster liberty.'

Lucie could think of only two people who might wish to do that, and she could not believe they would sink to such depths. 'It cannot be the chancellor and dean.'

Owen rubbed the scar beneath his patch, a sign of deep weariness. 'At present I can think of no one else, my love.'

She was incredulous. 'You think it possible?'

He shrugged.

Lucie found the idea of Churchmen behaving so ignobly, with so little regard to human life, very disturbing. 'Nicholas could be put to death for such offences.'

'I know. Someone will be. *Someone* murdered those two men.'

She moved next to him and took his hand. 'Owen, do you think Nicholas might be guilty?'

'Could he be such a fool?' He leaned his forehead against Lucie's, and she wished he would gather her up and take her upstairs, though as she followed the thought she realised it would not be quite as romantic as her spontaneous thought. 'I don't know, Lucie, I think him a stubborn fool for challenging St Peter's School, but that does not make him a murderer.'

She moved a little so she could kiss Owen on the lips. She would never tire of him.

'No, that does not make him a murderer,' she agreed, 'just a foolish man. I suppose you'll return to the palace after supper?'

Owen sighed, then pulled her to him and gave her a lingering kiss. 'Yes, I must trudge through the snow to ask more questions. It is my duty, though I curse the need to leave you.' His quiet evening with Lucie was not to be.

Ten

SNOW AND ASHES

O wen could not believe his good fortune in Lucie's long talk with Drogo's widow. He did not know how long Nicholas had been the pastor in Weston, and he did not want to wait until morning to ask him whether he remembered Drogo. As soon as he'd eaten enough to quiet his hunger pangs he was out the door and turning up High Petergate towards the archbishop's palace.

Brother Michaelo expressed no surprise at finding him at the door, merely flaring his elegant nose and pursing his lips, then nodding back towards the dinner table. 'Master Nicholas is amusing, so awed by His Grace's presence that he cannot make conversation. He will find no peace here. I pray you have interesting news, Captain.'

'I do. And I hope that Master Nicholas will be able to fill in some of Drogo's past.'

'Do you? Hmm. I shall keep my doubts to myself.' Michaelo hummed as he escorted Owen to the table where the three had been dining. A servant brought a chair for Owen, and poured him wine.

Master Nicholas's greeting was surprisingly friendly, Owen thought, as if he was relieved by his presence. Only hours ago he'd accused Owen of persecuting him.

Archbishop Thoresby inquired whether Owen was hungry. The meat looked too tempting to refuse. Michaelo graciously led some idle talk about the snowfall until Owen had eaten a little, by which point Thoresby would wait no longer and interrupted his secretary.

'What is amiss, Archer? You are not in the habit of dining here without being ordered to attend me.' Thoresby studied Owen's face as he sipped his wine.

'I would have a word with Master Nicholas,' Owen said, 'and it is as well to do it over a fine supper as with just a cup of wine before the fire. Unfortunately, the topic is not pleasant, so I ask your leave to pursue it at your table, Your Grace.'

Thoresby gestured for him to go ahead.

Owen faced Nicholas with hope rather than suspicion for once. 'Today Drogo's widow spoke with my wife. Apparently the ring we found in the scrip belonged to Drogo's family, and that family ran a mill on the Gamyll estate until the parents died in the first coming of the pestilence. Drogo grew up on the estate.'

Nicholas inhaled sharply and then, tightly clasping his hands together on the table before

289

him he focused his gaze on them as if to will them to lie still. 'I know what you are about to ask, Captain, and I wish that I could help you, but I must instead disappoint you. I received the living of Weston only nine years ago.'

Owen bit back a curse.

Now that he'd begun, Nicholas seemed eager to talk. 'In my time the mill has been run by someone else. I've never heard mention of Drogo there. But it might explain how he knew to whom the cross belonged, why he brought it to me. I am the subject of enough gossip that he might have heard I had the parish of Weston.'

'This ring,' said Thoresby. 'Surely Drogo had not placed the ring in the scrip only to forget it when he handed it to the lad?'

Owen shook his head. 'Either the lads or Master John would have noticed the ring had it been in there. Drogo's widow was robbed, and that is most likely when it disappeared from her home.'

'She is not certain?' asked Thoresby.

'No. She seldom wore it.' Owen could see that Thoresby was not convinced. He wondered whether it was he who was jumping to conclusions.

'When did this happen?' asked Michaelo.

'During the funeral mass for her husband,' Owen said. 'She returned home to find that someone had searched the house. Some pennies were also taken.'

'Poor woman,' said Nicholas. 'She has suffered much.'

290

'I believe you can dismiss Master Nicholas from suspicion for the theft,' said Brother Michaelo. 'I can vouch for his presence at the service. You are cheated of an answer once more.' He spread his hands and tilted his head mocking sympathy.

'Of course I attended,' said Nicholas, 'despite the gossips' eyes on me. Drogo had reached out to me, and, though I did not know why he had done so, I felt a responsibility to pray for his soul.'

Owen tried not to wonder how the priest might have used that to his advantage. It was time to listen.

Thoresby drummed his fingers on the table. 'This is impossible. *Someone* stole the ring and the scrip, and murdered the two men, but all the evidence seems to steer us in circles.'

It was time for Owen to propose the journey he wished he did not need to make. 'Your Grace, I believe the answers lie in Weston. I propose that I take Alfred and ride hard at dawn.'

'Are you growing fond of riding through snow?' Brother Michaelo asked.

Owen was accustomed to Michaelo's sarcasm. He suspected that the monk envied him for his more active service.

Thoresby sighed. 'I pray that you resolve this long before Dame Lucie is brought to bed. Do what you think best, Archer. My stables and guards are at your disposal.'

'Might I be of use to you, Captain?' asked Nicholas.

'I doubt it,' said Owen. 'If someone is trying to convince us that you are the guilty one, I'd rather have you safely hidden in this palace.'

'Oh.' Nicholas sounded forlorn.

Michaelo smirked. Owen remembered what he'd said about Nicholas being awestruck in Thoresby's presence.

In the wee hours Hubert woke from a sad dream about a dog he'd once had. He'd been awakened by a rustling sound – the pallet that he shared with Aubrey near the hall fire was stuffed with straw – and he rolled over to discover his father with shoes in hand sneaking away. Hubert grabbed his own shoes and followed his father across the hall, taking his cloak from a hook just as Aubrey reached for his.

As his pale blue eyes caught the firelight's glow he looked blind. 'Go back to bed, lad, it's just dawn. You need your sleep.'

'You're going to the ruins, aren't you?'

'I won't lie to you, son. I want to see what there is to see. I'll tell you what I find.'

'I want to go with you.'

'It's snowing. You can go out later.'

'It might be snowing later today as well.'

Aubrey bowed his head for a moment, then nodded. 'You're old enough to have the sense to turn back if it's too cold for you, eh? You'd do that, wouldn't you?'

Hubert nodded.

His breath was ghostly in the pale light, and the snow seemed to whisper all about them. He followed his father's footprints, trying to keep his strides long and manly. What if they found his mother's bones – would he cry or would he be angry that she'd wasted herself? He did not know, and the uncertainty frightened him. He'd always lived for his mother, worshipped her, did everything with a thought to how she would react when he told her about it. If he no longer cared about her, his life was utterly changed. He wondered whether he was still really Hubert.

The dark hedge that separated his parents' farm from the manor grounds loomed up before him, stark against the whiteness, though softened above where pillows of snow rested precariously. He'd never liked the hedge, imagining horrors caught in its ancient prickly branches, the corpses of birds, bugs enshrouded in forgotten webs, lost kittens half-eaten by vermin. He could not remember why the hedge had been so populated in his imagination, but even this morning, trying as he was to be a grown man, he held his breath and hurried through the archway, shivering as he made it past.

But a worse horror lay before him, down in the hollow, the smouldering remains of the house in which he'd been born and lived all his life. Smoke still rose from the centre of the pile. Some of the outer parts were blanketed with snow. His home had been reduced to scattered piles of charcoal.

Aubrey put an arm round his shoulder.

'We thank thee, O Lord, that we have each other. What we have lost is but a shell against the weather.'

'And Ma?' Hubert whispered, unwilling to say it louder.

'I still hope that she was away, son. It is most likely that she escaped.'

In the quiet morning a shifting piece of wood echoed loudly as a figure rose from the edge of the rubble.

'Who's that?' Hubert pointed to him.

'That cursed Osmund,' Aubrey said, withdrawing his arm and striding forward through the drifts.

Hubert tried to keep up with him, but quickly fell behind. He shared Aubrey's irritation about Osmund beating them to the ruins. He had no right. She was theirs. *God forgive me for not telling Da about Osmund's visits. I swear if Ma isn't in the ruins I'll tell him today.* Bargaining with the Almighty might not be the most respectful approach, but Hubert thought that if man had truly been made in God's likeness, the Lord would not be adverse to making a deal.

The blackened grass was encased in brittle ice that slowed Hubert even more. His father was already shouting at Osmund, who continued picking up bits of wood and crockery, dropping them, and then moving on.

'What right have you? Leave us. Do you hear me? Leave us!'

Aubrey finally grabbed Osmund by the elbow and caught him off balance. The young man flapped his arms trying to right himself. Aubrey grabbed his shoulders and turned him so that they were nose to nose.

'How dare you accost me!' Osmund growled, shrugging him off.

'Don't play lord with me, young sir. Get out of my personal belongings.'

Osmund glanced around. 'Belongings? Hah! You are welcome to what's left of them, Master Aubrey.'

For a few moments the two men stood facing each other. Hubert tried to neither breathe nor move.

'You're a fool, Master Aubrey,' said Osmund, beginning to pick his way out of the ruins. 'She's probably run away with a new lover.'

Aubrey cursed and threw a piece of debris that caused Osmund to jump as it landed at his feet.

After he left, father and son sifted through the blackened remains. They found no trace of Ysenda. Hubert was grateful.

Trudging back to the hall, Aubrey asked Hubert if he had any idea what Osmund might have been looking for.

Hubert just shrugged, distracted by a sudden disturbing memory. *Why, it's Ysenda's lad. What treasures have you stolen from her hoard, boy?* Drogo's question had frightened him. That's why he'd run away from him. He'd told no one what

295

the pilot had said. He hadn't remembered. He hadn't wanted to remember his mother's darker side.

In the courtyard Sir Baldwin was organising servants and tenants into search parties. Lady Gamyll greeted Hubert and Aubrey at the door with hot cider and concern.

'Did you find anything?'

'We found no sign of Ysenda, my lady,' said Aubrey. 'You are kind to ask. God grant that I shall see her again in this life.' He broke off at that and strode briskly towards the fire.

Hubert realised that his father had hurried away so that Lady Gamyll would not see him weep.

'Go comfort your father,' said Lady Gamyll. 'I'll bring bread, cheese and some broth to warm you.'

Hubert joined Aubrey. 'We'll find her, Da. We will.'

Yesterday's high wind had scoured the sky, making room last night for billowing clouds and snow to rush in from the North Sea. This morning the heavy, wet snow delighted Gwenllian and Hugh. They were rolling it into small balls and having raucous battles in the garden. Lucie and Alisoun sat at the window watching them.

Alisoun sighed for the hundredth time. 'How long will the school be shut? What fool believes that Master Nicholas is a murderer and a thief?'

'The evidence is against him, Alisoun,' Lucie said quietly as she smiled at Hugh's desperate efforts to form a snowball as firm as his sister's. Contradictory feelings were a matter of course during pregnancy.

But Alisoun took offence. 'Do I amuse you, Dame Lucie?' Her face was pinched with resentment. Her hair tucked into a white cap, Alisoun looked more vulnerable than usual with her exceedingly thin neck exposed.

Lucie took her hand, realising how insecure she must feel about her future. 'Not you, child, Hugh. He is so earnest. As for Master Nicholas, I am no happier about his troubles than you are. His sister-in-law is my good friend, and well you know that. Let's talk of something else. You say you are keen to be a healer. Have you always wished to be one?'

Alisoun shook her head as she slipped her hand from Lucie's. 'I wanted to work with horses. That is all I wanted to do.'

'Yes. I recall how you tended your family's horse,' said Lucie. 'What made you change your mind? What has inspired you to become a healer of men?'

'Meeting the Riverwoman. When I was biding in her home I saw that she did not fear what would happen if she weren't like others. She knew how to live in the world in her own way. Her life is free of pain.'

Lucie opened her mouth to comment that in any craft she might develop strength of character, but Alisoun did not pause.

297

'Master Nicholas is so discouraged by the threat of excommunication, and now the charges and suspicion that hound him, that he spoke to us and withdrew all the brave and inspiring things he'd said about the Church so that they could not be used against him. He's a coward. The Riverwoman would never be so meek.' Alisoun's colour had risen as she spoke, and her eyes flashed with anger. 'And the dean and chancellor – they're so keen to accuse him of all the wrongs in the city that they are letting the true murderer go free.'

Lucie knew that was a danger. 'It is the city's fortune that my husband is not convinced by their accusations and is still searching,' she said. 'But you are wrong about Magda feeling no pain. She has a heart as do we all, Alisoun, and she has known great sorrow. It is from her knowledge of pain and sorrow that she heals.'

'She knows all about roots and healing plants,' said Alisoun.

Lucie nodded. 'That, also.'

'What sorrow has she suffered?'

'That is for you to ask Magda. But tell me, what draws you to healing besides wanting to be like her?'

Alisoun, grown sullen, shrugged and peered out the window. 'The children look too wet. I must bring them in to sit by the fire.' She rose.

'Stay a moment, Alisoun. You have been here more than a year, yet we are almost strangers.

You are so gentle and loving with my children. That is a great strength in you. Is that what you wish to use in healing?'

Sinking back down, Alisoun slowly shook her head. 'I don't feel the same about people once they're grown. Just animals and children.'

'Why do you think that is?'

She regarded Lucie with her dark brown eyes, an unwavering gaze that she used to keep people at a distance. 'I don't know. I get impatient. People can be very disappointing.'

The gaze, the comment – Lucie would never quite know what inspired her, but she believed she'd just seen through the role Alisoun had been playing for a long while, as long as Lucie had known her. She hesitated to point it out to the girl, doubting that she could express it in a palatable way. She tried a question.

'What do you expect of people?'

'More,' Alisoun said with a bitter little laugh.

'What do you think people expect of you?'

A flinch was quickly replaced by a harder stare. Lucie saw it so clearly now, the girl's fierce defences.

'I don't care what people expect of me,' she said through clenched teeth.

'We regret the need for a wet nurse, Alisoun. I pray you believe that. Dame Magda never intended for you to be our children's nurse for so long. She said you wanted to be a healer. But I would still be your friend.' Lucie reached for one

299

of Alisoun's hands. The girl jerked away. 'Forgive me. I thought that perhaps as you love my children, you might accept my friendship,' Lucie said. 'Let me just sow an idea in your mind, Alisoun. You sit in stern, unforgiving judgement over yourself and others, allowing no joy but in children and animals. If you are ever the judge you'll find no joy in life.'

Alisoun shot up, already facing away from Lucie as she said, 'I must see to the children, Dame Lucie.' She walked stiffly to the door.

Holy Mary, Mother of God, I tried. Give me the grace to reach my children as they grow. I would know their hearts, and they mine. Lucie had experienced difficult times with Jasper, but it was his nature to want to understand and cooperate with those around him, so his sullen moods had never lasted. She wished that Alisoun would open her heart, even just a little.

A rapping on the street door brought Lucie to her feet, but Phillippa reached the door before her. Thank the lord that she was clear today. She escorted Emma Ferriby and her servant into the hall.

'Do not cross the room to greet me,' Emma said, hurrying towards Lucie with her arms outstretched. 'I am lighter than you at present.' She laughed as she embraced Lucie, but quickly sobered as she settled on a bench, reaching her hands out towards the fire. 'So here I am again, my friend, begging you for encouragement about

300

Nicholas's misfortunes. William came this morning to tell us that they've shut Nicholas's school, have you heard? Peter says they've imprisoned him at the archbishop's palace. What does Owen say of that?'

Lucie covered her smile and nodded to Kate to bring wine. 'Biding with His Grace is hardly imprisonment, Emma. Archbishop Thoresby lives well, eats well, and ensures that his surroundings are pleasing and restful. Nicholas is most fortunate, truth be told.'

Emma thanked Kate for the cup of wine, but set it aside. 'There is more, Lucie. William says that Chancellor Thomas had brought up Nicholas's heretical opinions in chapter, accusing him of teaching them to his young scholars and thereby endangering their faith. It was inappropriate to discuss in chapter, but of course he was merely sowing the poisonous seed.'

'By the saints, that is troublesome news.' Lucie glanced out at Alisoun, who was still trying to convince the children to come inside. 'Alisoun says that he withdrew those comments, telling the students he was in error.'

Emma tapped an elegantly shod foot. 'William says he's prepared to accept Nicholas's vow to abstain from such controversial comments. He believes that most of the chapter would be satisfied with such a promise. But Nicholas must be cleared of all suspicion regarding the murders and the thefts.' With a shake of her head she took

Lucie's hand and pressed it. 'We all count on Owen for that.' Her eyes sought reassurance.

'He is doing all he can, Emma. Indeed, he's riding to Weston this morning, convinced that it is there he'll find the answers.'

'He's left you again? Now I feel guilty. But we are desperate.'

'Your good friend the archbishop will not rest until he is assured that all is well with Nicholas. It is not you who is pushing Owen away.'

'William had something to say about the archbishop's interest in clearing the Ferriby name, you can be certain, for he's heard it too often in the chapter. They say that John Thoresby forgets that he is the Archbishop of York with a duty to represent the interests and needs of the North in Westminster and at court. To their minds he is so old and his illnesses have so weakened his mind that he believes he is a parish priest again.'

Lucie said something banal in support of the archbishop but she was saddened by such gossip. Owen had expressed concern for Thoresby's weakened health, but she had hoped it was not apparent to the public. Yet how could it go unnoticed when he was the second highest-ranking churchman in the realm, and a former Lord Chancellor, a man expected to make his presence felt in Parliament, in Westminster, and subtly in Canterbury, ensuring that the highest-ranking churchman in the realm did not forget the North.

* * *

As the light faded early, the sun hidden by snow clouds, the search parties straggled back to the stables, cold, weary, and frustrated. Though the snow the previous afternoon had begun late, and so had not been deep, the wind would have limited the amount of walking Ysenda would have managed, certainly if she'd been injured. Yet none of the neighbours had seen her, none of the outbuildings sheltered her.

'Perhaps Osmund was right.' Aubrey cursed as he sank down before the fire in the hall. 'She rode off with a lover, and we'll never track her. Christ, to never know.' He groaned as he tugged at his sparse hair. One of his hands was bandaged and needed tending – a huge splinter had sunk into the meaty part of his thumb when he'd pried open the door of an outbuilding. 'Cursed door.'

Hubert wished he weren't in his lord's hall, because he thought a scream would help him release the tight band around his chest. For now, he went in search of a servant who could see to his father's hand. He was directed to the kitchen behind the hall, and brought Aubrey there to an elderly woman who with perfectly steady hands soaked the wound and gradually coaxed out the splinter in one piece. She smiled and nodded at Aubrey's profuse thanks. All the while she'd worked on him she had said not a word.

When they returned to the hall everyone grew quiet as they turned to look at father and son.

Frightened to think what it meant, Hubert thought his heart stopped beating.

And then Lady Gamyll came to them, smiling and reaching out for their hands. 'Dame Ysenda has been found. She is weak, injured, and in a fever sleep, but she is alive.'

'God be praised!' Aubrey cried and kissed her hand. 'My lady, my lady, God bless you.'

Hubert fell to his knees and bowed his head to say a prayer of thanks for his mother's deliverance. Lady Gamyll knelt to him.

'They are bringing her in a wagon. She'll be here very soon.' She hugged him. 'I thought my mother was dead in a flood when I was about your age. I remember how that felt, young Hubert, I remember.' She smiled at him with such understanding that he clung to her.

When they rose, he saw his father wiping his eyes with his bandaged hand, and was glad for him. People crowded round them with offers of drink and pats on the back. Hubert discovered his appetite once more.

It was a brief interlude of happiness. When they carried in his mother he thought she looked pale as death, with a deep gash in her head and a bandaged hand hanging limply from a blackened sleeve. Lady Gamyll called servants and they disappeared with her into a room screened off from the main hall.

Aubrey rushed out of the hall to talk to the farmer who had found her, and Hubert followed.

The farmer lived outside the range of the day's search, but even so he'd searched his outbuildings for her when he'd gotten word she was missing, even before he'd joined them in the morning. He'd found no sign of her.

'But when I returned home, my daughter was babbling about a woman at the pond, an old weedy place I hardly ever go, but the young ones play there in summer. God must have sent her there today, for that's where I found your good wife, Aubrey, lying with her hand out in the icy water. She'll lose it, I trow, it did not look good and who knows how long she'd been lying there. Poor Ysenda.' He took off his cap and wiped his eyes.

Lying there all night with her burned hand in the freezing water. Hubert wondered whether she could have still been drunk. He remembered Aubrey carrying her in the previous winter, having found her snoring in one of the outbuildings, her clothes soaked in cider. Hubert had thought she'd been knocked out as a jug of cider fell on her, and that's how it had opened and soaked her, but he knew better now. God forgive him for thinking ill of her when she might be dying.

'God bless you and your family,' Aubrey said as the man and his son prepared to leave.

'You'd do the same for me,' said the farmer. 'God watch over you and yours. We'll be praying for Ysenda.'

They stood there a while, Hubert standing close

to his dad and looking up at the stars that twin-kled in the patches of clear sky in between the scudding clouds. He had an ache deep down in his stomach. This growing up was frightening. He understood too much yet not enough, and he feared it would only get worse.

'How do you bear it, Da?'

Aubrey looked down at him. 'Bear what?'

'Everything. Nothing's what I thought it was.'

'Let's go in, see if they'll let us see your mother.'

Folk clustered around the fire, quiet now, the efforts of the day beginning to show in their faces and their slumping shoulders. Hubert's feet ached, but not so badly as they had on his journey home from York.

They met a servant coming from the screened room. She was carrying a bowl of bloody rags and frowned at them as she hurried past.

Lady Gamyll stood in the doorway holding a tray with a cup, a small spoon, and small bottle. Her sleeves were covered with protective rags and her apron was already blood-stained and streaked with something darker. She was watching the silent woman who'd tended Aubrey – she now sat at the edge of the bed in which Ysenda lay, wrapping her head as a servant held it. Ysenda's burned hand was propped on a cloth-wrapped board, glistening – with grease, Hubert guessed. The rest of her arm looked much better than the hand, red to the elbow, then fine as far as he could see from the doorway.

'Could we sit with her?' Aubrey asked Lady Gamyll.

'In the morning,' the healer called out. So she did have a voice, and a strong one. 'We have work to do tonight, and then she must rest.'

'Will she live?' Hubert asked.

The woman shrugged. 'If God so wishes.'

'I am her husband.' Aubrey's voice rang out so loudly Hubert expected his mother to respond. But even that did not wake her.

'God watch over you,' said the healer. 'I know this is painful for you. I am doing all that I know how for her.'

'God bless you,' said Aubrey, crossing himself and turning away.

Hubert felt numb as he followed his father back out into the still-crowded hall. 'Can we walk outside and talk, Da?' He intended to tell him everything. He could think of no benefit in secrecy.

But Aubrey shook his head. 'On the morrow, son, on the morrow. Tonight I want to forget.' He poured himself a full mazer of wine and settled by the fire, staring into the flames.

So that was how he bore it. And tomorrow he might forget how he felt tonight? Hubert thought it a poor solution. But it made him wonder what his mother tried to forget with all the cider. The loss of his brother and sister, perhaps, or maybe she still loved Sir Baldwin and resented his new lady. Or was the bargeman someone she tried to forget? Hubert headed out to the stables to see if he could find kittens or puppies or a lonely horse for company.

A wan sun did little to warm Owen as he rode hard, Alfred just a little ahead of him. At least they'd dried their cloaks by the fire in the wretched inn in which they'd tried to sleep the night on the floor, visited by curious rats and ravenous fleas. The snow had chilled them too much to keep riding until they might find a better place to stop for the night.

A groom greeted them in the yard before Sir Baldwin's hall, helping them dismount and then taking their horses away to be rubbed down and fed. Lady Gamyll met them at the door, looking tired.

'Captain Archer, you are most welcome in our hall. But I pray you, how are you come so soon? News of the fire cannot have reached York so quickly.'

'I know nothing of a fire, my lady. Tell me, if you would.'

'Aubrey's house – oh, here, my lord will tell you . . .'

They'd been joined by Sir Baldwin and a dark-haired man with startling blue eyes who was introduced as Aubrey, the missing spouse. Owen studied him with interest. He looked every bit a soldier, great strength in shoulders and thighs, a scarred face and hands. They told Owen and Alfred about the fire and Ysenda's injuries.

'When her fever is down the hand should be removed,' said Sir Baldwin. 'We feared to do it sooner.'

Owen crossed himself and said a prayer for Ysenda remembering the horror of amputations in the field camps when he fought in France.

'May God ease her pain, and yours,' said Owen.

'Now it is your turn to tell us what has happened since you departed,' said Sir Baldwin.

Aubrey was quiet, and, having heard about the condition of his wife and his loss of property, Owen understood his silence.

'Another man was murdered in York,' Owen began, 'by the name of Nigel, a goldsmith's journeyman. The pilot Drogo had shown him your cross, Sir Baldwin, and someone did not like that he'd done so.'

'Drogo,' said Baldwin. 'He grew up at the mill on my land, Captain. I'm sorry I'd forgotten.'

'I found that out.' Owen turned his eye on Aubrey. 'Do you remember him?'

Pale blue eyes considered Owen's face, making him conscious of his scars, the leather patch over his left eye. Aubrey removed his hat and bunched it in his hands. 'I knew him to speak to, Captain Archer, but his da and his older brother saw to us when we brought corn to be ground and then picked up the sacks of flour, so I know nothing of his life, his state of grace. And that was so many years ago.' His eyes were swollen – from

weeping and fighting the fire, Owen guessed –
and seemed sensitive to light.

'As I recall he was a good lad,' said Sir Baldwin.

'Did your wife live here as a child, Master
Aubrey?' Owen asked.

He nodded, with reluctance it seemed to Owen.
'I'd like to talk to your son. Is Hubert here?'

'He's sitting with his mother,' said Aubrey. 'I'll
ask you –'

He was silenced by a look from Sir Baldwin.

Owen asked Aubrey how Hubert was faring.
He said that Hubert felt responsible for the fire,
that he believed that if he'd been at home it would
not have happened. The boy had not explained
why he was so certain of that.

Lady Gamyll escorted Owen across the hall.
'I'll bring wine,' she said as she left him in the
doorway.

The stench of burned flesh was familiar to
Owen. Ysenda's right hand was burned as if she'd
tried to rescue something from the fire. The burn
extended midway up her forearm, so she'd either
reached for something very near or realised too
late that she'd extended her hand into flames. The
gash on her forehead might have happened as she
fled, falling forward.

The lad sat on a stool beside his mother, holding
her good hand.

Owen crouched down beside him. 'Might I look
at your mother's palm, Hubert?'

'Captain Archer,' the boy said, his eyes welling

with tears. 'If I'd gone with you to York –' He turned away, sniffing.

Owen lifted Ysenda's good hand. The palm was bruised and scraped, as it would be if she'd tried to break a tumble forward.

A servant brought a tray with a flagon of wine and a mazer. Owen thanked her, then sat back to study Hubert, who still averted his face.

'Do you think the fire wouldn't have happened if you'd been in York?' Owen asked as he poured the wine. 'Is that what you were going to say?'

Hubert shrugged. 'Why did you come back?'

'I learned that Drogo grew up here. Another man was murdered, Hubert. Father Nicholas's school is closed. I'm worried that more people will suffer. If you have anything you've not yet told me, I pray you, trust me with it.'

He noticed a subtle change in the boy's breathing. He'd raised his shoulders a little as if protecting himself.

'Why do you feel so guilty about your mother's injuries?'

'She's always counted on me to be there to help her.'

At least he was talking. 'Does she need a lot of help?'

'When Da's not there.' Hubert's voice caught and he looked away. 'It's all gone. Our home. Everything.'

Owen remembered how hard it had been for him as a boy when his family moved from the

311

home in which he'd been born, how he'd missed every nook and corner.

'I am sorry. I know it is a great loss.'

The boy took a deep, shuddering breath and nodded.

'Did Drogo say anything to you when he took the scrip, Hubert? Did he know you?'

It was clear that the question startled the boy. He moved his head this way and that as if he didn't know where to look.

'He did, didn't he?' Owen asked, pressing him in this vulnerable moment.

Lady Gamyll came in, explaining that she was to smooth more grease on Ysenda's burned hand.

Owen silently cursed.

'Why don't we stretch our legs, Hubert?' he said, rising. 'I'd like to go to the scene of the fire. Will you take me there?'

'I want to stay by Ma.'

Lady Gamyll gave Owen a sympathetic smile.

He wanted to grab up the boy and take him away from the stench, but he respected his wishes and left alone.

Closing his eyes, Hubert struggled with the urge to run after Captain Archer to tell him what Drogo said to him the day he took the scrip. He wanted to tell him, but he was afraid that the captain would push his mother to talk. She needed rest. He might be too angry – two men had died – to be patient with her. And Hubert was frightened.

Aubrey had sat with him earlier. He looked awful. Hubert had asked him whether the wine had helped, and he'd groaned. Hubert wondered how someone like Captain Archer, who seemed to know so much, dealt with the hard things in life. He bet he didn't drink to forget.

Enough thinking now. He was here to pray for his ma. He tried to push everything else out of his mind and concentrate on his prayers for his mother's recovery, and her safety. She frightened him sometimes, and hurt him, but she was his mother and he loved her. Nothing would ever be all right again if he lost her.

Eleven

COVETOUSNESS

O wen carried the flagon and mazer with him into the hall and looked around for Aubrey. He found him sitting by the fire and settled down beside him despite Aubrey's unfriendly look.

Owen held up the flagon. 'I've more than enough for both of us.'

Aubrey groaned. He sat with his elbows on his knees, his hands supporting his head. He smelled of stale sweat.

'I have a head full of last night's wine, Captain. I hoped if I sat very still I might survive the morning.'

Owen was familiar with that feeling. 'If we were in York I'd offer you some feverfew in watered wine for your aching head, with some additional herbs for your belly. My wife is an apothecary.'

'Your wife?' Aubrey winced as he turned towards Owen. His colour was pale and dull. 'I didn't think of you as a married man. But my lord did say you'd had your son with you last time.' He paused for breath. 'I suppose you have more questions?'

'Aye. It would help to know where you were for several days.'

Aubrey pressed his temples. 'How would that help? Do you think I went to York and murdered those men?' He'd returned his gaze to the fire, his speech listless, not angry.

'No, I'm accusing you of nothing.'

'Are you blaming my son?'

'No, I am not blaming Hubert.'

An elderly woman with an air of authority strode through the hall towards Ysenda's room. The local healer/midwife, Owen guessed, expecting Aubrey to go talk to her. But he stayed where he was.

'I believe that your wife began a chain of misfortune that led to the death of two men, Master Aubrey. Your wife took the Gamyll birthing cross, though no one thinks she was with child, and she kept the cross hidden in her belongings. Your son found it when he was searching for something of his mother's to carry with him, to feel she was near him while he was away and worried about her. In York he lost it to Drogo, a man who grew up on this manor and seems to have understood what the cross was. He showed it to a goldsmith's journeyman, I presume to discover its worth, but then gave the cross to Father Nicholas, your parish priest, to return to the Gamylls. Then Drogo was murdered. The journeyman was murdered. Father Nicholas is now frightened for his life, and I would think your family might be as well. In fact, when Sir Baldwin mentioned a fire I feared I'd come too late.'

'All for a birthing cross,' Aubrey muttered.

'I don't know why a simple gold cross that has long protected the women of your parish in child-birth has become deadly,' said Owen. 'That is why I'm here. That is why knowing anything about your family's activities since this all began might help me find the murderer.'

Owen drank down the wine in the cup and was considering whether to pour more when Aubrey sat up and turned to face him.

'I hadn't strung it together like that. I don't know much about what my son and wife have done in my absence. I've been home less than a fortnight. My son came home without an escort, without his master's permission and unwilling to talk about his reasons except to say he was worried about his mother. Ysenda kept whining about wanting to go collect firewood, go to market, go here, go there. I know while I was gone she went about as she pleased, but when I am here I try to keep her at home. You can see why – look what she's stirred up.' He looked haggard beyond the discomfort of a night's heavy drinking, his pale blue eyes dull with weariness.

'Why do you wish to keep her at home?' Owen asked.

'I told you – look what trouble she's begun. She's a beautiful woman, Captain, but there's something lacking in her, God forgive me for saying so. She is a bit of a fool.'

Owen did not believe Aubrey thought his wife a fool, not at all, but he did not think it a good idea to contradict the man when he was finally talking.

'As for where I've been, Captain,' Aubrey continued, 'I have a shed I once used for sheep where I stay when I fear I'll lose all control of my temper with Ysenda. It's over the hill, at the edge of my land. Hubert was there with me the afternoon of the fire. I'd seen him walking and took him in to get warm by the fire. He's a good lad.' Aubrey closed his eyes. 'He fell asleep, and I let him rest until the sun was low in the sky, and then I woke him so he would be home before Ysenda began to worry. I walked back with him. As we came over the crest of the hill we saw the fire. The lad wanted to run in to search for his mother. Osmund and Sir Baldwin had come by then, and Sir Baldwin held him fast.' He took a deep breath. 'And that's all there is to tell.'

All he'd said was helpful, but incomplete, the motions, but not the content. Owen chose his next questions with care. 'What do you suppose your wife was reaching for when she burned her hand? Was there something in the house precious to her?'

'For the love of God, a burning door, a burning

cloak, how clearly would she have been thinking by then?' In Aubrey's eyes was a desperation that Owen read as a plea for time to calm himself.

Perhaps that would serve Owen's purpose. 'I've bothered you long enough,' he said. 'A walk in the cold air might help your head and your belly. I swear I'll be quiet.'

'I am comfortable here.' Aubrey's words were barely out of his mouth when his son appeared. 'Hubert?'

The boy did not look at his father but planted himself in front of Owen. 'There was a man who sometimes came and Ma would walk out with him, never asked him to come in.' The words poured forth as if Hubert were desperate to be rid of the secrets. 'When I saw Drogo at the barges I thought he might be that man. And he noticed me watching him. He pulled so hard at the scrip the knot gave way, and he said, "Why it's Ysenda's lad. What treasure have you stolen from her hoard, boy?" and he bounced the scrip in his hand, feeling its weight.' Hubert took a breath. 'He frightened me. That's why I ran. I didn't even wait to see if he'd give it back. I just ran. I wanted you to know that, Captain. I'm going back to Ma now.' As suddenly as Hubert had appeared, he rushed away.

Owen looked at Aubrey, who was shaking his head. He looked neither dismayed nor confused, but guarded. 'Do you know anything about a hoard?' Owen asked.

'I don't know what the lad's talking about,' Aubrey flatly declared.

Owen did not believe him, but right now thought Hubert seemed a more likely informant. Leaving Aubrey, Owen went in search of the boy and his mother. The elderly woman he'd noticed earlier stood in the doorway to the room in which Ysenda was lodged. She put a finger to her lips and shook her head as he approached. The woman had a powerful presence, almost as powerful as Magda Digby's.

'I want to talk to the lad,' Owen whispered.

The woman nodded towards the bed, where Hubert had his forehead pressed to his mother's uninjured hand. He could tell by the boy's trembling shoulders that he was weeping. 'He is in no wise so disposed,' the woman said.

Owen could see that, and though he grumbled to himself that the lad had all the time in the world to be with Ysenda later he withdrew, having not the heart to wrest him from her.

He found Alfred and led him out of the hall. 'Let us see the ruins,' he said. 'Aubrey's land is not far – just beyond that tall, old hedge.'

They took off across the snow, exchanging the facts they'd collected. They agreed that so far it was pitifully little except for what Hubert had just told Owen.

'Have you talked to Sir Baldwin about Ysenda?' asked Alfred. 'She's plainly at the centre of the web, Captain.'

'No, I haven't. I wish the boy had told us about Drogo's comment earlier. We've wasted precious time.' Owen slapped the hedge with a stick as they ducked through, dislodging the shrivelled corpse of a small animal.

'Country,' Alfred growled, kicking it away. 'Full of death the country is. Give me a city – full of life, a city is.'

They were upon the outbuildings of Aubrey's farm before Owen realised it, so changed was the clearing without the house. The charred remains were a scant memorial to a home in which a family had lived.

'God was watching over her, to have escaped that,' said Alfred as he crossed himself.

They stepped with care through the slushy debris in the ruin, gently nudging piles with their boots, but they found nothing of help. Footprints in the ashes gave evidence that others had already moved things about, so even had Owen found something of interest he wouldn't have known whether or not it had been moved.

'A hoard.' Owen gazed round. 'Let's search the outbuildings while it's light.'

Alfred looked doubtful, already stomping and blowing on his fingers. 'What are we searching for?'

'I don't know,' Owen admitted. 'But I'll know when I find it.'

Despite opening the doors of the outbuildings as wide as the snow and terrain allowed, they found the interiors dark and difficult to search. In the one closest to the house, scorched on one corner but remarkably intact for having been so near, they found four large jugs of cider and a small barrel of wine.

'They enjoy their drink,' said Alfred. 'Their food stores were likely in the house – ashes now, but I doubt they'll starve. Their lord seems a generous man, eh?'

'Dried apples here,' Owen said, poking a sack hanging from a rafter.

Avoiding the building with the livestock for now, they tried one farther away from the house. When Alfred tripped over something near the rear wall they both crouched down, feeling with their hands how the floor bulged there. Alfred went for a shovel they'd noted in another building, while Owen kicked a hole in the wall to let in what little light was left.

'This will warm me,' Alfred said as he began to dig.

Gradually he uncovered a chest an arm's length long and half as wide. He rested on the shovel once he'd uncovered the lid, watching Owen lift it.

'God's blood,' Alfred murmured.

Owen gazed down at the contents: cloth, a pewter plate, a mazer, several lamps. He reached beneath the cloth, which felt like silk, and found a small box – inside were perhaps two dozen sterlings.

321

'A hoard indeed,' he said, sitting back on his heels. He wondered whether the gold cross had been but one minor part of this treasure, and who had helped Ysenda bury it. 'I have a feeling Sir Baldwin might recognise some of this. Let's dig it out and carry it back to the hall.'

'I feared you'd want to do that,' said Alfred.

'I'll share the work,' Owen assured him.

By the time they reached the hall the shadows were very long. It was no small hole they'd had to dig, and though the chest was not full it was heavy and awkward to carry so far in the snow, across unfamiliar ground.

Lady Gamyll expressed great relief at their return, having feared for them in the dark and cold. 'But what is this? Did you salvage some things from the fire?'

'From one of the outbuildings,' said Owen, sighing with relief as a servant pulled off his boots. 'Where is Sir Baldwin?'

'In the stables,' said Lady Gamyll.

The servants asked where to put the chest.

'By the fire,' Owen suggested. 'Sir Baldwin will wish to see it. Where is Aubrey?'

'In the stables with my husband. Might we talk before I send for them?'

Owen readily agreed. 'It has lain hidden a long while, there is no cause for hurry now. What is it?'

'Dame Ysenda. She's frightened the boy, moaning and calling out for my lord's son.'

'Osmund?'

Lady Gamyll took a deep breath and nodded. 'I was glad that she spoke – it is a sign that the fever is abating and that she is still with us. But I cannot explain her calling for him.'

'And it frightened Hubert.'

She met his eye, and he saw that she was worried. 'He ran out to the stables. Perhaps it was not so much whose name she cried out but how she sounded.' As Janet spoke she led them to a small table set with drink, near the fire. 'I do not know her well, but I trow her voice sounds too weak for him to bear. Come, rest yourselves. We are quiet here this evening, but do ask for whatever you need.'

Owen thought that the tragedy had brought out a calm strength in her. Sir Baldwin was a fortunate man.

'Where is Osmund?' Owen asked as he took a seat. 'I've not yet met him.'

The question made her ill at ease. She fussed with the drape of her wimple. 'He was in a temper after the fire, arguing with his father about the smallest things. My husband said it was best that we leave him alone. Osmund would likely stay in his room behind the stables and take his meals at the inn in Weston for a few days, then rejoin us in the hall when he'd forgotten his anger. It is their way.'

'You've not seen him since the searches yesterday?'

'I have not seen him since the evening before.' She looked embarrassed. 'I know it must sound as if we're a family at war, but my husband was away, and I'm not so much older than Osmund . . .' her voice trailed off. Owen guessed she realised that he had not asked for an explanation and felt she'd revealed too much.

'Ysenda's calling out his name has you wondering what there is between her and Osmund,' Owen said.

Blushing, she nodded.

'Might one of the servants show us to Osmund's room?'

Lady Gamyll seemed to finally grasp the significance of Owen's questions. 'To his – have you had news of him? Has he done anything wrong? Has something happened?'

Owen thought the order of her questions interesting. 'Not so far as I know,' he said, 'but his name being the first on Dame Ysenda's lips when she woke is of concern to me.'

'I thought perhaps I should tell my husband – out of Master Aubrey's hearing, of course. He might –' She shook her head. 'I cannot think but that they have been lovers.' She called a servant over. 'Escort Captain Archer and his lieutenant to Master Osmund's room behind the stables.'

A weariness was settling over Owen despite thinking that he might finally get some answers. Riding so hard for a day and part of the morning was no longer the pace of his life, had not been for a long while, and the aches were settling in and stiffening his stride. As they passed the front of the stables he could hear Aubrey's deep voice and he realised how like his own father's voice it was, a powerful singing voice. He must be tired to be thinking of the father Owen had not seen since leaving Wales as an archer in his youth. When Owen had at last returned to Wales a few years past he'd learned his father was long dead, and that he'd died horribly, struck down by lightening. It was not something he wished to think of right now.

The stables were of more solid construction and fabric than Aubrey's hall had been. In the back was a high stone wall that broke the wind from the fields beyond, and in the courtyard a wooden stairway led up to a well-fitted oak door. The servant knocked, and another servant answered.

'Master Osmund is away,' he said.

'You said naught of this at dinner,' said Owen's guide.

'I don't need to inform the household of my master's comings and goings.'

Having no patience for servant chatter, Owen thanked their guide. 'You are free to return to your duties in the hall.'

Clearly disappointed, the man shuffled down the steps.

'He isn't here, sir,' said the servant, a man of perhaps twenty years with a deformed ear and a drooped eyelid.

'What is your name?' Owen demanded.

'George, sir. I know you're Captain Archer. I heard about you in the kitchen.'

'You did, did you, George? Then you know that I'm on the archbishop's business and you'll stand aside while I look round your master's room.'

Alfred put his hand on the door and pulled it open wider, startling the servant. 'Whether you will or no, we will come in,' said Alfred.

George moved aside, muttering something about hell.

The room was high-ceilinged though small, with one shuttered window. It was furnished with a curtained bed in the far corner, a brazier, several chests, and a small table with a pair of campaign stools. Owen thought it strangely lacking any indication of the man who lived there.

'When did your master depart?'

'Not sure, Captain.'

Weariness made Owen impatient. He grabbed the man by the shoulder. 'If you bide here in this room you know when he departed.'

'Morning after the fire,' the servant gasped. 'At dawn.'

Owen let him go. 'Did he tell you where he was going, or when he'd return?'

The servant shook his head. 'I knew he wasn't just going to the inn in Weston because he took another shirt.'

'Thank you for your help. You might want to

sit with your friends in the kitchen while we are here.'

'I don't think I should leave you unattended.'

'I do,' said Owen.

The servant nervously departed, peering in once more before shutting the door.

'Let's search the chests,' Owen said.

One contained a number of documents and a ledger indicating a wide variety of business transactions.

'He's not an idle young man,' said Alfred.

'He's certainly not sitting back to await his father's passing,' Owen agreed.

Another chest was filled with linen and hides, and Alfred was straightening out what he'd rumpled when he called out, 'Here, now.' He drew out a casket, no larger than two hands long and shallow. 'Captain,' he said, holding it out to Owen.

'Remember the poison. Wipe your hands.' Owen was thinking of the knife used on Drogo. He used some linen from the chest to protect his own hands as he took the casket and set it down.

Within were several small pouches of powder and a jar of unguent. Physics or poisons, Owen could not immediately tell.

'What is the likelihood that he would save the poison?' he wondered aloud.

'If this were his chamber in York, I'd say it was most unlikely – he doesn't sound like a fool,' said Alfred. 'But so far from York, and in his father's home, he might have felt safe.'

Owen nodded. 'We'll take this back with us, for Dame Lucie to examine.'

In the third chest they found an elegant pair of boots and several elaborate hats, including a green one trimmed in fur that sported several peacock feathers attached with a circular brass pin. Owen wondered whether Osmund was the finely dressed man whom Alice Tanner had seen on the riverbank with Nigel, the man with the furred and feathered hat. Many men might have such hats, but that Osmund owned one was of particular interest to Owen.

As they passed through the yard, Owen noticed Hubert standing in the stable doorway, cuddling a cat. He was glad the boy had found something warm and living. He'd looked so forlorn when sitting with his mother.

As Jasper headed down past the minster towards home, the late afternoon light reminded him of the afternoon less than a week earlier when he'd hurried after his friends and boarded the abbey barges. So much had happened since then. Drogo's murder, Jasper's journey to Weston with the captain, Nigel's murder. And now, nothing. Waiting. For all the captain had praised his help on the journey, he'd left him behind this time. Dame Lucie had explained that this time might be more dangerous, and he should not miss more school. But Jasper was still upset. He felt betrayed, that he'd believed the captain's praise only to learn it had been false.

He was fuming when he passed a finely-dressed man heading into the minster gates, but something made him turn to look again. He was glad that he had, for it was the young man who had talked to Father Nicholas the night of Drogo's death, the one called Osmund, who Jasper had later realised must be Osmund Gamyll. He wondered what he was doing in York. The captain would be sorry to have missed him. Jasper turned back through the gate to follow him, but he'd vanished. He hurried towards school and, catching sight of Osmund just turning down Vicar Lane, he followed, trying to stay hidden in the long afternoon shadows.

Osmund stopped at Master Nicholas's school and when the guard had passed around the corner on the near side, he tried the door. Jasper thought that worth the chase to witness. Failing to open it, Osmund turned down the alley on the far side. Jasper followed and peered round the corner, watching the man try a door farther down the alley that would lead into the same building. Jasper ducked back as Osmund looked around. Waiting what he hoped was long enough for the man to be walking away, Jasper peered around the corner. The alley was empty. Might he have broken in? Jasper crept carefully down the alley, listening for footsteps, and then tried the door himself.

'Why is Captain Archer's foster son following me?'

Jasper jumped. Osmund stood less than a hand's breadth behind him, breathing down his neck.

'Christ Almighty,' Jasper cried. 'I wasn't following you, I'm looking for Master Nicholas.'

'He does not seem to be in,' said Osmund.

He was quite obviously Sir Baldwin's son, though his hair was paler and his build much slighter. He was studying Jasper in a disturbingly focused manner as if he was boring into his soul.

'Father Nicholas's parish needs him,' Osmund said. 'One of his flock has died – Ysenda de Weston.'

'Hubert's mother?' asked Jasper. 'How? What happened?'

'A fire. May she rest in peace,' said Osmund.

'What of Hubert?'

'He was with his father. He is a friend of yours?'

'We're in school together.'

'Ah. If you should meet Father Nicholas, do tell him to hurry back to Weston.' He made Jasper an exaggerated bow, and sauntered off.

Jasper's heart was in his throat, but he cursed that he had no way of quickly getting word to the captain that Osmund Gamyll was in York looking for Master Nicholas. He stopped in the minster to pray for Ysenda's soul, and for Hubert, as well as saying a prayer of thanks for having dealt safely with Osmund, and then he trudged on home.

After helping Edric close the shop, Jasper joined Alisoun in the corner of the hall where she was watching Gwenllian and Hugh play with a paddle ball. He told her about his encounter.

She listened with rapt attention, almost forgetting her charges. When they fussed over her distraction, she offered them each a piece of dried apple and returned to Jasper.

'What will you do?' she asked with a conspiratorial air.

'I don't know. I might tell –' He stopped himself, uncertain whether or not she knew where Master Nicholas was biding. 'I might tell His Grace, and ask him for advice.'

'Can you do that? Just walk into the archbishop's palace and speak with him?'

Jasper nodded, pleased to have impressed her. 'I'm sorry for Hubert. He was devoted to his mother. She was very pretty.'

'Do you wonder what you would be like now if your parents were still alive?' Alisoun asked.

'I'd be apprentice to a carpenter,' said Jasper. 'What about you?'

'I don't know. Betrothed to some farmer, I think, and hating the thought of it.'

Jasper was delighted to have her attention, and let her lead the conversation. He would make his plans for seeing Master Nicholas once he went to bed.

On their return from Osmund's room, Owen and Alfred found Sir Baldwin and Lady Gamyll gazing down at the opened chest, quietly talking. Aubrey sat nearby with his head in his hands. Perhaps some answers might come out of this, Owen thought.

Their hostess came over to greet them, looking worn and anxious. 'How did you find Master Osmund?'

'He has been gone since dawn yesterday,' Owen said.

Baldwin glanced up at that. 'Since then? So soon after the fire?' He shook his head. 'My son is a riddle to me.' He lifted a length of silk from the chest and let it drop back. 'It is good you are here. We have much to learn from Aubrey and his son, I think.'

'Shall I go for the boy?' asked Lady Gamyll.

Sir Baldwin's expression softened. 'That would be best.'

As she passed Owen she whispered, 'My husband showed the chest to Master Aubrey against my advice.'

'I thought as much, my lady,' he said.

She moved on.

'You've seen some of that before?' Owen asked Sir Baldwin, taking a seat near the chest.

'All of it,' said Baldwin. 'It's all from this hall. Aubrey, tell the captain what you've just told me.'

Aubrey slowly lifted his head, and when he looked at Owen his face was lined with suffering. Now it seemed less the pain of too much wine that tormented him than a more profound wounding.

'My wife was ever bringing home small things

332

from the hall when she worked here, as if her admiration for them made her foolish, unable to let go of them,' said Aubrey. 'I would find things and return them as soon as I might. It seems I was good at it, for Sir Baldwin was aghast when I confessed it just now, though now and then he'd noticed things gone missing.'

'I never thought of Ysenda,' Sir Baldwin said.

'But this –' Aubrey gestured at the chest '– and her calling out for Master Osmund.' He closed his eyes, his forehead pleated with suffering. 'Were they his gifts to her?'

'Perhaps because of Hubert, Ysenda felt she was owed more,' Baldwin suggested. 'The boy is my son, Captain. Aubrey took her to wife knowing that, protecting her honour.'

'Her honour,' Aubrey said with a bitterness in his voice. 'No, I failed at that, it is certain.'

Owen poured a cup of wine, using it as a prop to excuse a few moments of quiet thought. 'So the cross was just one thing of many that she'd taken.'

'It seems so,' said Baldwin. 'When I returned from France, cook complained of many items that had disappeared, including two casks of wine and several silver goblets as well as a plate. I note the silver is not in this chest. Then I discovered that the circlet I intended to present to my lady on her first evening in our home was missing. Osmund expressed outrage and threatened to beat all the servants. My steward, having more sense

333

than my son, instead searched all the servant's quarters and the stable. Of course we did not find it. Nor is it in the chest.' Baldwin rose with a curse and began to pace, but halted when he caught sight of his wife.

Lady Gamyll was crossing the hall, Hubert and the cat following close behind her. Baldwin sank back down on his chair.

'Come, sit beside me, son,' said Aubrey, patting his bench. 'We are in need of your counsel.'

Bits of hay stuck out of the boy's curls, and he'd looked half happy until his father spoke. Now he sat down too quietly and stiffly for a lad his age. Owen was glad when the cat leaped up onto the boy's lap and curled up, awaiting no invitation. Hubert stroked the cat's head as he looked around, then at the chest. Owen detected no spark of recognition in the boy's eyes.

'Son, do you remember when I asked you whether Master Osmund had accused your ma of thieving?' Aubrey sounded weary and sad.

Hubert's nod was jerky, hesitant, and he glanced at Owen and Sir Baldwin as if wondering why his father was repeating such a question in this company.

'Now let me ask you this,' Aubrey continued in an unsteady voice, 'while I was gone last summer, did Master Osmund come to our home?'

Hubert stopped petting the cat and closed his eyes. 'Yes,' he mumbled.

'Often?'

Hubert nodded.

'Did he bring presents to your mother?'

Owen pitied the man, for by his questions it was plain the depths to which he suspected his wife had sunk.

'Sometimes,' said Hubert. 'Jugs of cider, wine, a duck once.' His voice was tight, but he'd opened his eyes and was gazing down at the sleeping cat.

'When he came – oh, lad, just tell us all you can about his visits.' Aubrey looked away.

Hubert looked round at all the faces watching him, then leaned towards Aubrey and said softly, 'I tried to tell you last night, Da, I swear.'

Owen's heart ached for both of them, the boy edgy and the man bowed, both ashamed.

'Tell me now, son, and that will be good enough,' said Aubrey.

Hubert nervously licked his lips. 'There's not much to tell because they sent me out when he came. When I'd return sometimes Ma was humming, but more often she would go out to gather firewood – I thought she was upset and wanted to walk.'

'Did she ever talk about Master Osmund? Try to explain his presence?' asked Owen.

'She told me he reckoned he was responsible for us while Da was serving Sir Baldwin.' His blush was witness to his understanding.

'I know this is not easy for you,' said Baldwin. 'But I pray you, tell us how often my son visited your mother.'

'He'd come a few days in a row sometimes, but more often once between Sundays. But the last time I was there when he came it was different. Ma told me to stay.'

'When was that, son?' Aubrey prompted.

'The day before the fire.' The boy described how he'd soon run out of the house. He expressed such regret despite his mother's unseemly behaviour. He clearly felt somehow responsible for her, the child parent to his mother.

'You told me yesterday about the man who sometimes came to the house,' Owen said, 'that you thought of him when Drogo took your scrip and wondered what treasure you'd stolen from her hoard, and that is why you ran.'

'Hubert, is this so?' asked Baldwin.

The boy nodded.

'Do you think now that Drogo was the one who came?' Owen asked.

Hubert looked up at Owen as if he expected to be struck. 'I don't know, Captain. He always wore a hood, and Drogo always wore that green hat.'

'But there was something about Drogo that reminded you of him,' said Owen. 'Do you have any idea what it was?'

Screwing up his face, Hubert looked down at the floor, thinking. After a while, he looked up at Owen. 'The way he held his head to one side,' he tilted towards his left shoulder, 'like this. And he sounded like he was holding his nose.'

336

'His oft-broken nose,' said Owen.

'Long ago there was talk that Ysenda and Drogo had pledged marriage,' Aubrey said. 'But she always denied it. I saw her with him at the fair once, and once in Sir Baldwin's woods when she said she was gathering firewood. But I've not seen him in a good long while.'

'God bless you, Hubert,' said Baldwin, smiling at the boy. 'You've been a great help. I pray that Dame Ysenda can soon talk.'

Aubrey mumbled something unintelligible, but by his angry expression Owen guessed he'd cursed his wife. He thought the boy had been through enough for now.

'You're a fine lad, Hubert,' said Owen. 'Sir Baldwin, might we walk out into the air?'

'What are you going to do with my wife?' Aubrey cried, rising so fast he almost tripped over the cat, who'd leaped off Hubert's lap at the cry.

'We shall take care of her until she is recovered,' said Janet. 'I'm certain my lord agrees?'

'I see no cause to do anything less,' said Baldwin.

'And us?' Aubrey asked.

Baldwin's face softened. 'You have done nothing I would not have done to protect my wife, Aubrey. And as for Hubert – you need not ask.' He turned to Owen as Aubrey's eyes swam. 'Captain.' He gestured for Owen to lead the way out to the yard.

'Wait,' said Hubert. 'There's something else.

Ma would drink a lot while Master Osmund was in the house, and after she'd just keep drinking until she fell asleep. Maybe that's when the fire happened.' He described the recent near accident, when she'd upset a lamp.

Aubrey sat down again and took Hubert in his arms. 'Brave lad. You're a brave lad. You've been a good son. Do not blame yourself for your mother's suffering.'

'Come, Captain,' said Baldwin.

Outside, clouds with the look of snow approached along the river valley. Sir Baldwin led Owen across the yard to the stables.

'The horses keep the air much warmer in here,' he said, taking off his felt hat and raking a hand through his hair that was so much like Hubert's. 'I don't need to tell you that the lad's revelations chilled my heart. I've often wondered whether I should have acknowledged him and brought him up in my own household. But Aubrey is a good man, and – I suppose we've all been blind to the fair Ysenda.' His pale eyebrows rose and fell, a facial shrug. 'I'll find a way to do more.'

'Tell me about Ysenda.'

'I think she'll live, Captain.' Baldwin did not meet his eye.

'You know what I mean. What was she like when you loved her? How were you drawn to her?'

Baldwin walked over to a handsome stallion with slightly wild eyes, the sort that's never entirely tamed, but loyal to one man. He murmured to him and stroked him between the ears.

'Like Sultan, she was exciting. I'd loved her for a long time, and I finally took her. She was mischievous, daring, and she made me feel a little wild. I didn't know myself sometimes, never knew what to expect when I was with her. But I loved my wife, deeply loved her, and I knew I must put Ysenda aside. I knew Aubrey lusted after her, so I asked him to wed her, telling him about the child she thought she was carrying. That's my great regret, Captain, that I did not recognise Hubert. He is everything Osmund is not.'

'What about Osmund's part in all that has happened?' asked Owen. 'For example, what do you think this might be?'

Baldwin, stepping away from the horse, looked at the box in Owen's hands. 'This is something you found in his chamber?'

'Among other things.' Owen opened the box and held it out. 'They might be physicks, but they might be poisons.' He looked up at Baldwin's face, saw not anger at such a statement, but fear.

'Poison?' he said softly.

'The reason I suspect poisons is that we also found a hat that matches what a possible witness described, and papers indicating that Osmund has a considerable trading interest to protect. All of that added to how often his name has arisen . . . Let me ask you, Sir Baldwin – what do you think?'

Baldwin closed the lid on the box and dropped

his hands as if in defeat. 'I do not know where I erred in the raising of my son. His mother worried about what she called his godlessness, a lack of fear of God's wrath. She also thought him too proud of his cleverness. I did not at first agree with her, but I gradually came to see that she was right. Without ever speaking of it we made a pact of secrecy, hoping that he would change and so we did not wish to have irreparably sullied his name. You ask what part I think he might have played in the deaths of the two men.' Baldwin had moved back to the horse, and pressed his forehead to the animal's head for a moment. 'If he believes I'll disinherit him, he'll do what he can to gather wealth – indeed, you have found evidence that he has done so. He has costly tastes.'

'He would take lives?' Owen pressed.

'I pray he would not.' Baldwin moved away as the horse grew restive, sensing his discomfort. 'But there have been times when I've feared what I saw in him. I once asked Father Nicholas about the difference between a sinful man and an evil man. I told him that I saw evil as a darkness so much a part of someone that prayer and the sacraments could not reach it, could not rescue the person, but that a sinful person could be saved.' He made a strangled sound and walked to the doorway, breathing deeply. In a moment he returned to Owen. He shook his head. 'I've not told Janet this, though I should, I should. Father Nicholas knew I was speaking of my son. He *knew*. I have prayed over that moment of terrible doubt, Captain. That I even entertained such a thought about flesh of my flesh.'

'Yet you allow him to live separately here, come and go as he likes.'

Baldwin sighed. 'He is of age, Captain. When his mother died I lost my patience – or perhaps my faith. I gave up on him. But now I wonder whether I irresponsibly unleashed him to prey on innocent people. I pray I am wrong.'

Owen looked out at the gathering storm, wondering whether he'd be able to ride home on the morrow. He feared that Osmund had gone to York. He realised he'd already condemned him without ever having met him. But with the apparent evidence and such a confession from his father, he felt justified in believing Osmund guilty.

Twelve

a Length of silk

The snow that had been threatening all afternoon with huge, heavy clouds and a cold
wind that sent debris skittering down the streets
and alleyways finally began in the evening.
Gwenllian noticed it as she closed the shutters in
the chamber she shared with Hugh and Alisoun,
and ran to the landing to shout the news to those
down below. Lucie laughed at her excitement.

'When you wake in the morning the world
might be white, as if someone played a trick on
you in the night, covering up everything that
points the way for you,' said Lucie.

Gwenllian clapped her hands and skipped back
to her room, but Lucie toppled headlong into
worry about Owen's journey home.

'He will not ride if the snowdrifts are too deep,
Lucie,' said Phillippa. 'Your father is not in the
habit of taking such risks.'

How strangely her aunt's mind worked, reading
Lucie's mood but mistaking the one about whom

she worried because she'd slipped back into the past, confusing Owen with Sir Robert. Lucie patted Phillippa's hand and thanked her.

In the morning, Owen cursed the weather. Snow drifted to several feet against parts of the buildings circling the yard. Making his way from the hall to relieve himself was a cold, wet business. But the sun had risen in a clear sky, which could mean that he would be able to set out for home later.

Lady Gamyll reported that Ysenda had been able to sit up to drink the tisane the healer had left as well as some broth. 'I believe you might talk to her this morning, Captain.'

Owen and his hostess had enjoyed a quiet conversation the previous night about Lucie and her joy over being with child. Lady Gamyll had asked many questions about his children, winning his devotion, and she seemed to have decided she might consider him a friend. She knew he wished to depart as soon as possible, believing the reason to be Lucie's imminent lying in. Which was as well, for despite all they'd said about Osmund the previous day, Baldwin had been clear about not having shared his feelings about his son with her, so Owen did not wish to explain his fear of what Osmund might do in York.

Owen asked Aubrey and Baldwin to join him in talking to Ysenda, hoping to save time. Hubert was incensed about not being included, despite Lady Gamyll's attempts to engage him in some activity with her.

Aubrey knelt to him, and looked him straight in the eyes. 'I pray that your unease about some of your mother's actions may soften in time, Hubert, and that you will once again feel that deep love for her that has always given me such joy to witness. That is why I don't want you to come with us. I fear that you might hear things that would increase your unease. You're too young to grasp how vulnerable any of us sometimes are to temptation. Do you understand?'

By the boy's expression Owen could tell that he understood to an extent, but was unconvinced.

'She scared me, Da, and then I got angry and ran. I didn't want to stay with her and listen to her apologies. I left her again. That's when the house burned, and she was hurt. *I* hurt her, like I thought I would when I lost the cross. I want to know what really happened.'

'I will tell you.'

Hubert narrowed his eyes. 'Will you tell me the whole truth about how it happened, even if you think I'm too young to understand?'

Aubrey dropped his head.

Owen was not certain what his own decision would be if Hubert were his son.

Looking up at Hubert, Aubrey asked, 'Do *you* swear to believe me?'

Hubert shrugged.

Rising, Aubrey nodded to his son. 'Then come with us. I don't want you to doubt.'

Owen hoped Aubrey did not later regret his decision.

Ysenda was resting against a pile of pillows, her face swollen and the eye beneath the wound blackened and swollen almost shut. But she forced a weak smile for her visitors.

'I don't remember how I came to be lying by the pond,' she said with an embarrassed laugh. 'Is that not strange?' She noticed Hubert, who'd entered last, and held out her arm. 'Come kiss me, my dear boy. I thank God you were not in the house when it happened.'

Hubert hung back. 'What happened, Ma? How did the fire start?'

She turned with a frown towards Aubrey. 'Where have you been? I was so worried.'

'Not far, but too far to save the house. How did the fire begin?'

She lifted her bandaged hand, then settled it back on a pillow with an unconvincing whimper. 'Let's talk of pleasant things this morning. I'm not well.' She anxiously looked at Hubert and Aubrey.

There was no doubt of the truth of her last words, for the skin on the forearm of her wounded hand did not look healthy, and there was still an odour of rotting flesh about her.

'We'll talk of pleasant things later. We must talk this morning of important things, Ysenda,' said Aubrey. 'How did the fire start?'

Biting her lip, Ysenda frowned at Sir Baldwin. 'God bless you for taking us in, and taking care of me, my lord.'

Owen thought it time to tell her about his discovery. She closed her eyes when he mentioned the chest, and her breathing quickened.

'How did it begin, Dame Ysenda?' Sir Baldwin suddenly interrupted. 'When did you begin to steal from me?'

She looked at him with an injured expression. 'My lord?'

'Ysenda, I've spent years returning the things you took from the hall,' said Aubrey in a weary tone. 'You cannot pretend it is not so. But I thought you'd taken only little things.'

'Hubert, leave us,' Ysenda cried, a desperate expression in her eyes. 'They are being cruel. You don't want to hear this. I don't want you to hear this.'

Aubrey shook his head at Hubert and gestured for him to stay. 'Your son deserves to hear the truth.'

'It does not sound as if truth will be heard in this company,' she said, and despite her obvious discomfort she struggled to sit up straighter.

Owen assisted her with the pillows. She thanked him in a half-heartedly flirtatious undertone.

'Now, Dame Ysenda, you must understand that we have the evidence in the hall,' Owen said, pulling her down to earth. 'A chest we dug up from your outbuilding. Neither your son nor your

346

husband knows anything about how it came to be there.' He spoke quietly, but loud enough for all in the room to hear. 'As your husband said, you cannot pretend it isn't so.'

Ysenda looked at Sir Baldwin, Aubrey, Hubert, her eyes lingering on her son as tears rolled down her swollen and bruised cheeks. 'I am so ashamed. Pretty things – I love pretty things. I see them and I think just this one little ribbon, this pretty glass, I will take it for a little while and then put it back. And then I cannot part with it. God forgive me. When I was caught, I was frightened for my husband's good name.'

Owen, next to Aubrey, heard him grunt.

'Caught by whom?' Owen prompted.

Ysenda lowered her eyes. 'Master Osmund. He's always watched me, coveted me. He found his way when he saw me take a length of silk. He followed me home and pulled it out from my gown. I was so ashamed. Then he searched the house. He found a cup from the hall. After that he was often at my house when Aubrey and Hubert were out, demanding *payment* for his silence.'

'Evil,' whispered Sir Baldwin.

Aubrey pulled Hubert close and asked him if he wanted to leave. The boy shook his head. One benefit of the boy's presence, Owen thought, was that Aubrey would guard his tongue, which might speed the inquiry.

'Could you not have stopped taking things?' Owen asked.

347

'I had stopped. You cannot believe –' she closed her eyes – 'of course you can. But I *had* stopped. Then Sir Baldwin took a young wife. Osmund feared he would be disinherited and left with nothing. Now he told me what to steal, and where to hide it.'

'What?' Aubrey cried.

'For pity's sake, why did you not come to me?' asked Baldwin. 'Surely you knew to trust me?'

Ysenda frowned at him. 'He frightened me. Hurt me. I don't know.' The tears fell faster and she began to sob. 'I know I've said it over and over again, but I was so ashamed. At least only he knew.'

'Tears will not send us away,' said Baldwin. 'Calm yourself, Dame Ysenda.' It was a crisp command.

Ysenda covered her face and gradually quieted.

'What did my son intend with the hoard?' Baldwin demanded. Owen was surprised by his lack of sympathy.

Ysenda took a few deep breaths. 'He sent Drogo to me now and then for particular items to take downriver to Hull, to sell them.'

Drogo's frequent absences, Owen thought. 'You knew Drogo well?'

She nodded.

'You said little when I told you of his murder.'

Ysenda dropped her gaze. 'I was afraid to say aught for fear I would be next. I'd known Drogo was in danger. He'd kept talking about how stingy

Osmund was, that his part of the sale was worth far more than what Master Osmund allowed him to keep. Master Osmund had threatened that if either one of us ever turned greedy or if we betrayed him he would kill us, and I believed him. I knew Drogo was too stubborn to listen.'

'But how did Osmund know that Drogo had the cross?'

'The cross? I don't believe he knew that Drogo had it. I don't know that he would have cared. One little cross. He was angry that Drogo had been lying about prices, keeping more than his share of the profit – I think he thought Drogo had been doing it much longer than he had. Poor Drogo,' Ysenda cried, looking as if she would burst into tears. 'He wanted to send his daughters to Father Nicholas's school. He was a good father.'

'There has been another death – a goldsmith's journeyman,' said Owen as he poured her some wine. 'It seems Drogo showed him the birthing cross.'

Drying her eyes, Ysenda shook her head. 'I don't know why he would do that. He knew what it was – his mother was one of the first to survive a terrible delivery because of the cross,' said Ysenda. 'Unless he meant to sell it.'

'Osmund had not told you to steal the cross.'

Ysenda shook her head.

'I wish you'd told me why you wanted me to stay the last time Master Osmund came,' said Hubert.

She tearfully thanked Owen for the wine and sipped it, seeming to calm a little. 'I could not bring myself to tell you, my son. I could not.'

Owen believed she loved Hubert in her way, and that it pained her to be exposed in front of him. But he had to ask the final question.

Ysenda spoke first. 'Captain Archer, is your son with you?'

'No.' He did not like the question. 'Why do you ask, Dame Ysenda?'

'I've been trying to remember what Osmund said about him. It was that day he came and called me a whore and a thief, and held my hand in the fire.'

'Ysenda, no,' Aubrey cried. 'Did he start the fire?'

She'd bowed her head and was now sobbing quietly as she cradled her bandaged hand.

'Why was he so desperate?' Baldwin asked.

She drew a jagged breath. 'Drogo said I was only one of several thieves – and he reckoned he was only one of several sellers. Osmund has much to protect.'

Owen could not wait in courtesy. 'Dame Ysenda, is my son in danger?'

'God protect him, for I fear that he might be,' she whispered. 'Osmund might use him to distract you.'

'Then I must leave as soon as possible for York, you can understand that. I must get to Jasper before Master Osmund does. I beg you, tell us about that day.'

She took another deep breath. 'He'd heard from Sir Baldwin of your coming to Weston asking the questions, and that you'd stayed at the hall. He said I must have known I must die, that he could not risk my talking about what he'd stolen. We'd had some cider, too much for me. I stood up and was dizzy. I stumbled, and when he grabbed me he put my hand in the flames and held it there. He said that was the way they dealt with thieves in the city. I fought him. Holy Mother of God, the pain was worse than childbirth. Then he hit me in the head.' She touched her bandaged forehead. 'I remember that, I remember falling, and my hem beginning to burn. I remember rolling away. Snow – I remember snow. Icy water that stopped the pain. A wagon ride. Then I woke here.'

Aubrey sat down on the bed, took her good hand and kissed it.

'And sometime in the attack he mentioned my son?' Owen asked.

'Yes,' she sobbed.

'There was a ring in the scrip Hubert had taken to York,' he said, 'Drogo's mother's ring.'

'Sweet Jesus, oh dear Drogo –' Her voice broke and she looked away from Aubrey.

Owen asked Hubert to find Alfred and tell him to get their horses ready.

'And mine,' said Sir Baldwin. 'If you apprehend Osmund, I want to be there.'

Hubert nodded and withdrew.

'Thank you, Captain,' said Ysenda. 'At least he won't hear – I loved that ring. Drogo had given it to me when we made our vows long ago, in front of friends. But then I discovered I was with child, my lord's child, and – I confess I thought I might do better. I went to Sir Baldwin and he named Aubrey as a man worthy of me.'

'You were wed to Drogo?' Aubrey cried. 'Do you even know whose son you bore? Christ, how could I have loved you?' It was his turn to look away.

'I was too far along for it to be Drogo's child,' she said. 'A woman knows these things. Was the ring in the scrip when Drogo returned it?'

'No.'

She looked crestfallen. 'I thought – I'm foolish, but I thought for a moment that Drogo meant for me to have the ring. That he'd put it in the scrip to give to Hubert.'

'We believe it was stolen from Drogo's home after he died,' said Owen. 'Did Osmund know the significance of the ring?'

'I spoke of it to him, yes. I wanted him to know that someone had truly loved me, wanted to wed me – he liked to remind me that his father had coaxed Aubrey into wedding me.' She was looking at the back of her husband's head. 'I learned to love you, Aubrey.'

'You were never my wife,' he said in a broken voice.

Owen still did not understand why Osmund or

anyone would add the ring to the scrip, but at present that was not his greatest concern. He must protect Jasper.

As Jasper stepped out to the street on his way to school he laughed at the shrieks coming from the garden – Gwenllian and Hugh had rushed out to attack the snow. He remembered feeling that way about it.

He had not told Dame Lucie about seeing Osmund Gamyll the previous evening, fearing she'd worry and find reasons to keep him home until the captain returned. That would not do, because Jasper felt a responsibility to let Master Nicholas know the man had been trying his doors. He'd felt guilty all night for not having told the guard. He headed for the archbishop's palace.

Brother Michaelo showed him in at once, escorting him to the chapel where Master Nicholas knelt in prayer. Jasper was awed by the great hall they passed through, and the stone passage to the chapel. It was a house such as a king might live in, he thought.

His account frightened Master Nicholas, that was plain.

'I have never trusted Osmund Gamyll,' the master said, 'and he's betrayed me to my brother, telling him about my admiration for John Wycliff's honesty. William could not hide his disappointment in me.'

Alisoun had told Jasper about his heretical ideas.

'They'll add it to their case for my excommunication.' Nicholas groaned. 'My dear boy, thank you for telling me this. I will be careful once I'm back in my school. If I'm ever so fortunate.'

As Jasper was leaving, Michaelo warned him to go to school and leave the sleuthing to his father. He did not need to warn him of that, Jasper thought. He must think him a fool.

When they found an inn for the night, Sir Baldwin went to the church across the way to pray. He had talked a little whenever they paused to rest the horses, about his hopes for more children, his memories of Osmund when young and innocent, and it was plain the man was struggling with the knowledge of his son's guilt – for it seemed certain that Osmund had murdered both Drogo and Nigel.

The inn was a much better one than the last, and Owen and Alfred settled near the fire with well-deserved tankards of ale. Owen recounted all that Ysenda had said, as much to mull it over as to fill in Alfred.

'Now I understand why he's not talking,' said Alfred. 'Poor man. Do you think he'll tell all to his new lady? I don't think I would.'

'How else would he explain his son's arrest? She must know all in order to understand Sir Baldwin's acceptance of Osmund's guilt.'

'If Osmund's hurt Jasper, do we kill him?'

Owen closed his eyes, trying not to picture Jasper floating in the river, but there it was, a horrible image. 'Yes. We kill him.'

It was a dreary morning, the icicles dripping from the rooftops, the snow, so pretty the day before, now slush. Jasper felt left behind, powerless, frustrated that there was nothing more he could do than he'd done the previous day, warning Master Nicholas. It seemed a puny thing. Alisoun had given him a warm smile last evening when he'd returned from school, and she'd been impressed that he'd been to the archbishop's palace, asking more questions than he could answer. But when she'd asked him what else he meant to do, he'd admitted he didn't think there was more that he could do until the captain returned, and she'd lost interest.

He'd been watching his feet as he walked along the city streets, avoiding puddles, but he had to look up to navigate around the people crossing every which way at the meeting of Stonegate and Petergate, and he thought he saw Osmund Gamyll walking quickly in the direction he'd taken the last time Jasper had seen him. His mood lifted. He did not think the man would risk trying the doors at Master Nicholas's school again, for surely he'd think it possible Jasper had told the guard of his attempt the previous day, but he was curious where Osmund was headed. It might prove important.

Rounding the corner to Vicar Lane he saw

Osmund walk past the guard in front of Master Nicholas's school and continue down the street, turning left at Goodramgate. Jasper hurried after him, but by the time he reached Goodramgate there was no sign of Osmund. He rushed through the gate of Holy Trinity churchyard. No Osmund. He kept going down the house backs until he found the alley to Master Nicholas's chamber. By now his feet were wet and icy, but he thought it would be well worth the pain if he picked up Osmund's trail again. He had expected a guard here in the alley by the school, but no one was watching the side door. He wondered whether the man would be so bold as to slip in when the guard was out front – but he had tried the handle the previous day. Jasper tried the door handle. Unlocked. Perhaps another guard hid within. That would be clever. But it was only a guess. He decided against opening the door, though it was tempting. A guard might mistake Jasper for Osmund, or a thief. And if Osmund Gamyll were hiding behind the door he would be armed and ready. Feeling foolish for having made the chase but failed to bring the prey to ground, he told himself that at least he had some information for the captain. He turned his back on the door – it was time to continue on to school. He gasped as someone grabbed him and put a gag to his mouth.

It was late afternoon by the time Owen, Alfred and Sir Baldwin led their horses into the archbishop's stables. Thinking to avoid another lecture from Thoresby on his late reporting, Owen stopped at the palace before heading home. Sir Baldwin seemed reluctant to see the archbishop in his present state, but he accompanied Owen.

Brother Michaelo welcomed them, and as he led Owen into the hall he inquired whether he'd been home as yet.

It was a chilling question. 'No. What is wrong?'

Michaelo paused, and his expression lacked even a suggestion of his usual playfulness. 'I have a bad feeling about Jasper.' He told him of the boy's visit the previous day.

Owen's heart sank. 'You could not have delivered worse news.' He had feared that Jasper would recognise Osmund and follow him. It's what he would have done at Jasper's age.

'Then I am glad I have told you,' said Michaelo. 'I can assure you that Jasper attended his classes yesterday, for I spoke to Master John in the evening. But there was a taste of adventure in the lad's eyes that has worried me.'

Jasper had been all right the previous day. He prayed that was still so. 'Have you spoken to Master John today?' Owen asked.

'No. Not yet. His Grace has kept me busy. Go to Master John now – before you go home.'

'I will.' Owen cursed under his breath. 'Didn't they put one of the guards on the school?'

'Yes, and I am likely worrying for nothing. But we know that Jasper is resourceful, Captain.'

357

'Keep Master Nicholas here, Michaelo,' said Owen.

Sir Baldwin was right behind him as he hurried out.

A servant at St Peter's School directed them to the Clee, where Master John was dining. Owen cursed. It was too long a walk to the Clee when he was in a hurry to find his son.

Sir Baldwin asked where Nicholas's school was. 'So near?' he said. 'Why don't we talk to the guard? He might have seen Jasper today.'

Owen thanked him – he wasn't thinking clearly or he would have come up with that himself. Memories of another time when he'd feared for Jasper's life crowded his mind. They almost ran down Vicar Lane, startling people who unwittingly got in their way.

Seeing that the guard was Edmund, one of Owen's newest men, he cursed himself for leaving Rafe in charge, with his philosophy of pushing inexperienced men into the thick of things, convinced that it was the only way they would learn because that is how he'd learned.

'I've been here since midday and I've not seen the lad,' said Edmund.

'Who's in the alley?' Owen asked.

'It's just me, Captain. And this morning Colm. You might ask him if he saw Jasper.'

Owen could not believe the carelessness of Rafe's command. 'Do you check the alley at all?'

'I do. I walk round the building, so I pass it often.'

'Go to the barracks. Fetch Rafe and Gilbert here.'

Startled, Edmund hesitated.

'Now!'

He took off.

'What do you intend?' asked Baldwin.

Owen was already at the door of the school, trying the latch. Locked. He headed round to the alley, Baldwin striding alongside him. It was mid-afternoon, but the alley was already dark. He wished Sir Baldwin were not with him, for if he found Jasper harmed . . .

The alley door was unlatched. Owen drew his dagger, then slowly opened the door. It was too dark to see, but he heard nothing. Crouching down, he crept into the chamber. Baldwin followed his lead, shutting the door behind him. Owen let his eye adjust before rising to look around. In the dimness he saw that the room was in disarray.

Baldwin tapped him on the arm. 'I hear breathing.' He moved towards the corner of the room taken up by the vestment press. Crouching by the trunk, Baldwin gestured for Owen to come. 'In here. What's in here?'

'Clothing,' Owen said softly. He heard footsteps in the alley, and opened the door a little to peer out, relieved to see that it was Rafe and Gilbert.

359

'Stay! Who goes there?' Rafe demanded.

'Your captain, you fool.' Owen swung the door wide seeing that Gilbert had the sense to bring a lantern, bold now that he had light and backup. 'Open the shutter,' Owen said.

Baldwin was trying to lift the lid on the press with one hand, his dagger in the other. Rafe crossed over to help him.

'God have mercy,' Baldwin sobbed, reaching into the chest and straightening with Jasper in his arms, bound and gagged and frighteningly limp.

'He'd dead? No!' Owen cried. 'Holy Mary, Mother of God. You said you heard breathing, damn you!'

'He's still warm, Captain. But stuffed into that chest – he couldn't have had much air.' Baldwin laid Jasper on Nicholas's bed. 'My son meant to kill him. Thank God he failed.'

'For now,' Rafe muttered as he cut the bonds and removed the gag.

'He should be coughing,' Owen moaned, pressing an ear to Jasper's chest. He almost wept with relief to hear his strong young heart beating. He checked his limbs – Jasper groaned when Owen touched his right shoulder.

Baldwin began to rub Jasper's wrists, Owen did the ankles. A shudder ran through the boy's limbs and he opened his eyes. At first unfocused and confused, he fought them.

'Steady, lad. You are safe. It's your da,' said Owen, knowing well this state of confusion on waking from such an attack as this must have been.

'Da!' Jasper cried, trying to prop himself up on his elbows. 'You're here.'

Owen helped him sit up. 'I am, I'm here, you're safe.'

'I thought I was dying in there. I was so mad.' Jasper knuckled his eyes. 'So stupid.'

'You're alive. That is not stupid,' Owen said. 'Tell me what happened.'

Rafe and Gilbert came from the schoolroom shaking their heads.

'Someone's gone through it, but they're not there now,' said Gilbert.

'There's not much to tell,' said Jasper, 'but that I did just what he wanted by following him here. He was pleased with himself. He said he was burying me alive because he didn't kill boys.'

'Who, Jasper?' Owen asked, wanting to be sure.

'Osmund Gamyll. Remember I saw him –'

'I'll crush him,' Baldwin growled.

'Sir Baldwin?' Jasper had not noticed him. 'How are you here?'

'There's no time to explain,' said Owen. 'Do you have any idea where he's gone?'

Jasper shook his head.

'We need to get you home,' Owen said. 'Can you walk?'

Jasper inched his legs over to hang off the side of the pallet. Owen helped him stand, holding him as he struggled for his balance.

'Not yet.' Owen helped him sit back down.

'Jasper! Praise God,' Alfred exclaimed from the doorway. 'Captain, the bailiff –'

Hempe pushed Alfred out of the way. 'Dame Lotta's servant came for me. Osmund Gamyll is at her home, threatening her. The servant is old, Osmund must have thought he would not muster the strength to go for help. Lotta was Nigel's landlord.'

'Rafe, stay with Jasper,' said Owen. 'Gilbert – no that won't work, Lucie can't come through the snow, not now.' He couldn't think what to do. They would waste time sending for Brother Henry, for he might not be in the infirmary.

'We'll take him home, Captain, don't worry,' Gilbert said. 'You've got three with you.'

Hempe led the way. A neighbour was pacing in front of Dame Lotta's house. The street door stood wide open.

'What has happened?' the neighbour asked Hempe. 'I've never seen old Paul rush like that, and there were shouts. They're in the lodger's room, down the alley.'

Alfred thanked him and told him to go home now.

'There's a door in the alley, the one from the hall, and a window on the very back,' said Hempe.

'Let's see if we can look in the window,' Owen suggested, his head clearer now that Jasper was safe.

A shutter was partly opened. Owen first saw only Dame Lotta, who was sitting on a bed shaking her head with a look of disgust, but he heard a man's voice, slurring and broken with drink and fear. Standing on Alfred's knee, he was able to see enough to locate Osmund off to one side of the window, a large mazer in his hand. His speech was too slurred and muffled to understand.

But Dame Lotta spoke quite clearly. 'You'll find no sympathy here. You should have thought about God's vengeance before you committed such deeds. You're not a child, you know better.'

Owen was relieved to hear her strong voice, but concerned that she would antagonise a man who had little to lose in murdering one more. He climbed down and withdrew to the street with Baldwin and Hempe.

'I heard her,' said Baldwin. 'Too late he comes to a healthy fear of the Lord. She sounds un-injured, how does she look?'

'I saw no sign of injury,' said Owen.

'Thank God,' said Hempe.

'But that could change at any time,' Owen said. 'He is drunk, he may lose control of himself.'

'Aye,' Baldwin agreed.

They quickly conceived a plan. Baldwin would confront his son by entering through the hall door which faced him. Hempe would guard the window, though it was unlikely Osmund would attempt to crawl out, and Owen would be at the alley door. Ready to kill him, Owen thought.

He waited until he heard Baldwin thunder his son's name before he cracked open the door.

363

Osmund was standing with open mouth, the mazer tilted, spilling wine.

'What? Are you here?' Osmund looked confused, then angry. 'Get out!'

'What have you done, Osmund?' Baldwin's voice was harsh with agony, but powerfully loud. 'How many have you killed in your greed?'

Osmund tossed the cup aside and tried to straighten. His eyes flickered from Sir Baldwin to Dame Lotta, and then he clumsily bolted for the door.

Owen grabbed him and kept his forearm to his throat as he turned him to face his father, pressing as hard as he could without crushing his windpipe though it was all he could do to resist the instinct to kill him. Sir Baldwin stood in the middle of the room staring at his son with a world of pain in his eyes and in the twist of his mouth.

Hempe pushed past Owen and Osmund to go to Lotta. She shook her head at him. 'Not now. Get this drunken murderer out of here first, the mewling beast, creature of the devil. He murdered them both – Nigel and the pilot – and now he fears God's wrath and that of his fellow man. Get him out of my house.'

Owen dragged Osmund into the alley. Baldwin's martial form blocked the light in the doorway.

'What will you do with him?' he asked.

'Take him to York Castle gaol until the sheriff and the archbishop come to some agreement,' said Hempe. 'That is the law.'

It was not what Owen wanted to do with him, but in his heart he knew Lucie would want him to cooperate with Hempe, to let the man take his punishment from the king's men. 'I'll go with you there,' he said.

Sir Baldwin nodded. 'I'll accompany you as well.'

In a room lit only by a rush light, Osmund mumbled his confession, a jumble of self-righteous resentment and misplaced pride. Drogo he'd murdered for his greediness, for his betrayal, as Ysenda had feared.

'And Nigel the journeyman?' Hempe barked. 'What threat was he to you?'

'He wanted me to pay him for his silence. He shouldn't have been any threat to me. I had nothing to do with the birthing cross Drogo showed him. Drogo should rot in hell, not me!' Osmund's voice was little more than a forced whisper.

Owen opened the box he'd found in Osmund's room. 'Which poison did you use on Drogo?' he asked.

Osmund shook his head and looked away.

'Why did you go to Dame Lotta?' Hempe asked.

'I went to a dead man's chamber to hide while I thought about what to do.'

'Why did you put Drogo's ring in the scrip?' Owen asked.

Osmund rubbed his face with his hands. 'I can't think. I need sleep. My throat hurts.'

'Answer the question,' Hempe said sharply.

'Confusion! It was worth too little to risk selling, so I tucked it in. You thought about it, didn't you?' Osmund's laugh was eerily high-pitched, then dissolved into a wheeze.

'Let him sleep off the drink,' Baldwin said in a voice flat with disappointment.

Hempe nodded. 'I want him clear-headed in my court tomorrow, and able to speak.'

It was dark by the time Owen opened his hall door and crossed the room to hug Lucie as hard as he dared.

'You are a welcome sight,' she murmured, reaching for her cap, which he'd knocked back. 'Oh, my love, what a horror. But Jasper will be fine. He will.'

Jasper sat by the fire in a high-backed chair, his feet propped up on a stool. He smiled at Owen. Phillippa was massaging one of his wrists. Alisoun sat beside him, and Edric nearby.

'I see you are well attended,' said Owen, unable to modulate his voice to hide his emotions. 'I did not think to see –' He dropped his head, took a breath.

'I wish I could have seen the three of you at Dame Lotta's,' said Jasper, already sounding stronger. 'Did Osmund crawl?'

'No, but he will find it difficult to talk or swallow for a while.' Owen managed a grin.

'So I helped?'

'I doubt he would have felt confident enough to get drunk had you still been sneaking around.'

Jasper smiled, but quickly grew serious. 'He said Dame Ysenda is dead.'

Owen shook his head. 'He left Weston too soon to know she'd been found alive. She has survived to give witness against him.'

'I'm glad she's alive,' said Jasper. 'Hubert's suffered enough.'

Lucie tugged Owen's arm. 'Come to the kitchen, my love. Gwenllian and Hugh will be so happy to see you.'

Owen accompanied her across the hall. In the space between the hall and kitchen doors, beneath the stairs, he paused. 'He's my son, there's no question of that,' he said. 'When I thought he was dead –' His breath caught. 'If Sir Baldwin hadn't been there I would have thrust deep into Osmund's heart and watched him bleed to death.'

Lucie pulled his face down to hers and kissed him long and hard. When she let him go, she said, 'Come back to me now, my love. It is over. Your part is finished.'

He took her hand in his and breathed more easily. 'It is. It is done.'

For George Hempe it had only begun. The bailiff's court was crowded with people who suspected Osmund Gamyll of selling goods stolen from their homes and businesses, as well as the usual onlookers, curious what sort of heir to a knight of the realm would stoop to theft and murder merely to accumulate wealth. He judged that with so many already making claims there would be more to come, and in the interest of recovering as much as possible he postponed Osmund's execution for a fortnight or longer – most likely he would be in the castle gaol until after the Yuletide. Archbishop Thoresby agreed to the delay.

His notoriety as the bailiff who'd scotched the thief brought him even more trade. He felt he was too busy to sleep. But even had it not been good for business, Hempe would not have regretted assisting Owen with the investigation, for he did not see how he might otherwise have begun his courtship of Lotta.

EPILOGUE

As Jasper gazed down on the wonder of Emma Archer, her impossibly tiny fingers wrapped around Captain Archer's calloused one, he felt at peace. This was Jasper's family, this was where he belonged, where he would always belong. He was at ease as he laughed with Archbishop Thoresby and Brother Michaelo over Gwenllian's and Hugh's efforts to dominate their new sibling. He was comfortable helping Kate and Alisoun greet people at the hall door, helping them out of their snow-encrusted cloaks and directing them to the refreshments. He felt himself moving in time to Tom Merchet's merry fiddling.

He'd had the honour of taking the beautifully wrapped mazer from Brother Michaelo on his arrival and delivering it to the captain. He'd watched as Emma Ferriby, first godmother, had cradled her namesake in her arms so that Dame Lucie – his ma – could unwrap her gift. She'd exclaimed in wonder at the beautiful workmanship and held it up to

Jasper to examine while the captain – his da – beamed and the archbishop proclaimed loudly, 'Well done, Archer.'

Maud, the wet nurse, stood with Magda Digby off to one side, awaiting her charge, her own pretty babe in her arms. Jasper was glad Magda had been there when his mother's labour began, even though the Gamyll birthing cross had made an easy delivery likely. Sir Baldwin had gladly let the captain keep it until after the birth. Still, Magda's presence had eased everyone's fears.

It was a wonder how everything changed with the birth of a healthy child.

'We've all much to be grateful for,' Master Nicholas said, quietly joining Jasper. 'May God watch over this household.'

'Amen,' whispered Jasper. He noticed Alisoun sitting down, free for a moment. He went to her.

She smiled up at him as she fanned her face with her long-fingered hands. She had beautiful hands. 'Come, sit beside me, tell me all the gossip,' she said.

'I'd hoped to hear of your meeting with the shipman's daughter,' said Jasper.

Alisoun shrugged. 'She found me unsuitable. I know nothing of cloth and ribbons, jewellery, shoes, hats.'

'That's part of what's so pleasant about you,' Jasper said. He reached for her hand.

She gave it to him, curling her long fingers through his.

AUTHOR'S NOTE

This tale is told against the larger historical background of Prince Edward's declining hold on the Aquitaine, the south-western expanse of present-day France that had been added to the kingdom of England by Eleanor of Aquitaine. Several factors were turning the tables on King Edward's war with France in the favour of the French: King Charles V of France proved a far more formidable opponent than had his predecessor King John; in joining Pedro the Cruel's fight to regain the throne of Castile, Prince Edward had wasted his resources, thereby jeopardising his ability to hold the allegiances of the Gascon lords, and had also contracted a virulent illness, most likely dysentery, on the mission that hastened his untimely death (in 1376 at the age of forty-six). But King Edward planned a double offensive against the French in the summer of 1372, the Earl of Pembroke striking first with a campaign in the Aquitaine, to be followed by the king himself and Prince Edward campaigning in northern France. The offensive was abandoned when a Castilian fleet trapped the Earl of Pembroke's fleet in the harbour of La Rochelle, capturing the earl and destroying the fleet. Few on the English ships survived. At the beginning of the story, Aubrey de Weston and his lord are feared lost in this battle, but they had fortunately been away from the fleet on a separate mission. An absent father provided a necessary piece of the foreground I planned for the book, the minster's grammar school, St Peter's.

One summer afternoon I was sitting in York Minster Library with a collection of the present-day St Peter's School newsletters, which often carry titbits of school history – I'd decided that it was time to give Jasper de Melton, Owen and Lucie's adopted son, a larger role in a book, and that it was high time I explored the Minster grammar school. I found a historical account of a bargeman who fell into the Ouse during a skirmish between the scholars and the bargemen; I was struck by the image of him being carried to the statue of the Virgin outside St Mary's gates, and the fact that despite the prayers he died – particularly because the event actually took place in the month of May, which told me the man did not die of hypothermia. I found Angelo Raine's book on the history of St Peter's School that same day. Apparently the tension between the young scholars and the bargemen had existed for a long while, a variation on 'town and gown' conflicts in many university towns. This brought the past alive for me – suddenly the young scholars were mischievous and the bargemen gruff and resentful.

I'd earlier discovered Jo Ann Hoeppner Moran's paper and book regarding education in York in Owen's time, and had adopted the real-historical Ferriby family in the previous Owen Archer mystery, *The Cross-Legged Knight*, with an eye towards using Nicholas Ferriby's struggle with the dean and chancellor regarding his grammar school in a future book. Happily, this controversy did not ruin Nicholas's career, not by any means. In 1379 he was a canon of York Minster and in 1393 he was master of the grammar school at St Leonard's Hospital in York. His brother John (see the note below) went on to become subtreasurer of the Minster. [Note: the name of Nicholas's brother 'William' was actually John, but Master John de York, Dean John, and Archbishop John Thoresby made too many in the book so I chose the second most popular name of the time.]

I also thought it an excellent example of Archbishop Thoresby's reasoned thinking that he had, in fact, condemned a song school five years earlier, but did not support the move to excommunicate Nicholas for his grammar school. The grammar schools taught children Latin grammar – the students might be destined for any walk of life; the song schools were for young men who were training to sing in the choir and therefore learning to read portions of the liturgy, and so those schools were appropriately connected with a church.

FURTHER READING

Richard Barber, *Edward Prince of Wales and Aquitain: A Biography of the Black Prince* (The Boydell Press, 1978, reprint 1996)

Jo Ann Hoeppner Moran Cruz, *Education and Learning in the City of York 1300–1560* (Borthwick Paper No. 55, 1979)

Jo Ann Hoeppner Moran Cruz, *The Growth of English Schooling 1340–1548: Learning, Literacy, and Laicization in Pre-Reformation York Diocese* (Princeton University Press, 1985)

Angelo Raine, *History of St Peter's School: York, AD 627 to the present day* (London: G Bell and Sons, 1926)

Clifford Rogers, *The Wars of Edward III: Sources and Interpretations* (The Boydell Press, 1999)

The Cross-Legged Knight

Candace Robb

An Owen Archer Mystery

England, 1371. A solemn convoy wends its way into York. William of Wykeham, Bishop of Winchester, is bringing home the remains of Sir Ranulf Pagnell. But the Pagnell family holds the bishop responsible for Sir Ranulf's death . . .

An accident in the grounds of York Minster nearly kills the bishop. Then, only a few days later, his townhouse is found ablaze. When the body of a young woman is discovered in the undercroft of the house, scandal threatens to destroy Wykeham.

The one-eyed spy Owen Archer is called to the scene and immediately starts asking questions. Was the fire an accident or arson? Was the woman trapped or the fire started to conceal a corpse? When it appears the dead woman was a midwife known to many of the city's women, including Lucie, Owen's wife, his quest becomes personal.

'It's . . . the Machiavellian intrigue that makes this such an enjoyable read. When the iron curtain came down people said the spy-thriller genre was dead. They were wrong. This is as full of intrigue as a Deighton or a Le Carré'
Guardian

arrow books

A Spy for the Redeemer

Candace Robb

An Owen Archer Mystery

Late spring, the year of our Lord 1370. Owen Archer, ex-soldier and spy, is preparing to depart Wales, his work for John of Gaunt completed. But his attempts to arrange safe passage home to York are thwarted by a mysterious suicide.

In York Lucie Wilton is disheartened by her husband's long absence and concerned by allegations against her apothecary. Then Brother Michaelo brings upsetting news, forcing her to journey to her father's manor outside the city. Increasingly desperate, she accepts the company of a stranger, who proves invaluable when they face danger.

Angered by Owen's prolonged absence, aware of malicious rumours, John Thoresby, Archbishop of York, orders his return. But Owen's stay in the land of his birth has created divided loyalties in him. And those who serve the Welsh rebel leader would have Owen sign up to fight and never go home . . .

'A real page-turner with lots of intrigue, murder and general derring-do' *Historical Novels Review*

arrow books

A Gift of Sanctuary

Candace Robb

An Owen Archer Mystery

Through the wet spring of 1369 a pilgrimage wends its way to the sacred city of St David's. Owen Archer, ex-soldier and sometime spy, accompanies the party to recruit archers for the Duke of Lancaster, who prepares to fight the French. But he and Geoffrey Chaucer have another, covert, mission: to ascertain whether the Duke's steward at Cydweli is betraying him to Welsh rebels.

Trouble precedes them: a body in the Duke's livery is left at the city gates. And when Owen rides on to Cydweli he finds the household of the steward and his beautiful young wife rocked by the theft of money from the exchequer and riven by tension, culminating in another violent attack. He must work fast to investigate charges of treachery, infidelity and murder if he is to prevent further deaths.

Political skulduggery, passion and ambition clash in this intriguing, evocative and compelling novel which vividly conjures up the medieval world.

'Robb deftly interweaves a complex story of love, passion and murder into the troubled and tangled fabric of Welsh history, fashioning a rich and satisfying novel'
Publishers Weekly

arrow books

The Riddle of St Leonard's

Candace Robb

An Owen Archer Mystery

Anno Domini 1369. The much loved Queen Philippa lies dying at Windsor, and the plague has returned to the city of York. In an atmosphere of fear and superstition, rumours spread that a spate of deaths at St Leonard's Hospital in York is no accident. The hospital is in debt and has suffered thefts: Sir Richard de Ravenser, Master of the Hospital, returns from Winchester painfully aware that scandal could ruin his own career. Anxious to avert a crisis, he requests the services of Owen Archer, spy for the Archbishop.

With plague rife and the city's inhabitants besieging his wife, the Apothecary, for new cures, Owen Archer is unwilling to become involved. There is too little to link the victims to each other: the riddle seems unsolvable. But careful enquiries reveal a further riddle, connected to one of the victims. Is this where the truth lies?

'A vivid portrait of 14th-century England which gives us a hero who is cunning and capable'
Time Out

arrow books

ALSO AVAILABLE IN ARROW

The King's Bishop

Candace Robb

An Owen Archer Mystery

A snowy March, 1367, and King Edward is impatient. He wants William of Wykeham confirmed as Bishop of Winchester, but Pope Urban V is stalling, deterred by the man's wealth and political ambition.

Thus Owen Archer finds himself heading a deputation from York to Fountains Abbey, to win support for Wykeham from the powerful Cistercian abbots. Ignoring advice, he places his old comrade Ned Townley in charge of the fellow company to Rievaulx, hoping to dispel rumours of Ned's involvement in a mysterious death.

But just days out of York trouble erupts: a friar and Ned both vanish, following news of murder at Windsor. Owen asks John Thoresby, at Court in his role as Lord Chancellor, for help, little knowing it will involve him with the King's mistress, Alice Perrers, ever a dangerous enemy . . .

'A complex and ambiguous tale . . . Robb continues to adeptly blend politics with period detail and three-dimensional characterization'
Publishers Weekly

arrow books